Emperor's Knife

ALEX GOUGH

EMPEROR'S KNIFE

CANELO

First published in the United Kingdom in 2019 by Canelo

This edition published in the United Kingdom in 2020 by

Canelo Digital Publishing Limited
Third Floor, 20 Mortimer Street
London W1T 3JW
United Kingdom

A CIP catalogue record for this book is available from the British Library.

Print ISBN 978 1 78863 829 6
Ebook ISBN 978 1 78863 089 4

Look for more great books at www.canelo.co

Printed and bound in Great Britain by Clays Ltd, Elcograf S.p.A.

Chapter One

On the approach to Eboracum, saddle sore, tired as a quarry slave and wanting nothing more than a large beer and a soft bed, Silus pulled up his horse and said, 'Fuck.'

He exchanged glances with his equally fed-up-looking companion.

'Fuck,' agreed Atius.

Ahead of them was the north gateway of the city walls, flanked by formidable towers, the cobbled north road leading straight through the invitingly open gates to rest and healing. And before them, dressed in full uniform, armour gleaming, red cloaks spotless, were half a dozen Praetorians, blocking the road, spears bristling.

Silus looked behind him. A hundred yards back was a carter, his plodding oxen hauling a cart laden with pottery, and a little nearer, a hunched old man, a sack of garden vegetables slung over his shoulder. Silus had to conclude that the welcoming party was for Atius and himself.

'Look at the bastards,' said Atius. 'Bet they've never drawn a sword in battle. Just sit in headquarters, occasionally beating someone up when their commander orders it and the rest of the time stuffing their faces and fucking the women the real men have left behind.'

Silus sighed.

'I'm sure Menenia has had nothing to do with the Praetorians while you have been gone,' he said.

Atius looked somewhat mollified until Silus said, 'How could she have time when she has had half of the Sixth Legion between her legs?'

Atius' brow creased and his lips drew back in a snarl.

'Silus, say that one again, and I'll spill your guts on these cobbles right now, even after everything we have been through together.'

'Calm down,' said Silus, a half-smile playing across his face. It was rare enough he found anything to smile about these days, but irritating his friend was one of his favourite pastimes. 'You know I'm joking.'

'I don't care. Say it again and my knife will be in your belly before you can draw breath to laugh.'

'Hey!'

They both turned to face the Praetorian centurion who led the small detachment.

'Are we interrupting something?' asked the centurion in mock-politeness.

'Yes,' said Silus. 'You are interrupting an important discussion. And you are in our way. Who the fuck are you, anyway?'

The centurion gaped, and he puffed his chest out and straightened his back. He was obviously not used to being spoken to without huge ladles-full of respect.

In a voice as deep and full of authority as he could make it, the centurion asked, 'Am I addressing Gaius Sergius Silus and Lucius Atius?'

'Lucius?' said Silus. 'You know, all this time together and I never asked you your praenomen.'

'You just don't care,' said Atius.

'Am I addressing Gaius Sergius Silus and Lucius Atius?' roared the centurion.

'You are,' acknowledged Silus. 'Pleased to meet you. And you are…?'

'I am Pontius Calvinus, centurion of the Praetorian Guard, and you two are under arrest.'

'By whose orders?' asked Silus.

'By the direct orders of the co-Emperor, Publius Septimius Geta Augustus.'

'What a surprise,' muttered Silus under his breath.

'I reckon we can take them,' said Atius in a whisper deliberately loud enough for the Praetorians to hear.

'Come on,' said Silus. 'Let's go with the lovely men.'

He dismounted and surrendered his weapons, and Atius reluctantly did the same. Two Praetorians grabbed each of them and escorted them roughly into the city, not to a soft bed with a large beer, but a damp cell with a stone bench.

They sat in the prison and stared at the walls. There was a variety of graffiti scratched into the brickwork.

'*Tertius buggers eunuchs.*'

'*Verica is the best whore in Eboracum.*'

A crude picture of a phallus, with the words, '*Handle with care*,' next to it.

'*Crotus shat here.*'

There was indeed a pile of faeces in the corner, filling the cell with a fetid smell.

Silus put his head in his hands and softly said, 'Fuck.'

–

The door to the cell flew open and four well-built Praetorians entered. Calvinus the centurion came in next.

'Stand,' he barked.

Silus and Atius looked at each other and shrugged, then got wearily to their feet.

'Gaius Sergius Silus. Lucius Atius. You are both charged with desertion and disobeying orders. You are found to be guilty of this crime. You are to be taken from here to the parade ground and stoned to death. Men, take them.'

Before Silus could say a word, each of his arms had been taken in a firm two-handed grip by the Praetorians, and Atius and he were being dragged from the cell.

'What the fuck is this?' yelled Silus at the centurion's back as he marched in front of them, but Calvinus continued to stride forwards.

'This is bullshit!' cried Atius.

'Fetch Oclatinius,' demanded Silus. 'He'll vouch for us.'

The guards exchanged worried glances at the mention of the old man's name, but Calvinus did not turn, and continued his march to the exercise ground beyond the city walls. Arrayed in one line were a dozen Praetorian Guards, immaculately turned out as always. Before them was a pile of fist-sized rocks. Two posts had been sunk into the ground. Silus and Atius were dragged to them and their hands were tied behind them on the other side of the solid wood. All their humour had vanished like a puff of smoke.

The reality of the danger hit Silus like a blow to the gut. 'Wait,' he cried. 'I demand a hearing with my commanding officer. We were acting on the orders of the Emperor himself!'

'Gag them,' ordered Calvinus, and strips of cloth were forced into their mouths and tied behind their heads.

Silus struggled and roared, but his words were muffled. Atius looked over at him with a helpless look in his eyes. Could this really be the end, after everything they had been through? The battles, the fights, the torture, and the escape from imprisonment and near-execution. To die at the hands of their own side, purely for doing their duty. It was so unfair as to be laughable.

'Take a stone each,' ordered Calvinus.

The guardsmen reached down and each picked up a rock. Some hefted them thoughtfully, some smiled sadistically, some looked sombre.

Silus' eyes darted back and forth, looking for an escape, a saviour. His heart raced and a cold sweat dripped down his brow.

'First two, throw!'

Two guardsmen stepped forward and hurled a stone each at Silus and Atius from a distance of ten yards. The missile headed towards Silus' head, but he ducked, and the rock hit the wood behind him. Atius took his in the gut, letting out an oof that was muffled by his gag. Some of the guardsmen teased the fellow who had missed, and mocked Atius' reaction. Others looked on impassively.

Silus roared against his gag. This couldn't be happening.

'Second two, throw!'

This time the rock hit Silus a glancing blow on his upper arm and he cried out against the cloth in his mouth. Atius took the blow in his chest. Silus heard a crack as a rib broke. Atius slumped forward, nostrils flaring as he gasped for breath.

'Third two...'

'Stop!'

The voice was authoritative and brooked no argument. The Praetorians turned and stood to attention. Silus saw an old but sturdy man striding towards them. Oclatinius. Thank the gods. His knees weakened in relief.

'Centurion. Explain yourself.'

'Sir, you have no business to interfere—'

'Do you know who I am?' roared Oclatinius.

'Yes, sir,' said the centurion, voice small.

'Would you like to tell me again where I do and don't have business?'

'No, sir.'

'Then explain yourself.'

'These men are deserters. They are being executed by stoning as decreed—'

Oclatinius turned his back on the centurion and gestured to two Praetorians. 'Cut them loose, and fetch a medicus.'

The Praetorians hurried to obey.

'But sir,' protested the centurion. 'I am acting on the direct orders of the Emperor.'

Oclatinius turned back to him, eyes narrowed.

–

Caracalla, Geta and Domna sat on thrones in the audience chamber of the palace that Septimius Severus had built for the Imperial family when he first arrived in Eboracum. Severus himself was in bed, too infirm to attend the morning of petitions that were being brought before his wife and sons.

Caracalla found himself drifting off as the two supplicants before them argued their cases. It was some sort of dispute regarding the ownership of a runaway slave, a beautiful red-headed young British girl, who stood between the two men, head bowed and cheeks flushed. The plaintiff complained that the girl was rightfully his, but had absconded. The defendant complained that she had been captured and sold at market, and he had paid full value for her, and it wasn't his fault if her first owner could not keep his property under control.

Geta seemed to enjoy this sort of thing, Caracalla reflected. Maybe he liked the sense of power, the ability to give orders and see them obeyed, without having to experience the danger of the battlefield. Or was he being unfair? Their father had groomed and trained Caracalla for military leadership and glory in battle, and held Geta back, so the younger son had never had the elder's opportunity to prove himself in arms. That was just the way it was. Caracalla, the older son, martial, powerful, loved by the troops, was the leader that the Empire deserved. And soon their father would be no more, and they would have to see if they could rule as co-Emperors, or whether there was only room on the throne for one. If it came to that, Caracalla had no intention of letting his half-brother be that one.

Still, maybe there was hope for co-operation. If Geta could deal with administrative problems like this and leave Caracalla to the important job of defending the Empire, maybe they could make a success of being co-Emperors.

He looked over to where Julia Domna sat, back straight, hands folded in her lap, head tilted to one side to demonstrate her attention. Fifty years old. How did she remain so beautiful, how did she keep such a hold over him? He tried to catch her eye, but she stayed focused on the case before her. She was always completely proper with him in public, and she was very wise to do so. If anyone found out about the relationship between the Emperor's wife and her stepson, if the Emperor found out, or Geta, the consequences didn't bear thinking about. Severus would demand they both be executed for treason. Caracalla would be forced to rally his supporters. There would be civil war, again. But would his allies support him, if they found out the truth?

No, it must remain secret. At least until his father had passed on. Even then, while any threat to his rule existed, he must not give his enemies ammunition to hurl at him. And when did an Emperor not have a threat to his rule?

He turned his attention reluctantly back to the case, where the supplicants were summing up. Caracalla got the impression that this was about more than the monetary value of the girl. She was a beauty, and with the way they both talked about her, and looked at her, he thought there was probably a large measure of lust involved, maybe even a dusting of love.

The men finished speaking, and there was a silence.

'Brother, do you have any thoughts on how to proceed?' asked Geta.

Caracalla wasn't sure he had been concentrating hard enough to come to a judgement, so he simply waved a dismissive hand.

'Empress Julia?' asked Geta. His tone towards his mother was always respectful, but often soft and loving as well, even on public occasions such as this.

'It is certainly hard to choose, and I can see why both parties feel they have right on their side. Let us consult our distinguished jurists.'

Aemilius Papinianus, the Praetorian prefect, was a Syrian and a relative of Julia Domna. He was also a noted legal scholar, and had written thirty-seven books of *Quaestiones* and nearly completed nineteen books of *Responsa*. Caracalla had read none of them, but had flicked through his work on the law on adultery, the *Lex Iulia de Adulteriis Coercendis*, which Caracalla had found a bit too uncomfortable.

As Papinianus stood to speak, Caracalla thought of his own wife, Plautilla, in exile on Lipari, a tiny island just north of Sicily. The woman was an embarrassment and an impediment. He had sent her into exile some six years before when her father Plautianus was executed for treason. It had been no hard decision. The marriage had been forced on him by his father in order to strengthen his ties with the prefect of the Praetorian Guard at a time when Severus was planning to leave Rome to campaign in Africa. Although Plautilla was pretty, Caracalla despised her. She was unintelligent, profligate with his money, unfaithful and had a hugely irritating tendency to whine like a mosquito. Of course, it hadn't helped their marriage that Caracalla was in love with Julia Domna, and it hadn't helped Plautilla that Domna resented sharing the title of Empress with the younger, prettier woman. His estranged wife was lucky to escape with her life, but Severus had insisted that she be spared the full punishment of the sins of her father and merely exiled. Caracalla was glad she was out of his beard, but would rather she was gone from this world entirely.

Papinianus was now arguing with his subordinate, Domitius Ulpianus, another famed lawyer. They seemed to be discussing a technical point of law which Caracalla could not follow. He couldn't believe he was wasting his time here, when he could be practising chariot racing, or in the gymnasium, or in bed with Domna. All over a slave worth a handful of coins. Yes, the men involved in the dispute were local dignitaries of some sort, but even so, it was intolerable.

'Enough,' said Caracalla abruptly, cutting off Ulpianus in mid-declamation. All turned to look at him. 'We have heard enough of the arguments for and against and it is clear that there is right and wrong on both sides. I therefore declare that I will purchase this slave for double the market price, which will then be split between the two supplicants here. The slave will join my personal household. Case dismissed, everyone get out.'

The plaintiff and defendant looked confused as they bowed and shuffled out. It was a generous deal where neither lost financially or reputationally, but both were clearly upset about the loss of the pretty girl. Geta and Domna also glared at him angrily. Domna no doubt would be jealous that he had purchased the young girl, and would need some reassuring in private that he had purchased her not for his own use, but merely to end the stalemate in the case. Not that he wouldn't mind taking his new slave to his bedchamber at some point.

Geta was presumably angry about the high-handed over-ruling of his authority in the case. Well, he would have to get used to it when their father was no longer around.

Geta turned to the guard at the door, and attempting to regain some control over the proceedings, said in a firm voice, 'Next.'

Caracalla was surprised to see Oclatinius Adventus, the spymaster, escorted into the Imperial presence. The balding, grey-haired old man walked confidently up to the thrones and bowed deep.

'Oclatinius,' said Caracalla. 'If you need to speak to me about affairs of state, a private audience would be preferable.'

'Yes, Augustus,' said Oclatinius. 'But a situation has arisen where I considered a mediation between yourself and your brother the co-Emperor might be of use, and I thought this could be a good forum, given the presence of you both in the company of such great legal minds.'

Papinianus and Ulpianus inclined their heads in acknowledgement of the compliment.

Caracalla was curious. He looked over to Geta who was shifting uncomfortably in his seat.

'Well, brother, shall we hear what Oclatinius has to say? I presume there is nothing you are hiding from me?'

'Nothing of importance to trouble you with, brother Emperor,' said Geta.

'Good. Oclatinius, speak.'

'Thank you, Augustus. As you all know, I have individuals working for me who sometimes use unconventional methods to achieve the goals that the Empire requires of them.'

'They are called spies,' said Geta flatly.

'Yes, Augustus, and many other names besides. Exploratores, speculatores, frumentarii. Arcani.'

The room grew quieter and colder when Oclatinius spoke this last word. The guards stood straighter and stiller. The jurists and other advisors paled. Geta leaned forward.

'We do not talk about the Arcani much, do we?' he said.

'Indeed,' said Oclatinius, 'and with good reasons.'

'Such as?' asked Geta.

'They carry out their tasks on behalf of the Emperors and the Empire in secrecy. People may know who they are, but not what their mission is, or how they carry it out. The clandestine and mysterious nature of their work is part of their legend. People talk of them in whispers. No one writes of their deeds, for fear the author will receive an unwelcome visit in the night. And yet, one of my finest men languishes in a prison cell in this city.'

'One of your finest men, and yet he allowed himself to be captured like a common criminal?' asked Geta.

'He surrendered peacefully to the Praetorians in order to avoid shedding the blood of fellow Roman soldiers. But despite this, they took him for execution without trial. I was only just in time to prevent their deaths.'

'What was his crime?' asked Caracalla.

'He and his companion returned from a secret mission in Caledonia, and there appears to have been some misunderstanding as to the authority under which they acted.'

Realisation slowly dawned on Caracalla.

'Oclatinius,' he said. 'Who are these men?'

'Their names are Lucius Atius and Gaius Sergius Silus.'

Caracalla sighed. Always these two. But why was Oclatinius being so circumspect, when it was Caracalla himself who had ordered the men on their mission? He answered his own question. Because Septimius Severus had not authorised it, and with the old man struggling desperately with his health, Caracalla could ill afford to alienate him at a time when the succession was being decided. Caracalla told himself to remember to thank Oclatinius privately. For now, he would keep some distance from the situation.

'What was their mission, spymaster?'

'The barbarian chieftain who caused us so much trouble was still at large after the battle at Cilurnum. I felt it imprudent to allow that situation to continue. I sent Silus and Atius to track him down and kill him.'

There was an audible intake of breath from around the room. Even Domna, who usually paid little attention to military matters, narrowed her eyes.

'I see,' said Caracalla. 'And were they successful?'

'They were,' said Oclatinius.

Caracalla smiled inwardly. That damned barbarian would no longer be a thorn in his sole. The war in the north was all but settled, bar some sweeping up of pockets of resistance.

'And who authorised you to give them their orders?' asked Geta, voice cold.

Caracalla held his breath.

'I gave the orders on my own authority, Augustus. When I was appointed to my role, I was given considerable latitude in how I went about my duties. If you feel that I have acted inappropriately, I am happy to stand aside for another to take my place.'

'That won't be necessary,' said Domna, a bit too hastily. Oclatinius had a network of spies so complex and vast that no one but he fully understood it. Despite that, and the vast power it brought, he had stayed staunchly loyal to the three Augusti. Although he favoured Caracalla privately, he was careful not to flaunt this. Putting another into his position could easily upset the delicate balance of power between the two brothers and their father, or worse, embolden someone from outside the Imperial family to make a bid for the purple. On top of this, no one was sure what secrets Oclatinius held close to his chest. Caracalla had no idea whether the old man knew about Domna and himself, but he had to assume that he did.

'So why are they imprisoned?' asked Caracalla, trying to keep an air of nonchalance in his voice.

'They are accused of being deserters. Or of carrying out an unauthorised mission. The exact charge is unclear. Either way they have been threatened with being stoned to death.'

'And who gave the order for their arrest?'

'It was the Emperor Geta, Augusti.'

Caracalla turned to look at his co-Emperor.

'That seems odd thanks for their service, brother.'

Geta reddened. 'It was brought to me that two deserters had returned and I was asked to authorise their arrest and punishment. I had no further details than that and no interest in the fates of two men such as these, so I simply gave my assent and moved on to the next problem.'

It didn't ring true. Why would the officers bother Geta with it at all? He was right that it was beneath him to bother with a couple of deserters. And why was it Praetorians who arrested them, not officers from the legions? Then Caracalla understood. Geta must have suspected it was Caracalla behind the mission. Either to spite him, or to stop him getting any reflected glory from the successful mission, it was Geta who had demanded the two spies were arrested and executed.

'Thank you for bringing this to our attention, Oclatinius. Clearly there has been some confusion. Release the men, and let it be known they are pardoned of any possible crime of desertion or disobeying orders.'

'Yes, Augustus,' said Oclatinius, bowing and turning to leave.

'Wait!' said Geta.

Oclatinius turned back, one questioning eyebrow raised. 'Augustus?' His tone bordered on insolent.

'I gave the order to have these men arrested. My brother does not have the authority to rescind that order.'

Caracalla gritted his teeth, about to retort, but Oclatinius spoke first.

'But Augustus, now you know it was a mistake, surely you would wish to reverse your decision?'

'Don't presume to tell me what to do, spymaster,' said Geta, his voice rising. 'Technically these men are still deserters if they were not acting under lawful orders from their superior officers. And pardoning them after I ordered their execution will make me look weak.'

'You are weak,' muttered Caracalla, before he could stop the words from coming out.

Geta rose to his feet and pointed at his brother, finger trembling, face white with unconcealed rage.

'Just because you are older, because you have fought in battle, does not make you my senior, brother,' he spat. 'I am Augustus, Emperor, the same rank as you, and no one has the authority to countermand my orders!'

'No one?' The voice that came from the doorway was quiet but penetrating. All eyes swivelled from the outraged Geta to the source of the new voice. Leaning on the arm of a strong male slave, the Emperor Lucius Septimius Severus, victor of the year of the Five Emperors, conqueror of the Parthians and the Africans, stood on shaky legs. 'Did I hear rightly, my son, that no one has the authority to countermand your orders?'

'Father,' said Geta. 'You made me your co-Emperor. You never said that I was still your subordinate.'

'You're not a fool, boy, stop behaving like one. Papinianus, make sure Oclatinius' men are freed and pardoned as Antoninus has decreed. Oclatinius, Domna, attend me. I wish to be apprised of current affairs.'

Domna hastened to her elderly husband's side, and Oclatinius, still strong despite his own advancing age, replaced the slave in supporting the Emperor from the other side. They left the audience chamber to a silence only filled by the old man's laboured, dyspnoeic breathing.

When he had gone, Geta whirled on Caracalla.

'This is your doing!' he shouted, voice squeaky in high-pitched indignation. 'You set this whole thing up to humiliate me.'

Caracalla shook his head sadly. 'You have done a good job of humiliating yourself, brother. Ulpianus. The petitions are ended for today. Dismiss those waiting and tell them to come back tomorrow.' He stood up and strode from the room, leaving a speechless and apoplectic Geta in the company of the embarrassed courtiers.

–

A Praetorian released them from their cell, looking shamefaced. Pontius Calvinus was nowhere to be seen. Silus helped Atius to the medicus, who gently removed Atius' tunic and put a tight bandage around his chest to much complaining from Atius.

'Christos' wounds, that hurts,' he hissed through gritted teeth.

'Stop whining like a baby,' said Silus, rubbing his shoulder.

'Fuck you,' said Atius, but then kept quiet until the medicus came to the end of the bandage and pinned the end down.

'Do you want me to look at you, too?' the medicus said to Silus.

'I've healed from a lot worse,' said Silus.

'Fine. Stop clogging up my valetudinarium then. Six weeks rest and pray twice daily to Aceso.'

'I pray only to Christos,' said Atius.

'What's he like at healing?' asked the medicus.

'He had his moments,' said Atius.

'Come on, let's report to Oclatinius,' said Silus, and offered Atius a hand. Atius moved more freely now he was strapped up, and he managed the walk to Oclatinius' headquarters without

Silus' help. Oclatinius received them without making them wait outside, but then made a show of ignoring them while he attended to some administrative work before looking up. The two spies stood at attention, Atius grimacing at the pain from his ribs.

Oclatinius looked up, frowned, then gestured to them to sit. Atius slumped down onto the bench with a relieved exhalation.

'More trouble,' Oclatinius sighed.

'Hardly of our own making,' said Atius resentfully. Then added a grudging, 'Sir.'

'We were arrested for obeying your orders, sir,' added Silus.

'I'm aware of that,' said Oclatinius. 'But it was always a risk. Your mission wasn't strictly official.'

'And we nearly paid with our lives. What the fuck was all that about? Sir.'

'It's above your salary to know the details. Just understand that you were caught up in some politics among the big people.'

'Little people die when big people argue. Was this all because of a dispute between Geta and Caracalla?'

'Listen, you're fine, you got a pardon and you're free. Stop whining like a baby.'

Atius sniggered as Silus' own insult was thrown back at him.

'What's funny, soldier?'

'Nothing, sir. Sir, what will happen when Severus dies? Will there be civil war?'

'Firstly, to talk about the death of the Emperor could be construed as treason. Secondly, what will be will be. And thirdly, keep your nose out of stuff that doesn't concern you. Now, to business. Despite your reception, your work has been noticed and appreciated by at least one of the Augusti. And by me. Silus, you have proven yourself a worthy Arcanus. I am promoting you to centurion. I am attaching you nominally to the Sixth Legion, officially as a speculator. In reality you will report directly to me.'

'Thank you, sir.' Silus thought about how proud Velua would have been of him. The promotion and, of course, the extra pay.

The recognition was bittersweet, and tears stung the corners of his eyes. If Oclatinius noticed, he didn't acknowledge the fact.

'And Atius, you are worthy too to be inducted into the society of the Arcani. What do you say?'

'It would be an honour, of course.'

'On your knees,' commanded Oclatinius.

Atius got off the bench and knelt, jaw clenched in pain as he got into position. Oclatinius took a knife from his desk and pricked his thumb, then rubbed the blood into Atius' forehead, the way he so recently had for Silus. He placed his hands on Atius' head and gave the words of induction.

'Diana, triple goddess of the hunt, accept this man Lucius Atius into the secret order of the Arcani. Let him never breach our trust or confidence, on pain of death and eternal damnation.'

Then he said, 'Lucius Atius, swear your allegiance to the Emperor and to the order of the Arcani.'

'I swear my allegiance to the Emperor and the order of the Arcani.'

Oclatinius wiped his thumb on a cloth and sat back down. He looked up to see Atius still kneeling.

'Get up, man.'

Atius got slowly to his feet. 'Is that it?'

'That's it,' confirmed Silus.

'I don't feel any different.'

Oclatinius let out a barking laugh. 'We haven't gone through a magic ritual. You've just been given a new job. But have no doubt, it's a job where total obedience is expected, on pain of a horrible death.'

Atius bowed his head.

'What's our next mission, sir?'

'Your mission, soldiers, is to go into Eboracum, find some quarters, get drunk, get laid, and heal up.'

'Sir?'

'Winter is coming. There will be no more campaigning this year. The Emperor is ill but still in control, so his sons are not in open conflict. For now, there is nothing for you to do. Get fit, keep your skills honed, stay out of trouble. I'll call you if I need you. Now get out.'

Silus and Atius saluted and left the spymaster's office. They stood in the street, watching soldiers march past, market traders hauling wares, slaves hurrying on errands, Imperial messengers carrying satchels and scrolls.

'What now?' asked Atius.

Silus scratched a flea bite on the top of his head. 'Beer?'

Chapter Two

For someone used to the thrill of battle, the excitement of a scouting mission, and of course his more recent dramas, a winter in Eboracum bored Silus to tears. He sat now, with a particularly bitter-tasting beer and a particularly chewy meat pie and waited for Atius to join him. Not that his friend would alleviate the boredom. The conversation would turn to Menenia, how beautiful she was, and if Silus was really unlucky, how good she was in bed. He sighed, took a bite of pie, then fished a piece of gristle out of his mouth and tossed it to Issa. His elderly little dog, whom he reclaimed from Menenia once he had settled into some quarters in Eboracum, wolfed it down without chewing. She had lost many teeth over the years and those that remained were wobbly and covered with calculus, so Silus always made sure she had bite-sized chunks of meat when he fed her.

The door to the tavern opened, and a chill air blew in with some spots of rain. Atius entered, slowly closing the door behind him. A few of the patrons in the tavern glanced up, then resumed their conversations and games. Atius walked slowly over to Silus' table, pulled out a chair and sat with a long sigh.

Silus ordered a beer from a waiting slave, and passed it to Atius. Atius tipped the beer into his mouth, swallowing in long gulps, the excess dribbling down his cheeks, until the jar was empty. He wiped his face on his sleeve and ordered another. Silus waited patiently while he downed that one too.

'Is two enough for you to tell me what's wrong?' asked Silus.

'She ended it with me,' said Atius, his tone flat.

'Why?'

'She said she didn't like me fucking other women.'

'Ah. Women can be like that.'

'She says she has met someone else,' said Atius.

'Oh, shit. Atius, I'm so sorry.'

Atius nodded.

'Do you know who it is?'

'No, she wouldn't say.'

'Probably sensible, if she wanted him to keep his bollocks. Which presumably she does.'

Atius looked at him sharply.

'Sorry, sorry. No time for jokes.'

'What am I going to do, Silus? I love her so much.'

'I don't know, friend. All I can tell you is that you can survive loss.'

Atius reached out and grasped his friend's hand. 'I don't want to.'

'These things aren't always in our power.'

Atius looked at his empty jar. 'I want to get drunk.'

Silus thought about talking his friend out of it. What good would it do? But he couldn't think of a better solution right now. He clicked his fingers at the waiting slave.

'Two beers,' he said.

'And two for me,' said Atius.

–

The night was black as charcoal, overcast, with a freezing wind and icy needles of rain stinging their faces as they staggered home, rolling drunk. The beer warmed them from the inside, and they sang a bawdy marching song about a whore from Deva, arms around each other. The streets were quiet, windows shuttered so no light from within illuminated the way. Eboracum was not a big city compared to Rome, but it was bigger than the two drunk friends were used to, and the alcohol and lack of light didn't help. They were soon thoroughly lost, and they stopped at a street corner, leaning against a wall for support.

'We could just sleep here,' said Atius.

Silus wasn't quite as drunk as his friend. 'I think we might freeze to death.'

'I feel fine,' said Atius. 'But I could do with a lie-down.'

'We should really get back to quarters. We will thank ourselves tomorrow, I think.'

'Which way, then?'

'No idea. Let's ask those men over there.'

Sheltering in an open-sided, roofed temple, crowded round a smoking brazier, was a group of five men. Silus and Atius approached them, and as they got close, they saw they looked like veterans. One had a hand missing, one used a crutch for support, and all bore scars. Although they had served their twenty-five years, none had run to fat, yet neither did they seem malnourished. They turned to look at Silus and Atius with unfriendly faces, and an alarm bell began to ring at the back of Silus' mind. Atius showed no sign that he was wary of danger, though, and strode forward unsteadily, hand raised in greeting.

'Good evening, friends.'

'What's good about it?' said one. 'Pissing down and freezing.'

'Beer in your belly helps,' said Atius.

'Not much money for beer on the pension the army gave us. Not much work either for injured veterans.'

'Maybe we could give you a coin for a beer,' said Silus. 'We are just trying to find our way home.'

'One coin won't keep us in beer for long, will it now?'

'Are you from the legions?' asked another of the men. 'Auxiliaries?'

'Yes,' said Atius. 'Both. I think.'

'Then maybe you could be a bit more generous to your comrades in arms.'

'We need to get back to the Legio VI barracks. Can you point us in the right direction?'

The first man held out his only hand and waited. Silus sighed and retrieved his purse from under his tunic. He opened the drawstring and pulled out two copper coins. The man took them, then looked pointedly at the purse.

'Looks like you have quite a bit more in there.'

He was right. Despite the night's drinking, Silus' purse was full. He had just been paid, and was surprised to find out how much more a centurion in the legions got than a scout in the auxiliaries.

'Don't do this,' said Silus, sobering up fast.

'Do what, comrade? We are just asking for some help, brother soldier to brother soldier.'

'I'll give you four copper coins if you tell us the way home.'

'Well, that's not very generous, is it?'

'You're right. I'm not known for my generosity.'

'Hey, lads,' said Atius, slowly coming to the realisation that this meeting wasn't as friendly as he had hoped. 'Why don't you tell us the way home, and we can fuck off, and no one gets hurt?'

The men looked at each other and laughed. Silus and Atius certainly seemed like hard men to the casual observer, but they were completely drunk, bedraggled as sewer rats and outnumbered.

'Last chance,' said Atius.

'Or what?' said the one-handed man.

Atius' knife was in his hand before Silus could speak. The big Celtiberian took one step forward and stabbed the blade deep into the side of the one-handed man's neck. One-hand gripped at the handle, tried to pull it out weakly. Then his legs went from under him and he toppled to the ground.

There was a moment of stillness, then the other veterans let out a roar of anger and rushed forward as one. This was no ordinary untrained street gang – they had drilled and trained and fought together, and they knew the power of acting together. And Atius and Silus were badly impaired by the drink.

On the other hand, Silus and Atius were younger, fitter, especially now Atius' ribs had healed, and they knew how to fight dirty. The two Arcani reeled back under the initial onslaught, ducking and dodging fists and kicks, evading bear hugs. Silus' spinning head made his retaliatory blows inaccurate, and his arms felt like they had lead weights attached to them.

A thump to the side of his head sent him back further, but sharp fingers to his assailant's throat had the man on his knees clutching for air. His second attacker had a club, however, and a glancing blow to his temple staggered him. He stumbled and tripped over backwards.

Atius was having similarly mixed fortunes. His knife still stuck in the one-handed man's throat, he had to fight with fists and feet, and his strength was keeping the other two at bay, but he made no headway.

The man with the club bent down to Silus and ripped his purse away. 'Come on, lads,' he said. 'I've got the money. Let's get out of here.'

The three men still standing limped off into the darkness, leaving two fallen comrades behind. Atius came over and helped Silus to his feet. He gingerly touched his head where the club had caught him, feeling an egg-sized lump already swelling up under his fingers.

'Fuck,' he said. Then he looked at his belt, where his full purse had been moments before, and said, 'Fuck' again.

–

Aulus Triarius Rufinus was a crushing bore, Titurius decided as he walked home from the Senate meeting. As the previous year's consul, he had every right to be heard out, but couldn't he find something more interesting than the forthcoming cabbage harvest to discuss? He sighed and pulled his toga closer. Before him, two well-built slaves pushed aside anyone too slow to get out of his way of their own accord. An old man with one leg reached out his hands in supplication for a coin, and a slave shoved him hard, so he fell face first into the shit and mud that ran down the street towards the sewers. It had been raining hard, and the cripple sent up a big splash of ordure as he fell with a cry. Brown droplets splashed across the front of Titurius' pristine white toga, and he stopped abruptly.

'Look what you have done!'

The muscular slave turned and his mouth formed an O when he saw the muck on his master's clothing.

'Dominus, I am so sorry,' he said, and rushing to his master, tried to rub off the dirt, only succeeding in smearing it in deeper.

'Stop, stop,' said Titurius, 'you are just making it worse. Let's get home.'

'Yes, dominus. Out of the way, fools,' cried his slave, and began clearing a path again, although this time making sure that he directed any shoves well away from his irritated master.

They made their way out of the forum and up the Esquiline Hill to Titurius' residence, a beautiful town house high enough above the city to escape the worst of the noise and smells, although nowhere in Rome could compete with the tranquillity of a country villa. As he reached his front gate, the porter stood to attention.

'Dominus, you have a visitor.'

Titurius sighed. Of course he did. His clients queued from before the break of dawn to beg indulgences – favours, resolution of disputes, or just straight cash. Although most disappeared by mid-morning, some lingered. Several hopefuls hung around outside the gate now, attempting to catch his attention.

'He is waiting in the atrium.'

Ah, that was more interesting. The household slaves only showed important visitors inside.

'Who is it?'

'Dio Cassius, dominus.'

'Hmm.'

The trouble with the design of houses in the city was that there was only one way in and out, through the vestibule and into the atrium. There would be no way of getting into a fresh toga before greeting his guest. He brushed himself down as best he could, straightened the folds, and strode inside.

The atrium was floored with a beautiful mosaic of satyrs frolicking amongst woodland creatures in leafy groves, and the impluvium was well-stocked with eels that broke the surface of the water with their sinuous bodies. Two marble benches sat against the walls that bracketed the door leading into the interior of the domus. On one sat a grey-haired grey-bearded thin man with a receding hairline over a wide forehead. He stood as Titurius entered, and Titurius couldn't help but notice that his visitor had a perfectly clean toga. Titurius advanced to greet him, and Dio Cassius looked down at his smutty clothing with a momentary sneer of disdain that was quickly gone. It was replaced with an easy smile as he shook Titurius' hand.

'Good afternoon, Dio,' said Titurius.

'And to you, Titurius.'

'Is this a passing visit, or would you care to join me for a Falernian? My agent has managed to acquire a particularly fine vintage which I think will amuse you.'

'You know how much I like to be amused,' said Dio without a trace of humour.

'It's a bit chilly to sit in the peristylium, I fear. Shall we recline in the tablinum and I will have some morsels brought as well?'

'That would be delightful.'

Titurius escorted Dio through to the dining room, and offered him a couch. Titurius lay next to him, propped up on one elbow, and after Dio had accepted a goblet of wine from the serving slave, Titurius took his own. Dio swirled the liquid around the goblet, sniffed, took a sip and swished it around his mouth ostentatiously. Then he swallowed.

'That is entirely satisfactory,' he said.

Titurius inclined his head, and took a sip himself. It was in fact excellent, and had cost a fortune, but he didn't expect Dio to acknowledge that.

'I didn't see you at the Senate,' commented Titurius. They spoke in Greek, the language of the higher echelons of the Empire, especially those who considered themselves educated and cultured.

'Rufinus was speaking, wasn't he? What was his diatribe regarding today? The inflationary pressure on the price of asparagus?'

'The crisis in the cabbage supply line, actually.'

The corners of Dio's mouth turned up marginally.

'And you wonder why I wasn't there? Besides, I was working.'

'Your history? Which era have you reached now?'

Dio's face lit up. It was an easy way to get the senator in a cheerful mood, prompting him to talk about his passion and life's work.

'It is a work in progress, and as it approaches the present day, I will likely continue it until I die, and describe the events that unfold around me. I am already making records about the Emperor's British expedition for a future volume. As of now, though, I am working on the fortieth book. Crassus' Parthian disaster, and the beginning of the rift between Pompey and Caesar.'

'The start of the civil war,' commented Titurius.

'Would that all Rome's wars were so civil.'

The sound of children's voices reached them, laughter mixed with outrage, and in a moment a young girl burst into the triclinium hotly pursued by an elder boy. The girl was screaming, and the boy was yelling at her to stop and see what present he had for her. On seeing their father with a togate visitor, they both stopped abruptly and stood still, expressions sombre. The boy hastily hid something behind his back.

Titurius held back a smile and adopted a stern expression and tone.

'Children, explain yourselves.'

The siblings – they were clearly brother and sister from their close resemblance of jet-black hair, and thick dark eyebrows – looked at each other guiltily but said nothing.

'Tituria, what is going on?'

'Nothing, Father,' said the girl.

'Quintus,' said Titurius. 'What are you hiding behind your back?'

Reluctantly, the boy brought his hands in front of him to reveal a fat, wart-covered toad. Tituria took a step away, grimacing in disgust.

'Quintus—' began Titurius. Then with a loud croak, the toad kicked out its powerful back legs. Quintus grappled with it for a moment, but couldn't hold it, and it leapt onto the floor and hopped towards Tituria.

She screamed and ran to her father, hurling herself into his lap.

'By all the gods!' exclaimed Titurius. 'Quintus, catch that creature and throw it into the peristylium.' But despite his angry voice, he clutched his daughter close against him as she wailed in fear. 'Shh, Tituria, everything is well. I won't let anything hurt you.'

Quintus chased the amphibian around the floor for a few moments before managing to recapture it.

'I'm sorry, Father,' he said, panting and red-faced.

'Get out of here, boy, and send your mother in.'

Quintus bowed to his father and his father's guest and hurried out. Moments later, a plump, middle-aged woman hurried in. Her face was whitened, and she wore a heavy wig with a centre parting and waves the width of a finger, modelled on the look made fashionable in Rome by Julia Domna.

'Autronia, I am having a meeting with the senator here. Would you please take this child away somewhere where we can't hear her sniffling? And I would also suggest you think of a suitable punishment for your son.'

'Yes, Titurius. Dio Cassius, I am so sorry for my children's behaviour.'

Dio waved her apology away. 'Think nothing of it. I have children of my own. I know what a trial they can be.'

Autronia reached out to take Tituria away. As she went, Titurius gave her hand a small squeeze and Tituria turned back and gave him a smile through her tears. He watched his wife and daughter go, then turned back to Dio.

'Apologies again, senator. That was unacceptable. But if I may, can I enquire as to the nature of your visit?'

Dio took a deep sip of his wine, and swirled the goblet, looking deep into the contents as if he could divine some future there.

'Rome has had three co-rulers before, of course.'

Titurius nodded agreement. 'Of course. I did pay some attention to my grammaticus and my rhetor. We read Caesar and Tacitus and Suetonius.'

'Pompey and Caesar were always destined to be rivals. Both were too proud to share power. Only Crassus, the eldest in the partnership, held the first triumvirate together. And when he was captured in Parthia, his molten riches were poured into his mouth.'

'Do you believe that story to be true? I understand there is some doubt.'

'Of course it is true,' snapped Dio. 'I have researched it myself!'

'Interesting,' said Titurius. 'Do go on.'

'My point is this. Imagine Caesar and Pompey as two bull elephants – powerful, angry beasts. Imagine Crassus as a strong iron chain that binds their yokes, holds them together even as they strain against each other. Now what happens when the chain snaps?'

'They part ways,' said Titurius.

'Yes. And then what?'

'Well, I'm no farmer, but my understanding is that two bulls will likely turn on each other.'

'And woe betide anyone standing in their way when they charge.'

Titurius acknowledged the point and sipped his drink.

'And when those two bull elephants turn on each other, bent on destruction, where would you rather be? On the ground between them? Or on the back of the more powerful elephant?'

'What are you saying?' asked Titurius, the first sensations of unease fluttering in his belly.

Dio looked around him. Satisfied that there was no one in earshot, he lowered his voice and said, 'Severus is a strong chain binding his sons together.'

'I would hardly call Geta a bull elephant,' scoffed Titurius. 'More of a suckling calf. And as for Antoninus – a boar maybe.'

'Titurius,' said Dio earnestly. 'Severus is weakening. My reports from Britain say he will not survive until the spring. With the time it takes messages to reach Rome from that barbaric country, he may already be dead, for all we know. The time is approaching fast. The chain is about to snap. You will need to choose which elephant to ride.'

'Senator,' said Titurius. 'Our loyalty is to Rome. Rome currently has three equal co-Emperors. To talk of Severus' death borders on treason. May it be many years before he leaves us and is deified. But when that time comes, Rome will still have two co-Emperors, and it is our duty to serve them equally.'

'Don't be naïve,' snapped Dio. 'It will be war, be it overt or covert. You are right our loyalty is to Rome. And for that reason, we must get behind the side that will bring most stability to Rome. One who is educated and who listens to advisors, not one who charges off headlong into battle seeking personal glory.'

'You mean one who is most easily manipulated. I think I see which side you are favouring.'

'There are some men, fine men, patriots, who want the best for Rome. All I ask is that you meet some of them, and hear what they have to say.'

'I'll think about it.'

'Titurius. Rome is not the power it once was. Our legions no longer sweep all before them like they did in the days of

Augustus or Vespasian or Trajan. Even the great Marcus Aurelius barely kept the tide of the barbarians dammed back. Yes, our glorious Emperor Septimius Severus has reversed the decline in our fortunes, but do you expect that to continue under Caracalla? Do you think he has his father's skill, temperament and wisdom?'

Titurius looked doubtful. Neither of the younger co-Emperors inspired in him any particular confidence. Their loose-living, quarrelling, drinking, gambling and chariot racing were legendary in Rome, and were thought to be the main reasons why their father had wanted a foreign war, in order to occupy them. Dio was right that there were threats to the Empire. Constant pressure on the borders from the Marcommani kept those who knew the danger awake at night. Financially, Rome was struggling. An Empire that for hundreds of years had been based on plunder and expansion was now having to live within its means, and it was finding this a challenge. The economy was a threat to the Empire from within to match the barbarian threat from without. It would take strong leadership over the coming decades to prevent collapse. And Caracalla and Geta were both young. If they survived war, disease and assassination, either one of them could be the leader of Rome for the whole of the coming crisis. Maybe Dio was right. Maybe they should be thinking about choosing a captain to weather the coming storm.

'It has been an interesting discussion, senator,' said Titurius, standing. 'I'm sure you are very busy. And as you will have noticed, I need to get the grime of the city from my clothes and my person. But perhaps we should continue this discussion another time. With some colleagues, if you think that appropriate.'

Dio stood, face grim. 'Someone will be in touch,' he said, and took his leave.

Titurius walked slowly into the peristylium. The open-roofed, colonnaded garden looked dour in the late winter weather. It had started to rain once more. At the far end, sheltered from the weather by the overhanging roof, Tituria teased a kitten with a length of twine. The kitten batted the string with its claws sheathed, and Tituria giggled at the game. He looked at the sky. A storm was coming. He shivered, and he didn't think it was from the cold.

Chapter Three

Warm air from the underfloor heating wafted upwards. A bowl of hot water sprinkled with rose petals on a stand in the corner filled the bedroom with a light fragrance. Domna's trusted lyre player picked out a slow tune on the sheep-gut strings with an ivory plectrum while tapping out a driving rhythm on the skin of the lyre.

Domna rode Caracalla to the beat of the rhythm, sinking down hard with each downbeat, lifting herself up to his tip with the upbeat. Caracalla's eyes were narrowed, his hands on her thighs which were spread outside his hips, watching her move. The combination of sensations was exquisite: the music, the scents, the pleasure radiating from his groin in time with his stepmother's movements.

The tempo increased, the beat coming faster, Domna keeping time. Her lips were parted, her fingers clutched in his wiry chest hair, her breath leaving her with a quiet moan on each exhalation. The music became louder, faster still, and then he was there, pulsing inside her as she ground down onto him and let out a cry.

They held still like a tableau, the music fading from the vibrating strings. Then Domna leant forward and kissed Caracalla firmly on the mouth. He slid his arms around her, held her still, then rolled her sideways, still breathing hard. The lyre player started up again, a light tune but with complex harmonies.

Caracalla kissed Domna's lips, her cheek, her neck, and ran his fingertips down her back. She sighed and cuddled up closer to him, eyes closing, head on his chest moving up and down with his breathing.

Caracalla regarded the lyre player, who blushed under his stare and concentrated on her instrument. Her hands started to tremble, and she fumbled a note.

'You play beautifully,' he said.

Her hands froze on the instrument and she stopped playing abruptly.

'Thank you, dominus.'

'It was a Phrygian tune, I think. Aristoxenian enharmonic?'

'I wouldn't know, dominus. My mother taught me the tune when I was a little girl.'

Caracalla was secretly relieved. He had gambled that the girl had not had a classical musical education. Although he had an interest in music himself, he had never had the patience to develop any expertise in the theory, so his comments had been something of a bluff from half-remembered childhood lessons. Hopefully, though, it had served its purpose of impressing the cultured Domna. If it had, she gave no sign, her eyes remaining closed, as if she was drifting into sleep.

'Pass me the lyre, girl.'

He sat up, gently easing Domna onto the bed, where she rolled onto her back and watched curiously. The girl passed him the instrument. The upright arms and the tuning knobs were bronze, and it had seven strings of equal lengths but varying thickness, stretched over a calf skin which spanned the lower halves of the arms. He made a show of altering the tuning somewhat, though in reality he knew he had probably made it worse, and began to pluck out a tune.

It was amateurish even to his own ears, but Julia listened with an indulgent smile on her lips. His tutor had taught him the song, and it had left the teacher perpetually disappointed with his pupil's level of competence. But when he finished, Julia clapped her hands together in delight.

Caracalla waved away the praise and passed the instrument back to the slave.

'I think we should let the expert continue,' he said.

The lyre girl began to play a much more melodious harmony as Caracalla rejoined Julia on the bed. He lay on his back, and Julia lay beside him, propped on one elbow, index finger stroking his chest.

'How long can he last?' asked Caracalla.

Julia sighed. 'He has always been as strong as an elephant. But even elephants don't live for ever. Time catches up with them eventually.'

'It's pitiful really. I remember when he could wrestle against two strong men, fight a professional gladiator and win, then run ten miles and not break a sweat.'

'He was always a physical man,' said Julia, and Caracalla gave her a sour glance. She had the good grace to look down, abashed.

'Time is growing short,' she said.

'Are you sure?'

She nodded. 'His illnesses worsen. His gout and arthritis leave him writhing in agony, and every breath is a constant struggle.'

'And yet he lingers.'

'Antoninus,' said Domna reprovingly. 'You sound like you want him gone.'

'Of course not. Not really. I love my father, I'm proud of him. But this man, this hollow shell of what he once was. Is he still my father?'

'Of course he is!' snapped Domna.

'Yes, yes. But surely he is suffering now. In body and in spirit. Wouldn't it be a kindness now to help him on his way to meet Serapis?'

Julia drew in a hiss of air, and looked over at the lyre player, who was staring straight ahead, trying desperately to look like she hadn't heard anything. Trusted slave she might be, but talk of murdering the Emperor in front of anyone was reckless.

Caracalla realised he had crossed a line, and put an apologetic hand on Julia's arm.

'I'm sorry, of course I didn't mean that. It is just sad to see him in this state.'

'And frustrating waiting for your turn to rule?'

'Julia...'

The Empress sat up and clicked her fingers for her slave. The lyre girl stopped playing and hurried over with a robe. Julia snatched it from her impatiently and covered herself up.

'I should attend him. I shouldn't be here with you when my husband is suffering.'

'Julia, I'm sorry...'

Julia swept out of the room, the lyre player hurrying after her. Caracalla slumped back onto the bed, let out a frustrated grunt and thumped the mattress with his powerful fist. Soon though, surely, it would be all over. And then he would have it all, everything that now belonged to his father.

The army.

The Empire.

The woman.

—

'You're a disgrace, the pair of you,' said Oclatinius, his voice not loud, and all the more frightening because of it. Atius and Silus stood before him in his office, dishevelled, unshaven, bruised and smelling of beer and piss. Silus had a dark lump on the side of his head, and Atius kept probing his ribs, wondering if they had re-broken.

'You do understand the concept of *secret* police? Of spying? Blending in? Remaining unseen and unnoticed?'

The two Arcani said nothing. Silus' head throbbed from the hangover and the injury, and the only saving grace of their current situation was that Oclatinius wasn't shouting at them.

Their superior shook his head. 'I expect better from you. I know that this winter has been tedious, but that is no excuse. How will you keep your discipline in the field, if you can't remain focused in the comfort of a Roman city?'

'Sorry, sir,' they both mumbled.

'I'll think about your punishment later. For now, I summoned you to my office for a reason. You two are not the only Arcani. The order does not number vast amounts, though, and they are spread thinly throughout the Empire. Sometimes, replacements are needed, for obvious reasons.'

'Retirement, sir?' enquired Atius.

Oclatinius looked at him steadily. 'No one retires from the Arcani.'

Atius dropped his gaze.

'So, replacements. I have a youngster I intend to bring into the order. This one has had some instruction from me already, and shows promise. You two aren't my most experienced men, but you are the only ones available. I want you to take them under your wings, give them some training, show them the ropes.'

Silus groaned inwardly. Teaching some rookie how to sneak and spy and fight dirty was not his idea of fun. 'It will be our pleasure, sir.'

'I don't really care whether you enjoy it or not, soldier.' He raised his voice. 'Daya, get in here.'

The door opened, and a dark-skinned young woman sauntered in. She had a swaggering step and a half-smile on her lips. Her frame was slight, and she was short, but she held herself with the confidence of a famous gladiator. She looked Atius and Silus up and down, and her half-smile changed to a sneer. Silus was aware that they weren't looking their best, but this cocky young whelp's condescension irritated him.

'This is her?' asked Atius. 'This little girl?'

'Don't be so quick to judge by appearances, Atius,' said Oclatinius.

'Training her is one thing, but you can't fix puny.'

'Strike her,' said Oclatinius.

'Sir?'

'Hit her. Punch her in the face. Grab her throat. Whatever. Attack her.'

35

Atius turned to face the girl. Silus estimated she was about twenty years old, and when he looked closer, he could see that the slim limbs were finely muscled. Oclatinius was smiling, and alarm bells were going off in Silus' mind.

But before he could say anything, without warning his friend aimed a jab straight at Daya's nose.

The movement was too quick for Silus to follow. Somehow, Daya had deflected the blow, grabbed Atius' wrist and twisted it behind his back, then slammed the big Celt face down into Oclatinius' desk.

Oclatinius regarded Atius' squashed visage for a moment, then looked up at Silus. 'As I said, she has promise.'

'Yes, sir,' said Silus.

'Yes, sir,' said Atius, his voice muffled by the woodwork. 'Could you ask her to let me go now, please, sir?'

–

Caracalla and Geta reclined on a couch on either side of Julia Domna and Severus. The Empress had insisted they dine together as a family, although she was probably the only one of the four of them that had the slightest desire to be there. No officials were with them, nor was there any entertainment. Only serving slaves were present, and the mood was sombre. Severus ate sparingly, his breathing noisy. His face was pale behind his grey-white beard, and his eyes were bloodshot. He said nothing, slowly picking up morsels of meat, and masticating noisily with his mouth open. Caracalla couldn't help but feel disgust when he looked at him, though it shamed him. His magnificent, powerful, terrifying father reduced to this shade of his former self.

Geta was in a foul mood, stabbing his meat with the point of his knife, and chewing aggressively. The two brothers had seen little of each other recently, keeping themselves to themselves, surrounded by their own adherents and loyalists. It was obvious to all that Severus would not be Emperor for much longer, if he even was now, and the intriguing and tussling for position amongst the senior officials and courtiers was intensifying.

Court politics was greatly to Caracalla's distaste. He preferred the rigid hierarchy of command that was found in the legions. Men below you to take orders. Men above you to give them. In Caracalla's case, one man above him. The one who was currently dribbling saliva and meat juice down his beard. And when that man was no longer his superior and commander, he fully intended that there would be no man higher than him in the Empire. Nor even his equal. He did not even want to be primus inter pares.

Domna made an attempt to break the awkward silence.

'I dined with Papinianus yesterday,' she said. 'He really is a remarkable man. His knowledge of the law is second to none.'

Geta stifled a yawn and looked away. Caracalla feigned interest.

'Yes, he is certainly a man of intellect.'

'People say his books on the law will last for ever.'

'As will Father's renown.'

'Of course,' said Domna, looking over at her husband to check she hadn't inadvertently offended him.

'He is the greatest general of our times,' said Caracalla. He believed it and he was genuinely proud of his father's achievements, but it didn't hurt to get on his father's good side, especially with the succession so close to being decided. Unfortunately, Severus appeared to be concentrating mostly on getting more of his food into his mouth than down his front.

'Father's military prowess is inarguable. His victories prove it,' said Geta, obviously deciding he needed to get in on the sycophancy. 'But what of the greatest general of ages past?'

'That's easy,' said Caracalla. 'Alexander. It is beyond doubt.'

A mischievous look came over Geta's face, and Caracalla knew that he was about to take a contrary view for the sake of annoying his older brother.

'It's clearly Hannibal,' said Geta.

Caracalla took a sip of wine, deciding whether to engage. But he was bored, and a good argument was better than this excruciating family gathering. He shook his head.

'You know nothing of military matters, brother. Stick to administration.'

'You should study harder, brother, and you would understand these matters better. And maybe you would be able to conquer a small primitive country at the furthest reach of the Empire without bogging the cream of the legions down for two years.'

Caracalla's jaw clenched. The slow progress in Caledonia had been a frustration, but the tactics of the Caledonian and Maeatae barbarians had made it impossible to win a quick victory. Geta was also coming dangerously close to criticising their father, whose idea the whole British expedition had been, and who had dictated the grand strategy. But he had obviously decided that Severus was concentrating too little on their conversation to register the slight.

'Tell me then,' said Caracalla. 'Why is Hannibal so clearly superior to Alexander?'

'Because he defeated Rome. Alexander never attempted that.'

'When Alexander came to power, Rome was beneath his notice. He wished to conquer the greatest Empire in the world, which was Persia. If Alexander had turned on Rome at that time, he would have crushed us, and the Roman Empire would never have existed.'

'You think little of your forefathers, Bassianus.' The use of Caracalla's childhood name always grated, and Geta knew it.

'I know war, little brother.' He knew calling Geta little brother was just as annoying. 'I know that Rome wasn't yet mighty enough to resist the Macedonians. It's like saying you are being disrespectful to a gladiator just because you don't believe he could win a fight as an infant.'

'Nevertheless, Hannibal did in fact defeat Rome when it was becoming a proper regional power. And he did it in enemy territory, and stayed there undefeated for ten years. He did it after his country had lost a disastrous war against Rome. Alexander inherited a powerful land and army from his father that was already in the habit of winning.'

'Yet in the end, Hannibal lost, defeated by Scipio. Alexander was never defeated, except by ill health.'

'Hannibal was only defeated after he was betrayed by the elders at home.'

'Alexander conquered vast territories, further east than even the Roman Empire has ever reached. For all his tactical skill, Hannibal had no strategy. He never conquered anything.'

'In the end, though, he is African, like our family. Family loyalty is everything, is it not?'

It was strange how Geta gravitated to the African side of the family through their father, with most of his close circle coming from the province, while Caracalla tended to be closer to Domna's Syrian relatives such as Papinianus, despite not actually being related to Domna except by his father's marriage.

'Yes, little brother. Family loyalty is everything. Every Roman owes allegiance to their paterfamilias. Right now, Father is our paterfamilias. When, gods willing many years from now, Father is no longer with us, I will be paterfamilias of the Severans. Then you will owe your loyalty to me.'

'I owe you nothing,' said Geta, his voice rising. Severus looked up now, stopped chewing, frowned. Geta didn't notice. 'We are co-Augusti. Co-Emperors. When Father is no longer here, we will rule as equals.'

'You are not my equal,' said Caracalla, his voice even.

'Maybe you are right. There are some notable men that say that I am your superior. In every respect.'

'And would those same notable men say this to my face?' demanded Caracalla, finally letting his anger show. Domna put a restraining hand on his arm, but Caracalla shook her off.

'Maybe they fear you as a tyrant. A Sulla? A Caligula? "Let them hate me as long as they fear me?" Is that what Rome needs? What Rome deserves?'

'What Rome deserves and needs is a powerful leader to keep it safe. These aren't the days of Seneca's Pax Romana. The Empire faces threats on all sides. It needs a man like me to protect it. Not some boy who has barely stopped wetting the bed!'

At this, Geta leapt to his feet.

'You go too far with your insults,' he said, stabbing a finger in Caracalla's direction, and Caracalla stood too, only the parents between the two brothers preventing them from laying hands on each other.

'Enough!' said Severus, his voice cracking through the air with the power and authority of old. 'That is... enough.' His voice trailed away, and he grabbed at his chest, then slumped backwards onto the couch. His breath came fast and shallow, a groan on each expiration.

'Slaves!' cried Domna, leaning over her husband. 'Fetch a medicus. Fetch Galen! Now!'

The slaves hurried from the room, while Domna loosened Severus' toga and stroked his face, which was now covered in a light sheen of sweat. He looked into her eyes, and reached a hand up to her.

Caracalla and Geta looked at each other in alarm. Moments later, Galen bustled in with three assistants in close attendance.

'Augusti, Augusta, your pardon, please give me some space.'

Galen was an elderly man now, his long beard white, his hair receded high on his head, deep sacks under each eye, and deep creases in his cheeks and forehead. Nevertheless, he still retained the full strength of his formidable intellect. The renowned doctor was an important part of Julia Domna's intellectual circle.

He immediately began assessing Severus with the eyes of a medical practitioner of many decades' experience. He looked at the Emperor's tongue and eye colour, felt the pulse in his neck and wrist, palpated his abdomen, bared his chest and pressed an ear against it to auscultate it, all done briskly but thoroughly.

'Excess of phlegm,' he muttered. 'Excess of black bile. Stagnation of the blood.'

He flicked his fingers. 'Slaves, take him to his chambers. You, fetch my phlebotomy knife. You, go and prepare a paste of ginger, thyme and liquorice. You, fetch hot water.'

Galen's attendants hurried away, and the slaves carefully and respectfully put their arms beneath the Emperor's shoulders and knees and carried him out of the triclinium. Domna followed them out, her hands clasped together, face creased in worry. The Praetorian Guards who had been standing watch at the door followed anxiously behind. The two junior Augusti were momentarily alone together.

Caracalla glared at Geta. 'This is your fault, provoking a stupid argument.'

'My fault?' retorted Geta. 'Maybe we should be looking at what was in his food tonight? Did you bribe the food testers and threaten the kitchen slaves to put something in his meat?'

Caracalla stared at his brother aghast. 'You can't be serious. Father has been ill for months. He didn't suddenly become ill because someone poisoned him tonight.'

'Maybe not. But people will speculate. Maybe they will think that you tired of waiting and helped him on his way.'

Caracalla gritted his teeth. It was unsettling that Geta had inadvertently touched on his own recent musings. But in fact, Caracalla had done nothing. As far as he was aware, Severus' illness was entirely the work of nature and the gods.

'And maybe you will encourage them in that belief?' he asked bitterly.

Geta looked offended. 'Brother, would I? But know this. When Father is gone, you will not rule alone.'

There were just the two of them. The dinner knives were sharp. Caracalla was far more physically powerful than his brother. While the household was distracted with the Emperor's collapse, he could take his chance and end this question of succession once and for all. He clenched and unclenched his fists. He thought of all the slights, the insults, the scheming. He thought of how disastrous it was going to be, to rule the Empire with his petty, incompetent younger brother.

He thought of how when they were children, they used to wrestle in the grass in the palace gardens, the much older Caracalla tickling Geta until he cried for mercy amidst howls of laughter. How they used to bet on quail fights, and Geta had a knack for picking a winner from the weediest-looking specimens. How, as soon as Geta had been old enough to wear his toga virilis for the first time, Caracalla had arranged for a party with just the two of them, a huge amount of wine, and some experienced pleasure slaves. What a night that had been.

Geta looked at Caracalla curiously, and Caracalla realised he must have been showing a faraway expression. He shook his head and sighed.

'Get out of my sight, little brother.'

Geta held his gaze for a moment, then his face curled into a sneer, and he turned and left Caracalla alone.

Chapter Four

The room was quiet apart from the rattle of dyspnoeic breath and the slow drip, drip of blood from the Emperor's wrist into a copper bowl on the floor. Galen sat on a stool, holding Severus' non-lacerated wrist, two fingers on the pulse. Julia Domna was seated by his head, dabbing his cheeks with a damp flannel. Caracalla and Geta stood at the foot of the bed, watching. Hovering near the door were Papinianus and two Praetorian Guards. It had been some hours now since the collapse. Night had fallen. The palace beyond the Imperial chambers was deathly silent. Even those slaves and servants who had business to be up at this time tiptoed around, aware that something momentous and terrible was happening.

Lucius Septimius Severus Pertinax Augustus Parthicus Britannicus was sixty-five years old and had reigned as Emperor of Rome for nearly nineteen years since the year 966 Ab Urbe Condita. His predecessor was the egregious Didius Julianus, who had tried to purchase the purple as the highest bidder in an auction instigated by the corrupt Praetorian Guard. Severus had been the ultimate victor of the wars stemming from the Year of the Five Emperors, and had gone on to defeat the Parthians, expand and refortify Africa province as well as defeat the barbarians of Caledonia. He had ruled the Empire for longer than any since Marcus Aurelius.

Now here he lay, surrounded by his family, body ravaged by time, sickness and an intemperate climate, weaker than a newborn kitten. Caracalla was in his prime, strong and fit, and couldn't imagine ever being in such a physical condition. Maybe

43

he never would be. Severus was something of an exception in recent years in his length of reign, and to die of natural causes while wearing the purple was unusual. No one wanted to die before their time, but Caracalla was realistic – when he took the throne, he would be a target for everyone with an ambition to rule. Not least his younger brother.

Galen's prognostication had been grave. The old doctor was not a seer or a haruspex and did not claim to be infallible. Nevertheless, even Caracalla could see that his father was fading fast. His belly fluttered with excitement. Much as he loved his father and admired his achievements, his time had gone. Caracalla had served his apprenticeship. He was ready to be the master now.

Severus opened his eyes, and raised a hand to Domna. She bent her ear close to his lips, and Severus whispered to her. She nodded and closed her eyes, tears overflowing and rolling down her cheeks. Caracalla felt mixed emotions at this display of affection from the woman he loved towards his father. But soon, Domna would be his alone as well.

Severus spoke aloud, his voice weak and breathy but audible.

'Julia. Antoninus. Geta. Come close. Everyone else. Out.'

Papinianus bowed, and nodded to Galen. The physician hesitated, then stiffly stood and was escorted out by the two Praetorians. The door closed. Geta and Caracalla stepped forward and knelt on either side of their father's bed.

For a moment Severus just breathed heavily. His lids fluttered, and Caracalla wondered whether there would be any last words. Then he opened his eyes again and looked at Caracalla and Geta in turn.

'You boys have made me proud,' he said. The words came slowly, punctuated by struggles for breath, but they were clear. 'You will both be an asset to Rome. You have different qualities, complementary...' He trailed off and his eyes closed again.

Caracalla waited. The time was very near now. Severus took a deep breath, and Caracalla wondered if it was that last agonal gasp that he had witnessed so many times on the battlefield. But it was merely a prelude to more words.

'The Empress and I...' More breaths. 'We wish you to rule together. Co-Augusti. Like Marcus Aurelius and Lucius Verus.'

Caracalla and Geta both bowed their heads. Caracalla sighed inwardly. He had hoped, even at this late hour, that Severus would come to his senses. That he would realise that making them equal could only lead to conflict. Caracalla and Geta were not Aurelius and Verus. They did not have that deep brotherly love. Nor would Geta subordinate himself to his older brother the way Verus had to Aurelius. He could only hope now that Geta would succumb to an untimely natural death like Verus had.

'I know that the two of you have conflicts. But heed these words. Live with each other in harmony. Enrich the soldiers. And damn the rest.'

'Yes, Father,' said Caracalla, wondering already how he could live up to his father's dying wishes.

'Yes, Father,' said Geta sombrely.

'Julia,' said Severus. 'My love. For ever.'

He closed his eyes. This time he did not open them. His breathing became deeper and more erratic. Then it slowed. Slowed. Stopped.

Domna laid her head on his chest and wept. Caracalla's thoughts whirled. He was now the most senior Augustus, by age, experience and length of time in the purple. Maybe he could make this work with his brother, if Geta could be persuaded to accept him as the senior partner.

He looked at his father's still body, and offered a silent prayer to the gods for his swift passage to the afterlife.

—

Februarius in Eboracum was a foolhardy time to go swimming in an open-air pool. But Daya didn't seem to feel the cold, and Silus could not let himself be shown up by this young woman. Atius, Daya and he swam lengths of the thirty-yard pool that was the centrepiece of the Fortress baths. Apart from the three of them, the pool was unsurprisingly empty. The snow had only just melted from Januarius' biggest fall, and the water could not have been much above the temperature at which it would freeze. He gritted his teeth and swam on, using a steady breaststroke. Daya was half a length ahead of him, Atius just behind, grumbling loudly, then choking as his mouth filled with water.

He reached the nymphaeum at the south end, where a statue of a group of dolphins played in the water coming from the fountain that supplied the pool. The freezing spray splashed his face as he came near it and he squeezed his eyes shut.

They had agreed ten lengths, and he had one more to go. His limbs were tired and his breath short, but the cold was absolutely numbing. He put in a burst of speed, but actually lost ground to Daya who reached the far end and hauled herself out. She stood there, water dripping off her slim, naked body, waiting for Silus to arrive, and when he reached her, she offered a hand and helped haul him out of the water.

It was even colder out than in, he felt, as the cool breeze played across his wet body.

'Gods, that was horrible,' said Silus.

'To the caldarium,' said Daya, and set off at a run.

Atius was at the far end of the pool, and got out without completing the ten lengths. He stared daggers at Daya's retreating back, then looked at Silus. Silus shrugged and set off after her.

They ran briskly through the frigidarium and tepidarium, but it was too fast to acclimatise. The heat of the caldarium hit Silus like a slap, and he suddenly found it hard to breathe, difficult to properly fill his lungs. Daya didn't hesitate and jumped straight into the hot plunge pool, a big splash making some nearby legionaries who were sitting on stone benches soaking up the heat look up and send curses her way. Silus gritted his teeth and jumped in after her.

It felt like he had landed in a cauldron of boiling water and he yelped aloud. The hot plunge pool was a high enough temperature to make him wince even when he had already acclimatised in the caldarium room. Going straight from freezing cold to boiling hot instead of the usual, civilised build-up through frigidarium and tepidarium prior to entering the caldarium was excruciating. He jumped out as quickly as he had jumped in.

'Are you trying to kill me?' he gasped.

Daya wallowed in the hot water for a moment, then leapt out.

'That felt amazing,' she said, a huge grin painted across her face. 'Atius. Your turn?'

'Fuck that,' said Atius, and sat down heavily on one of the stone benches.

Daya and Silus joined him. The hot air circulated around them. Silus thought his body didn't know whether to shiver or sweat. It had certainly got the blood pounding, though, and he felt strangely alive.

The great bathhouse had become a regular haunt for Atius and himself over the winter, as they exercised, gambled, chatted, and in Atius' case, found women to entertain him, especially after Menenia had thrown him out. Atius had encouraged Silus to take a woman, and he had actually thought about it, but though it was almost a year since the loss of his family, he still could not bring himself to be near anyone else. He knew that the memories, and the sense of betrayal of his beloved Velua, would be too intense.

Daya now wore a breast band and thong, and it only now really occurred to Silus that he was sitting next to a barely clothed woman. There had been no time to look when she had stripped and dived into the swimming pool, and he had been too cold and exhausted afterwards to even think about her nudity. Now, when he had time to contemplate her, he found himself strangely uninterested. He realised that women generally had little interest for him after the loss of his family, but he was a man, and not entirely immune to feminine charms. Yet Atius, the womaniser, was showing no interest either. Maybe it was her handsome but androgynous features, her boyish build and face, her short-cropped hair.

Or maybe it was just that it was so unusual to have a female warrior. Yes, history and legend were littered with examples, such as Boudicca, Cartimandua, Camilla and Antiope. He had even seen gladiatrixes who fought in the arena, although most aficionados considered them an amusing diversion rather than a serious contest. So maybe Silus and Atius were just not viewing this athletic, martial young woman as female at all.

'So is that your idea of fun?' Silus asked Daya.

'Why not? I live for extremes. Why spend your life in the tepidarium, when there is a frigidarium and caldarium out there?'

'There speaks someone without enough experience of life,' said Atius. 'There will be times when you long for tepid.'

Silus' body decided the heat was here to stay, and his pores opened and sweat began to pour down his head and back.

'Daya. You are a master of unarmed combat. A fast swimmer. You don't seem to feel heat or cold. Is there anything you can't do?'

'I don't know,' said Daya. 'I haven't found anything yet.'

'I bet she can't piss standing up without getting her feet wet,' muttered Atius.

'Maybe you have a challenge for me?' Daya suggested.

Atius regarded her steadily. 'Maybe I do. Come with me.'

Atius led Daya to the gymnasium. Some dedicated legionaries and auxiliaries were working out, lifting weights, doing squats and press-ups, keeping themselves in shape through the winter inactivity. More of them would be drinking, gambling and whoring, mocking those who did work they didn't have to. Silus wondered who was more likely to survive a battle. It wouldn't necessarily be these men striving to be the best. They were often found in the front line, or taking part in a hopeless charge. The shirkers and wastrels had a tendency to survive.

Two round stone balls, about the size a man could encircle with his arms, sat at one end of the gymnasium. Atius stood behind one, and motioned to Daya to stand behind the other.

'What's the game?' asked Daya, still cocky. The young woman was much slighter than Atius in build, both in her natural frame and the lack of muscle that developed as one matured. Yet she seemed to show no doubts.

'Simple,' said Atius. 'Pick up this ball, and carry it to the far end. First there wins.'

'What's the prize?'

'If you lose you have to find the finest whore within a hundred yards of the bathhouse and pay for me to spend half an hour with her.'

'And if I win?'

'Well, it's not likely, is it? Do you want me to find you a man whore?'

She gave him a contemptuous look.

'Fine, I'll buy you some jewellery to the same value.'

She didn't look like the sort who was interested in pretty trinkets, but she shrugged and accepted. It was not the sort of wager to bankrupt either of them. The finest whore to frequent the bathhouse was hardly the sort of high-class courtesan that might attract the attention of a senior commander or high-up civilian. But the motivation for the contest was far more about proving prowess than financial gain.

'Silus, you're the judge,' said Atius. 'Count us off.'

'Right,' said Silus. 'First to carry the stone between those two pillars over there. Get ready. On three. One, two, three. Go!'

Both the contestants bent their knees, wrapped their arms around the stones, and heaved them up. In unison, they took their first steps.

Silus was impressed with how Daya had started. He had doubted whether the young spy could even lift the weight, and it had certainly taken some effort. But once she had it in her arms, she did not hesitate. Slowly, one steady foot after the other, she began to make progress.

But she did not have Atius' bulk. Though the larger, older man was not finding the task easy either, breathing hard through gritted teeth, his steps were longer and firmer. Silus watched the muscles stand out in bunches around Atius' arms, the veins on his neck bulging, his legs rigid as tree trunks.

The total distance was around twenty yards, and by the halfway point, Atius had opened up a gap between them of three feet. The strain was showing on both. The temperature in the gymnasium was neutral, but sweat poured down both contestants' bodies.

When Atius reached the three-quarter mark, Daya was only at the halfway point, and her legs were beginning to tremble. Her breathing came in a ragged hiss, and her back stooped. Suddenly, the ball slipped from her hands and crashed to the gymnasium floor, cracking a tile, and narrowly missing crushing Daya's foot. Atius looked back, and gave a smile that was more of a grimace. He lowered his own stone to the floor and took some deep breaths.

'Ready to quit?' asked Atius, unable to keep a mocking tone from his voice.

In answer, Daya bent down and with immense effort hefted the stone back into her arms. She set off again, a determined look on her face, and Atius suddenly seemed alarmed as the young woman began to close the distance between them. He reached down and hastily grabbed his own stone. The effort of carrying the boulder with already fatigued muscles was even worse now, and he grunted with each step. The finish line was yards away, then feet. Atius glanced back over his shoulder.

Impossibly, the young woman was gaining on him. Only a few feet separated them now. Silus saw Atius start to tremble. His legs shook, and his face showed concern through his pain. He took another step. Another. Silus thought he would drop the boulder, and doubted he would manage to pick it up again if he did.

And then he was there, crossing the line, letting the boulder crash down to the floor.

'The winner,' declared Silus. 'Well done, Daya, good effort. You can stop now.'

The young woman said nothing. She continued to take one step after another, eyes focused only on the finish line.

'Daya, it's over, you lost,' said Atius. 'You did a lot better than I thought, but you can rest now.'

It was as if she was deaf. Her face was white, her legs trembling violently. The pulse in her neck was thumping fast. Silus became alarmed.

'Daya, you are going to hurt yourself. Stop.'

Others in the gymnasium who had initially paid only a passing interest to the wager now stopped their exercise to watch. Some shouted at her to stop. Some laughed. Some yelled encouragement. Inevitably some started to bet on whether she would make it or not, and one even wagered that she would die before reaching the finish.

Step.

After.

Step.

It was fascinating. Time seemed to slow down. The fantastically stubborn young woman, moving more slowly than a tortoise, approached the finish line.

Three feet left.

Two.

One.

She staggered over the line, let the ball tumble down, and collapsed onto her back beside it, gasping. An attendant slave rushed over with a damp towel and patted her head and body.

Atius and Silus stared in amazement.

'Christos,' said Atius. 'What were you trying to prove, girl? You had already lost.'

Her eyes slowly refocused, and she looked up at them.

'There,' she said between heavy breaths. 'Still nothing I can't do.'

Silus shook his head and laughed.

'You are something, Daya. I don't know quite what, but you are definitely something.'

He offered a hand, and when Daya took it he hauled the young woman to her feet. Daya put a hand on Silus' shoulder for a moment, looking momentarily dizzy. Then she straightened and smiled.

'Anyone for a run?'

'I think we're done with exercise for the day,' said Silus. 'Let's get a massage.'

'And then go and find me that whore,' said Atius.

–

Silus sipped his beer at the table outside the brothel, watching Daya curiously. She drank water and ate chestnuts sparingly. Silus figured he had seen about fifteen more years than the prospective Arcanus, and yet the young woman held herself with an air of unperturbable confidence. Her back was straight, her limbs relaxed, her eyes watchful and alert but not anxious.

They had time to kill while waiting for Atius. Daya had been true to her word and had found Silus' friend a beautiful prostitute, a mature Caledonian slave, and paid for Atius to spend half an hour with her. Silus decided to indulge his curiosity.

'Where are you from, girl?'

Daya took a sip from her cup, looked around, then looked at Silus steadily, saying nothing.

'Lost your tongue, girl?'

'Are you talking to me?' said Daya.

'Who else would I be talking to?' asked Silus, confused.

'It's just you seemed to be addressing a girl, and I don't see any girl within earshot.'

Silus sighed.

'Fine, fine. Can I call you young woman?'

Daya seemed to consider for a moment, head tilted to one side. Then she nodded. 'That will be acceptable.'

'Then I'll try again. Your accent is Syrian?' It was a guess. Not only had Silus never travelled outside Britannia, but he was exposed to a relatively small mix of ethnicities.

Daya shook her head. 'I'm from Mauretania. Mauri tribe.'

Silus racked his brain for mental images from the maps of the world that his father had shown him as a child. He had a vague recollection that Mauretania was to the west of the province of Africa.

'So how did you end up at the other end of the Empire?'

'Why do you want to know?'

Silus shrugged. 'Listen, girl, young woman, whatever you are. I don't really give a shit about you. But right now, I'm bored, freezing my ass off, and was looking for some conversation. We can sit here in silence if you prefer.'

Daya sipped her water again, and Silus resigned himself to seeing out the rest of Atius' prize half-hour in tedium. Then Daya spoke.

'My mother and I were kidnapped by pirates when I was young. My father was killed trying to save us. We were sold into slavery.'

Silus nodded, and waited. It seemed like Daya would tell her tale at her own pace, and with her own level of detail.

'We were bought by a merchant from Byzantium, who travelled a lot. He kept my mother as his mistress for when he was away from home. She became pregnant. But she died in childbirth. My baby sister only lived a few days.'

So far so ordinary, thought Silus. A tale replicated thousands of times every year across the Empire. Still, he felt sorry for the lass. Traumatic as Silus' upbringing had been, he had never been a slave, and his wife and daughter were freeborn. He couldn't imagine what it did to a person's soul, even if they later became free, to have been owned, entirely at the whim of their master or mistress, to be put to work or beaten or used sexually or killed as they willed it.

'I'm sorry,' said Silus, realising how inadequate that sounded. Daya dismissed the sympathy with a wave.

'I was left behind at the merchant's domus in Rome and raised by the house slaves. The mistress of the house resented me. I think she found her husband's closeness to my mother upsetting, and I was guilty by association. I ran domestic chores for the household, but I was regularly beaten and whipped for minor mistakes. I think the mistress was a little bit insane. She drank a lot of unwatered wine and then would lose her temper and strike out. She once threw a serving girl down some stairs. The girl broke her leg and never walked straight again afterwards. The girl's father, the steward of the house, lost his temper and struck the mistress. He was crucified.'

Less ordinary now, thought Silus. What an environment for a girl to grow up in! A stout, middle-aged man walked past them and into the brothel without a sideways glance. Daya watched him until he was out of earshot.

'So what happened?' asked Silus. 'How did you get out of there?'

'Her money started to run out. She carried on drinking the best wine. She looked for a lover to support her, but no one was interested in this drunk old woman. So she sold possessions. Furniture. Jewellery. Me.'

'I see. So who was your next master or mistress?'

'I have had no owner since that evil woman.'

Silus raised his eyebrows. 'So you...'

Daya nodded. 'I ran away.'

Silus whistled. 'Does Oclatinius know that he has recruited a runaway slave?'

'Of course,' snapped Daya.

Of course, thought Silus. No way that Oclatinius would entertain allowing someone into the Arcani who he didn't know inside and out.

'Well, your story doesn't end there. It's a long journey from a runaway slave in Italy to a candidate for the Arcani in northern Britannia, any way you measure it.'

'Why are you so curious? I've been through all this with Oclatinius.'

'Like I said, mainly boredom. But also, if we might be working together, I think I have a right to know more about you.'

'You have no rights over me,' snapped Daya. 'I have pledged my loyalty to one man. The rest have to earn my trust.'

Silus opened his mouth to snap back, then closed it again. He had never been a slave. How would he feel if he had had that humiliation in his past? He made an open-handed gesture.

'Tell me what you will.'

Daya paused, then nodded.

'I got out of Rome in the back of a cart taking empty vegetable sacks back to the latifundia. The carter found me a few miles out of the city and chased me, but I had nearly fifteen summers by then and he was fat and out of shape. I disappeared into the countryside and survived by stealing food from farmers.'

'Brave. And hard. The slave hunters are pretty thorough in Italia, I hear. And aren't there bandits? I don't believe you made it long on your own.'

'You're right. I thought I was doing fine, until one day I was caught by a vicious slaver. He beat me, put an iron collar around my neck and threw me into a cage on the back of a cart to take me back to Rome.'

'You were enslaved a second time?'

'No. I was rescued.'

'Rescued. Who would rescue an escaped slave? Spartacus is long dead.'

'Bulla Felix,' said Daya, in a flat, matter-of-fact tone.

'What!'

'Greetings, brothers,' said Atius, strolling out of the brothel, his face flushed, and his hair a mess.

Silus looked round at Atius, then back at Daya, his mouth hanging open.

'What did you say?'

'I said, "Greetings,"' said Atius.

'Not you, you idiot,' said Silus, causing Atius to adopt an offended air. Silus ignored him and looked pointedly at Daya.

'Bulla Felix rescued me,' said Daya and took a long drink of his water.

Atius looked confused. 'Who? What? When?'

'Atius, sit down, have a beer and try to catch up. Daya is telling us how she ended up in Britannia. She is an escaped slave who was rescued by Bulla Felix.'

'I don't know who that is,' said Atius.

Silus waited for Daya to interject, but when she showed no inclination to do so, with a sigh, Silus spoke.

'Bulla Felix was a bandit who terrorised the Italian peninsula with six hundred men for two or three years, what, five years ago?'

Daya nodded.

'So it was Bulla Felix who taught you to fight?' asked Silus.

'Yes,' said Daya. 'He took me under his wing and trained me. He was a great man. Brave, cultured, strong and a skilled warrior. He only took what he thought was fair from those he robbed, and distributed the gains to the local community.'

'Oh, a kind-hearted thug,' commented Atius dismissively.

'Don't talk about what you don't know about,' said Daya and her tone was low in warning.

'There are all sorts of tales told about Bulla Felix, Atius,' said Silus. 'I can't believe you haven't heard of him. Once he rescued two of his men who were about to be killed in the arena by disguising himself as a provincial governor, telling the prison warden he needed prisoners for labour and describing the type of men he needed so that the warden himself picked out Bulla's men and handed them over. Another time he ambushed a centurion who had been sent to capture him, gave him a mock trial, shaved his head like a slave, then sent him back with the message for his masters to feed his slaves properly so they didn't become bandits too.'

'Fine, maybe I would like him if I met him,' said Atius.

'He is dead,' said Daya, and her face showed real grief.

'Were you lovers?' asked Atius bluntly.

'No!' said Daya vehemently. 'I've never...' She stopped speaking and reddened uncharacteristically.

'The Emperor was furious,' said Silus, smoothing over the embarrassing moment. 'No one could catch Bulla Felix, and he seemed to be mocking authority at every turn. Severus sent out a military tribune and a bunch of Praetorians and told him that either he came back with Bulla or he would suffer dire punishment himself.'

'So the Praetorians actually did something useful?' said Atius.

'It was no skill of theirs,' said Daya. 'He was betrayed.'

'Really?' said Silus. 'I just heard that the Praetorians tracked him down.'

Daya shook her head. 'Bulla was sleeping with the wife of one of his soldiers. The soldier found out, and told the Praetorians his location for revenge.'

'So Severus got his man in the end,' said Atius. 'I think he defeated everyone who opposed him.'

'Bulla was thrown to the beasts in the arena,' said Daya. 'Many of us from the band went along in secret to witness his end. He was a brave man to the last. The Emperor himself watched. I was close enough to see his expression. He showed no compassion or admiration for a defeated enemy. Only contempt.'

She paused, then said, 'After Bulla was gone, everyone went their separate ways. Without him, we were nothing.'

'He sounded like a great leader,' said Silus. 'But I still don't understand how you got from there to here.'

There was silence. She seemed to be wrestling with something. Silus and Atius waited for her to ready herself to tell them.

She opened her mouth, then something over Silus' shoulder caught her eye. Silus turned to see two Praetorians in full uniform approaching at a brisk march. He thought it odd that they should visit the brothel in that dress, until he realised they were approaching the three of them at the table.

The guardsmen came to a halt, saluted, and said, 'Centurion Gaius Sergius Silus?'

Silus hadn't really got used to being addressed as a centurion. It seemed to him a purely honorary title since he didn't command a century. He nodded acknowledgement.

'Greetings from Oclatinius Adventus. He said we would find you here.'

How did the wily old man know where they were? They had only come to this place because of Atius' stupid bet. Did he have spies following them? Spies spying on the spies? Or was it just his natural intelligence and intuition? He reminded himself never to underestimate the spymaster.

'Yes, what does he want?'

'I presume these with you are Atius and Daya.'

'They are. Speak.'

'Oclatinius orders you to attend him immediately in his offices.'

Silus' eyes narrowed.

'Why?'

'Oclatinius said you would ask why, and said to tell you to obey your orders, you insolent bastard.'

Atius let out a laugh, which he had to choke back after a dagger glare from the silent Praetorian.

'But he did authorise us to tell you this. The Emperor, Lucius Septimius Severus Augustus Parthicus Britannicus, is dead.'

Silus, Atius and Daya looked at each other in stunned silence. Atius spoke first.

'Fuck.'

Chapter Five

Argentocoxos, the Chief of the Caledonians, was an imposing figure. Tall, broad, with a long red beard and flowing long red hair which had been streaked and shaped with lime. He wore an ornate bronze helmet, and blue tattoos of animals and plants decorated his bare chest. Around his neck was a beautiful golden torc, flattened into a ribbon and twisted into a tight helix along its length.

Beside him was his wife Barita. She was tall and flat-chested, with a thin nose and narrow chin. Her long blonde hair was braided with gold balls fastened to the ends of the strands, and her eyebrows were darkened with berry juice.

The royal couple stood before Caracalla's throne, where Caracalla was seated next to Julia Domna, backs straight and gazes steady, but Silus was sure he could see the defeat and despair in their eyes. Silus wondered if he should be feeling hatred towards the man who had commanded one half of the confederation that Rome had been fighting for years. But the Caledonians had not been the ones who had initiated the attack, and it had not been Caledonian tribesmen that had attacked the vicus at Voltanio and killed his wife and child. So all he could muster was some pity, and some admiration for their attempt to keep their dignity in the face of the utter destruction of their peoples.

Caracalla's campaigns of the previous year had followed his father's instructions to the letter. *Not a man left alive, not a woman, not a child, not even the unborn in its mother's womb.* Silus had seen first-hand the results of those orders. Old men, children, pregnant women, massacred without mercy. Those who escaped doomed to death by starvation after the destruction of their crops and herds. Even Argentocoxos and Barita looked thin-faced, no doubt sharing the deprivations of their subjects.

Silus, Atius and Daya had accompanied Oclatinius on this diplomatic mission from Eboracum to Caledonia. Oclatinius seemed to like having the two Arcani and the apprentice spy close. Silus guessed that the old man wanted some dependable bodies around him in case they became needed. Certainly the political situation was very uncertain right now. After they had reported to Oclatinius on being told the news of Severus' death, the spymaster had detailed them to mingle with the soldiers and ascertain their loyalty. He had given them some simple spying assignments, checking out some middle-ranking officers of suspect allegiance, but they had found no wrongdoing.

The funeral had been tense. Domna had seemed genuinely upset, while the two sons had been brooding and nervous. All three of the Imperial family had given speeches, praising Severus' achievements as Emperor: defeating the usurpers, the Parthians and the northern British tribes and leaving an Empire in magnificent military and financial health. But everyone was scared of what was coming next, now the man who had held everything together was no more, and there was no sign of a united front from the two surviving co-Emperors. Anyone Silus spoke to about the situation prayed to the gods that Julia Domna would remain in good health and continue to act as a mediator and conciliator between the two feuding brothers.

Oclatinius had explained to Silus that despite the fact that all power had been centralised into the hands of the Emperor since the time of Augustus, and no one would have dared to question Severus' authority, with Rome now in possession of two antagonistic co-Emperors of similar standing, both Augusti would need to travel to Rome as soon as possible to start to gather support for their positions.

Hence why they were here now. If Severus had survived in good health, he would no doubt have continued his campaign until the whole of Caledonia was subdued and made into a province of the Empire. But despite the wholesale slaughter and destruction of the Maeatae and Caledonians, pockets of resistance remained in the further-flung parts of the island, and it would take a long time and a lot of soldiers to complete the subjugation. Caracalla declared that the objective of the Expeditio Felicissima Britannica, the securing of the borders of Britannia province, was achieved, and that a peace treaty should be concluded as soon as possible.

Silus couldn't imagine the relief and celebration that news of the death of Severus must have been greeted with in Caledonia. It was like some miraculous intercession, to prevent the total annihilation of their people. Now, with an entourage of Caledonian nobles, Argentocoxos greeted Caracalla, while Silus lurked in the background with Daya and Atius, watching Oclatinius for instructions.

The negotiations had already been carried out prior to this meeting – the concessions of territory, the agreements to withdraw military forces from buffer zones, the payment of hefty reparations and tribute by the Caledonian tribes and the handing over of hostages. This meeting was the formal acceptance of the terms of the peace treaty.

Silus noted that the Maeatae were sparsely represented. Argentocoxos had pleaded that the aggression was mainly Maeataen in origin, and the Caledonians had only joined the fight reluctantly when the Romans had invaded. While this was probably true, it meant little to most Romans. Barbarians were barbarians after all, and none of them could be trusted.

Argentocoxos' voice was deep, and he spoke loudly for the benefit of all present on both sides. His Latin was heavily accented, but fluent.

'I accept the generous terms of peace offered by the Emperor Antoninus, who men call Caracalla, on behalf of the Senate and People of Rome,' he said. 'I pledge that in perpetuity the peoples of Caledonia will leave in peace their neighbours to the south, and will not wage war. Moreover, we will pay the agreed sum in tribute, and hand over the agreed hostages. I swear this by my ancestors, and by Teutates, Esus and Taranis.'

'And I,' said Caracalla, 'pledge the peace of the Roman Empire to the people of Caledonia, as long as the terms of this treaty are honoured. The boundary of the province of Britannia will once again be set at the wall of Hadrianus. I swear this on my father's ashes, and by Jupiter Optimus Maximus and Serapis.'

Caracalla stood and shook the barbarian chief's hand. Argentocoxos was much taller than Caracalla, and despite his recent poor nutrition, was still a well-built man. And yet Caracalla, with his broad chest and thick arms and square jaw, looked physically superior. They locked eyes and gripped hands for an uncomfortably long moment, testing each other's wills, even at this late hour in their conflict. Then Caracalla smiled, safe in his victory and superiority, and let go. He clapped Argentocoxos on the back.

'Come, let us drink. Though I'm afraid I have never become fond of this beer of yours.'

'And I have never understood the appeal in wine,' said Argentocoxos.

'We can toast each other with our own preferred beverages then,' said Caracalla, and he led the chief away. Domna rose from her throne smoothly and offered a hand to Barita. The small party moved to a sumptuously laid-out tent, with fine wines and foods from around the Empire, specially selected to impress the barbarians.

It all seemed so easy. All that death and destruction, all the misery. In Silus' mind, not least of which was the suffering inflicted on himself and his family. Now the Emperor and the barbarian chieftain treated each other like they had been combatants in a friendly wrestling match. He shook his head and spat.

Oclatinius approached the spies. 'Get in there, stay out of the way, listen to what the barbarians are saying to each other, and tell me if there is anything I should know about.'

Silus doubted there would be anything of importance. Everyone was glad to see the back of this war, the Romans to be going home, the barbarians to be rid of the invaders. But Oclatinius hadn't grown old by being lazy or incautious.

Silus, Atius and Daya entered the dining tent, and began to circulate. It was a sizeable space, and there were Roman officers, Caledonian nobles and serving slaves, drinking, eating and talking. Mostly, people talked to their own compatriots, sending suspicious glances across to their recent enemies, but in some cases curious individuals approached and struck up halting conversations with the other side. Daya kept herself to herself, standing near the entrance to the tent, her darting eyes missing no details. Atius, on the other hand, was already chatting up a young red-headed barbarian girl. Though neither spoke the other's language particularly well, Atius leant in close and whispered in her ear which sent her into fits of giggles. Silus shook his head and turned his attention to where Julia Domna was talking to Barita.

The two noblewomen were similar in age, similar in height, and both had retained fine features, despite traces of lines around the corners of their eyes and mouths. There seemed to be a tension, but a respect and understanding between them, as they spoke. Silus moved a bit closer so he could eavesdrop. He doubted that Oclatinius had meant him to spy on the Empress when he had sent him in here, but he could see nothing else of interest going on, so he decided to indulge his curiosity.

Domna was admiring the gold ornaments that decorated Barita's hair. She reached out to touch one, flicking it with her finger so it swung back and forth. Barita smiled, then indicated Domna's hair. Domna had created her own fashion which was much imitated among the wealthy Romano-British, especially after she arrived in the country and Britons saw her in the flesh rather than just on coins. The style was of waves set in tight lines running from forehead to the back of the neck, with smaller waves within the larger ones at right angles, the overall effect being of a beautiful seashell.

'How long does it take your slaves to make it look like that?' asked Barita.

'My personal slaves spend about two hours when I wake attending to my hair and make-up. How long does your braiding take?'

'About an hour, but I leave it in overnight.'

'Doesn't the jangling wake your husband?'

Barita laughed. 'My husband, or whichever man I am sharing my bed with that night. They seem to think it is worth it.'

Silus saw Domna's eyes widen slightly, though she otherwise kept her composure.

'Of course, I was told that your men share their women around like they are meats to pass around at a banquet. In Rome, we comport ourselves to higher moral standards, and swear ourselves to just one man.'

'Oh,' said Barita. 'I have heard about your Roman morals. To the world, so right and proper. But we fulfil the demands of nature in a much better way than do you Roman women. For we sleep openly with the best men, whereas you let yourselves be debauched in secret by the vilest.'

Domna blanched at these words, even beneath her white lead make-up, and cast an involuntary glance towards Caracalla, who was talking seriously to Argentocoxos. Barita was not looking in the right direction to see the recipient of her glance and no one but Silus was paying them any attention. Domna looked away quickly, but Silus had caught the look of distress on her face. He remembered another glance between them he had seen when he had first met the Imperial family at a banquet in Eboracum, and his mind started whirring. Was it possible? Surely not. She was his stepmother and at least fifteen years

64

his senior. He considered telling Oclatinius his suspicions, then shook his head. It was ridiculous. The old man would laugh in his face, then have him beaten for making treasonous remarks.

Silus looked across to Atius. His friend was getting closer to the barbarian girl, and as Silus watched, Atius started to pucker his lips. Silus was on him in two long strides, taking his arm and guiding him away.

'Silus,' protested Atius. 'What the fuck are you doing? I was on a promise there!'

'Jupiter and Mithras, Atius,' said Silus as he led him out of the tent. 'Do you want to create a diplomatic crisis? Peace is breaking out here. An end to war, and an end to us being in constant danger. Don't fuck it up for everyone.'

But even as he said the words, Silus thought of the conflict between Geta and Caracalla, and knew that he was talking bollocks.

—

Euodus walked through the camp, straining his eyes in the darkness. Praetorians patrolled the streets of the marching fortification that the Imperial party had erected for the night, built on the remains of one of the Severan camps from the previous summer. A pair of owls called to each other in the distance, and a vixen let out one of those weird screams that always chilled Euodus to the core. He couldn't sleep, and now his bladder was full and he would need to look for somewhere to piss.

He wasn't entirely sure where he was. He had been wandering for around half an hour, occasionally being challenged by a patrol, but otherwise alone with his thoughts.

It was Septimius Severus himself who had selected Euodus as the tutor to Caracalla and Geta. He had seen the boys grow into men, watched them develop in intellect as well as physique. Neither were stupid, and Caracalla was prepared to apply himself when he found an interest. Geta was the more bookish of the two, however, and had always secretly been Euodus' favourite.

How would things play out now? he wondered. Severus had been so dominant for so long that it was hard to imagine a world without him. And what would happen between the two boys he had tutored? Caracalla was clearly the more ambitious of the two, but Geta was not prepared to give up his right to rule merely to appease his older brother. And if Caracalla did win power for himself, where would that leave Geta?

And then Euodus thought about his own role. He had been the boys' tutor for so long that he had retained their confidence as trusted advisor. Even now, a week would rarely pass when one or the other didn't turn to him for advice on a weighty matter. Would they continue to do so now they were rulers, with a court of experienced men and intellectuals at their beck and call?

He looked around him, trying to remember the way back to his own tent. Then, full bladder overcoming him, he hitched up his tunic and sighed as a long stream came out. Good flow, he thought, for a man of his age. Galen would be impressed.

The nearest tent was nondescript, some sort of depot, but he heard low voices coming from inside. He wondered who was awake and desperate for supplies at this time of night. He edged closer, expecting to hear sounds of a theft in progress, ready to raise the alarm. But instead he heard a woman's voice.

'And then she said, "For we sleep openly with the best men, whereas you let yourselves be debauched in secret by the vilest."'

It took a moment for Euodus to place the familiar voice, but with her next words it all became clear.

'She besmirches Roman honour, with the ashes of my husband, bless Septimius, barely cooled.'

Domna? thought Euodus. What was she doing here? And then he heard the unmistakable, deep voice of Caracalla.

'Let it go,' he said in a half-chuckle. 'She is a defeated queen. Give her no more thought.'

'Doesn't it anger you that she considered you vile?'

'She wasn't referring to me specifically, now, was she? She can't have known about you and me. Anyway, all that matters is whether you think I am vile.'

'I'm not entirely sure about that,' said Domna, her voice playful.

'Hmm, then maybe I should show you just how vile I can be,' said Caracalla, laughing.

'Antoninus, what are you...' Her sentence was cut off by a gasp, and then some low moaning.

Euodus stood frozen like a statue, his hand over his mouth, mind whirling, terrified of being caught. He backed slowly away from the tent, and as soon as he judged he had retreated a safe distance, he ran.

It took a few false turns and some directions from a helpful Praetorian, but eventually he found his way back to the tent he shared with Castor, the bedroom attendant of Severus, and Proculus Torpacion, Caracalla's childhood attendant.

He let the tent flap close behind him, and stood in pitch darkness, sucking in wheezy breaths. Castor stirred, sat up.

'Euodus? Is that you? What's all the noise? Do I need to fetch Galen?'

'No, no, I just... need to catch my breath.'

'What's going on?' asked Torpacion, his voice slurred from being freshly woken. They spoke Greek, the language of the cultured and educated elite of the Empire.

'It... I...' Euodus slumped onto a small wooden stool. 'Shit.'

'Tell us, old friend,' said Castor. 'Is something wrong? Can we help?'

'I just... heard something. When I was out walking. I shouldn't say.'

'Come on,' said Torpacion. 'We tell each other everything.'

It was true. The three old men had known each other for decades, and there were no secrets between them.

67

'I heard...' He swallowed. 'I heard the Augusta and the Augustus together.'

'Domna and Geta? Has our little protégé had a nightmare and needed his mother?'

'Not that Augustus. The other one.'

'Oh,' said Castor. 'That one.'

'And when you say together...' said Torpacion.

'I mean *together*!'

'Oh,' said Castor.

'Oh,' said Torpacion.

Then in unison they all said, 'Shit.'

They sat in silence for a while. Then Torpacion spoke.

'Should we tell someone?'

'Who?' exclaimed Euodus. 'He is the Emperor now!'

'Not the only Emperor,' said Torpacion.

'You think we should tell Geta? How would that go down, to discover his brother is fornicating with his mother?'

'It's disgusting,' said Castor.

They all murmured agreement.

'He is the poorer of the two of them, isn't he?' remarked Euodus.

Although such an indiscreet remark could be construed as treason, it was nothing they hadn't discussed many times before. Caracalla wasn't stupid, but Geta had more of a natural inclination to learning. He was also more malleable, and they found it much easier to guide Geta, or manipulate him, depending on your point of view. That was partly his age, being much younger than Caracalla, but partly it was Caracalla's innate stubbornness and self-belief.

'He would certainly make a more... pliable Emperor,' said Castor.

'We would retain much more influence with Geta than Antoninus.'

'But Geta doesn't have Antoninus' strength, nor his influence with the army. If we took this information to him, what would he do with it? Could he confront Antoninus directly?'

'Maybe, but not here, in Britannia, with the army behind Antoninus. He would have to wait until getting back to Rome to secure a power base. Get the Praetorians on side, by gaining their respect, or just plain bribery.'

'But if we wait until he gets to Britannia, it will be old news, dismissed as a rumour spread on campaign. And Antoninus will have had time to consolidate his power.'

They fell silent again.

'How bad would it be if we just announced what we know? Told the council, the army commanders, the troops?' asked Torpacion.

'It would be devastating for Antoninus. And sadly for Domna too.'

They all shook their heads at the damage it would cause the Empress – they bore her no ill will. 'But as bad as it would be for Antoninus, it would be worse for us. He would have to deny everything, regardless of whether we were believed, and he would have to execute us for treason to make his point.'

'But surely this is too good an opportunity to waste?'

They sat and thought for a while. In the darkness, Euodus could only dimly make out the forms of his colleagues and friends, Torpacion skinny and bent, Castor corpulent, while he had maintained himself with good diet and regular exercise as Galen had recommended.

Suddenly Castor thrust a finger into the air.

'Heureka!' he said, mimicking one of his philosopher heroes.

'What is it?' asked Torpacion.

'We blackmail Caracalla into giving power to Geta.'

There was an intake of breath, then silence as they all worked through the implications.

'But he would just kill us,' said Euodus.

'Not if, not if,' said Castor, working it out as he went, 'I go alone and tell him the three of us know his secret. And if anything happens to any one of us, the others will make it known far and wide.'

'It could work,' said Torpacion.

'If we do this, it has to work, or we are all dead men,' said Euodus.

'And if it works and we persuade Antoninus to cede at least some power to Geta to make him the senior Augustus, then the Emperor will be someone we can manipulate to our advantage,' said Castor.

For a while there was only the sound of the stertorous breathing of three old men.

Then Torpacion said, 'I'm in.'

Euodus hesitated longer and then said, 'Very well. Me as well.'

'Then there is no point in delaying. Tomorrow, we arrive back in Eboracum. I will request a private audience with Antoninus, tell him what we know and present our demands.'

There was no conversation to be made after that. Nor sleep to be had. Just three old men, lying on their beds, staring into the darkness with cataractous eyes, contemplating the morrow.

–

Caracalla looked around the room in the palace in Eboracum that had been designated a council chamber. While a few men of rank remained in Rome to continue to govern, Severus had brought with him to Britannia the majority of the most important men in the Roman elite. Domna too had her own circle of intellectuals, philosophers and poets, some of whom had travelled with her and acted as her advisors. Domna was seated between the two Augusti, Caracalla to her right, Geta to her left. Aemilius Papinianus, seated next to Caracalla, was the more senior of the two Praetorian prefects. He had been truly loyal to Severus and was a relative of Domna. Caracalla felt that Papinianus' loyalties tended towards himself, but he tried to maintain an air of neutrality which irritated Caracalla. On the other hand, Caracalla didn't trust the other Praetorian prefect, Quintus Maecius Laetus, who was still in Rome, at all.

Domna had many members of her intellectual circle in attendance – Ulpianus, the renowned jurist; Galen, the world-famous physician; Philostratus the philosopher. All men who were jealously proud of their intellect and could be trusted as a group to have sincere, deeply held and contradictory opinions on almost everything.

Geta's adherents included Gaius Septimius Severus Aper, their cousin, who had been consul a few years before, as well as others of north African heritage related to Severus.

The Syrian faction of the court, most of them related to Julia Domna, was more closely allied to Caracalla. Sextus Varius Marcellus, the husband of Julia Domna's niece Soaemias, was as loyal a follower as he could wish for. Other notables present that Caracalla could count on included Severus' Imperial companion Julius Avitus, who was married to Julia Maesa, Julia Domna's elder sister, Gaius Julius Asper, Julius Paulus who had long sat on Severus' council, Quintus Marcius Dioga and Fabius Cilo, the former urban prefect. And of course, sitting inconspicuously at the far end of the room, but nevertheless a presence noted by all, was Oclatinius.

Quiet conversation filled the room, low voices talking in sombre tones. Caracalla rose to his feet, and silence fell.

He paused, locked eyes with loyalists and antagonists, gauging their mood and challenging them, holding the moment to make sure everyone could see that the authority in the room belonged to him. When the tension started to become uncomfortable, he spoke.

'Friends, family, compatriots. We are in mourning. Rome has lost an Emperor the likes of which it has never seen and may never see again. My father was a brilliant general and an accomplished ruler. He took the throne that was rightly his from a horde of usurpers, and went on to achieve stunning martial victories throughout the Empire. He left the Empire in rude health, financially and militarily.

'Now he is gone, and while he can never be replaced, Rome needs a new ruler. My father had two sons, and we sit before you as co-Augusti and co-Emperors. But I must ask you, trusted advisors and counsellors, is this what is best for Rome? Are the people and Senate best served by a divided rule, or will they be stronger under a single Emperor?'

'And you believe that Emperor should be you, of course,' put in Geta.

'Little brother,' said Caracalla. 'I am the older, I am more experienced, and I am more respected by the legions. It would be a disaster for the Empire to be run by you.'

'I have experience in administration and I am better educated and more intelligent than you,' retorted Geta. 'Tell me, did Caesar Augustus' lack of military experience make him a poor ruler?'

'Augustus had Agrippa and Tiberius to fight his battles for him. Who do you have but me?'

Domna stood before Geta could argue back.

'Augusti,' she said, and her voice was mellow but firm. 'Your father was clear. He made you both Augusti before he died so that you could rule together.'

'Do you really think that is possible?' asked Caracalla.

'I believe it is the duty of both of you to do your utmost to work together in harmony. It was your father's dying wish.'

Caracalla pursed his lips, and Geta looked down abashed. Papinianus took the opportunity to speak.

'If I may be so bold, Augusti, Augusta. It was your father's wish that you rule together. Maybe it will be a challenge, but I believe with the right spirit on your part, and the right advice, you can successfully rule as co-Augusti and co-Emperors.'

Caracalla looked across at Geta, who was glowering down at the table before him. Papinianus was right that this was what his father wished. And maybe it was the path of least resistance, to at least try to rule with his brother. Besides, what was the alternative? Could he rule as sole Emperor and let his brother live, agitating and plotting against him? Despite their conflicts, he did love his little brother. He remembered when he was born, how he had been both delighted and jealous of the baby's affection from his father and from Domna. Even then, he had worshipped Domna discreetly, and resented Geta while he loved him. Growing up had been typical of two rival siblings —pranks, contests, fights, arguments. Now, though, they were both adults, and maybe if they behaved like adults and not like children vying for their parents' attention and affection, they could make joint rulership work. Maybe.

'But that is irrelevant right now,' continued Papinianus, causing Caracalla to look at him and frown. 'We are at the furthest extremity of the Empire. When Commodus died, the Empire suffered the year of the Five Emperors, and thank the gods, your father, your husband, was victorious. But he was not in Rome when Commodus died and maybe if he had been, the succession would have been less chaotic.'

'What are you saying?' asked Caracalla.

'I am saying that although an Emperor can be created outside Rome, as Galba discovered, he cannot rule until he is confirmed by the Senate, and has taken his throne in the capital. And until he, or they, do that, there is a risk of a usurper. A Didius Julianus maybe, buying the loyalty of the Praetorians.'

'You are Praetorian prefect,' said Caracalla. 'Can't you guarantee the loyalty of your own men?'

'I am not the only prefect,' Papinianus reminded him. 'Quintus Maecius Laetus commands the guard in Rome.'

Caracalla's eyes narrowed. He wouldn't put it past Laetus to do something underhand.

'Do you have any evidence for your defamation of Laetus?' asked Geta.

'I am making no allegations,' said Papinianus, 'and I have no reason to doubt the loyalty of my colleague. I am merely reminding you both that while you sit so far from the centre of power, unconfirmed as Emperors, you are vulnerable.'

Caracalla looked around the room. There was no disagreement. His and Geta's followers looked at each other distrustfully, but no one spoke up against Papinianus. Caracalla caught Oclatinius' eye, and the old spymaster gave him a subtle nod.

'You speak wisely,' said Caracalla. 'We could easily argue among ourselves here for so long that we both lose the Empire. And I, for one, am ready to honour my father's wishes, and rule in harmony with my brother. What do you say, Geta?' Caracalla held his hand out.

Geta hesitated, then stood and grasped it. Spontaneous cheers broke out around the room, and the tense atmosphere lifted. Members of the rival factions smiled and clapped each other on the back. Caracalla pulled his brother to him, and hugged him tight. Over his shoulder, he looked at Domna. She looked back at him. Her face wore a smile, but in her eyes he could see worry and doubt etched deep.

He let go of his brother and turned to the assembly, raising his hands for quiet. When the noise had died down, he said, 'After too long an absence, it is time to return to Rome. Generals, ready your legions, allocate your garrisons, and prepare the ships. The rest of you, pack your bags.'

–

Castor lay on his front on a massage table in the steam room of the bathhouse, trying to let the heat and the firm hands of the masseuse rid him of the worries that had plagued him since that morning. Had they made a monumental mistake?

Caracalla had seen him privately as requested, and listened politely as Castor stuttered and stumbled through his story about what Euodus had heard, and what it meant for Rome and the Empire, and for Caracalla and Domna personally, and how it was their opinion that he should cede his powers to Geta, and serve in a purely ceremonial role, and...

He had trailed off when Caracalla had simply regarded him, emotionless and silent. He had expected an explosion, shouts for the guards to kill him outright, or even to plead for his mercy. Nothing. Caracalla had thanked him for his time and dismissed him. Castor had stutteringly pointed out that Euodus and Torpacion also knew and if anything happened to one of them, the others would shout the information from the walls to anyone who would listen. Caracalla nodded and told him that he understood, and bade him a good day.

So here Castor lay, after reporting back to the others and leaving them equally confused. They had decided all they could do now was wait, and so Castor had gone to the baths for his regular early-evening massage in a vain attempt to relax. There was a knot of anxiety in his guts, though, and the humid air felt oppressive and left him short of breath.

If this worked, the pay-off would be immense. The three of them could become the power behind the throne. Yes, others would try to manipulate Geta too, and jostle for influence, but the lad would always listen to his childhood tutors and companions. If Caracalla did not play along, though – well. It would all be over.

He sighed as the masseuse kneaded his muscles through the layers of fat that encased him. He could feel some of the tension easing with the pressure on his spine and neck. Then the masseuse took the strigil and began to scrape away the oil.

There was a sharp pinch on his neck, like a little bite, and he grunted and let out a curse.

'Be careful with that thing,' he said.

There was no reply. He propped himself up and looked around, but the masseuse had gone. Other patrons were having massages, some were sitting on benches soaking up the heat and steam, but the masseuse who had offered her services when he had first arrived, the new young girl with the dark skin, was nowhere to be seen.

He put his hand to the back of the neck, which was starting to sting, and when he looked at his palm, he saw it was spotted with blood. Damned new slave girl must have got scared when she had accidentally cut him and run off.

He suddenly felt weak, and lay back down on the massage table. All this stress was not good for him at his age. He was aware how much he was sweating suddenly, more than usual even for the steam room, and the walls and floor began to move in a nauseating motion. His heart started pounding in his chest, an irregular rhythm, and he began to feel scared. What was happening to him? Was this some sort of stroke, or problem of the chest? His fingers and toes started to tingle, and a numbness crept up his limbs. He began to struggle for breath, but couldn't force his chest to move enough to get the air he craved.

Oh, no.

Realisation hit him. Caracalla had given him his answer. Would the others realise he was dead and spread the co-Emperor's secret before the young assassin reached them too?

He felt a strange fluttering in his chest, and darkness began to move in from the periphery of his vision. And suddenly, he didn't care about Caracalla, or Rome, or power and influence, or anything else at all.

–

Torpacion lay on his back on the bed in his cubiculum. He had retreated there while he waited to hear from Castor about Caracalla's decision. He was being attended by a young Greek boy he had taken a liking to – clean-shaven face and chest, well-muscled. Torpacion had bought him at market just a few weeks ago, but had not yet taken his pleasure from him.

Maybe this evening was the time to sample him for the first time. A celebration. He started to become aroused. He was sure that Caracalla would accede to their demands, and give Geta the purple. And through Geta, Torpacion and his two elderly friends would finally get the power and respect that years of service to the old Emperor and his sons deserved. First, though, a drink.

He snapped his fingers for the Greek lad to bring him wine. The boy filled a cup of lightly watered wine from a jug and proffered it to him. He sat up, drank deeply, then handed the cup back to the boy. To his irritation, the slave wasn't paying attention, but looking towards the doorway. Torpacion followed his gaze and saw a tall, well-built man, a knife loose in his hand.

The cup fell from Torpacion's fingers and smashed on the stone floor. The slave rounded the bottom of the bed and stepped forward, begging for mercy in Greek. The intruder strode forward and thrust his knife up into the boy's belly and through his liver. The boy gasped, held on to him, then slid to the ground.

'I have money,' said Torpacion. 'I can pay you more than whatever the Emperor is paying you. A fortune. Just spare me.'

He knew it was hopeless. He could see in the assassin's eyes that he was not here for financial reward, but from loyalty to the Emperor. They had gambled and lost. He slowly stood, legs weak, trying not to let his bowels loose.

'Very well. Please make it quick.'

The assassin nodded, and plunged his dagger straight through Torpacion's eye into his brain.

—

Euodus was already packing a small bag. It was madness. What had he been thinking, agreeing to this stupid plan? He had been caught up in the enthusiasm. They had goaded each other into it. And to what end? They were old men. They were comfortable. Respected. They had money. They should have sat out the rest of their lives in quiet retirement. What need had they of power?

So what if Antoninus was fucking his stepmother? So what if Geta was the more cultured of the two? What did it matter to him?

He thrust some jewellery into his leather satchel, then threw in a purse with some gold coins. He looked around the room for anything portable and valuable. He didn't know yet where he would go. Flee to Londinium maybe, then take a boat to

Gaul, then from there travel south, maybe to Sicily or Greece. Somewhere quiet and rural, where he could live out the rest of his days with a small library, a couple of slaves and a supply of decent wine. That was all he wanted from his life. All he wanted, if he lived.

What else could he take? Obviously no furniture, no ornaments. Maybe some personal correspondence. He bent down to open a drawer in his desk. Which ones? There was a letter from Caracalla, a poem written by Geta, an order from the old Emperor. And he should take his seal, not least to stop anyone forging a letter from him.

He suddenly became aware of a presence behind him. He let the scrolls drop out of his hand, stood slowly, and turned. He recognised the man standing there. Short brown hair, short beard streaked with the beginnings of grey, lean but well-muscled. Hands behind his back. A sad expression in his eyes. He had remembered seeing him at more than one banquet and meeting, usually in close company with Oclatinius.

Oh.

'I'm sorry, Euodus,' said Silus. 'It's too late.'

Euodus looked down, trying to compose himself. When he trusted himself to speak, he said, 'You don't understand.'

'I don't need to,' said Silus. He brought his hands round in front of him and Euodus saw he was holding a short length of thick rope, knotted at either end. Terror rose in his chest and he fought it down.

'I know Antoninus sent you. You have to go back to him. Tell him that if you kill me, my friends will tell his secrets.'

'Your friends are dying right now. Even as we speak. Castor and Torpacion.'

All hope deserted him at the news, but the desperate desire to live remained. He sank to his knees.

'Please.'

Silus stepped behind him and looped the rope around his neck.

'I know things,' babbled Euodus. 'I heard them together. Antoninus and—'

Silus pulled the rope tight, cutting off the end of the sentence. Euodus reflexively reached for the garotte, fingers digging into his neck to try to relieve the pressure, his nails scraping the skin ineffectually, making it bleed. His back arched, eyes wide, mouth gaping like a fish on a line, sucking no air in.

Madness, he thought as the darkness approached. Utter madness.

–

'That was well done,' said Oclatinius. 'The timing was critical, and you all pulled it off flawlessly.'

Silus, Atius and Daya acknowledged his praise only with slight smiles and nods.

'Sir?' said Atius. 'May I ask why the Emperor wished those three men dead?'

Silus winced at the indiscreet question. But Oclatinius simply said in a mild tone, 'Yes, you may.'

There was a pause, then Atius realised he was expected to speak.

'Sir, why did the Emperor wish those three men dead?'

'None of your damned business!' yelled Oclatinius, the sudden ferocity of his voice making Silus and Atius flinch, though Daya appeared unperturbed. 'You are Imperial assassins. You carry out your orders without question and without hesitation. Do you understand?'

'Yes, sir,' all three replied in unison.

'Good.' Oclatinius' voice returned to normal. 'Now, soon the bulk of the legions with the Imperial court will leave for Rome. Atius, you will remain with me. You never know when someone with your muscles may come in handy. Silus and Daya, I have another mission for you.'

'Yes, sir, how may we serve?'

'The Emperor Antoninus wishes you to travel to the island of Lipari.'

'Um, where is that, sir?'

'It's a small island just north of Sicily.'

'Sicily?'

Silus had never travelled as far south as Londinium, let alone to a location in the middle sea near the centre of the Empire. He felt both nervous and excited at the prospect.

'And what are we to do when we get there?'

'You are to kill the Emperor's wife and all her household.'

Chapter Six

Only five pieces remained on the board out of the original thirty-two. Titurius retained three black counters to his daughter's two white. But he did not feel confident. His daughter always surprised him with her tactical sense and quick thinking. Maybe he was just old, or distracted by affairs of the state, but the nine-year-old girl won as often as he did.

They were playing a speeded-up version of ludus latrunculorum. After each move, they both tapped the table three times, by the end of which the next person had to have made their move. Not only did it prevent endless internal strategising, but it forced errors, meaning the game could be completed within an hour, rather than take a whole day.

Tituria's two white pieces were close together, while his were spread further apart. He moved his more distant counter sideways to reinforce the other two. Tituria advanced a piece. He brought his piece closer again. Once it was nearby, he could force a win with superior numbers.

Damn. It was the speed of the game that made him miss the obvious trap. She advanced her other piece, and caught one of his counters between the two, blocking it so it was no longer allowed to move. He turned this piece, called alligatus, upside down and brought his outlying piece to just one square away from the beleaguered two. Tituria used her next move to take the alligatus piece out of play. He moved a counter away from him down the board in a way that he hoped would be able to bring it into play in a move or two, and then realised his error too late. Triumphantly, Tituria leapfrogged his counter, pinning the other.

There was nothing he could do. He let the game play out – resigning at this moment of victory would be robbing her of the glory. He played his only counter that wasn't alligatus in a pointless move, and she took his alligatus piece off the board with a huge grin on her face. With only one black counter remaining to him, he was defeated.

Titurius leapt to his feet, and upended the board with a roar, sending the last three remaining pieces on it flying across the room.

Tituria giggled at his mock display of anger, and he stepped forward and hugged her tight. Weren't well-brought-up Roman girls supposed to respect and fear their fathers? He wouldn't change a thing about her, his precocious, fearless, loving daughter.

Autronia entered, and rolled her eyes. Titurius knew that his wife did not approve of educating girls, or encouraging them in sports of the mind. As far as she was concerned, the only training the daughter of a noble family needed was in running her husband's household – controlling the finances, managing the house slaves, rearing children, spinning and weaving. The qualities she needed were piety, chastity, strength and an absolute devotion to her family. Not like the loose-living, hard-drinking, hard-partying women who made up most of their social circle. Autronia was a model matron, a rare Cornelia, Lucretia or Verginia for the modern times, and Titurius loved her for it, even while he secretly wondered what it would be like to be married to someone a bit more fun.

Titurius exchanged a knowing look with his daughter that spoke of Autronia's displeasure, and wordlessly agreed to humour and ignore it.

'Tituria, it's time for your wool-working lessons with the slave girls.'

Tituria grumbled but her father gave her a glare, and she reluctantly left.

Titurius noticed now that Autronia was holding a folded parchment letter. It was closed with Dio's seal. He broke it and read quickly, digesting the news. He looked at Autronia.

'The Emperor is dead.'

Autronia put her hand to her chest and inhaled sharply.

'When?'

'The day before the nones of Februarius.'

'So long ago. Why are we only just hearing it now?'

Titurius sighed inwardly. The education she despised would have helped her here.

'Eboracum is over a thousand miles from here as the crow flies. When the Augustus died, they would have dispatched a messenger by ship to inform the Senate as the quickest way to reach Rome. But it would have to sail down the coast of Britannia, round Gaul and round Hispania before travelling along the Mare Nostrum to reach Ostia. That is some journey.'

'And who is now the Emperor?'

That was the question on everyone's lips. Severus had reigned for nearly two decades, and it had been fourteen years since he had defeated his last rival for the throne. Rome had got used to uninterrupted and uncontested rule, and now found itself anxiously waiting for what came next.

'Antoninus and Geta will rule together as co-Emperors.'

'But don't they hate each other?'

Titurius looked at the ludus latrunculorum board on the floor, the counters scattered. When he had last spoken to Dio about the succession, a storm had been coming. Surely, this news was a distant crash of thunder.

–

Not long into his first day at sea, Silus had decided that he hated ships even more than he hated horses. He grudgingly accepted that horses got him from one place to the next in a faster time than he could walk or run, that they were of use in battle, and had even saved his life in the past, such as when he was escaping from imprisonment by Maglorix at Pinnata Castra.

Ships, though, were unnatural. Men were not supposed to ride the waves like dolphins. They had no flippers on their feet, no webbed hands, and they couldn't breathe underwater like fish. And clearly the gods thought he had no right to be there, either, and had visited on him feelings of nausea and bouts of vomiting such as he had not experienced since his father forced him to eat raw squirrel as a child. He had spent the first day of their voyage hanging over the side rail of the ship, heaving himself dry, while Daya looked on with ill-disguised condescension.

After a few days of misery and sickness, Silus began to find his sea legs, as the sailors put it. Being unable to keep food down, he was sure he had lost pounds of weight, and once his stomach was up to it, he ate hungrily to regain his strength. After the sickness had passed, though, the boredom set in. Every so often, the captain would point out a feature on the coast they were passing, but it interested him little. Only when they passed through the Pillars of Hercules into the Mare Nostrum did he show any real interest. The Mare Nostrum was also notably calmer than the waters of Oceanus that they had just left, which was kinder on his stomach.

Daya spent the voyage exercising and training on deck, running the short distance the space allowed, doing squats and push-ups, practising knife play and archery. Once he started to feel less like a victim of poisoning, he joined her for some of the exercises. Archery was the only thing in which he was her equal, and he was even able to teach her a few tricks. Despite some initial doubts, once she saw his prowess with bow and arrow, she listened carefully to his lessons about breathing, aim and visualisation of the target, and soon she was incorporating his teaching into her shooting. He understood now how she managed to be so good at everything. She practised continually, not just until she got the hang of it, but until she was as good as she could be, and then she practised some more. He wondered if her background as a slave, and the accompanying feelings of worthlessness, pushed her to prove her worth, if only to herself.

In the evenings they slept near each other. A horny sailor had once approached her bed. Silus had only woken at the man's cry as he retreated with a broken wrist. The captain had been angry about that. Apparently, he was one of their best rowers, and the captain had to find a port, put him ashore and employ another oarsman at increased expense when the new employee realised that the captain's need of the oarsman was greater than the oarsman's need for employment. Nevertheless, the rest of the crew left Daya well alone after that.

Silus tried to engage Daya in conversation numerous times, but she tended to give one-word answers to questions when she could get away with it. Used to Atius' garrulousness, it was disconcerting to sit in silence with the young woman, and so he sought the captain and the crew for company, leaving her to herself. He exchanged war stories with the sailors, told them tales of Caledonia, of battles with barbarians, of capture and torture. They told him stories of pirates and mermaids, and battles against storms that nearly carried them to the bottom of Poseidon's kingdom.

They asked about Daya, and he told them what he knew. They listened with fascination and frustration at her incomplete history. The crew knew they were being conveyed on a military or diplomatic mission of some sort, but Silus had obviously told them nothing about their assignment, nor even that they were Arcani. Still, they wanted to know more about the slight girl who fascinated and terrified them.

They were around two days out from Lipari when Daya ignited. He had been standing by the rail, watching Sardinia disappear over the horizon behind him, when he felt two hands grab the collar of his tunic and thrust him forward. His feet left the ground, and he balanced precariously, like a lever with the rail a fulcrum pressed painfully into his midriff. He cried aloud and flailed his arms for balance, seeing the dark sea passing by a few feet below, knowing that if he fell, he would likely drown before the ship could turn and rescue him.

A face came near his cheek, and a female voice hissed in his ear, 'What have you been saying about me?'

'Daya, Daya,' he cried out frantically, his fear of drowning crowding out all thought. 'Let me go. What are you talking about?'

'I overheard two sailors talking about me,' she said, and her voice dripped venom. 'They didn't know I was there. They said that I fucked Bulla Felix. They said I sucked his dick, that I was his mistress and whore. They said that he liked to give it to me up the arse because I look like a boy. Now, Silus, think carefully before you answer,' and she tipped him forward a little further to emphasise the point. 'Who might have told them that?'

'Daya, I never said that,' he said desperately.

'But you were talking about me?'

'Yes, but I never said—'

'You told them about me and Bulla?'

'Well, I said that you were part of his gang—'

'You sullied his honour and my reputation? For what? A laugh? Some pats on the back and some increase in your standing among these rough men?'

'Daya, listen to me. Yes, I talked about your time with Bulla Felix. I didn't know it was a secret. I'm sorry, I should have known better. You are right, I talked about you to become better liked by them, because I was bored, because...' He was babbling, he knew, but the rail in his guts was getting painful, and making it hard to breathe.

'But I never said any of those other things about you. They are just gossiping. Making things up for their own amusement. You have to believe me. Daya!'

He teetered over the edge of the ship for a moment. Then she yanked him backwards and he fell to the deck, breathing heavily and holding his bruised abdomen.

'Daya,' he said. 'Forgive me. I was indiscreet. But I never said a bad word about you. I only praised your courage and abilities. I… I respect you. I want you to know that.'

She knelt over him, gripped his tunic and brought her face close to his.

'What sort of an Arcanus are you? Is this the standard I am supposed to be aspiring to? I am supposed to be learning from you? Someone who runs his mouth off at the first opportunity because he is bored and seeking approval?'

'Daya…'

'Fuck you, Silus. Leave me alone.'

She stood abruptly and walked to the prow of the boat where she sat cross-legged on the deck and stared out at the horizon, as if she were the ram of a trireme, her furious stare enough to cut a ship in two.

You're so fucking stupid, Silus, he thought. Then he felt a lump in his throat as he remembered who had told him that before. Menenius and Geganius, his commanding officers. Velua his wife. All now dead. They were right then, and Daya was right now. What was he thinking?

Daya and Silus avoided each other for the rest of the day. Silus knew he should be reaching out to her, trying to apologise again, but her silence was like armour, and he didn't have the energy or courage to try to batter it down.

After night fell, they lay in their beds. In the close proximity of the cramped quarters, he could hear her breathing. Steady, even, but not slow and deep enough to indicate sleep.

'Are you awake?' asked Silus quietly, tentatively.

'No,' replied Daya.

Silus said nothing for a moment. Then, 'Will you accept my apology?'

'We have to work together.'

That wasn't a yes. Should he push?

'This wasn't just about our reputation among the sailors, was it?' It was a guess, but her reaction had seemed quite extreme to a little bit of gossip. 'Was it about Bulla Felix?'

87

'Shut up,' she said. 'You know nothing.' Her voice was quiet, and he detected a little tremor in it.

'Did you love him?'

No reply.

'Oh.'

Silence. Silus tried one more time. 'I didn't know. I am truly sorry.'

After a moment, Daya said, 'It's not like you think. He loved me like a daughter. I loved him... more strongly than that. But it never transformed into anything... physical.'

'That must have hurt,' said Silus.

'No!' she said vehemently. 'He was a great man. Being with him was enough. He saved me from a life of slavery. He taught me how to survive. How to be free. Being with him didn't hurt, even if I loved him in a way that he didn't love me back. It was losing him that...'

She broke off. Silus reached out a hand to hers but she jerked away from his touch. He folded his arms across his chest.

'I know what it's like to watch loved ones die,' he said.

There was a pause, then a small hand reached out, squeezed his shoulder briefly, and was gone.

'Oclatinius told me about your family. It's my turn to be sorry.'

The old spymaster was a gossip too? No, he always had a good reason to do anything. Maybe he wanted to bond Silus and Daya more closely. That might even be the reason that Daya was on this mission instead of Atius.

'He told you that, huh?'

'He did. But I haven't blurted it out to the crew to gain their favour.'

He took the reprimand stoically. Was the conversation, the brief rapprochement, over?

'I still don't understand something though, Daya,' he said tentatively. 'How did you go from running with the outlaws to trying out for the Arcani, the Emperor's spies? Don't you hate the Emperor for what he did to Bulla Felix?'

'I do,' she said vehemently. Then, more uncertainly, 'I did. Now, the Emperor who ordered him hunted down and executed is dead. His sons had nothing to do with his death.'

'So it was the man himself you hated, not the position, not Rome itself.'

'Bulla was always kind to the people, and merciful to the soldiers he defeated and captured. That makes his end even more bitter. They gave him a wooden sword and set two lions on him. He didn't attempt to fight. He was never cruel to animals any more than to people, and I believe he knew these animals held him no personal animosity. Hating them was as useless as hating the executioner's garotte.

'Before they attacked, he looked around the crowd. For a moment, our eyes locked. I was so far away, I don't know if he recognised me. But I must believe that he knew I was with him to the last. After that, he disappeared beneath the beasts, and I couldn't hear his screams over the cheering of the crowd. After the beast handlers had used their whips and spears to get the animals off him and out of the arena, his body was dragged away, leaving a long trail of blood in the sand. His head was hanging half off, one arm ripped clean away. I looked at the Emperor, and I knew what I had to do.'

'What?' asked Silus, spellbound.

'I had to kill him.'

—

Plautilla looked out across the narrow sea that separated Lipari from mainland Sicily and sighed. A short distance away was the island of Vulcano. She could probably reach it by swimming, but what was the point? Vulcano was even less interesting than Lipari, as it was primarily used for forestry and mining. Lipari at least had some interesting ruins from when it was owned by the Greeks before the Romans conquered it. Occasionally wealthy

Romans still visited to use the baths that were fed by the island's hot springs. Sometimes she was able to obtain news from the Empire. Her guards were taciturn and grumpy, resenting their posting to this isolated place to act purely as gaolers, and they told her next to nothing. But the visits to the island had become less and less frequent. She didn't know if people were avoiding her out of fear of incurring disfavour from the Imperial family, or because there were more interesting places in the Empire to visit.

The last time anyone of importance from the mainland had come to see her was before the Saturnalia. A Romano-Gallic nobleman was looking for warmer climes to see out the winter and he had stayed about a week. She had squeezed every bit of information she could out of him. Severus and Antoninus were still in Britannia, campaigning against the Caledonians, she discovered, but the Emperor's health was failing.

Knowing that the seemingly invincible Severus was ill sent a frisson of excitement and fear through her. When the old man who had executed her father and exiled her was gone, would she be recalled from exile? Would she be reunited with Antoninus, her father's sins forgiven?

Her brother Plautius threw cold water on that idea. In his years of exile, he had grown fat, drunken and morose. He did little but eat and drink and bathe, for what else was there for a man of his age to do here?

'When Severus is gone, Antoninus can do what he likes. Geta isn't strong enough to restrain him. We are an inconvenience from his past. He hated Father, and he never liked you. When the old Emperor dies, our own time will be about to run out.'

She detested her brother on occasion. Even if what he said was true, why say it so cruelly? But he was the only adult Roman company she had, and sometimes she just needed someone to have a mature conversation with. Their elderly Greek house slave, Loukia, was no Socrates, or even a Julia

Domna. Catching Plautius in the brief moments between his being too drunk and too hungover was the key to a discussion worth having.

Right now, he was a little too drunk, but at least he was entertaining Hortensia. Plautilla's daughter was her delight and the only thing that kept her sane. Just one year old at the time of Plautianus' execution and Plautilla's expulsion from Rome, she was now nearly eight, and had never known anything except exile, first in Sicily and now on this tiny, broken-down island. Despite this, or maybe because of it, she was a happy child, delighting in her lessons from her mother in Greek grammar and poetry, from Loukia in weaving and sewing, from Plautius in philosophy and history. She explored the island and befriended one of the feral dogs that roamed near the rubbish tip. She played board games and sang and played the lyre beautifully.

Sometimes she asked Plautilla why they couldn't leave the island, and Plautilla was always evasive, even as her heart was breaking. Her daughter should have been in Rome, her education preparing her for a life married to a Roman nobleman, caring for his household and bearing his children. Was that future to be denied to her?

She turned back to the sea, looking towards Sicily where any news or visitors would come from, and resumed her watch.

–

'And how did that work out?' asked Silus, incredulous.

'The Emperor is dead, isn't he?'

Silus gaped. 'You? But it can't have been. He was ill. He died of natural causes. How did you…?'

He realised Daya was chuckling quietly, and he shut his mouth abruptly. Bitch.

'Very funny,' he said. 'But were you serious about wanting to kill him?'

'Deadly,' she said. 'He was the man I held responsible for Bulla's death. Merciless and cruel. I vowed to make him pay.'

'How?'

'You may have noticed I have some skills.'

'One or two,' admitted Silus.

'I planned to infiltrate the palace as a serving slave, and stab him to death right in front of his family and the Praetorian Guards.'

'And your escape plan?'

'There was no escape plan.'

'I see. So what happened?'

'It took years. I allowed myself to be taken slave again, and worked domestically. Sometimes I couldn't believe I had put myself back into slavery voluntarily, but it was the only way. I manipulated my masters into selling me to people that I wanted to be near. A word in the right ear about how much such-and-such a noble would pay for a particular skill I had, for example. Playing the lyre. Cooking a certain dish. I became a valued commodity, and eventually I was purchased by the Imperial court, much to my current master's annoyance.'

'So you got your chance? What went wrong?'

'Oclatinius, of course.'

Silus nodded. Of course.

'I had finally been selected to serve at an Imperial banquet. They were all going to be there. Caracalla, Geta, Papinianus, Julia Domna. The Emperor himself. I had a small knife, tipped with belladonna to make extra sure, hidden up the sleeve of my tunic.

'I was on my way from the kitchens to the triclinium with a tray of sweetmeats and my knife, when Oclatinius intercepted me in the corridor. He had been watching me for some time, apparently. I pulled the knife and tried to stab him, hoping I could make a run past the guards for the Emperor. He grabbed my wrist, made me drop the knife and had me pinned against the wall before I could take a breath. Then before anyone came along to investigate the noise of the dropped tray, he whisked me off to a side room.'

Silus knew the old man had prodigious fighting skills, but Daya was good. To disarm her so easily was impressive. He reminded himself once more never to cross him.

'And from attempted assassination of the Emperor, to training for the Arcani, the most trusted and feared spies in the Empire, was a short step?' asked Silus, bewildered.

'Of course not,' said Daya. 'Oclatinius took me into his household and talked to me. I didn't understand why I wasn't being arrested and executed, or just cut down on the spot. And he did tell me that if I tried to escape, or showed disobedience, he would have me flayed and left out for the crows. But he also told me he saw something in me. He asked me about why I wanted to kill the Emperor, what had led me there, what skills I had, made me demonstrate them to him. I think that if I hadn't been sufficiently interesting to him, he would have put a knife in me.

'But he liked me. And for my part...' She trailed off, swallowed. 'For my part he was the first person to treat me like a human being since Bulla.'

'He is an extraordinary man,' said Silus.

'He showed me what use I could be to the Empire. How it would give me a sense of value and purpose. He told me how ill Severus was, and persuaded me that there was no point in continuing my attempt on his life, as he would be dead before long anyway. And he told me that Bulla would have wanted me to be happy and successful.'

'That must have been hard, given Bulla's attitude towards the state.'

'At first. But Oclatinius showed me that Bulla was running his own little empire, and that despite his mercy, he used violence to keep it running smoothly. And he told me that admirable as Bulla's mini-empire was, how much better it was for the life of the people of Rome to live in a big, stable empire, where laws were upheld, everyone was fed, and everyone was safe from violence.'

Except the slaves, thought Silus. Oclatinius had done a good job of persuasion on the impressionable, idealistic young woman. Converts and turncoats were often the most passionate of believers, he knew.

'And so he trained me, and judged me, and finally decided that I was good enough for a mission. And that's when he introduced me to you.'

'You aren't a sworn Arcanus yet, are you?'

'After this mission, he promised.'

'And how do you feel about this mission? Off to kill an innocent woman and her family.'

'No one is innocent,' said Daya with a sneer. 'Besides, she is a threat to the peace and stability of the Empire. And Oclatinius orders it. That is good enough for me. And it should be for you too.'

'It is, certainly,' said Silus. He may have been tasked with assessing Daya, but he was sure that cut both ways, and he had no desire for her to report back to Oclatinius that he had doubts about his mission.

'Good,' said Daya. 'Do you want to know anything else?' Her tone suggested she was done talking now.

'No, no. I think that covers everything.' Silus lay back on his bed and was quiet. Soon, Daya was breathing deeply. But Silus found it hard to drift off, unsure how he felt about the scary young woman asleep by his side.

—

There were few things Tituria enjoyed in life more than eavesdropping on adults. For a nine-year-old girl, the world of grown-ups was a mysterious place. Her mother and father instructed her on what was to be expected from a young unmarried Roman girl, and then a married Roman woman, and while some aspects seemed nice, such as being in charge of the household, others seemed less so. Why could she never be a senator like her father, for example? What happened when a man married a woman, and how did they make babies? Her parents were silent on these matters, and the explanations that the household slaves attempted seemed implausible.

Hearing the words straight from the horses' mouths was Tituria's preferred method of self-education. And since the horses were unwilling to communicate with her directly, listening in on their discussions was the next best thing.

At this particular moment, Tituria was hiding inside a wide, tall vase that sat in her father's study. It had been one of her preferred hiding places for several years, but now that her limbs were starting to lengthen, she had to pull her knees up to her chest and tuck herself in more tightly than in the past, and she knew that it wouldn't be long before she had to give up this spot. For now, though, she had an excellent position to listen to her father's conversation, even if the words came to her through the aperture of the vase in a ghostly echo.

When she had heard Dio Cassius announced at the door, she had taken a gamble on where her father would meet him. Last time he had come she had rushed to hide beneath a couch in the triclinium, and been disappointed when they had retreated to the tablinum. Father had become more secretive when Dio Cassius visited these days, and Tituria was desperate to know why.

It was difficult being silent in the darkness, unable to see what was going on. She was sure the vase amplified the sound of her breathing, that they might even be able to hear her heart thudding with excitement and fear of capture. But she had not yet been discovered, and her luck seemed to be holding out again today.

She heard a slave take orders for drinks, her father and Dio Cassius exchange pleasantries while they were served, and then dismiss the slave. When they thought they were alone, Dio Cassius spoke.

'Have you given the matter any further thought?'

'Of course I have,' said her father, his voice uncharacteristically curt. 'I have been thinking of little else.'

'Good. This is no light matter. And where do your loyalties lie?'

'To the Emperor, of course.'

'Come now, Titurius. There is still more than one Emperor, even after the passing of Severus. This isn't the first time we have discussed this matter.'

Her father sighed and she heard him lift his cup and drink. She imagined his face now, brow furrowed as always when he was concentrating or concerned.

'You know there were two wolves seen at the Capitol this week,' said Dio. 'They were chased away. One was hunted down and killed in the Forum. The other was killed later, outside the city walls.'

'You and your omens, Dio Cassius.'

'It doesn't matter if you believe them, Titurius. If the common man, or even the average senator, gives it credence, then it matters.'

'Do you really think there can only be one?'

'Do you really think they can rule together?'

'No, I don't think they can. They even messed up their joint sacrifice to Concord.'

'Both Emperors and the superintending consul searching for each other all night. What a farce. So you have two options. Which charioteer will you bet on? Blue or Green?'

'There is another option. Not to place a bet.'

'Titurius. Would you really stand on the sidelines when the fate of the Empire is being decided? Besides, do you think that the victor will be any more magnanimous to those who stayed out of the battle than those who opposed him?'

'So we all have to choose a side, and we all have to pick the winner or else?'

'And once we have picked a side, we have to do everything in our power to help them win, or we will suffer the consequences.'

Tituria shivered. She didn't like the sound of that.

'Who is the more likely to win then?' said Titurius. 'Blue is the more powerful. He has the support of the army and the Syrian faction.'

'Green is more popular with the people. Blue always seems so stern. And the army won't turn against Green. He is physically very like his father, whom they loved.'

Tituria supposed that Dio Cassius and her father thought they were being clever talking in codes. But she knew that Caracalla liked to race in the arena in the colours of the Blue faction, and Geta consequently had chosen the Green and raced for them.

'I am inclined to back the more powerful man, regardless. I want to be on the winning side, for my own sake and the sake of my family.'

Again, Tituria felt a chill.

'I still assert that Green is the more powerful. He may not have as much support among the legions, but true power is decided in Rome by the Senate and the Praetorians. It is the Praetorian leadership and the Senate we must work on. And remember, we must not only back the winner, but ensure that the winner is the best one for Rome and for ourselves. Blue will never take our guidance on matters of state. Green is much more malleable. I believe the key is convincing both Praetorian prefects to our way of thinking.'

'Laetus is no lover of Blue, that's for sure,' said Titurius. 'But Papinianus seems undecided. His loyalty was to the father. And he is related more closely to Ge… I mean to Green. But he is part of the Syrian faction who support Blue.'

'Papinianus is the one we need to work on,' agreed Dio Cassius. 'Let's wait for the Imperial party to return to Rome, and then look for an opportunity to spend some time with Papinianus.'

Titurius let out a long breath, then Tituria heard the scraping of two chairs as the men stood. Moments later, they were gone, and Tituria was alone with what she had heard.

She eased herself out of the jar, stretched her cramped limbs, and tiptoed to the door. Once she was sure no one was nearby, she hurried away, heading for the peristylium. There, she watched the birds gathering material for nesting, while thoughts of what she had heard churned through her mind.

–

Silus and Daya landed on Lipura at night. A small skiff had taken them inland and dropped them near enough to the shore that they had only got wet up to their ankles. They followed a narrow path up a cliff, lit by enough moonlight to avoid twisting an ankle or taking a nasty fall. At the top was the villa where Plautilla lived in exile with her family.

Silus knew that two Praetorians guarded the house, but he doubted that they would be very alert. Silus reckoned that they felt their jobs were fairly superfluous anyway. The imprisoned family had no means of escape from the island, and where would they go if they did manage to flee? And the guards had no reason to worry about attack from the outside. There were no riches here and no one would pay a ransom for these hostages.

Their orders were to kill Plautilla and all her familia. That meant her slaves as well as her family. But they had been ordered to spare the Praetorians if at all possible, and if it wasn't possible, to ensure that they both died, so neither Praetorian could report back on the murder of the other.

Daya had argued that their orders gave them scope to go in and kill both guards quickly and quietly, before moving on to the rest of the household. But Silus, nominally in charge, although he feared the level of control he had over Daya, had vetoed this, and laid plans to incapacitate them peacefully.

They climbed the wall at the back of the villa, made simple by missing bricks and large cracks to give hand and footholds, and slipped into the peristylium. From there they moved silently into the main house and took stock.

The villa was not huge, and some parts had been abandoned to the elements, roofless or with doors nailed shut. That considerably narrowed the number of rooms to search. As usual, Oclatinius had been short on detail, never one to hand-hold his spies in their mission, expecting them to be competent and independent enough to need nothing from him but the barest of orders.

They split up and scouted the layout efficiently. As they had suspected, no one was awake. Some doors were partially open, and some they had been able to peep through a crack. They located the two Praetorians sharing a bedroom just off the atrium, snoring loudly. They could only find one slave: a plump, elderly woman who lay on her back and moaned intermittently. One man slept in a bedroom alone, tossing and turning and smelling strongly of alcohol. And in the final room was Plautilla. He glimpsed her through the crack made by the partially open door. She was lying in bed under a light blanket, face serene in sleep, breathing lightly. He sighed and returned to Daya.

'Guards first,' he whispered. She nodded.

They entered the guards' bedroom, and at a nod from Silus to coordinate their actions, they both pressed a knife to their victims' throats while clamping hands over their mouths. Both guards woke up, trying to gasp and struggle, gripping their attackers' wrists, until the pressure from the knives quickly made them still.

While Daya held her captive motionless, Silus eased his victim upright, and whispered to him to put his hands behind his back. When he complied, Silus quickly bound his wrists tight, then slipped a gag into his mouth and tightened it painfully. He then tied his feet together, tied his hands, then attached the wrist and ankle ropes together behind his back, so the guard was well and truly trussed. Once the first guard was immobilised, he helped Daya do the same to the second.

Daya stood over them while Silus crept to the door and made sure that they hadn't been overheard.

'I still think we should kill them both,' said Daya. 'It's safer that way.'

The guards started to struggle, eyes wide. Silus made calming motions, then drew his knife when they continued to wrestle with their bindings.

'We aren't going to kill you,' said Silus. 'Unless you do anything to give us away before our mission is finished. Do you understand?'

The guards nodded, calming down.

'Come on,' said Silus. 'Let's get this over with. Quick and silent, right? You take the slave woman and I'll take the brother. Then we will do Plautilla together.'

Daya nodded and was instantly out of the door. Silus followed quickly, entering the small bedroom where Plautius slept. He was a large man, once fit, although long since gone to fat. Strangulation might not be quick enough, and might alert others to the sound of a struggle.

He stepped forward to the bedside, pressed a hand over the drunkard's mouth, and slit his throat from side to side. Blood spurted sideways, and Plautius woke, staring in terror at his attacker. The fear lasted only moments though, before all awareness left his eyes. Silus cleaned his hands and blade on the bedcover, and went out into the corridor to find Daya. She had also cleaned her knife and herself, but blood was leaking out from under the door of the room she had just vacated. He nodded to her and she nodded back. Then, taking a deep breath, they approached Plautilla's room.

When they opened the door, the young woman was standing in the middle of the room, her bedclothes in a lumpen mess behind her. A tiny oil lamp was the only illumination in the windowless room, but Silus' eyes had adjusted enough to the dark that he could make out all her features. She wore a plain white smock. Her skin was smooth and unblemished, her nose petite, her eyes wide and round and full of tears.

'Did my husband send you?' she said, voice tremulous.

'Yes, Augusta,' said Silus. 'I'm sorry.'

'Did he say why?'

'He did not, Augusta.'

'Silus,' hissed Daya. 'What the fuck are you doing? Get on with it. Or are you too much of a pussy? Shall I do it for you?'

'Be silent, Daya,' said Silus. He pulled out his knotted rope where it had hung from his belt. He took two brisk steps forward to stand behind her, then slipped the rope over her neck.

'If you have any last prayers to say, say them now,' Silus whispered in her ear. Then he pulled hard to tighten the rope around her neck. Reflexively, she reached up to try to loosen the pressure, opened her mouth to draw breath which would not come through her collapsed windpipe. He leant back, lifting her feet from the ground, increasing the pressure on her neck. His face was by the side of hers. He could see the tears in her eyes. And strangely, in the last moments before she lost consciousness, he saw her eyes dart towards the bed.

Daya had seen it too, and looked curiously at the bedcovers, piled up as they had thought in disarray when Plautilla had arisen in alarm. But when he looked closely, he thought he could see movement.

As he pulled tight one last time, making sure he had squeezed the last of the life out of Caracalla's wife, Daya stepped forward and pulled the bedcovers away with a sharp tug.

Lying exposed on the bed, trembling violently, was a young girl.

Daya and Silus looked at each other. Silus let Plautilla's lifeless body fall to the floor, and the girl gasped and covered her mouth with her hand.

Daya moved quickly. Silus cried out, 'Daya, no!'

Daya put a hand on the girl's chin, another behind her head, and twisted sharply. There was a crack, and when Daya stepped back, the girl collapsed, dead.

'Daya,' whispered Silus. 'What have you done?'

Daya looked puzzled. 'We had our orders. Kill everyone in the household apart from the guards.'

'She was just a little girl.' Not much older than Sergia had been when she…

'Kill everyone,' repeated Daya.

'I didn't know that Caracalla and his wife had a daughter.'

'Neither did I. And Oclatinius clearly didn't think he needed to mention it, as his orders were so clear. Kill. Everyone.'

Silus looked at her in anguish. Daya shrugged and walked out, leaving Silus alone with the bodies of the young mother and the little girl that they had just killed.

Chapter Seven

Their arrival in Rome should have been a victorious return, but was in fact an occasion of public mourning, the whole city observing both festivities and religious ceremonies. The Senate was clad in black, and the women of the city wore plain white, unadorned with any jewellery. Choirs of children and women from noble families sang both joyful and mournful hymns. Some of the ceremonies involved in saying farewell to an Emperor had already been carried out at his cremation in Britannia, but this interment was an opportunity for Rome to pay its respects to the man who had now become a god.

The Imperial party had rested outside the city walls the night before, so they were refreshed to start the journey in the morning. The Praetorians led the way, with Geta and Caracalla riding behind them, flanking the carriage that conveyed Julia Domna with their father's ashes.

The ashes were contained in an urn of purple stone that Severus had selected himself. Not long before his death, he had held the urn in his hands, and said gravely, 'You shall hold a man that the whole world could not hold.'

And it was true – his mortal remains, those few ashes that were all that was left when the rest of the flesh was burnt away, were now held in that small pot. It hardly seemed real to Caracalla that the presence which had dominated his entire life was now in that small container. And soon to be interred and never seen again.

The procession went across the Pons Aemilius and through the Forum Boarium, through the Forum Romanum at the bottom of the Palatine and Capitoline Hills, and circling the Flavian Amphitheatre, before heading west past the theatres of Marcellus and Pompey, then back over the Tiber at the Pons Aelius to the Mausoleum of Hadrian. All along the way, crowds thronged the sides of the street and threw flowers and laurel branches in the path of the two Emperors and the Augusta. From the rostra in the forum, Hedius Lollianus Terentius Gentianus and Pomponius Bassus, the consuls, gave flowery speeches praising Severus' merits and achievements, as well as those of the two new Emperors.

While it was technically a funeral procession, and the Imperial family was in mourning, this was the first time in more than three years that an Emperor of Rome had visited the city, and Caracalla and Geta were celebrating a devastating victory over the tribes of Northern Britannia. Both Geta and Caracalla had been awarded the titles Britannicus, along with their father, although Caracalla grumbled privately to Domna that Geta had done little to deserve it. In those moments Domna would usually silence him with a kiss.

The Mausoleum of Hadrian contained the ashes of the Emperor Hadrianus, who had built the great wall that had proven so important in the war against the northern Britons waged by Caracalla and his father, and most subsequent Emperors had also been interred there. They were famous names, now gods, like Antoninus Pius, builder of the more northerly wall that had taken such a beating in the Maeatae raids, and the brothers Marcus Aurelius and Lucius Verus, who had ruled together in such harmony. He still wondered how that had been possible. Lucius Verus surely deferred to his older, more experienced sibling? If only things were so easy for Geta and him.

The Mausoleum itself was magnificent. A square base, topped by a large cylindrical structure, shaped like a layered cake, it was the tallest building in Rome. It was faced with blocks of marble, and marble statues thronged the first layer.

Rising from the middle of this small neat forest of figures was a columned tower. On top of the tower was a marble statue of a quadriga, a chariot drawn by four horses abreast. Severus had restored and built some impressive structures during his time in power, not least his arch at the other end of the Forum celebrating his victories over the Parthians. It was still a source of pride, even all these years after its dedication, that Caracalla himself was honoured on the arch, although he was obviously annoyed that his younger brother was also honoured, given that Geta had only been ten years old when the Parthian wars ended.

The procession halted before the gate in the bronze railings that surrounded the monument. Domna, holding the funerary urn, together with Geta and Caracalla and a small entourage of the most prominent nobles, entered the mausoleum.

Caracalla looked around, impressed despite all the wonders in Rome and around the Empire that he had seen. He had never been inside, and he stared at the resting places of the previous Emperors, situated in this enormous, magnificent structure. At the far end of the chamber was a colossal statue of Hadrian, looking down on them. Caracalla felt uncharacteristically small. He wondered if the great Emperor would approve of him as the ruler, or would prefer Geta.

A steep spiral ramp led up into the central tomb chamber, and Geta, Domna and Caracalla climbed alone. The Pontifex Maximus, as chief priest of the state religion, would have been expected to play an important role in the interment ceremony of an Emperor, but as the Emperor had also been the Pontifex Maximus since the time of Augustus Caesar, it was difficult to achieve unless the old Emperor was buried after the Senate had bestowed the title of Pontifex Maximus on the new one. At the moment it wasn't clear which of the two, Geta or Caracalla, would be given the honour, although Caracalla naturally thought it should fall to him as the elder.

When they reached the niche that had been prepared for Severus, Domna gently placed the urn in its spot. Once the ashes were interred, Severus' shade could finally cross the Styx. Caracalla was relieved that he would no longer be hanging around. When he made love to Domna, he wondered if the shade of Severus had been watching in impotent outrage. Now, the shade would be gone, and he would no longer feel his father watching him have sex with his widow.

Domna stepped back, and they all bowed their heads, alone with their thoughts. Caracalla's own thoughts never strayed far from his future, and a quiet moment just meant more time dwelling on the difficulty of sharing power, and what he could do about it.

After a few moments, Domna led them back down to the rest of the waiting party, then out into the light. It was Domna who had been chosen to give the funerary speech, since it could not be agreed if Geta or Caracalla would have the honour, or if it was to be both who would speak first.

Domna stood at the entrance gate and raised her hands for quiet. The crowd which lined the bank of the Tiber and the pons Aelius hushed, although only the most important who dominated the front ranks would properly hear her.

'Citizens of Rome. We have laid to rest Imperator Caesar Lucius Septimius Severus Pius Pertinax Augustus Arabicus Adiabenicus Parthicus Maximus Britannicus Maximus, Pontifex Maximus, Tribuniciae Potestasis, Father of the country.'

Caracalla only ever heard his father's full list of titles and honorifics at formal occasions. They were usually greatly truncated given how long they were, but Domna had pronounced them all correctly from memory without hesitation or faltering.

'He was one of the greatest of all Emperors,' continued Domna. 'A man who claimed the throne that was rightfully his and held it against a horde of usurpers. Who conquered some of Rome's oldest enemies, the tribes of Caledonia and the Parthians. Who ruled with justice and authority.

'Now he has been laid to rest, and his shade has departed, waiting to ascend when he is deified. Rome will never see the like of him again, and I will miss my husband for the rest of my days.

'But Rome is fortunate. My husband clearly decreed that Rome will be ruled jointly by his two sons, Geta and Antoninus. The chaos of the civil wars is not to be repeated, as our two Augusti reign in brotherly harmony. Rome is about to move forward, from the wondrous situation my husband has left it in, into a new Golden Age!'

The crowd went wild. It was a good speech, Caracalla thought, as he applauded and put on his best smile. Maybe it was even true. Maybe he should try to make it true. Was it possible? He could talk to Geta at the funeral feast, see if they could find a way forward together.

Geta leant across to him, still clapping.

'I have given orders for the palace to be partitioned. The interconnecting passages are being bricked up. My mother will have the central portion. I will take the north wing and you can have the south. We will not need to talk to each other unless on official business.'

Geta walked forward and placed an arm around Domna, and saluted the cheering crowds. Caracalla kept his smile plastered to his face and stepped forward to do the same.

—

Caracalla had his elbow on the arm of his throne, and his head was resting on his hand. Oclatinius stood to his right side, and apart from the two Arcani, the room was otherwise empty. Two tough-looking Praetorians stood on the other side of the door, forbidding entrance to anyone except by the express permission of the Emperor. Silus and Daya stood at attention in front of Caracalla and waited.

Daya was breathing slowly and calmly, her nostrils flaring and a gentle movement of her chest the only indication that she wasn't actually a statue. Silus' heart was racing, and he felt as though he couldn't get enough air into his chest, but every time he took a deep breath, it seemed to him like a yawn, and he became even more terrified that Caracalla would think that he was showing boredom at the wait.

Caracalla paid no attention though. He seemed uncharacteristically indecisive, opening his mouth to speak, then closing it again and stroking his beard while looking at the two assassins uncertainly. Finally, he broke the silence and spoke.

'Let's hear it then.'

Silus was the senior officer, and the full Arcanus, so it was his duty to deliver the report.

'Augustus,' he said, struggling to keep his voice steady. 'I can report that our mission was entirely successful.'

It seemed that Caracalla had been holding his breath, and with Silus' news, he let out a long sigh and his shoulders slumped.

'So, it is done,' he said, and his voice was a whisper.

Silus looked at Oclatinius, uncertain whether he should respond. Oclatinius shook his head slightly, and Silus held his tongue. Caracalla wiped his palm across his eyes.

'All of them?' he asked.

'We were able to spare the guards as instructed,' said Silus. 'Everyone else in the household was taken care of. The slave, the brother, the mother and the...' Suddenly his tongue felt too big for his mouth, and tears blurred his vision. Get a fucking grip on yourself, Silus. This display of emotion could get you thrown from the Tarpeian Rock. 'The child,' he finished.

After Daya had killed the little girl, Silus had been stunned and distraught. He had felt uncomfortable enough about killing the defenceless woman, but it was the Emperor's wife, and he could do with her as he wished. But his daughter? That had been a surprise. He wondered what would have happened if Daya hadn't coldly performed her duty. Could he have gone through with it himself?

Daya and he had talked little about what happened that day. When Daya saw that he was angry and upset, she had tried to bring it up with him, had explained that it was just a job, and as paterfamilias, Caracalla had every legal right to order the death of his wife and child. On their trip north through Italia, Silus had slowly thawed. Intellectually, he knew that Daya was right, and that in fact they had had no choice but to carry out their orders, but as a man who had lost his wife and daughter to violence, it felt like Silus had done violence on himself.

By the time they reached Rome, riding all day together, sharing their food, and sleeping next to each other, Silus had put it behind him. He wondered if part of his shock was that it was the young woman who had done this dreadful deed. But Daya's life had been one of brutality, as a slave and as an outlaw, and he could not expect her to behave like the sheltered daughter of a free man. They had entered Rome together shortly before the arrival of the legions and the new Emperors. They had watched the interment ceremony from the crowds, then reported to Oclatinius, who told them that Caracalla himself was keen to hear their report personally.

Fortunately, Caracalla did not react to his hesitation, nor his careful avoidance of using the names of the murdered mother, brother and child. His eyes had unfocused, staring over Silus' shoulder into the distance. After a moment he turned back to Silus.

'Did she suffer?'

'Plautilla was brave, and the garotte is very quick—'

'Not her,' interjected Caracalla. 'I don't care about that bitch. The girl. Was it quick?'

Silus noted the Emperor couldn't bring himself to say his daughter's name out loud. He opened his mouth, then glanced across at Daya.

'I broke her neck, Augustus,' said Daya matter-of-factly. 'Her death was instantaneous.'

Now a tear crept down Caracalla's face. The Augustus, ruler of the civilised world, was crying?

Silus opened his mouth, then snapped it shut when he realised how suicidally stupid speaking now could be.

'What is it?' asked Caracalla, seeing that Silus had been about to say something.

'Nothing, Augustus,' said Silus, bowing his head.

'Speak your mind, spy. I command it.'

Silus felt the blood drain to his feet, and he felt light-headed. He looked to Oclatinius, who just shook his head sadly. He should have thought of something insipid and inoffensive to say, but his thoughts had frozen, and all he could bring to mind was the question that had formed when he saw Caracalla cry.

'Why did the girl have to die, Augustus?' he blurted out.

Daya turned to him, gaping. Even Oclatinius drew a breath. Caracalla's stare felt like a dagger through the eyeball. He rose from his throne, the dark skin that could be seen around his thick beard blanched with rage. For a moment, Silus thought the burly Emperor would beat him to death with his bare hands. Then he sat back down, put his head in his hands and wept.

For an uncomfortably long time, Daya and Silus stood at attention while their Emperor wept in front of them. When he had recovered, he fixed Daya and Silus with a stern glare each in turn.

'Needless to say, if you tell anyone what you just witnessed, I will have you both tortured to death.'

'Yes, Augustus,' said Silus and Daya hastily.

'The last thing I need right now is any rumours of weakness of character. The Senate and army might seize any excuse to turn against me.'

Silus and Daya remained silent.

'You asked me a question. And as someone who has done me great service, Silus, not to mention the fact of your own losses, maybe I should give you an answer.'

'There is no need, Augustus,' said Silus. 'I spoke foolishly—'

'Be quiet.'

Silus snapped his mouth shut.

Caracalla sighed. 'Plautilla had to go. My father had wanted her dead, the consequence of Plautianus' treachery. You do know that her father was my father's cousin and one of his closest friends. And yet he tried to kill my father and take his throne.'

Silus bowed his head in acknowledgement, not daring to speak.

'Plautianus was a cruel man. He abused his rank to indulge his whim to torture boys and girls and prey on them sexually, both free and slave. My father made me marry his daughter to cement a closer relationship with Plautianus and secure his position. But truly, Plautilla was a horrible woman. She had strings of lovers – slave, low-born and nobleman – and she had a love of spending money on any lavishly expensive pretty thing that caught her eye. Cornelia, mother of the Gracchi, would have wept to see an Empress behave so.'

Oclatinius was looking sombre behind the Emperor. Caracalla looked to the old spymaster for support, and Silus thought he had never expected to see this powerful man so vulnerable.

'Your Emperor speaks the truth, of course. It was my sad duty to keep the Augustus informed of the lovers that his wife kept. And sometimes, if the Augustus thought the person was particularly egregious, to do away with them.'

'There were too many to make an example of all of them, and to be honest I did not care that much. Can you be a cuckold over a woman you have never had sexual intercourse with?'

'Never?' said Silus, despite his resolve to be silent. 'But that means—'

'The girl was not mine,' confirmed Caracalla, his voice weighted with regret. 'Listen to me, Silus. You have earned my trust, and I hope I have earned yours. My position is precarious. As long as my father lived, there was a truce between my brother and myself. Now, the gods know what the outcome will be. Maybe we can work together. Maybe only one of us will survive, and if that is the case, I fully intend to be the victor. And I will do anything necessary to achieve it.

'Plautilla and her brother could have been rallying points for the disaffected. They are related to the African faction, which supports my brother. People like Caecilius Aemilianus and Gaius Septimius Severus Aper. For my part I have the loyalty of one of the two Praetorian prefects, Papinianus, and the urban prefect Cilo and his deputy Asper. But the young girl could have been a bargaining chip, maybe promised in marriage to give a legitimacy to a claim to Empire. What if she was betrothed to Geta? It wouldn't be the first time an Emperor has married his niece. And would my faction's followers remain loyal with such a claim to the throne?'

'Will you please forgive me, Augustus? I should never have questioned you.'

'Of course you shouldn't have, spy. Who do you think you are?' Caracalla's voice had risen. Silus quailed, shrank back.

'Calm yourself, Silus. I ordered you to speak. And I am not a man who is deaf to the opinions and advice of others. The senators just believe that to be the case because I don't listen to those old fools. I prefer the counsel of men who have experience of the real world, like Oclatinius here, like you.'

Silus bowed his head in gratitude.

'I think you have had enough of your Emperor's innermost thoughts and feelings, spy, don't you?'

'Yes, Augustus.'

'With the political situation as it is now, I'm sure Oclatinius and myself will have need of your skills very soon. For now, Oclatinius will reward you with a cash bounty for your service. You are dismissed.'

Silus and Daya saluted, and Oclatinius followed them out of the throne room, leaving Caracalla alone with his thoughts.

Once they were out of earshot of the guards, Oclatinius hissed, 'Fuck me, Silus. It's usually Atius shooting his mouth off. I thought better of you.'

'I'm sorry, sir. It's just… it was difficult.'

'Your job is difficult. Get over it. You chose this. You had the option to go back to your shitty life on the wall, scouting in enemy territory in the cold and the rain. You chose to work for me.'

'Yes, sir.' Silus had lost all will to argue, but he reminded himself that the only reason he had joined the Arcani was to have the opportunity to avenge his family.

Oclatinius looked at him, calculating.

'I hope I haven't misjudged you, Silus.'

'No, sir. You haven't.' Silus hated that the coldly efficient Daya was witnessing all this. What must she be thinking of him?

Oclatinius tossed him a bag of coins.

'Go and find yourself somewhere to live. Rome is your new home. Rent an apartment in an insula. Buy a house slave. Explore the city. Keep your head down. And report to me twice a day in case of orders. Daya, come to my office at dusk. You did well. Tonight I will induct you as a full Arcanus. I'll have some quarters in the Praetorian barracks allocated to you. A girl living on her own in the city could run into trouble.'

'I can look after myself, sir,' said Daya defiantly.

'I don't doubt it,' said Oclatinius. 'But if you are forced to repeatedly prove your fighting skills, you will quickly become well known, and that is a distinct disadvantage for a spy.'

'Yes, sir.'

Oclatinius looked from Silus to Daya and back again.

'It was a shitty job,' he said. 'No one is pretending otherwise. But it had to be done. And you did it proficiently. Well done, both of you. Now fuck off out of my sight.'

–

Rome was like nothing Silus had imagined. He had pictured a city like Eboracum, but a bit bigger. The difference between Eboracum and Rome was as large as the difference between Eboracum and a tiny Brigantian village. It was not just the size. It was everything. The streets were dirtier, the crowds were denser, the cacophony was louder. The markets were bigger, the ethnicities vastly more diverse, and the prostitutes more beautiful and more forward.

And the buildings. Vast structures reaching up into the sky. After being dismissed by Oclatinius, Silus had found Atius in the Praetorian barracks, and they had been reunited with a manly hug. Silus had given Atius a playful punch and commented how nice it had been to be out of his company, to disguise the fact that seeing him had made him realise how much he had missed his friend.

They spent their first full day together in the city just wandering around and staring. Their clothes, accents and general country-bumpkin ignorance marked them as outsiders, which led to interest from two types of entrepreneurs – guides and muggers.

After the third mugging attempt had ended, as with the previous two, in multiple broken bones among the assailants, and not a bruise on the two newcomers, word had quickly got around that these men were not such easy marks as their appearance suggested, and they were left alone.

On the other hand, prospective guides constantly pestered them, and Silus thought that it would be unreasonable and probably illegal to beat them up as well. Eventually, he decided the best way to stop the beggars, cripples and former slaves too useless to be retained by their masters was to hire one for the day and make it their job to keep the rest away.

The one they chose was a maimed veteran who had recognised them as fellow military men. He had an empty socket where one of his eyes had been, had lost one arm at the elbow, and had a crutch under the other to compensate for one of his legs, which had clearly been fractured and healed crookedly.

The crippled guide introduced himself as Lurco, a veteran of the Legio II Parthica, and it was in Severus' Parthian wars, he told them, that he had sustained his injuries.

'We knew the men of the Second Parthica in Britannia,' said Silus. 'Good fighters. For legionaries.' The rivalry between auxiliaries and legionaries was perennial, with the legionaries looking down on their less armoured, less trained juniors, while the auxiliaries always felt they had something to prove to their uppity comrades.

'I didn't make Britannia,' said Lurco regretfully. 'Invalided out before that.'

'What happened to your pension?'

'Most of it went on booze, dice and whores.'

'And the rest?'

'The rest I wasted.'

Atius gave a good belly laugh at this, and Silus could imagine Atius finding himself in the exact same position in years to come.

Silus paid Lurco a silver coin for the day's service, with the promise of another at the end of the day if he did a good job and kept the crowds away. The veteran was as good as his word, showing a highly illegal knife to anyone who tried to encroach on his clients' personal space, and taking them to some of the landmarks. It was a slow journey, the speed of their progress hindered by Lurco's infirmities and the thick crowds, but Silus wasn't complaining.

They stared in amazement at the Pantheon with its vast dome. They goggled at the Forum Romanum, full of politicians, priests and traders mingling in chaos. Lurco pointed up to the Palatine Hill where the luxurious villas of the ultra-wealthy sat, including the palace where the Emperors and the Empress lived. He took them to Trajan's Column and the Arch of Severus, where they could see the pictorial representations of the victories and triumphs of both those great Emperors. He took them around the outside of the Flavian Amphitheatre, and told them tales of mass executions, thrilling gladiatorial contests, and beast fights. He showed them the Circus Maximus, and told them where the best seats were to watch the chariot races between the Greens, Blues, Reds and Whites.

After lunch in a tavern near the Forum, Silus told Lurco that he needed to find a place to live.

'What's your budget?' asked Lurco.

Silus considered. His reward and the pay he had saved was generous, but he could see that Rome was a far more expensive place to live than northern Britannia had been.

'Let's say I'm looking for something economical.'

And that's how they ended up seeing the other side of Rome. The Subura had for centuries been the poor district of Rome, but with a character all its own. Despite some notable inhabitants over the years, including a young Julius Caesar, the rich avoided it like it was ridden with the plague of Antoninus these days, preferring to live in the hills above the city to avoid the noise and the stench.

Every sort of tradesman lined the streets, their stalls set out in front of the terraces of their tiny shops above which they slept with their families. Sandal makers, blacksmiths, wool workers, felt workers, linen weavers, perfumiers, spice merchants, cheesemongers, fishmongers, and sausage sellers all yelled out the prices of their wares, competing with the noise from the heralds and the prostitutes as well as all the shoppers trying to make themselves heard while they haggled for the best prices.

It was a hot day, and the ordure in the streets, human and animal, was steaming, the overwhelming acrid stenches making Silus gag. Chickens, pigs, dogs and dirty children scurried around Silus' feet, threatening to trip him up, and more than one urchin made an attempt on his purse. Lurco led them off down a narrow side street between two tall insulae and banged on a ground-floor door.

'This is the insula of my old friend, Tigranes. He is an ex-gladiator, and he went into the property business with his winnings. We go way back. He'll do you a good deal.'

A tall, dark slave opened the door and glowered at them. He took in Silus' and Atius' clothing, tatty and dirty from their travels, and Lurco's physical state, and spat at their feet.

'Fuck off. No beggars.'

Atius laughed out loud. 'Old friend, huh?'

Lurco gave him a sour look. 'New staff,' he muttered. He turned to the slave. 'Listen, slave. I am a close personal friend of Tigranes. Tell him Lurco is here to see him, or I'm sure he will give you a whipping you will never forget.'

The slave looked him up and down, sneered, then slammed the door shut. Lurco gave Atius and Silus a sheepish grin. 'Can't wait to see my old friend Tigranes.'

The door flew open again, and a huge man with a white scar across his olive-skinned face yelled at them in a huge voice with a Syrian accent. 'Lurco, you cunt, you'd better have brought me the money you owe me or I'm going to slice you into strips of meat and feed you to my fucking dogs!'

Lurco shrank back, and Atius and Silus both moved their hands subtly nearer their concealed blades. Then the huge man burst out with a deep laugh that echoed down the street.

'Lurco, your face! Have you shat yourself? Tell me, honestly. Is there shit running down your legs right now?'

Lurco let out a breath. 'No, Tigranes. I managed to keep my arse clamped shut, thank you very much.'

'I'm surprised you can keep your arse closed with all the piles dangling out of it.'

Lurco looked embarrassed, and Silus suspected this was a real detail that he had confided to his friend, and that he now regretted his openness.

'Don't worry, old friend,' said Tigranes. 'You still have a month to pay off your debt before I cut you up.'

Silus frowned. 'How much does he owe you?'

'Five denarii.'

'Is that all?' The silver coin he had given Lurco earlier was worth one denarius. 'Are your begging skills so poor you can't get that much?'

'Oh, he earns it,' said Tigranes. 'He just spends it as fast as he gets it.'

Silus reached into his purse and handed over five silver coins. 'Here. Consider his debt paid.'

Tigranes took the coins suspiciously, then looked at Lurco. 'Who is this? Your brother? Your lover?'

'Just someone new to the city who hired me as a guide for the day.'

Tigranes looked abashed. 'You shame me, stranger. If you can show this kindness to a man you met for the first time today, then surely I can forgive the debt of my old friend Lurco. Here.' He handed four coins back to Silus. Silus looked down at the four coins in his palm, and the one remaining in Tigranes' hand, in puzzlement.

'I forgave the debt, not the interest,' said Tigranes and dropped the coin into his purse. 'Now, Lurco, what brings you to my door? You had better not be looking for another loan after you have just become debt free.'

'No, no. Like I said, I'm a guide today. These men are foreigners and they are looking for lodgings at a reasonable price. And I thought who better to take them to than Tigranes the landlord, owner of the finest insula in the Subura.'

Tigranes smiled broadly. 'In that case, come in, have some wine. It so happens I do have a vacancy. The tenant on the top floor was behind in his rent. Sadly, he has no realistic prospect of making his back payments now.'

'Why not?' asked Atius.

'Because he broke his leg when I threw him down the stairs,' said Tigranes.

Silus and Atius exchanged glances, but Tigranes had already turned his back, beckoning them to follow him into the house. Lurco trailed after him, and with some trepidation, and their hands still close to their knives, Silus and Atius followed them inside.

The ground floor of an insula was always the most desirable, and Tigranes was obviously doing well for himself. A guard dog was chained in the vestibule and it growled at them, hackles up, as they edged past it. The atrium had colourful mosaics and frescoes, with several statues of nude tree nymphs around the well-maintained impluvium. The lararium contained ornate statues of Isis and Serapis rather than the usual household gods, and this helped confirm Tigranes' Syrian origins in Silus' mind.

Tigranes led them into the triclinium, where slaves brought dates and olives, and poured them cups of fine wine. Silus sipped, aware that this was probably a decent vintage, but knowing that beer was scarce in Rome, and feeling suddenly homesick.

'Where are you from, my new friends?' asked Tigranes.

'Britannia,' said Atius, before Silus had a chance to consider how much information they should volunteer.

'And what brings you to Rome?'

'Trade,' said Silus quickly before Atius could open his mouth again.

'May I ask what sort of trade? I have many contacts in Rome. I could open doors. And purses...'

'It is confidential at this stage. I'm sure you understand.'

'Of course, of course. But my door is always open any time you want to talk business.'

'I appreciate it,' said Silus.

'But for now, you wish to rent an apartment.'

'I do,' said Silus. 'Ideally something with a little space, not too draughty, with a comfortable bed and some furniture in good repair.'

'Then finish your wine and let me show you what I have.'

Atius drained his cup, and Silus set his down, half-finished. Tigranes led them outside to a staircase that led up the outside of the building. The wood had rotted through in places, and Silus watched carefully where he placed his feet. Progress was slow, as Lurco found the winding stairs hard to negotiate, and he refused all offers of help.

They ascended to the fourth floor, by which time everyone was fatigued, although the two Arcani were breathing much more easily than the crippled beggar and the overweight land-lord. At the top they faced a door made of four vertical planks with two planks nailed horizontally to keep it together. The top was splintered so there was a hole big enough for an eagle to get through, and there were gaps between the planks wide enough that it would have been easy to see inside if the interior hadn't been so dark.

Tigranes produced a rusty key the size of a sausage, and inserted it into the lock. He turned it one way, then the other, then wiggled it, cursed, and kicked the door. With a squeak that went right through Silus and made him shiver, the lock turned and the door swung open.

A stench of rat piss, garlic and human faeces hit Silus like a slap.

Tigranes strode inside and lit an oil lamp. Silus followed him in and looked around in dismay. There was a low table covered in stains and flies, and one chair with a broken back support. A brazier full of ash sat in the middle of the room. Behind a filthy curtain was a bedroom with a straw mattress on the floor against one wall. In the corner was a chamber pot, which had not been emptied, from whence much of the stench was emanating. One tiny window allowed the only light and ventilation, apart from whatever filtered in through the defective door. A rat scampered across the floorboards and out of a hole in the corner of the room, taking a mouldy crust with it.

Tigranes swept his arm around the room, a broad smile plastered across his face.

'Fully furnished, two rooms, spacious, with a wonderful view of...' He frowned and looked out of the window. 'A view of that building there.' Silus judged that with the tops of the buildings leaning in towards each other because of their shoddy construction, the building across the street was only around six feet away, and he could see through the window to where a round woman was applying make-up. She caught sight of him watching her and turned her back.

Atius suddenly burst out laughing. 'Let's go, Silus. We aren't staying here.'

'You won't find better in the Subura. Or maybe you are looking for something on the Palatine,' said Tigranes sarcastically. 'Something with hot baths and a spacious kitchen, and a separate wing for your servants' living quarters so you can't hear them farting and fucking at night?'

Silus looked to Lurco. 'Is he right? Is this as good as it gets?'

Lurco looked hesitantly at Tigranes, who gave him a meaningful stare. Lurco swallowed, but said bravely, 'Honestly, Silus, this place is a shithole.'

Tigranes opened his mouth to protest, but Lurco held up a hand to forestall him. 'Wait. It's a shithole, but so is everywhere in the Subura. And unless you own a fortune, then pretty much every place in Rome is. You said something economical – well, this is it. You can try for a better district, or a floor lower. But you will pay more and not get a lot of improvement. You can clean this place up and make it your own, and have some money from your pay left over for booze and women.'

'What's your price?' asked Silus.

'Are you nuts?' asked Atius, bemused.

'One thousand denarii per month.'

'Don't be absurd. I'll give you two hundred.'

'Five hundred.'

'Two fifty.'

'Deal.' Tigranes stuck his hand out and Atius grinned in disbelief as Silus shook it.

'Fuck this,' said Atius. 'I'm going to take up the offer of quartering with the Praetorians, like Daya.'

'I understand,' said Silus. 'But you will spend most of your evenings shacked up with loose maidens and whores. I want somewhere to call my own, like I had in Britannia.'

Atius nodded, losing his smile. 'Well, I will come to visit you, if I have no other company on a particular night. As long as you give the place a good clean out. I'll carry on looking after Issa in the barracks too until you are settled in.'

'One thing,' said Tigranes. 'Don't be late with your rent. Unless you want bad things to happen.'

Silus gave a half-smile. He took a step forward towards Tigranes, and said quietly, 'Let's be clear here. I will be a good tenant, and I will pay my dues. But don't threaten me again, or I will have your balls.'

Tigranes looked down to see Silus' knife pressed into his groin. He swallowed and held his hand up placatingly.

'No threat, my friend. I only meant that the gods hate a debtor, and I don't want divine misfortune to come your way.'

Silus held the blade and the silence until both became uncomfortable. When a single drop of sweat rolled down Tigranes' temple, he stepped back and smiled. 'We understand each other. The key.' Silus held out his hand, and Tigranes handed the bulky key over.

'Let me know if you need anything,' said the landlord, before he backed quickly out of the room and hurried down the stairs.

–

They ditched Lurco back in the Forum with an extra silver coin for his services, and the crippled veteran thanked them for their kindness. They met Daya in the mid-afternoon. She hadn't been interested in a tour of Rome – she had seen as much as she wished during her slave days. Silus noticed her hair was wet, and her face and upper chest, where it was visible above her loose-fitting tunic, were glowing. Daya saw him looking at her and frowned, and Silus turned away quickly.

'Been to the gymnasium?' asked Atius, not noticing this brief interaction.

Daya looked at Silus a moment longer, then turned to Atius as if only just hearing the question.

'Um, yes.'

'What exercises this time? Swimming ten miles? A quick run like Pheidippides did?'

'Just some weights, and then a bout in the ring with a boxer who was training.'

'You don't have a mark on you!' exclaimed Atius.

Daya just smiled.

'Come on,' said Silus. 'Time is marching on.'

The Saepta Julia was a huge porticoed structure built of marble, with roofed colonnades on two sides enclosing a vast open space which served as a market for the wealthy. The three Arcani wandered past the stalls, gaping at some of the amazing wares on offer. Silus could scarcely believe the contrast between the smelly, dirty shops in the Subura and these plush stalls, with tables covered in fine cloth and laid out with various luxuries. Many stalls sold jewellery – gold and silver earrings and necklaces inlaid with pearls and rubies and sapphires. Some sold exotic spices – saffron, cinnamon and nutmeg – while others sold perfumes which were like nothing Silus had ever smelt before, delicate scents of flowers and more exotic odours that made it feel as though his nose was getting a massage from a beautiful maiden.

Soldiers from the urban cohorts patrolled the market, alert for signs of theft or to move on beggars and prostitutes. The clientele here expected a much higher level of protection than the denizens of the Subura.

But the reason Silus was here was the slave market at the far end of the square. On a long raised dais, a constant flow of slaves marched up the steps, were paraded and auctioned, and then taken away by a new owner, or by a dealer with an eye for a bargain.

The first slaves up when the Arcani reached the dais were a pair of young Parthian boys, maybe fifteen and sixteen years old, looking like brothers. They were dressed in neat plain tunics which were shorter than was customary, showing off firm, hairless legs. The auctioneer made them turn slowly for the crowd, then he opened up the bidding.

'What do you think?' asked Atius. 'Couple of nice little bum boys to warm your bed?'

The bidding started at one thousand denarii, and rapidly built up, with the final price over four thousand for the pair. A fat man in a fine toga collected them, licking his lips as he led them away. Next up was a thin Greek man, balding on top, with narrow eyes and a pointed nose. The auctioneer notified the crowd that the slave was a scribe, and also highly numerate. Two matronly women bid for him, and he went for three thousand denarii.

'It's a bit rich, isn't it?' commented Silus.

'Don't worry,' said Atius. 'Those ones had special talents. You just want a standard house slave to take care of your new palace. He or she will be much cheaper. Here, this one is more like it.'

The auctioneer brought a young woman onto the dais. She had a willowy figure, straight-backed, and wore a long, flowing stola. Her skin was free of pockmarks and she was lightly made up. Silus was close enough to see her eyes. They were a brilliant blue, and completely lifeless.

'One hundred denarii!' shouted Atius.

The nearby crowd members turned to stare at him in surprise. The auctioneer looked taken aback. Then he recovered his composure.

'I would like to start the bidding at five thousand denarii. Do I have any takers?' Hands immediately shot up.

Atius looked crestfallen. Silus looked at him and smirked, then saw Daya's expression. She was staring at the slave girl, and her eyes were filled with tears. Silus felt a lump in his throat, and he suddenly felt he wanted to hug her.

'Come on, Atius,' said Silus gruffly. 'This place is well out of our league. Let's get out of here.'

They pushed their way out of the crowd and left the luxury market behind them. Daya was quiet and Silus asked if she was well.

'I have a little stomachache,' she said, and wouldn't be drawn further.

Silus felt a tap on his shoulder and turned to find Lurco grinning at him.

'My friends! Was your trip to the market successful?'

'Not really. They didn't really have what we were looking for.'

'I did warn you that place wasn't for the likes of you. But if you still need a house slave, I have a contact.'

'Why doesn't that surprise me?' said Silus with a sigh.

'How about I find you a slave, and you give me ten per cent of the sale price as a finder's fee?'

Silus thought about it. 'Let's see what you can come up with.'

Lurco led them to the Caelian Hill, where he took them down several twisted alleys before finally stopping outside a brothel.

'I want a housekeeper, not a whore,' said Silus.

'Bear with me,' said Lurco and led them inside.

The room was dark, despite being lit by a handful of lamps burning cheap oil, and it took a moment for Silus' eyes to adjust. There was an overwhelming smell of smoke, cheap and powerful perfume, and sex. At one end of the room was a bar, with a couple of customers drinking wine and eating bread and nuts. Around the room were half a dozen cubicles. Five of the cubicles were open, and dull-eyed girls, completely naked, sat in them. Above each cubicle was a tablet, with the name of the girl and her price. When they saw the new customers, they plastered smiles onto their faces. Some began to dance seductively, one got on her hands and knees and wiggled her backside towards them, and one just lay on her back and spread her legs. The sixth cubicle had a curtain drawn across, and the tablet above it had been reversed so it read, '*Occupied*'. Sounds of male grunting and a creaking bed frame emanated from within.

'What are we doing here?' asked Daya in a low, angry voice.

A plump woman with long hair shot through with veins of grey came bustling over. 'Lurco, why are you in my establishment? I keep telling you that we don't do freebies.'

'You do keep telling me that, Aspasia, but I know how kindhearted you are.' He turned to Atius with a wink. 'When things are quiet, she gets one of the girls to give me a hand job, as long as I keep finding her customers.'

'Lurco, I don't understand why we are in a cheap brothel,' said Silus.

'Hush now, let me introduce you. Aspasia, these are my dear friends, Silus, Atius and Daya. Friends, this is Aspasia, the lena of this fine place.'

'It is a pleasure to greet new customers,' said Aspasia.

Atius was looking around at the girls and reading the prices. 'Bit more expensive than Eboracum, but quite reasonable for Rome,' he commented.

'We aren't customers,' said Silus. 'Lurco brought us here. For reasons as yet unclear.'

'My friend Silus here is new in Rome and he was attempting to purchase a slave to care for his new apartment. Unfortunately, he found the market in the Saepta a little on the extravagant side.'

Aspasia let out a short laugh. 'You astound me, Lurco. So why bring them here?'

'Well, rumour has it that one of your ladies is nearing... retirement.'

Aspasia looked straight at a cubicle, whose sign read, 'Apicula'. Silus followed her gaze. Apicula had the cheapest price, just a single copper coin. The woman inside the cubicle looked like she was approaching her fifties. Her belly was loose and saggy, as though it had borne children in the past. Her breasts were large but drooped down her chest. Her face was handsome but heavily lined, with bird's feet at the corners of her eyes and large bags beneath them. Her hair was almost entirely grey.

Aspasia turned back to Lurco. 'I don't know what you mean. Apicula is one of my most valued staff members. There are many men with an interest in the more mature and refined lady.'

'Come off it, Aspasia. Look at her price. Is she even paying for her keep? Why don't we take her off your hands?'

'I could be persuaded to part with her, for a good price. With deep regret.'

'How much?'

'One hundred denarii.'

Daya spat on the floor. 'How can you exploit these women like this, a woman yourself?'

Aspasia looked offended. 'These are slaves. They do as they are told. And I care for them as if they were my own family.'

'They are abused in any way their customers feel fit, and they have no choice in the matter. You make me sick.'

'Gentlemen, could you please restrain your slave or I will have to ask you to leave.'

'I am no slave!' protested Daya, but Silus held up a restraining hand.

'Mistress, I think there has been a misunderstanding. I am not looking to buy a whore. We are sorry to have wasted your time.' He turned to leave.

'Silus, wait.' It was Daya who had spoken. Silus turned in surprise.

'When she no longer makes enough money, if this woman can't find a buyer, she will throw her out on the street to beg or starve.'

'What are you asking me?'

'Buy her.'

Silus took Daya's elbow and guided her to a corner. 'Daya,' he said quietly. 'You were a slave yourself. I'm not sure you approve of me owning anyone. Why are you asking this of me?'

'I'm not Spartacus,' she said. 'I know that there will always be slaves. All I can hope for is that they will be properly looked after. And there are worse things than slavery. It's better to be fed and sheltered than left in the gutter to die.'

'But look at her. I don't really want her.'

'Oh, so you really were just looking for a pretty young thing to suck your cock in the morning?'

'No, I want a housekeeper. I don't want that. It's just I didn't think... I... oh, fuck it.'

He returned to Aspasia.

'Twenty denarii.'

Lurco protested, seeing that the deal was on, and clearly thinking about his share of the sale price, interjected, 'Twenty? For this experienced lady, who can take care of your home as well as your every need? Surely eighty.'

Silus ignored him, but said to Aspasia, 'Fifty or I walk away now.' She shook his hand avidly, and smiled as he counted out the money.

'Apicula, get out here.'

The slave walked uncertainly over to them.

'Apicula, you have been sold. Get dressed, get your things and get out.'

Apicula looked shocked, and suddenly on the brink of tears. Daya took her hand. 'Don't worry,' she said. 'He will be a good master to you. And if he isn't, he will have me to answer to.' The look Daya gave Silus left him in no doubt that she meant it.

—

Silus lay on his back on his mattress in the darkness, covered by a single blanket. Apicula lay on another mattress on the floor near the window, breathing lightly. Daya had helped pick out some basic clothes for her in the Subura market, a couple of dresses, and they had also got a new chair and table as well as two new mattresses.

Now it was the middle of the night, and Silus lay awake, struggling to sleep as his mind spun with all the sights and sounds and smells he had experienced that day. His thoughts flitted from temples to slums, from priests to beggars and he wondered at this amazing city of contradictions and extremes.

He heard the sound of a key in the lock. Strange, he thought he had the only copy. He tried to sit up, but seemed paralysed, his arms and legs not responding. A small dark figure crept into the room, and tiptoed over to his bed. He suddenly found it hard to breathe. The small figure slid under the blanket with him and kissed him on the lips.

'Daya,' he whispered in amazement.

'Shh,' she said and kissed him more deeply. She was naked and he felt her small breasts pressing against his chest. She was incredibly light despite her toned physique. She ran her fingers over his face, then reached down to grasp his rapidly hardening cock. She stroked it a few times, then straddled it and guided it inside her. Sitting up, she rode him, faster and faster, and he looked into her eyes as she moaned wordlessly. Suddenly he was there, spasming inside her as she cried out.

He sat up abruptly. The room was empty apart from Apicula breathing lightly. The door was still shut. He was panting heavily. He looked down, and saw his blanket was wet and sticky at the level of his groin. He squeezed his eyes shut. It had seemed so real. But surely he didn't think of her that way. Did he?

'Fuck,' he said quietly.

Chapter Eight

'Papinianus, sit, take some wine.'

The Praetorian prefect sat on the marble bench beside Cara-calla, and a slave handed him a silver cup of fine Falernian. He sipped, though he seemed not to taste it, his thoughtful gaze slipping across the butterflies fluttering from flower to flower in the palace garden.

'What am I to do, Papinianus? Counsel me.'

'Augustus? With respect to what?'

'With respect to my brother, of course. As soon as we arrived in Rome, he set builders to work on the palace. He has walled up the communicating passages and set up his residence in the north wing. I have the south, and the Empress has the central portion.'

'I am aware of the changes to the living arrangements in the palace, Augustus.'

'At the interment, there was a moment where I really wanted to make it work. To find a compromise that would make it possible for us to rule together. Some acknowledgement that I was the senior Augustus, even though it was something small. An agreement on the order in which our names went on monuments, or who spoke first at official meetings. I don't know, anything. But I think it will never be. He cannot accept me as senior in any way.' Caracalla sighed and pressed his fingers against his perpetually lined forehead. 'What was in Father's mind, when he raised him as co-Augustus? When he bequeathed the Empire to us both equally? Did he really think it could be done without friction?'

'Maybe he thought it was the best way to preserve his younger son's life.'

Caracalla looked sharply at Papinianus. 'Be careful with your words.'

'Apologies, Augustus. It is no aspersion on your character. I merely point to history, where siblings who threaten a claim to a throne are done away with. Nero and Britannicus. Cleopatra and Ptolemy XIV.'

'And many brothers happily accepted their elders' claim to the throne. Titus and Domitian. Alexander the Great and Philip.'

'I cannot tell you the inner workings of your deified father's mind, I'm afraid, Augustus.'

'So now my brother and I live in a divided palace, with a divided rule. Maybe we should just divide the Empire and be done with it.'

There was a moment's silence, as the Emperor and the Praetorian prefect looked at each other, eyebrows raised in reflection of each other's expressions.

'Is it possible?' asked Caracalla quietly.

'I... don't know. It has never been considered. Not a peaceful division in any case. The Second Triumvirate divided the responsibility for governance geographically, but it remained one Empire under Rome. Antony and Cleopatra had ideas of setting up an independent eastern Empire with Alexandria as its capital. But Octavian would not allow that to happen. A peaceful, planned splitting of the Empire of Rome into two equal, independent halves? It is a radical idea, Augustus.'

'But is it possible?'

'All things are possible, Augustus.'

'Then let's talk about how it could work.'

–

The council chamber was divided along factional lines, as had become the norm at meetings of state. Domna sat in the centre as the unofficial mediator of the two factions, Syrian supporting Caracalla and African supporting Geta. Caracalla sat on Domna's right hand, with the Syrian faction arrayed to his right, facing the opposing African faction, which was ranged alongside Geta, who was seated on Domna's left.

Domna, as the former Emperor's widow, had in theory even less power than when she had been the Emperor's wife, and any influence she had was advisory. In practice, with the two current Emperors in conflict, if not open war, her role as peace-maker and intermediary gave her a position as important as any Empress in Roman history, including the deified Livia, the wife of Augustus and grand-matron of the Julio Claudian dynasty. So here she sat, at another meeting in which nothing would get done while the two factions argued and the two Emperors sniped at each other.

The current discussion was the important one of army pay. Geta and Caracalla had both taken seriously their father's dying wish that they should enrich the soldiers and damn the rest, although they had been less diligent in observing the wish that the two brothers should live in harmony. However, there was disagreement on the amount of donatives they should give out, and on the amount by which they should raise the standard pay. The Africans, who tended to be members of the civil service and had the state of Rome's treasury in mind, wanted a modest increase; while the Syrians pushed for something more substantial, arguing that with the passing of Severus, the position of neither of the Augusti was secure from a third party, a usurper in one of the provinces with a few legions willing to support him in a march on Rome, or in creating a breakaway province. Caracalla's natural inclination was also to reward the army which he had marched with and led, while Geta had a much less personal relationship with the military, although they were still fond of him because of his close resemblance to his father.

Caracalla ran a fingertip through the curls of his beard as he listened to an African official drone on about the drain on the treasury from the maintenance of the aqueducts and sewers, and wished for the tenth time that day that he was sole Emperor. It was intolerable enough that every decision he wanted to make had to be ratified by Geta, but his brother seemed to take perverse pleasure in opposing his every suggestion, while making entirely impractical suggestions of his own. The coins that had been struck with Caracalla and Geta shaking hands and sacrificing to Concordia seemed like a perverse joke. How long could this go on for? When would it reach a breaking point, and end in violence?

Caracalla stood abruptly and spoke in a loud voice that cut over the boring bureaucrat.

'Enough!'

The civil servant stopped talking in surprise, and all eyes turned to Caracalla. He held the room for a moment, milking the silence. Then he spoke, in calm measured tones.

'This cannot go on. The Empire is paralysed. We cannot make a decision on the most basic issues, let alone work out who should really be in charge. I have a proposition. We should divide the Empire.'

This led to gasps all around the room. Geta stared at him, but Caracalla kept his face impassive.

'I have given this matter some thought.' It was true. He had racked his brains trying to find a solution that involved neither violence nor the death of his brother. This was all he had come up with. 'We will both be Emperors, and the Roman Empire will still be one, but it will also be two. Geta would have the east. I would have the west, including North Africa as far as Cyrenaica. It is equitable and practical. What do you say?'

Everyone turned to Geta, who was looking at his brother with a thoughtful expression, clearly trying to work out if this was some sort of plot or trap.

'Tell me more,' said Geta cautiously.

'Don't you see?' asked Caracalla. 'We can both have what we want. We will both have unchallenged power, answering to no one else. I will have most of the more challenging military situations under my purview – Britannia, North Africa, Germania. You will have the richer, more peaceful states of the east, with only the Parthian threat to worry about. The distribution of the legions will be even, so neither has the power to overthrow the other. And there will be benefits for the Empire too. Not just that the decision-making will be smoother without the two of us arguing over everything, but that each half of the Empire will get the close attention of a full Augustus. Just think of the benefits that increase in focus could bring, the ability to crack down on local corruption, to raise military forces whenever required, to manage taxes and finances by the requirements of each region. It's perfect.'

Geta nodded, then looked to his advisors and the other council members. Papinianus spoke first.

'I must confess, Antoninus brought this proposal to me for discussion, and although I did not advise him for or against, I could not see a flaw in his plan. Antoninus' capital would remain in Rome, and Geta's could be Alexandria or Antioch. The senators and council would divide according to their origins, and legions would be stationed in Byzantium and Chalcedon.'

Ulpianus spoke next. 'I cannot see a legal impediment, if the Senate will support the move. Nor any insurmountable logistical problems. Although drafting the legal documentation to enable this move will be quite fascinating.'

Sextus Varius Marcellus stood. Marcellus had always been a loyal supporter of Caracalla, and wanted Caracalla to be sole ruler of the entire Empire. Nevertheless, he could obviously see the practicality of the idea, and as the suggestion had come from the man he had pledged himself to, he argued in favour. Others in turn around the council spoke in favour of the proposition, and an uncommon agreement broke out in the council chamber.

Until Julia Domna got to her feet.

'I say no.'

The harmonious chattering that had been bubbling around the chamber abruptly stopped.

'You two young men! I am your mother!' Only technically, Caracalla quickly told himself, but legally she was correct. 'How are you going to divide me? How am I going to be cut up and assigned to each of you?'

'Julia, what are you doing?' hissed Caracalla under his breath. She ignored him.

'You should kill me. Cut me in two, and bury each part. Then you can share me properly between you, like you are dividing the land and sea.'

Caracalla saw genuine tears in her eyes. Maybe he should have discussed this with her before, and no doubt she would be angry that he had confided in Papinianus instead of her. But surely she could see this was the only way? The only way that would resolve this conflict without bloodshed?

Domna suddenly threw her arms around Caracalla and Geta and pulled them into a tight three-way hug. Both men resisted briefly, then allowed themselves to be gripped by the Empress. She held them there, and for a moment, Caracalla felt like they were a real family, two brothers who had grown up together in love and rivalry, fought and laughed and cried together, and Caracalla felt tears coming to his own eyes. Then he pulled back, and looked at Geta, and his brother was frowning, eyes clear and dry, looking like a man who had won a prize and had it snatched away from him.

Caracalla felt his stomach lurch, and he was suddenly nauseous. There would be no reconciliation, and as he looked around the council chamber, he saw the sympathetic faces of the moved councillors, and realised that his plan was dead. There would be no division of the Empire, no peaceful solution.

Julia had tears running down her face as she tousled the hair of her son and her lover, and Caracalla couldn't believe that she was unable to see into Geta's soul, see the animosity and resentment that was now boiling into hatred. Didn't she understand the consequences? Did she really think that the Empire was better off this way? Or was she being entirely selfish, having her son and her lover remaining in the same city so she could continue to see them both?

'Oh, Julia,' he whispered, loud enough only for himself to hear. 'What have you done?'

–

Silus lay on his back on his mattress, covered by a single blanket. Apicula lay on another mattress on the floor by the window, breathing lightly. He had a strange feeling this had all happened before, then he remembered his dream of Daya from two nights before and flushed. He looked at the door, half-expecting it to open and his colleague to walk in once more. When nothing happened, he let out a breath he hadn't realised he had been holding.

He had spent most of the day in the company of Atius and Daya. He had no other real friends in Rome, and when there was no mission, he had little to keep him occupied. Daya trained in her free time, and Atius whored and drank, and made lifelong friends for the evening that he never saw again. Silus liked to think he was more normal and balanced than either of those two who were at opposite ends of the scale of introversion–extroversion. But in reality, he was probably neither normal nor balanced. He was a spy and assassin. What was normal about that?

His mind went back to the little girl that Daya had killed. He couldn't quite picture how she looked now, and whenever he thought about her, it was his own daughter's face that was there, conflated with Plautilla's daughter's. Sadness welled up inside, the loss threatening to overwhelm him, so acute even after all this time.

There was a knock at the door and he sat up abruptly. It must be near midnight. He lit an oil lamp, then reached for the dagger beneath his mattress, always nearby, and crept to the door. Apicula had also sat up on her mattress, and was watching suspiciously. Silus unbolted the door and opened it a crack. A young, nervous-looking girl was standing there. He looked past her, ascertaining that no one was lurking a bit further down the stairs, waiting to pounce on him. When he was sure she was alone, he opened the door fully.

The girl was maybe twenty years old, with long dark hair, almond eyes, a firm, round bust, and long, slim legs. She had an uncertain smile on her face. She was also completely naked.

Silus stared in surprise for a long moment, words completely absent from his mind. The girl's smile fell.

'Don't you like me, master?' she said in a small voice with a mild Eastern accent.

'What? I… No! I mean, yes, of course, but no!'

'Don't you want me?'

'I think there has been some mistake. You must have the wrong apartment.'

'No mistake, sir.'

'Did Atius put you up to this? If this is his doing…'

The confusion on her face told him it wasn't Atius.

'Look, I don't know who sent you to me, but go back and tell them it was a mistake. Goodnight.' The girl looked concerned, but he closed the door in her face and bolted it again. When he turned around, he saw Apicula smiling.

'What was all that about?'

'A neighbourly greeting, master, that's all.' She lay down again and turned her back to him.

He settled himself back onto his mattress, but had only just closed his eyes before there was another knock at the door.

'She is persistent,' he muttered, and opened the door again, with less caution this time. But it was not the same woman. This one was shorter, rounder, a little older, with blonde hair and blue eyes. And naked.

'Do you like me, master?' she asked with a hint of a Germanic accent.

137

'I'm sorry, but no,' said Silus. He closed the door and went back to bed. Why was he declining the offers? he mused. It wasn't the undoubted financial cost that the encounter would incur – he could afford a prostitute. It wasn't that he had any moral qualms about using a prostitute either – he had done it plenty of times in the past, both before and after his marriage. But not since Velua died. He had been with no one since then. Not only did it not feel right, but ever since that horrific night in Britannia, there had been no desire.

At least until he had met Daya.

The next knock came just moments later. He threw the door open to find a young boy, no older than twelve, his body hairless, his face made up like a woman.

'Leave me alone,' he yelled and slammed the door shut.

Apicula was chuckling openly now. 'What is going on?' Silus demanded.

'I think the local leno is trying to persuade you to sample his wares. And he obviously hasn't worked out how to tempt you yet.'

The fourth visitor was an enormously fat lady with a heavy growth of facial hair and a hunch. She had lost a leg at the knee sometime in the past, and supported herself with a crutch. Silus pitied her the walk up the stairs to his apartment and couldn't bring himself to shout at her.

'Listen to me. You tell whoever keeps sending you people to my apartment and disturbing my sleep that if I get one more visitor tonight I'm going to hunt down your leno and stab my knife up his backside. Can you pass that on for me, please?'

The lady nodded, and limped back down the stairs.

Silus wondered if the message would get through and was sufficiently threatening, and for a while he thought he had been successful. He had just started to drift away, when a knock came again. Silus jumped out of bed in a fury and threw the door open.

A tall, wide man with broad shoulders and a chest like a barrel grabbed him by the shoulders and shoved him hard back into the room, keeping the momentum going until Silus crashed backwards into the far wall. Apicula screamed, and then went silent as two more bulky men, armed with clubs, followed the first into the apartment. They had a brief look around, and one picked up the knife that Silus had carelessly left lying next to the mattress. Then they stood back, and allowed a much smaller man to enter the room.

The large man had his forearm thrust up against Silus' throat, keeping him pinned to the wall, but there was no point in struggling against such overwhelming odds. Silus used his hands in an attempt to keep enough pressure off his throat to breathe, and watched the newcomer.

The small man had a completely bald head, a long, narrow nose and a condescending sneer as he looked around the room, taking in its diminutive size and state of disrepair. He noticed Apicula, who had backed herself into the corner of the room, her blanket pulled up to her chin, her eyes wide with terror, and he smiled and approached her. He reached out to stroke her face and she shrank back. Then he spoke, Latin but heavily accented with Greek.

'Apicula, my dear. I heard that someone had made an honest slave of you. I do miss our times together. You were always very receptive to my tastes. And you were a good-looking thing once, too. Ah, well, it escapes, irretrievable time, as the poet said.'

'Who the fuck are you?' hissed Silus, voice attenuated by the strangulation, partly to distract this man from his terrified slave, and partly because he wanted to know who the fuck he was.

The man turned to Silus as if noticing him for the first time.

'I'm Sidetes of Alexandria.' The man watched for a reaction from Silus, and when he saw none, he shook his head with a wry smile. 'You really aren't from around here, are you? Because if you were, I would be terribly offended that the mention of my name doesn't instil more deference.'

'I've never heard of you. What the fuck are you doing in my apartment?'

'I wanted to see who was so discourteous to my employees earlier this evening.'

'That set of freaks you sent to my door were yours?'

Sidetes nodded to the man restraining Silus, who took a step back, then punched him hard in the midriff. Silus doubled forward with an 'oof' sound, then with an effort forced himself upright. He was no longer restrained, but the three strangers watched him like dogs ready to pounce.

'And there you were being discourteous again. I feel these slights to my employees as if they are against my own person. That is why none of my girls and boys have any harm come to them in the course of their duties. At least not since my colleague here cut off the cock of someone foolish enough to assault a young lad of mine.'

The man who had been holding Silus smiled to reveal a mouth full of blackened and broken teeth.

'I have introduced myself. Now tell me your name, stranger.'

'I'm Silus. What do you want with me?'

'Just to give you some, what shall we call it, orientation? I run this block. Everyone knows it, and respects it. But when a newcomer arrives, they need to know the score. I started off sending you employees with greetings to make you welcome. The experience and the price would have been most agreeable. Instead, you chose to send them away, insulted them, and threatened me. In fact, Aphrodite told me you had threatened to hunt me down and stab your knife up my backside.'

Even through his fear, Silus was able to feel sympathy for the poor woman who had no doubt endured much mockery for being named after the goddess of love. Sidetes looked down and noticed Silus' knife lying abandoned on the floor. Silus cursed his carelessness, and wondered what Oclatinius would say if he was here now. He almost felt more scared of the old man's disappointment than of the thug in front of him.

Sidetes bent down and picked up the knife, tested the point with his fingertip and flinched.

'A nice piece. You keep it in good order. I think it would slide very easily up a man's backside. Bend him over.'

The three men grabbed Silus by the arms and neck and thrust him face down onto the table. They grabbed the light tunic he wore and pulled it up over his back, so his hairy arse was exposed. Sidetes stepped forward, knife in hand, and suddenly Silus felt real terror. He tried to turn to see what was happening, but one of the men grabbed his hair and shoved his face into the table. He struggled desperately, and became aware of Apicula sobbing hysterically.

He felt the touch of sharp cold steel slide between his buttocks, the tip touching his hole. His breath hissed in and out in terror, and he leaked urine. The blade jerked forward and he screamed.

But Sidetes had only stabbed half an inch. It hurt like hell, and blood ran down the insides of his thighs, but it was a flesh wound, not fatal unless it got an infection.

The men let him go, and Silus sank to his knees, sobbing in pain and humiliation.

'I will send Aphrodite to your bed every night. And every night you will fuck her, and pay her a denarius. Or next time, the blade goes all the way in. Do you understand?'

Silus nodded, unable to speak.

'Then I will bid you a goodnight. I'm sure we won't have to meet under such circumstances again.'

Sidetes turned and swept imperiously from the room, followed by his chuckling thugs.

Apicula ran to the door and bolted it, then rushed over to Silus who was now face down on the floor, groaning. She took some of the rags she saved for her menses, wetted them from a jug of water, and pressed them between his buttocks.

Silus screamed at the sudden intensification of the pain, but he didn't resist. When Apicula had cleaned the wound and staunched the blood flow, she lay beside him on the floor and put an arm around him, stroking his hair. Silus turned to look at her. Tears were streaming down her cheeks, and she was trembling violently. Silus put his arm protectively around her, and spoke through gritted teeth.

'Don't worry, Apicula. I will sort this.'

–

Caracalla watched the young boy playing with his mother, his perpetually wrinkled forehead creased even deeper than usual.

'How old is the lad now?' he asked.

'Eight years,' said Sextus Varius Marcellus. Caracalla squinted. The sun was low in the sky, but the Emperor's vision was good, and he could make out his features clearly. Was there a resemblance?

The boy was named Sextus Varius Avitus Bassianus, and he was the son of Marcellus' wife Julia Soaemias, who also happened to be Julia Domna's niece. He was also, officially, the son of Marcellus. But Caracalla had always had doubts, and those doubts grew just as the child did. And he knew there were many who shared those doubts, and whispered them when they thought no one dangerous was listening. But in Rome, someone dangerously usually was listening, and Oclatinius dutifully reported the rumours on the streets, whether or not Caracalla wanted to hear them.

Marcellus had long been loyal to Caracalla and his father. He had married Julia Soaemias soon after Severus took the purple, and had been a Severan adherent ever since. But as Severus aged, he had subtly switched his allegiance to Caracalla, knowing that the old man would not be around for ever. There had been one particular occasion that Caracalla couldn't help but think back to every time he visited Marcellus.

Caracalla's wife Plautilla had just given birth to a daughter, and Caracalla knew full well that it wasn't his, as he never went near the spouse that he hated. Still, it was embarrassing, humiliating, that his wife had born another man's child and he had been drowning his sorrows with a variety of fine wines from Marcellus' Campanian estates.

Soaemias was around twenty-four at the time, six years younger than Caracalla, and fifteen years younger than her husband. Marcellus and his wife had laughed and joked with the young Augustus as they became drunker, and Soaemias had flirted ever less subtly.

Towards the end of the evening, Soaemias had excused herself to relieve her bladder, and Marcellus had nudged Caracalla and asked with a conspiratorial wink whether he thought his wife was a beauty. Caracalla had replied that of course he did, and it was then that Marcellus offered her to him for the night.

He still felt a stab of guilt at the thought, and that guilt was mainly to do with Domna. She had found out, of course. Soaemias had bragged about it until the Empress had had a quiet but severe word with her niece.

He knew he shouldn't really feel guilty that he had betrayed Domna. She had been with his father at the time, after all, not there for him when he needed her.

Soaemias had tried to seduce him on multiple occasions after that. Marcellus remained prepared to turn a blind eye and play the cuckold for the sake of preferment from the Augustus, but beautiful and tempting as Soaemias was, Caracalla could not bring himself to repeat the performance and disappoint Domna further.

The young lad was playing with his mother's make-up box, using a mirror to apply kohl with a hand skilled enough to suggest it was not his first time. He was wearing a stola he had taken from the daughter of a freedman who was a client of Marcellus. Caracalla raised an eyebrow. Marcellus reddened and made a dismissive gesture.

'It's just a phase he is going through, Augustus. He will be organising cock fights and playing soldiers with wooden swords before we know it.'

Caracalla said nothing, but he ached to ask, *Is the boy mine?* Instead, he turned to business.

'The division of the Empire seemed such an ideal solution.'

'The Syrian women are formidable when their ire is up, Augustus,' said Marcellus sympathetically. Caracalla nodded. There were a number of them that Caracalla regularly had to deal with, with Soaemias, Domna and Domna's sister Julia Maesa the most problematic. But even if Caracalla had wanted to clip their wings, their influence with the Syrian faction of court, as well as in their homeland, would make it challenging. Domna and Maesa were daughters of the high priest of the Syrian god Elagabal, and Soaemias' son would inherit that role one day.

Fortunately, he was generally content to let them have their way, finding it the easier path. But Domna's intervention in his plan to resolve his issue with Geta was disappointing as much from the mere fact of her opposition to him as the situation it left him in.

'What next, old friend?' Caracalla asked.

'Next, I believe, is the festival at the Circus Maximus that you are due to attend with your brother. Maybe you could speak to him when you sit by him in the Imperial box?'

'Maybe. But I fear that the last chance for compromise has passed.'

The young Sextus was now running in circles around his indulgent mother, crying out in a high voice, 'I'm a naughty girl, I'm a naughty girl.'

Marcellus sighed.

'It will pass,' he said, without conviction.

–

Naturally, Atius found the whole thing hilarious, nothing more so than the climax of Silus' account.

'Nearly buggered? By your own knife?'

He bent double, howling with laughter. Daya looked on in bemusement, while Silus fumed.

'Well, thanks a fucking bunch. I'm so glad I came to my best friend to tell him about this horrible experience. I knew I would find sympathy here.'

'I'm sorry, Silus,' said Atius, attempting to collect himself. 'Does it still hurt?'

'What do you think?' snapped Silus. 'Yes, it hurts, with every fucking step. And shitting is agony.'

That set Atius off again and Silus shook his head in despair. They were in a tavern in the late afternoon, and although it was busy, they had a corner table to themselves, with anyone approaching warned off by a glare from Silus and the flash of a blade from Daya. Apicula was also present, clutching Issa to her chest, who was loving being fed scraps from the table. The little dog had walked with a limp ever since she had suffered a fracture at the hands of the barbarians in Britannia, but she didn't seem to notice it unless she was playing on it to beg for food. Apicula still looked shaken, and Issa seemed to be a welcome distraction and comfort.

'What do you want to do?' asked Daya, ever practical.

'I think I need to send them a message. Let them know I am not someone to fool with.'

Atius, trying to recover himself, said, 'You could ask Oclatinius to ask someone to send the Praetorians round to have a word.'

'The Praetorians wouldn't dirty their boots in my street. And if I asked the Urban Cohorts to come round, what sort of message does that give? That I can't fight my own battles. No, I think I need to find out where he spends his time, and scare the piss out of him.'

'What do you think, then?' said Atius. 'Threaten to cut his balls off, roast them like chestnuts and feed them to Issa?'

'Something like that. Or maybe something more subtle, but that would worry him even more. Threaten to damage his business. Scare away the customers so they won't use his whores and his taverns any more. Spread messages that he and his men are marked, and any associating with him and his enterprises risks death.'

'Yes,' said Atius. 'We could beat up a customer or two, maybe give some of his thugs a scar or two, and let it be known we are not to be messed with.'

Daya was looking from Silus to Atius in confusion. Silus noticed her expression.

'What is it, Daya?'

'Why don't we just kill them all?' she said.

'Well,' said Silus, failing to find a good answer.

'I suppose we could...' said Atius.

Daya nodded, like it was decided. 'We just need to know where to look for him.'

'I can tell you where to find him,' said Apicula. Her voice was tremulous and she still look scared, but she seemed resolute, and Silus wondered if she was proud that her master was standing up to the bully. 'He spends most of his time at a brothel and tavern, two streets over from where I... where I worked. I can take you there.'

'No,' said Silus. 'You need to look after Issa. Just give us directions and we'll take it from there.'

–

The Circus Maximus was the biggest structure in the Roman Empire. Nestling in the valley between the Palatine and Aventine Hills, overlooked by the palaces of the super-wealthy, the Circus was the venue for chariot races. While the Flavian Amphitheatre could hold eighty thousand spectators, enjoying a day of gladiatorial fights and executions, the Circus could accommodate more than one hundred and fifty thousand avid fans screaming for their own teams, Green, Blue, Red or White, with the fanaticism of the most extreme cultist.

Caracalla looked down from the Emperor's box situated on the lowest tier at the northern end of the stadium. Arrayed above him were the other ranks of society in descending order of importance: senators first, then equestrians, then the wealthy humiliores, and then the poor. Sadly, he was not the only Emperor in the Imperial box, with Geta seated next to him, waiting excitedly for the race to begin. Papinianus, Dio Cassius and a few other honoured guests joined them in the box. Since boyhood they had supported opposing factions. The Greens and Blues had been dominant in the Circus for many years, with the Reds and Whites generally just making up the numbers.

Caracalla had supported the Blues ever since his first race, so Geta had naturally become a Green. Their rivalry had been fun at first, until they became more seriously adversarial. When the brothers started racing each other for their teams, the rivalry reached a dangerous level, culminating with Caracalla falling from his chariot, nearly being trampled to death by the horses behind him, and lucky to escape with a broken leg. To this day it still pained him in the winter, and he remained convinced it had been an attempt by his brother, furious at continually losing to his older and better sibling, to kill him.

The ceremonial procession before the race started was over, thankfully. Endless processions of priests holding statues of their gods and sacrificing at the altars and temples around the grounds had bored Caracalla to tears, waiting for the action to start, and while some of the crowd were respectful, most yelled for them to get on with it. Now, though, in front of him were arrayed twelve quadriga, the four-horse chariots, three from each team, ornately decked out in their respective teams' colours. The starting boxes were staggered so that no team got an advantage as they raced to the central barrier, although the boxes were allocated by lottery in any case.

They were waiting from a signal from the Emperor. But there were two. Julia Domna was not present – she was with her circle of intellectuals, and she and Caracalla, still angry and emotional, had been avoiding each other since the council meeting. So who would start the race?

The brothers looked at each other, and reached a silent agreement born of years of love and rivalry. They both stood and raised their arms simultaneously, then brought them down as one.

The starting gates sprang open, and the horses leapt out, taking up the slack on the reins and yanking the chariots forwards. The first challenge was to gain some advantage before the track narrowed at the white break line between the lower line which ran between the lower turning post and the right-hand wall of the stadium seating area. After this, they raced in parallel to the line before the judges' seats, after which they could cross lanes. This was when the action began.

The real race was between the lead chariots of the Blues and Greens. The other Blue and Green chariots played support roles, only really coming into their own if the lead chariot crashed out. As for the Reds and Whites, more poorly supported and funded, their financial survival tended to depend on deals done behind closed doors with the two major factions to assist one or the other to victory. Caracalla wondered how long it would be before the two small teams were simply absorbed into the larger ones.

The Red faction showed their allegiance early. One of the Red chariots was clearly weaker than the rest of the field, the horses less muscled, the charioteer less experienced, even the quadriga itself shabbier and more poorly maintained. But this chariot had never been intended to finish the race, or even the first lap. The charioteer yanked hard on the reins, steering his team outwards. One of the Green support team had made a move to pass him on the outside, and the Red cut across his path, forcing both chariots into the stone wall in front of the seating.

They impacted with a crash that momentarily drowned out the cacophony of the crowd. Both teams disappeared in a mess of dust, metal and flesh, human and equine. A wheel came loose and flew high into the crowd, impacting a spectator several rows back, who went down, skull caved in.

Course attendants rushed out from their sanctuaries along the central spine of the track to help the victims. The horses were likely all beyond rescue and those still alive would have their throats cut when it was safe to do so. The wreckage would have to remain until the race was over as an obstacle to the other teams. But it was accepted that it was reasonable to try to save the charioteers, not least because they were usually skilled men who could not be easily replaced. As the other chariots thundered on, the attendants dragged the two men out of the carnage. The Green charioteer was clearly dead, but the Red was moving weakly. If he survived his injuries, he would likely be richly rewarded. Caracalla decided to send a few gold coins his way himself.

The Green fans booed and jeered loudly as the Red charioteer was carried to safety, and some threw fruit and vegetables at him. A soft pear hit him in the face, which brought a cheer from the Green and White fans.

The lead chariots rounded the far end of the spine in a tight curve. The top Blue chariot held a slight edge over a support Green, while the top Green chariot was holding back, steering a wide course to try to keep out of trouble early in the race. The support Green tried to manoeuvre inside the Blue, but the quality of the Blue team and driver, not to mention a liberal use of his whip against his opponent, held him back. He dropped behind, allowing the Blue to accelerate down the back straight and open up a short lead.

As the leader passed the finish post, a dolphin statue was tipped over on the spine of the track to indicate the first of seven laps completed, drawing another cheer from the Blue supporters.

Caracalla looked across to Geta, and saw an expression of excitement and envy that mirrored his own conflicted feelings. Fun as it was to watch this spectacle, little beat the visceral excitement of racing itself. For the sons of an Emperor, protected from most of the dangers of the world, it was one of the few real thrills they could experience. Caracalla even rated the sensation above that of battle. Much as he loved to ride into a crowd of barbarians with his spatha swinging, his Praetorians protected him too well for him to be in genuine danger. Out in the Circus, the risk was very real.

One more chariot, a White, failed to complete the first lap as the charioteer, trailing the rest of the field, attempted the sharp turn at the far end of the spine clumsily, clipped a wheel and overturned. The charioteer was thrown clear, and managed to run to the safety of the spine before the field came round again. The horses continued to run, dragging the chariot on its side, for a further lap, the attendants unable to stop the beasts when they had their head. Eventually, a brave and athletic slave leapt from the side wall onto the back of the front horse of the four, and guided the team out of the Circus, to appreciative cheers from supporters of every colour.

'Wish you were out there?' asked Caracalla.

Geta turned to him, looking like he wondered if there was a trap in the question. Then seeming to accept it at face value, he said, 'Of course. What times we had.'

Caracalla was tempted to mention his suspicious crash again, but he felt suddenly weary. Was there no way to reconcile with his brother? He knew the answer to that. Geta would only be satisfied if Caracalla accepted him as an equal ruler in all things. And what sort of a man would that make him? Submitting to the wishes and whims of his younger, less qualified, less experienced, less skilled brother, purely for the sake of avoiding conflict. Is that the attitude that built the Empire?

But how he wished he was playing his brother at ludus latrunculorum, betting against each other at quail fights, listening together to their father's stories of his youth before he was Emperor. How he wished for those simpler times. Were they really gone for ever?

'Brother,' he began, then was interrupted by a huge crash below the Imperial box.

'What happened?' asked Geta, annoyed that he had missed the excitement because of his brother's distraction.

'One of the support Blues jumped into the Green leader's chariot and steered the horses into the barrier,' said Papinianus.

Geta rounded on Caracalla. 'Your team always cheats!' he spat, pointing a finger straight into his face. Caracalla strongly resisted the temptation to smack it away and follow that up with a punch to his brother's nose.

'Is this your first race, brother? That isn't against the rules.'

'There is such a thing as the spirit of the contest as well as the rule,' Geta snapped back. 'The Blues are dishonourable, and always have been, like all who support them.'

Caracalla felt anger rising up in him, his head aching with tension, and the pain in his leg from his old racing injury suddenly throbbing. He clenched one fist, his fingernails digging into his palm, using the pain to control his emotions. The race roared on beneath them, and he focused on the contest, blocking his brother from his hearing and his mind.

By the end of the sixth lap, only three chariots remained, the Blue lead chariot, which was winning, the slower of the Green support chariots, lagging a full length behind the leader, and a back-marking Red, which was close to being lapped by the Blue.

Caracalla watched intently as the Blue chariot took the turn to start the last lap. He went wide, slower than he could have, but showing caution as he had the luxury of a decent lead on the chasing chariot. The Green closed the gap a little, cutting the corner as close he dared, but they went out on the last lap with the Blue looking as though only a disaster would prevent his victory.

The disaster came at the final turn. The Blue caught the lagging Red at the corner. It was clear Red was supposed to be co-operating with Blue from the way the race had panned out so far, and so Red went wide as was customary for those being lapped.

But Blue was also taking the turn wide to avoid clipping the spine or turning over with too tight a circle, and in the confusion, the foot of one of Blue's horses connected with Red's wheel. The spokes shattered the coffin bone and the horse went down and rolled over its own head, breaking its neck and dragging the rest of the team down with it. The Blue chariot careered straight into the horses, pitching the charioteer out and into the path of the oncoming Green.

Whether the Green could have made more of an attempt to avoid the Blue charioteer was hotly debated and argued over for weeks afterwards. The Green fans said that there wasn't time to swerve without risking a crash, while the Blues said there was plenty of room to manoeuvre around, and that the Green just wanted to take out one of their best men. Many of these conversations came to blows, with even some permanent injuries and the odd death resulting from the debates.

Whatever was in the mind of the Green charioteer in that instant, the result was that as the Blue crawled on his belly towards the safety of the spine, the Green chariot rode over him at high speed. The thin wheel with the weight of the quadriga and the Green charioteer pressing down cut the unlucky Blue in two. The crowd gasped, roared, cheered and even laughed as for a moment, the Blue continued to drag himself towards safety by his hands, leaving his lower body and a mess of entrails behind him in the dirt. He made it a bare couple of feet before slumping face down.

The Green quadriga took the final turn and the home straight gently, not attempting to overtake the Red, and he passed the finishing line to an eruption of cheers and boos from the crowd.

The excitement boiled around the stadium long after the end of the race. Bookies paid out grudgingly, and drink and food sellers circulated, hawking their wares, as did the prostitutes. Greens continued to cheer the victory, as their charioteer performed his victory laps, while the Blues roared their disapproval, and the few fans of the Reds and Whites speculated in muttered grumbles why they ever bothered turning up.

The victorious charioteer stopped near one section of the crowd, and a broad-chested man with white hair, looking to be in his sixties, hopped over the barrier and with surprising agility jumped in beside him, joining him as the charioteer continued to drive around the track receiving the adulation of the crowd.

'It's Euprepes!' said Geta with excitement. Caracalla knew who it was. The bane of the Blues for years. He had been crowned seven hundred and eighty-two times, an extraordinary feat simply to survive that many races given the high mortality rate. He was adored by the Greens and the neutrals, and respected if not loved by the Blues. He was wealthy enough to become an equestrian, though he had never applied, preferring to remain with the people of his roots in the lower classes. Consequently, he enjoyed tremendous influence with the common people, and was well-liked by many in the ruling classes as well.

The crowd roared with excitement at seeing this legendary hero out on the track again, with many shouting that he ought to come back and show the youngsters how it should be done. It was as close to unifying the arena as had been seen for some time, and Caracalla marvelled at how much real power an important figure in one of the racing factions could hold. If all that pent-up humanity was united, whipped into a frenzy and pointed in one direction, what destruction could be unleashed? Nothing that even the combined strength of the Praetorians, the Urban Cohorts and the vigiles could stop, even if all those units remained loyal to the side of law and order.

A chill ran down him. He knew Oclatinius had been active on his behalf among the factions, and that the Blue faction, the charioteers, team owners, the associated employees as well as the fans, were his natural allies after his lifelong and vocal support for them. But allies of Geta were bolstering his brother's standing among the Greens and making overtures to the Reds and Whites. He had considered it something of a sideshow to the real power, control of the Praetorians and the legions, but now he wondered if he had misjudged the situation.

After two laps, milking the crowd for all he could, Euprepes and the much less famous Green victor pulled the quadriga up in front of the Imperial box. Geta and Caracalla stood to greet the victor and the famous veteran of the Circus, holding their hands aloft for quiet.

Although it was the winning charioteer's right to address the Emperor and dedicate his victory however he wished before receiving the Emperor's blessing, it was Euprepes who spoke into the hush.

'This was a tremendous victory,' he said in a loud voice, clearly audible to the Imperial box and the front few rows. His words were relayed back and round the stadium like a wave, with shouts and cheers coming at staggered intervals as the message reached different sectors of the Circus seating. 'It is a victory that I would have been proud of, even in my prime.'

Caracalla doubted that strongly. It was a fluke, and everyone knew it, but when had a lie ever stopped a good speech?

'Being a charioteer is a profession that requires immense bravery as well as strength and skill. This man has showered his team with honour and dignity today. But he has given me permission to dedicate the victory where I will.'

Dedications were usually to the Emperor, and then to a revered god, sometimes with the mention of a favourite girl-friend if the charioteer really wanted someone to swoon at his feet, although it would of course cramp his chances with the rest of the adulating women, and indeed men. With two Emperors present, it would be customary to dedicate the victory to both of them.

'This victory I present to a man who has worn the Green, and now wears the Purple. A man who, like his father, has the power, strength, courage and dignity to rule Rome wisely and for many years. I dedicate this victory to Imperator Publius Septimius Geta Augustus.'

Spontaneous cheers broke out around the stadium, and Geta stepped forward to bask in the adulation. He raised his arms high and wide, smiled broadly, and held the praise for a long while, before lowering his arms again in a request for silence to speak. He turned to Caracalla, smirked at the stunned look on his brother's face, then spoke in a loud voice.

'Euprepes, hero of the Circus, your loyalty to your Emperor is as strong as your loyalty to the Greens. And I know what a passion you have for the Greens. I accept your dedication, and I pledge to rule Rome wisely, the way you have spoken. I will use my power, my strength, my courage and my dignity to bring Rome glory, honour and riches.'

Caracalla stared at his brother in disbelief. He had gone beyond angry to a cold, calm, calculated fury. Geta stood there receiving the acclaim of the roaring crowd. The sun was angled so Geta's shadow fell on Caracalla.

Nobody casts a shadow over me.

Caracalla turned and swept from the Imperial box, the noise of the cheering crowds seeming to mock his exit.

Chapter Nine

The three Arcani walked into the tavern in the early evening and stopped just inside the doorway. Atius had scouted the place out already, as the one looking most like a customer, and they knew exactly how many clients, employees and guards were present, and where they were situated in the room. It took them a brief moment to confirm there were no major changes, and another moment to allow their eyes to fully adjust from the evening twilight to the more profound gloom of the tavern's interior.

Silus thought there were about twenty customers. Half were drunk, and the remainder were either gambling or chatting to the bar staff, who doubled as prostitutes of both sexes. On top of this, there were six bulky men whom Atius had spied out as being Sidetes' muscle. Silus recognised the three men from his apartment the night before, including the big one who had first assaulted him. He bit the inside of his cheek to control his emotions. His buttocks clenched involuntarily with his anger, and he winced at the pain, making him even angrier.

And there, sitting before the bar, was Sidetes. At his feet in the dirty straw knelt a slave boy, with a metal collar and a large tag. Sidetes was ignoring the miserable wretch and arguing with the barman about the day's takings which were spread on the bar before them.

Little notice was taken of them at first. A couple of nearby men had leered at Daya. One drunk customer had cursed them for being in the way when he wanted to go into the street to relieve himself and they had let him pass. Then one of the men who had been in Silus' apartment noticed him. He squinted before elbowing his neighbour in the ribs and pointing. The neighbour looked across at them, then opened his eyes wide in surprise. He pushed his way through the customers and other guards towards Sidetes.

Others began to take notice of the commotion. Sidetes' guards muttered, moved their hands towards nearby clubs and axes. They were uncertain, finding it hard to see how the two men and the little girl could be a threat, but bemused by their confident air. The customers and staff in the tavern quietened down as they realised something was up, and made calculations whether it paid to stay and be entertained, or to flee to avoid the possibility of being hurt in whatever was about to happen next.

The tavern was now quiet enough that only Sidetes' voice could be heard.

'Listen to me, you foul leper's vomit. I am telling you that there should be more in the cash box than that, and if you don't produce it for me immediately, I am going to have your testicles—'

'Boss,' said the thug. 'Look who's here.'

Sidetes turned with anger across his face.

'What is it?'

The thug pointed to the three Arcani.

Sidetes stood slowly, in wonder. Then he broke out into a low, mocking laugh.

'Isis and Serapis, what a surprise. Silus. It seems I wasn't clear enough.' He walked towards the Arcani, his hands spread. 'Last night wasn't the start of a negotiation. And we aren't going to be friends or colleagues. You are not to drink here, you are not to come and find me, you are not to talk to me. You are to follow your instructions to the letter, or you will die. Horribly.' His face twisted into a snarl as he spoke, pronouncing each word individually and precisely. 'Do. You. Understand?'

Silus took a stride forward, the knife concealed in his tunic sleeve dropping into his grip, and in one smooth motion buried it to the hilt in Sidetes' eye socket before withdrawing it neatly.

The Egyptian didn't even have time to flinch. His body stiffened, and he toppled slowly backwards, falling on the floor with a crash that was deafening in the silence.

The customers, the staff, the guards, all stood frozen in shock at the sudden and shockingly violent death of the man who had ruled over them all with terror for as long as they could remember.

But the Arcani did not freeze. Atius and Daya were moving the moment Silus struck. Six guards, and within a few heartbeats, two were down. The first had taken a blade through the ribs to the heart from Daya, and the second had his skull broken by Atius' club.

The remaining four scrambled for their weapons. Daya and Atius moved forward as Silus confronted the nearest thug. This one held a club with nails through the end, and without hesitation he swung for Silus' head. The weapons were mismatched, the club having superior reach, blocking power and ability to inflict damage than the knife. But one was in the hands of an Arcanus, the other in the hands of an unskilled thug from the slums. The thug feinted forwards twice, jabbing the jagged tip of his club towards Silus' face. Then he pulled the club back and swung it round in a wide arc aimed somewhere between Silus' shoulder and head.

If it hit, it would be fatal.

But Silus was not standing still. He bent his knees, ducked beneath the arc of the blow, then exploded upwards with both hands around the hilt of his knife, thrusting it up through his attacker's liver and into his chest. He turned to see Atius backing one of the other thugs into a corner with careful swings of his own club, while Daya was on the back of another, her garotte around his neck. Silus watched for a moment as the large man tried to shake the small woman from him, to check that she didn't need assistance. She didn't, of course. Silus felt a glow of pride as he watched Daya finish her victim off. Pride, and something else? For fuck's sake, Silus, get hold of yourself. You are in the middle of a fight!

As if to confirm his self-admonishment, he was hit in the midriff with a shoulder tackle that sent him flying backwards. He landed on his back with the thug who had nearly strangled him in his apartment on top of him. Silus lost his knife in the fall, and the big thug's club was useless at such close quarters. Silus fended off blows to each side of his head as the thug knelt astride his abdomen and punched him with fists like hammers. Silus tried to strike back, aiming for throat, eyes, groin, but he was in the wrong position to make the contact tell. He bucked and thrashed, trying to dislodge him, but the thug was too heavy and was mad with rage. Broad fingers closed around Silus' neck and he started to choke as they tightened. He gripped the wrist and tried to prise them away, squeezing his eyes shut in an attempt to fight off approaching unconsciousness.

Suddenly he felt warm liquid sprayed into his face, into his eyes and open mouth. At the same time the grip around his neck loosened. He opened his eyes, squinted through a red blur in time to see the thug topple sideways, crimson still pumping from the rent in his neck. Daya stood behind him with a reddened blade and a self-satisfied smile.

She put out a hand and helped Silus to his feet. He felt dizzy as he stood, and instinctively reached out his hand. She put her arms around him to steady him, and for a brief moment they shared a hug. Her firm, slight body against him did nothing to dispel his dizziness, but he pulled away despite this.

He wiped his eyes with the back of his tunic sleeve, and looked around him. All of Sidetes' men were as dead as their leader, who still lay on his back with blood and goo oozing from his ruptured eye. The rest of the occupants of the tavern were like statues, frozen in shock at the suddenness and completeness of the fight.

Silus cleared his throat and spoke to them.

'I'm not from round here. I don't know how things are done in Rome. But this is how we do things where I come from. I just wanted peace and quiet. This idiot,' he pointed to Sidetes, 'decided to disturb me. Hopefully the word will get out now. Leave me alone.'

He picked up his knife, and walked gingerly out of the tavern, Daya and Atius following. Once he was out of sight and earshot of the tavern, he groaned, leant against a wall and clutched his backside.

'Fuck, my arse.'

'Seriously, Silus,' said Atius. 'I don't think you should let anyone fuck your arse for a while.'

–

Silus thought that was enough excitement for the night, but Atius' blood was up, and he begged Silus to come for a drink or two. Daya sneered at the boyish behaviour and declared she was returning to her quarters and going to bed. Silus thanked her for her help and watched her go for a little too long, unwelcome thoughts flashing through his mind, until his reverie was broken by Atius slapping him on the backside, causing him to yelp in pain as his buttocks clenched.

'You're a cock, Atius.'

'Maybe, but I think you owe me at least a cup of wine for tonight's work.'

They chose a different tavern from the one in which they had fought, and selected a table in a corner. Like many taverns, this one served the multiple purposes of drinking establishment, gambling den and brothel.

Within moments of arriving, Atius had availed himself of the first two functions, and was making plans to utilise the third. He pulled out some knucklebones, and called for challengers. A couple of young men, beards sparse, no chest hair protruding from their tunics, joined them, and Atius took out his purse with a smile.

The game of tali could be played in two ways. One was by throwing the bones into the air and trying to catch as many as possible on the back of your hand, a game of skill. Gamblers preferred the other version, a game of chance, where your score was decided by which side up the bones landed. Because of their uneven shape, some sides were more likely than others, and it was not possible to land on the two curved ends. The four other sides were numbered I, III, IV or VI. The best throw was the Venus throw, where all four bones landed on different sides, and the worst was the Dog throw, where all the bones showed a I.

Atius reckoned himself an expert in the game, though Silus was convinced it was entirely chance. Nevertheless, Silus' friend was soon doing well, significantly up on his starting stake, and the two young men grumbled and made insinuations about cheating, although they weren't brave enough to outright accuse him.

But this being gambling and chance, and Fortuna being a fickle goddess, the game changed and swung against Atius. Silus had been gambling moderately, just enough to keep his friend company without taking any particular risks, and his purse was no heavier nor lighter than when he started. Atius, however, had watched his winnings grow, then shrink, until he was left with only a small pile of copper coins.

'Let's make it interesting,' said Atius, a few drinks inside him enough to slur his speech and alter his judgement. 'Everything on a Venus Throw. Everyone all in.'

'Don't be stupid, Atius,' said Silus. 'That will wipe you out.'

'Only if I lose.'

'I'm out,' said Silus, taking his coins off the table.

'I'm in,' said one of the young men, throwing his whole stake into the middle of the table. The other hesitated, then also added his coins to the pile.

Atius picked up the knucklebones and shook them in his cupped hands. He spat on them, shook them again. Then he said out loud, 'O Christos, bringer of light and life, look down on this your faithful servant, and guide these bones, that my good fortune can glorify your name.'

He gave Silus a confident wink, and threw the bones across the table.

He looked at the result.

'Shit.'

Two Is, a III and a IV. The young men smiled and took the winnings, splitting it between them.

'Thanks for the game,' said one. 'Any time you want a rematch, let us know.' They stood and walked off, laughing and clapping each other on the back.

Atius looked disconsolate. 'I can't even afford a whore now,' he said.

Silus tried to be sympathetic, but he was actually tired down to his bones, and was desperately wishing for his bed. 'Let's hit the road, friend. There will be other nights.'

A thin man with a long grey beard and a bald head who had been watching the game leant in to them. 'I know how you can make your money back.'

'Thank you, but—' began Silus.

'How?' asked Atius.

'You look like a strong man. Can you fight?'

Atius smiled. 'I have been in the occasional brawl.'

'I know a boxer looking for challengers. There is a fat reward for besting him.'

'Take me to him.'

Silus' attempts at dissuasion fell on deaf ears, and so he dutifully tagged along with his friend as they followed the stranger down some winding streets to a scruffy-looking tavern. Their guide left them to talk to a plump, well-dressed man sitting in a corner with two burly-looking slaves attending him. They spoke in whispers, and cast sidelong glances towards Atius, who straightened his back and tried to look intimidating.

The plump man came over to them and shook Atius' hand. 'I'm Nicator. I'm something of a lanista, but my gladiators aren't slaves, and they don't fight with swords.'

'I'm Atius. This is my friend Silus.'

Nicator ignored Silus and looked Atius up and down.

'Can you fight?'

'I can.'

Nicator considered, then seemed to come to a decision. 'Very well. I have a boxer who has yet to be beaten. There is a purse of five hundred sestertii for the first man who bests him.'

'It's as good as mine.'

Nicator smiled. 'Give me an hour. We need to get the word out to give everyone the chance to place their bets. Meet me at the crossroads by the fountain of Mercury.' Silus and Atius looked uncertain, so Nicator gave them directions. It was a couple of streets away. He then strutted off, still wearing a broad smile.

Atius continued to drink for most of that hour, subsidised by a reluctant Silus, who tried unsuccessfully to talk him out of the fight, or at least to moderate his intake of wine. Soon, though, the hour had passed, and Silus led Atius to the crossroads. A decent crowd had gathered, and bets were changing hands, privately and through a couple of bookmakers. The odds on Atius were good, enough to tempt Silus to place a bet himself. His friend was drunk, but he knew he was a good fighter, and he was tall and well-built.

The crowd had formed a large circle, and Nicator led Atius out into the centre.

'Please welcome our challenger, Atius the Celt,' he announced in a loud voice, holding Atius' hand aloft. Silus smirked. He might start calling him Atius the Celt himself. The crowd cheered, clapped and whooped, and Atius bowed and played to the audience.

'And now, let's hear it for Segimerus the German.'

The crowd parted, and all heads turned to catch a first glimpse of Segimerus.

Silus' heart sank. The man was a giant. At least six and a half feet tall, chest as wide as a bull's, legs like tree trunks, the veins winding round his muscular arms like ropes.

Atius stared open-mouthed. He looked around to Silus, who shrugged helplessly. He wondered if his friend might try to back out, but he knew better. Atius had too much pride, even if it might see him badly beaten.

'Let me remind you all of the rules. No weapons of any sort, edged or blunt. Stay within the circle. The loser is the one who submits, loses consciousness or dies.'

'Atius the Celt, ready?'

Atius nodded nervously.

'Segimerus the German, ready?'

Segimerus punched his chest with a fist like a blacksmith's hammer and just roared.

'Fight!'

Segimerus swaggered into the centre of the ring, hands wide. Atius cautiously moved forward, staying out of reach, circling around his opponent as he sized him up. Silus could see no obvious weaknesses. Against a man of that bulk, a smaller man would usually have superior speed, but every time Atius feinted a punch, Segimerus swayed, shuffled or ducked with respectable fleetness of foot. Atius still held the edge in quickness, but it was not a telling superiority.

Atius continued to stay at arm's length, while Segimerus tried to close the gap between them. Twice, he managed to dart in and land a jab to his opponent's face, and skip away from the retaliatory swings, but the German didn't seem to notice the punches. The crowd became impatient, and began to whistle and boo. One picked up some dirt from the street and threw it at Atius, and it hit him in the back, leaving a brown mark.

Despite the number of bets on Atius, who had the best odds, the crowd started to turn against him, cheering on Segimerus.

'Come on, you coward. Get in there.'

'Smash him, Segimerus. Pound him into the ground.'

Maybe inspired by the support, Segimerus lunged at Atius, managing to grab his wrist. Atius thumped his fist down on Segimerus' forearm, but before he managed to break the grip, Segimerus swung a roundhouse punch towards the side of Atius' head. He ducked, but the blow glanced off the top of his skull with a resounding thud, and Atius staggered back, shaking his head.

Segimerus followed up immediately, and Atius desperately dodged and weaved as a rain of punches flew in, each one powerful enough to knock him out cold if they connected. Some he avoided, some he blocked on his forearms, though Silus could see even that was painful. Some got through, the force attenuated by a block or a dodge, but still enough to make Atius grunt.

Atius managed to sneak through some punches of his own, to body and to head, but they had little impact. Then Segimerus managed to grab him in a clinch, his arm around his shoulders, his other hand punching the back of Atius' head. Fortunately, the close proximity meant that Segimerus couldn't get the angle to make the blows full power, but they were clearly still getting through to Atius.

In desperation, Atius sank his teeth into Segimerus' shoulder, drawing blood. The giant German howled and let go, turning to look at the bite marks deep in his flesh.

'You will pay for that, Celt,' he growled.

'Give it up, Atius,' Silus shouted. 'It's hopeless.'

Atius gave him a sour look, and Silus felt guilty for his lack of encouragement, but he had now become genuinely worried for his friend's safety. There was a very real chance here of a major injury or death. He wondered if he would have to step in, and whether he would even be able to with the crowd here determined to see the fight to its finish.

Then Silus saw there was a small cut above Segimerus' eye, and it was trickling a little blood. One of Atius' blows must have done a bit more damage than he first realised.

'Atius,' he yelled. 'The eye. Work on the cut!'

Atius looked closer, then waved an acknowledgement to Silus. Segimerus tried to close on Atius again, but Atius used his slight edge in speed to dance in and out. Now, every jab that Atius threw was aimed at Segimerus' bleeding brow, and soon the cut had extended across his forehead, and blood was streaming down into his eyes. Segimerus used the back of his hand to wipe it away angrily, but the blood continued to pour, worsening, as Atius continued to jab.

Soon the German was blinking, struggling to see at all. His punches went wild as he struggled to find Atius through the red blur across his vision. Atius stepped back, assessing his opponent's injury. Segimerus roared and flailed, wiping ineffectually at his face.

Atius took two steps forward, and using all his momentum, all his quite respectable bulk and strength, bending his knees and using the power in his legs to explode upwards, he landed an uppercut on Segimerus' chin.

The giant's jaw clanked shut and his head rocked backwards. Beneath the blood, Silus saw the German's eyes roll up into his head. He took one step backwards, another, then toppled over to crash onto his back and lie still.

There was a brief shocked silence, then the crowd erupted into cheers and roars of approval. Nicator came out into the middle of the ring, took Atius' wrist and lifted his arm high.

'Atius the Celt is the victor! Segimerus is defeated for the first time.' He presented Atius with the purse of money, and seemed to be genuinely happy that the prize had finally been won.

The bookmakers were pleased – the favourite losing was always profitable as the most likely winner attracted the most bets, even though the odds on Atius had been temptingly long.

The winning gamblers were delighted, and even the majority of the losers accepted their losses with good grace after witnessing a fight that would be talked about for weeks.

Segimerus had a bucket of water thrown over his face, and he sat up spluttering, looking around him in confusion. Silus decided it was time to make their exit. He stepped into the ring, put his arm around Atius. 'Come on, friend, let's get you home. Clean you up.'

'What a fight,' gushed Nicator. 'Such persistence. And what a punch. There is a place for you here among my fighters any time.'

'We'll be in touch,' said Silus, and guided Atius away.

When they were clear of the crowd and on their own, Silus turned to Atius and put his hands on his shoulders so he could look him directly in the face.

'Atius, you are an idiot. You are reckless, a gambler, a drunk. But by Mithras and all the gods of Olympus that was magnificent.'

He grabbed Atius' hand and gripped it hard as he shook it vigorously.

Atius let out a scream.

'What is it?' asked Silus in sudden concern.

Atius cradled his arm against his chest.

'That last punch,' he said. 'I broke my hand.'

–

'Kill him,' said Caracalla. He was pacing up and down his private study, while Oclatinius stood at attention, letting the Emperor rage. 'Cut off his balls and feed them to the dogs. Slice him into quarters. I know, flay him alive and paint the skin Blue before his eyes as he dies.'

'Can I be clear about who we are discussing here?'

Caracalla whirled on him. 'Haven't you been listening to a word I said? I told you what happened in the Circus, how Euprepes praised Geta and excluded me.'

'So it is Euprepes you want dead?'

'Of course, who else?'

'Well, it did cross my mind that maybe it was your brother...'

Caracalla's eyes narrowed.

'Careful, Oclatinius. I trust you with my life, but there are lines that shouldn't be crossed.'

Oclatinius bowed his head, though Caracalla saw little repentance in his expression. His old spymaster was no fool: he saw what was coming, even as Caracalla tried to lie to himself that it would not come to that.

Caracalla stopped raging, let the fire down, and let the ice take over. He took a few deep breaths and released them slowly.

'Was it premeditated, do you think?' he asked.

Oclatinius considered. 'None of my spies in the factions had any warning this was coming. Which means it was kept a closely guarded secret among only a few, or it was spontaneous. If you want my opinion, from what you have told me, your brother did not seem particularly surprised. I think this was all carefully planned. The victory could obviously not be guaranteed, but if the Greens hadn't won that race, they would have won another soon, and then they would have proceeded as they did today.'

'I want an example made of him, Oclatinius. I want people to know that if you support Geta, no matter how famous or loved you are, you risk your life.'

'Yes, Augustus. I'll get my best team straight on it.'

–

'You are without doubt my worst team!' yelled Oclatinius. Silus, Atius and Daya stood before him with heads bowed, taking the admonishment stoically.

'What did I say to you? Rent an apartment in an insula. Buy a house slave. Explore the city. Keep your head down.'

'To be fair, boss, he did the first three,' said Atius.

'Shut the fuck up, Atius. This is not the time to be messing with me. Things are starting to come to a head. You are going to need to be sharp, alert, at the very top of your game. Instead, what do I find out? You had some trouble with some pathetic lowlife, so instead of shrugging it off, doing as he asked, and acting like a cowering, submissive, ordinary person, you went in heavy-handed, and made sure everyone in the Subura knows that there is a new tough guy in town. So much for anonymity.'

'Sir, he wanted me to fuck a cripple every night.'

'If you need to arse-fuck a leper twice a day because the job demands it,' yelled Oclatinius, 'that is what you will do! Do I make myself clear?'

'Yes, boss,' said all three together.

'And then this idiot breaks his hand in a bare-knuckle boxing contest. Knocking out the infamous Segimerus at the same time, guaranteeing you will be remembered while simultaneously making you useless to me for at least a month.'

Oclatinius took a deep breath and stroked his chin. 'It may not be a complete disaster. Your missions aren't in the Subura anyway, and there is not a lot of overlap in the social circles of the Subura poor and the important people your missions will involve. That said, your next job doesn't involve someone of the noble class.'

Daya looked up, eyes suddenly bright. 'You have a job for us, sir?'

'Yes. You are to kill Euprepes.'

Oclatinius left a dramatic pause, awaiting their reaction.

The three Arcani looked at each other and shrugged.

'Right,' said Silus. 'Anything else?'

'Do any of you know who Euprepes actually is?' asked Oclatinius.

All three shook their heads.

'Fuck me, two foreigners and a girl. What should I expect? Euprepes is the most famous charioteer in the city. More famous than any gladiator. More famous to the common man than any senator or noble except the Emperors themselves.'

The three Arcani looked unimpressed and Oclatinius sighed and sank into his seat.

'I shouldn't have to explain this to you, but time is short. I know you have chariot races in the provinces, but it's different in Rome. And I know you, Daya, won't have had much chance to ever attend a race, nor probably the desire – it tends to be a man's interest.

'The races are huge. Almost every man in the city will have a favourite team, and the conversations in taverns and the street corners are far more likely to involve a discussion of the latest race than the latest fight in the arena.

'Charioteers have an unusual place in society. They are mostly lowborn, slaves or freedmen, and are often looked down upon by the elite. On the other hand, the successful ones can be fabulously wealthy. The richest ever, Diocles, supposedly made more than thirty-five million sesterces. That's more than most senators.

'And because charioteers take such massive risks every time they get on the track, they are considered lucky, at least the ones that survive. Men want to be them, women want to fuck them. People make lucky charms with their names on. Once, a fan even threw himself onto the funeral pyre of his favourite charioteer and burnt with him. Am I starting to get through to you how beloved and important charioteers are?'

The Arcani nodded.

'Well, Euprepes is the best known in the city. He is an old man now, but he won an enormous number of races, he is rich, and he is idolised by the common folk and not a few of the senators too.'

'So how has he upset the Emperor?' asked Silus.

'You don't need to know why,' snapped Oclatinius. Then he shook his head. 'Poor Euprepes. I remember watching him. No one could touch him in his day. Handsome and talented. Even I admired him. And now he has got himself involved in politics.' He pursed his lips. 'Just go and kill him, and make it obvious and public. But beware the fans.'

'And what about... incidental damage?' asked Atius.

Oclatinius sighed. 'Just try to keep the body count down.'

—

Lucius Fabius Cilo had a perpetually worried expression, Titurius thought. Even when Severus was in power, and Cilo was one of his closest friends, position entirely secure, he seemed constantly on edge. Now, sitting on a bench in Titurius' peristylium, the elderly senator looked close to breaking down.

'Were you there, Titurius? Did you see his face?' Cilo had never quite lost the Spanish accent he had acquired from his place of birth.

'I've told you already. No, I wasn't there, I'm not a fan of the horses. But I hear he wasn't pleased.'

Cilo worried at a piece of loose skin at the edge of a fingernail, peeling it back and leaving a tiny stripe of raw flesh beneath. He didn't seem to notice what he was doing, staring blankly at the far wall where roses climbed a trellis. Titurius saw similar red marks along his other fingers. His nails were bitten short and there were scratch marks on the backs of his hands.

'What is going to happen, Titurius? Will it be another civil war, but this time between two brothers? When has Rome ever seen the like of that before?'

'Rome was founded by warring brothers, and that worked out well in the end.'

'Don't be flippant, Titurius. This is serious. This could be the incident that pushes Antoninus over the edge and turns him into a murderous tyrant.'

'You think he has it in him?' asked Titurius more sombrely.

'Severus certainly did.'

'If it is a trait in his nature passed down from his father, then why are you more afraid of Antoninus than Geta?'

'Because Antoninus is more capable,' said Cilo, and Titurius nodded agreement.

'But this? A trivial incident in the Circus. A disrespectful charioteer?' Titurius couldn't keep the sneer out of his voice.

He didn't understand the men of senatorial rank who demeaned themselves attending the races, although given the love Caracalla and Geta had for the sport, he would be very careful who he said that to.

'You have never understood the allure of the Circus Maximus, Titurius, and I won't try to explain it to you again. Either it's in your blood or it isn't. Suffice to say that for men of all ranks of society, the races are of the utmost importance. When a big race is looming, or one has just been run, they talk of nothing else. They gamble huge sums on the outcome, they hang around the Circus, they harry the camps of the racing factions of their opposing teams. You know a man is far more likely to change his wife than ever to change allegiance to his team.'

'I know all this, Cilo, even if I don't feel it. But why are you here?'

'I used to be a brave man, you know, Titurius. I have been a legate, a military prefect, a proconsul, urban prefect and a consul. I fought for Severus against Pescennius Niger. I saw combat. I killed Roman soldiers.'

'You have had a career that I for one am envious of, senator.'

'Surely we should become braver as we age. And yet when we are young, we are anxious to risk all the life we have ahead of us, while when we are old, we cling to what we have left like frightened mice waiting for the terrier to dig us out.'

'Cilo, what do you want from me?'

'I'm going to talk to Antoninus. Plead for harmony and co-operation with his brother.'

Titurius kept his face impassive, but inside his heart sank. He couldn't see how that would end other than badly.

'Why would you do such a thing, Cilo?'

'Because it is my duty to the Senate and people of Rome. If Antoninus and Geta could come to an arrangement, could reign together in peace, then we could avoid the bloodshed that is to come. And maybe they could even augment Rome's power and glory better together than either on their own. Antoninus with his military prowess and strength of personality, and Geta with his more intellectual approach, and his willingness to listen to advice.'

'You know what a dangerous path this is, don't you? You risk alienating them both, and making it seem like you support neither.'

'It's the right thing to do, Titurius.'

'I know.' Titurius ran his hand through his hair, reflexively tidying a rogue quiff that tended to stand up at times of stress if he neglected it. 'Still, you haven't said what you want from me.'

'I want you to host a dinner for Antoninus and Domna, and invite Papinianus and myself. Papinianus thinks as I do, though he has a loyalty to Antoninus that restrains his tongue.'

'Why me?'

'You have not come out strongly in favour of either Emperor, though that may be just because you haven't been put in that position yet. But I'm sure Antoninus will be pleased to come and attempt to win you to his side. And I know you and trust you. Most other senators would use an evening with one of the Emperors solely for their own advancement. You aren't like that. You can seat me to Antoninus' left, while you are seated to the right of Domna, and give me the chance to try to talk some sense into him.'

Titurius touched his fingertips to his bearded chin.

'I don't like it, Cilo. I have a wife and a son and daughter. I don't want to do anything to put them in danger.'

'There will be no danger to you, Titurius. I'm not asking you to say or do anything that would be a risk to you or your family. I just want to be in close proximity to Antoninus, in a relaxed social setting, away from his more poisonous influences.'

'Such as?'

'You need me to list them? You really should pay more attention, Titurius. Sextus Varius Marcellus has long been an Antoninus loyalist, but Quintus Marcius Dioga, Julius Avitus and Julius Asper are all close to him. Marcellus is now urban prefect, and there are rumours that Dioga will be put in charge of the treasury. Their interests all lie with Antoninus as sole ruler. I need to speak to him without them present to contradict me.'

Titurius considered for a while, and Cilo sat in silence for his answer, biting at an already short fingernail while he waited.

'Very well.'

Cilo let out a breath Titurius hadn't realised he had been holding. But he couldn't tell if Cilo wore an expression of relief or despair. Maybe he had been hoping Titurius would decline, and then Cilo could feel his conscience was clear, that he had tried. Now, the course was committed.

'Antoninus might refuse my invitation, you know. I'm sure he has a hundred offers of social events to consider.'

'You have influence, Titurius, though you may not fully appreciate it. You have the respect of the senators. Antoninus will very much want to persuade you to his cause. I believe he will accept.'

'We will see. Cilo, you don't have to do this. Say now, and this is all forgotten.'

Cilo looked close to tears. 'Titurius, I must.'

Titurius nodded. 'I'll send the invitation today.'

Cilo rose, shook Titurius' hand, and left, walking slowly, head bowed and shoulders rounded. Titurius watched him go with sympathy, and then turned his attention to organising a banquet fit for an Emperor.

–

They hadn't had long to scout out their target's position, work out his habits and movements, and assess his strengths and weaknesses. Silus reflected how everything in Rome seemed hasty and rushed, not just his missions. Food was served in stalls and on street corners hot and ready to eat, and was consumed in moments before the customer got on with their day. Everyone was in a hurry to get somewhere, to see their patron for a handout, to get to the market early for the freshest produce and the best meals, or to deliver an urgent message that would get the messenger beaten if they were tardy.

In Britannia, he had sometimes spent weeks observing a target before getting back to his superiors with the intelligence they wanted. And when he returned home, it would commonly take hours for Velua to prepare him a meal – to fetch the wood for the fire, boil the water, and let the tough meat and vegetables stew until they were edible. Yes, some things were urgent, but generally there just seemed a lot less to fit into your day back home.

They had had less than a day to prepare for this mission. Oclatinius wanted the job done while the insult to Caracalla was fresh in people's minds, so there could be no doubt of the reason for his death. Daya, Silus and Atius had also had a brief meeting to discuss their approach. Daya and Atius had their own strong and completely opposing views. Daya had advocated a subtle and stealthy approach, involving kidnapping Euprepes, torturing him and then crucifying him at night and leaving him to be found by a shocked city the next morning. Atius wanted to find him and go in fast and hard, swords swinging, until the charioteer was dead, along with any who got in their way.

Fortunately, it was Silus who was in charge, and he got their reluctant agreement to follow his own plan. They had spent the morning making discreet enquiries about Euprepes – where he lived, where he ate, what he did with his day. It was less satisfactory and less secretive than observing those things directly with their own eyes, but time was not on their side, and it yielded enough information. While not a man of regular habits, Euprepes would usually visit the stables of the Green faction at least once a day to talk to the owners of the teams, the grooms and farriers, and the charioteers themselves, who were always delighted to receive words of wisdom from the champion, to accept his words of admonishment if he was disappointed in their performance, or bask in the glow of his praise if he was pleased with them.

Silus had ordered Atius to dress like a beggar – it wasn't hard, he just selected his unwashed outfit from his last night out on the town, which was sufficiently stained with food, wine and vomit to easily pass for the clothing of one of Rome's army of derelicts – and had him beg outside the Greens' stables. At least it was a mission for which his broken hand didn't hinder him. Daya and Silus played dice at a table on the street outside a nearby tavern. Graffiti on the walls and carved into the table displayed slogans such as, '*Curse Pollox the Red, and let him fall on the first lap*,' or simply '*The Blues are shit.*' Someone had gone so far as to paint a lengthy curse on the outer wall that read, '*O demons, I call upon you to torture and kill the horses of the Whites and Blues, and crush the drivers Felix, Alexander and Hermes so there is not a single breath left in their body.*' Silus wondered what sort of welcome a Blues supporter would receive in here on race day.

The sun was well past its zenith when Atius shuffled over to them, enjoying his acting role. He approached their table, cupped hand out.

'Copper coin for an old veteran, kind sir,' he said. 'I've got nothing since the army tossed me out for screwing the centurion's mother.'

'Sit down,' said Silus. 'Join us for a drink, brave soldier.'

When Atius sat at their table, Silus hissed at him, 'For Mithras' sake, Atius, what are you doing? You fancy a career on the stage or something? We are supposed to be avoiding attention.'

Atius gestured around him. Their exchange had gone completely unnoticed by the people on the streets and at the nearby tables, all occupied with their own conversations or activities.

'Fine. Speak.'

'Euprepes has just entered the stables with his entourage.'

'How many?'

'About twenty.'

'Twenty? Why so many?'

Atius shrugged. 'A couple of bodyguards, big Germanic types. A few slaves. The rest seemed to be fans.'

'And we know what we will face inside the stables,' said Daya. 'Charioteers, blacksmiths, grooms. Not to mention the guards. From what I have heard, the factions are constantly trying to get into each other's stables to see what advantage they can get, whether it is injuring their best horse or poisoning their best charioteer. If we go in there, we will be spotted and questioned immediately, and then we will be facing a very angry, very tough mob, armed with whips and hammers.'

'Then we have to catch him when he leaves,' said Silus.

'If we aren't doing it inside the stables, we should do it directly outside, for maximum impact,' said Daya. 'This isn't supposed to be a discreet doing away with. We are to send a message.'

'The timing will have to be just right, then,' said Atius. 'We will have to catch him the moment he comes out, execute him, then escape. And we will need to make sure we aren't recognised. The whole city will be looking for the murderer of Euprepes, half to kill us and half to congratulate us.'

Silus thought back to his time sitting in the cold, wet forests of Caledonia, scouting for the legions. He would never have dreamt back then that within a year he would have swapped those frigid environs for the hot streets of Rome, stalking not a Maeatae barbarian but a Roman sportsman. He marvelled at the position he found himself in, a board marker in a grand game of ludus latrunculorum between the two great players in the Empire, the brothers Augusti. And with no idea if he was on the right side. But that was the situation the Fates had handed him.

'Fine, this is how we will do it,' he said, and outlined his plan.

'I should cut you up and feed you to the dogs, you stupid bitch,' he yelled, grabbing her by the hair and throwing her to the ground. It had rained the previous night, and all the sun had done was warm the wet dirt and shit that coated the road rather than drying it out, so the ordure splashed her as she fell.

She landed on hands and knees, looking up at him with a pitiful expression which almost melted the heart of the watching Silus and made him intervene before he remembered they were both just acting. Atius jabbed a finger in her direction, and yelled curses at her again.

'This is the last time you disobey me,' he yelled, and gave her a backhanded swipe across the face with his good hand. Daya did a good job of rocking with the blow, just enough to take the force out of it, but not so much it didn't sound convincing.

Silus lurked in the shadows a dozen yards away. As soon as Euprepes had emerged from the stables and started to make his way back towards the main street, Silus had nipped ahead and given Atius the nod. Atius had started his performance with the enthusiasm of a Greek actor.

A few passers-by and people sitting on the floor or at nearby tables turned to watch in idle curiosity. Watching a master beat his slave was hardly a rarity, but it was uncommon enough to warrant a little attention if one was bored enough.

'Maybe I'll sell you to the quarries,' Atius said angrily. 'Then I'll get a little cash for you, and you will still be dead inside six months.'

'Please, master, no, I beg you,' said Daya piteously.

'I gave you every chance. I've had enough. Maybe I should just give you away to one of these good people.'

That attracted some notice. It wasn't every day that someone gave a slave away for free.

'You,' said Atius, pointing at an old man with a mouth full of sausage sitting at a tavern table. 'Will you take her from me?'

Before the man could hastily swallow and reply, Atius singled out a man too young to have more than the barest growth of beard lounging against a wall. 'How about you? You could take her as a bed slave, if you like girls that look like boys.' Silus was sure Atius would pay for that later. 'Come on, who wants her? All I ask is someone who is prepared to knock her about enough to keep her in her place.'

'I'll take her,' said a podgy man in a tight-fitting tunic.

'No, give her to me,' said a broad-shouldered man with a russet beard.

'I spoke up first,' said the podgy man.

'You'll get my fist down your throat if you speak up again,' said the red beard.

'Let me take the poor wretch,' said a middle-aged woman of middling wealth judging by her fine but not too fine dress and jewellery. 'I'll turn her into a decent house slave, with no need for beatings.'

A crowd was slowly drawn in, forming a circle around Atius and Daya, with jostling, shouting and even some bids to buy Daya on the cheap. Daya remained on all fours, face spattered with shit, looking down at the ground, while Atius whipped up the crowd.

The timing was perfect. The crowd fully blocked the street by the time Euprepes and his entourage arrived and attempted to pass.

'Clear the way!' yelled one of Euprepes' bodyguards. 'Make way for Euprepes the charioteer!'

But even the legendary hero could not tear the crowd away from the possibility of a free handout. Some started to push each other and one woman fell to the ground with a scream; a young man received a shove in the back as he bent to help her up, and retaliated by spinning and planting a brisk uppercut on the jaw of the man who had pushed him.

In moments the brawl spread, punches and kicks thrown, hair pulled, limbs bitten. From a short distance beyond the crowd that was now a mob, behind Euprepes' entourage, Silus saw Euprepes' bodyguards wade in with clubs, breaking limbs and skulls to clear a path, helped by the slaves and fans who accompanied him.

The charioteer looked impatient, shouting at his bodyguards to hurry up and make a path for him. He was dressed in a belted tunic made of fine wool, dyed green, and wore gold necklaces and bracelets, showing all his wealth and success. From his belt dangled his leather whip, a souvenir from his time in the Circus. He was still well-muscled, as any successful charioteer was. It took strength as well as skill and agility to win races, or even just to survive them. But Euprepes was an old man now, and the skin was wrinkled, the muscles flabbier than they once had been, and his gut bulged over his belt.

Suddenly Euprepes was alone. All the fans and slaves had waded into the crowd, and were themselves fully engaged in the fighting, shouting, kicking and punching, crying out that they should be showing respect to the great Euprepes.

Silus drew his knife from under his tunic and stepped out of the shadows. His tunic was hooded, as had become more fashionable since Caracalla had started wearing a Gallic cloak in this style, and his face was mostly hidden by drawing the hood up and forwards. Euprepes was concentrating on the small riot in front of him, his fist balled, looking like he was itching to wade into the action himself.

Silus didn't hesitate. His blade in his right hand, he grabbed Euprepes' chin from behind with his left hand, twisting it up left to expose the throat. His knife came round, edge honed to razor sharpness, ready to slice deep into the soft tissues, the vessels and pipes.

But you didn't win more than seven hundred victories in the Circus Maximus without having the reflexes of a cat and the strength of a bull. Before Silus could slash, Euprepes dipped his chin down, twisted his head right, and dipped his right shoulder. Atrophied by age though he was, he was still immensely powerful, and Silus found his left hand dragged by the old charioteer's neck muscles, round and over his shoulder, and as Euprepes bowed forward, he grabbed Silus' left wrist and yanked. Silus sliced deep into Euprepes' cheek, a wound that would scar but not kill, and then found himself flying over Euprepes' back to crash onto the muddy ground.

Euprepes stood above him, hand clamped to the wound on his face, and roared in anger. As yet there was too much din from the disturbance Atius had stirred up for Euprepes' entourage to have noticed his danger, but at that instant, it was Silus, stunned, squinting up into a terrifying expression of fury, who felt the most imperilled.

Euprepes clasped his fists together, reached high above his head, and brought them down hard towards Silus' chest. Silus recovered his wits enough to begin a roll to his right, but it was only enough to redirect the blow to his upper left arm, which immediately became numb. He continued his roll, and staggered to his feet, still clutching his blade in his right hand, left arm hanging loose, he hoped only temporarily paralysed.

Instinctively he moved into a blade fighter's stance, feet a foot apart, right side forward, blade out and low to easily stab upwards into the less protected vital parts. Euprepes adopted a wrestler's stance, face on, feet wide, knees bent, arms out and ready to grip his opponent and hurl him about like a little girl's rag doll. Silus wondered whether poison on the blade would have helped his position now, but he had never been a fan. It was too slow and unreliable, and it was too easy to cut yourself with your own weapon.

'Who sent you?' hissed Euprepes. 'The Blues? Surely not the Reds?'

Silus let out a chuckle, belying the level of confidence he really felt. 'There are some people in Rome even more important than the racing factions, you know.'

Euprepes narrowed his eyes. 'Caracalla? He was really so insulted?'

Silus gave a small nod of acknowledgement. He flexed the fingers in his left hand and felt the feeling slowly return.

'When Geta's men approached me to dedicate the next victory to him, I had no idea it could lead to this.'

'My boss is a fan of yours. He is going to regret your death. Me, I'd never heard of you.'

'I'm not dead yet,' said Euprepes, and rushed at Silus.

Maybe if Euprepes had been thirty years younger, maybe if he had been fighting a normal street thug with a knife who was trying to take his purse, the outcome would have been different.

But Silus was an Arcanus, raised by a spy, trained as a scout, honed by Oclatinius to be one of the elite, and Euprepes, for all his natural power and skill, was an old man. Once Silus had recovered from the mistake of underestimating his opponent, the contest was one-sided.

Silus sidestepped Euprepes' charge, leaving a straight leg trailing which sent Euprepes flying forward, face down into the dirt. Instantly, Silus was on his opponent's back, knees either side of his broad chest. He grabbed the charioteer's hair with his left hand, and pulled his head backwards. Although still weakened from the blow to his arm, he was strong enough to expose Euprepes' neck.

The old man seemed to realise the fight was lost. He drew a deep breath, and bellowed out, 'Greens for ever!'

One of the fans at the back of the crowd finally heard, and turned. 'Euprepes!' he screamed in anguish as Silus sliced deep into the famous man's neck. Blood jetted forward, the liquid splashing into the dirt and swirling in red eddies in the puddles.

'He's killed Euprepes!' yelled the fan, a balding man with wall eyes, a broad chest and a paunch. Silus' hood had slipped back in the tussle, and he hastily pulled it forward to protect his identity, just as all heads swivelled towards him. For a moment, the crowd stared in disbelief at the tableau, Euprepes face down in the dirt with a lake of blood spreading around him, Silus on his back with a dripping knife in his hand. Then cries of outrage broke out, and they surged towards him.

Silus leapt up, spun on his heels and ran.

He had a ten-yard head start on the foremost of his pursuers, and he was quick, but he had just been in a fight and had been injured. What was worse was that he was in unfamiliar territory. He sprinted, pistoning his arms and legs, taking deep lungfuls of air. He didn't turn round. He could hear the furious yells of the chasing crowd.

'Stop him! Murderer! He killed Euprepes!'

The streets were narrow in this part of Rome, the Transtiberim on the far side of the Tiber. Packed with immigrant populations such as Jews and Syrians, as well as warehouses and docks, it had a very different feel to that of the Subura in the centre of the city, but like the Subura, had the houses of the wealthy nestling up against insulae-filled slums.

Silus ran, mud and shit splashing as his boots landed, not sure where he was headed, just desperate to stay ahead of the baying mob. He had no doubt that if he faltered, if he fell, if one of them caught him, they would rip him to pieces, like hounds on a fox, and no agility or fighting skill would save him. Speed now was his only defence.

He rounded a corner and collided with a woman carrying a basket of clothing back from the fullers, beautiful stolae and pristine togae, no doubt for the household of someone important. The basket tipped, and the clean clothes fell into the dirt, soaking up the ordure. The woman screamed curses at him, likely in for a beating for this, but her curses trailed off into surprise, then redoubled in pitch and volume as the mob appeared, trampling the clean laundry into the shit.

Silus hurdled a pig snuffling in a pile of rubbish, trod on the tail of a cat that let out a spine-chilling screech, kicked a chicken that was too slow to get out of his path, and shoved a little toddler so the child landed face down in the muck and immediately started wailing.

He risked a look back. He was extending his lead on his pursuers, none of whom were too anxious to get ahead of their fellows, but he was conscious that one wrong turn down a dead end could finish the chase very quickly and very finally. Also, the numbers of those pursuing had grown as the crime was shouted to onlookers, who joined the lynch mob to assuage their righteous fury. He took another corner, a left, breathing heavily now, sprinting past curious traders, sailors, labourers and dock workers, then another right.

And there was a mob at the end of the street in front of him. Someone must have had the sense to split the crowd, and with their better local knowledge, had outflanked him. He came to a halt, but the sounds of pursuit immediately grew louder.

The mob before him saw him instantly, and with a collective howl, rushed at him, many holding makeshift weapons such as hammers, legs of stools, and butcher's knives. The street was flanked on either side by tight rows of shops and dwellings with no gaps between them. He chose the nearest one, a bakery, and ran in through the open frontage.

In the front of the shop, laid out on a long table with depressions for containers to hold the freshly baked bread, were the wares for sale – the oval panis quadratus with its two perpendicular grooves for easy division; the round lentaculum; panis nauticulum for sailors; artolaganus, a luxury bread made with honey and spices; and even panis furfureus, a tough bread reserved for feeding to dogs.

Silus hurdled the counter, his trailing leg sending ceramic dishes and baked goods crashing to the floor, and rushed into the back room. Here the baker looked up from where he had been bent over his charcoal-heated oven, an angry curse on his lips. When he saw the knife in Silus' hand, he backed away to the far wall, eyes wide with fear.

'Take what you want. I don't have much.'

'How do I get out of here? Quick!'

'There is only the front way in. Or that way to the upper floors and roof.'

The baker gestured to a side door and Silus ran for it, wrenching it open and dashing through.

'But the stairs—' said the baker, and the rest of his sentence was lost as Silus ran, taking the steps three at a time. The boards looked dry and rotten, and his pounding on them was making them groan and crack ominously. But below him he heard the sounds of the mob entering the bakery, demanding to know where Silus had gone, starting for the door.

Silus passed the apartment above the shop on the first floor, then the second. The board on one step split and he stumbled to the next as his foot went through. He steadied himself against the apartment wall for the briefest of moments, then heard shouts as someone lower down caught sight of him, and he forced himself onwards, heart pounding with the effort of the climb straight after the headlong flight.

He rounded a turn on the staircase that brought him close to the roof, and this time the poorly maintained woodwork, rotted in the sun and rain, let him down. The step split in two, and he plummeted straight through, stopping his fall by grabbing on to the next step. The staircase ripped from the wall and swung wildly around. He looked down and saw the mob leader, one of Euprepes' bodyguards, just a single floor below. In moments he would be on him, and Silus would be done.

The staircase swung back inwards, bringing him in reach of the next step, which was still attached to the intact staircase that led to the roof. He grabbed it with both hands and pushed the broken stair away from him with his feet. He hoped it would break, but it just wobbled around a few feet away from where he dangled, a fatal drop below him.

The bodyguard reached the top of the lower staircase, looking down uncertainly as it shook beneath him. He gestured to the other pursuers to stay back in case they brought the whole structure down with their weight. Then he looked at Silus' predicament and smiled.

'I don't know who you are, or why you killed our greatest living sportsman. But now you die. There is no way out from here.'

Silus tried to pull himself further up, but he was exhausted, and his left arm was still weakened by the blow from Euprepes. He dangled helplessly, hearing the roars of the mob below him cursing him and appealing to the gods that he fall. He looked down, and the world started to spin. His grip on the stair weakened.

A hand grasped his wrist. Then another hand grasped his other wrist. He looked up into the face of Daya, staring down at him, teeth gritted with effort as she pulled.

'Help me, you stupid bastard,' she hissed. 'Climb.'

He reached out with his feet to gain a purchase on the wall, and with Daya tugging on him like a dog playing tug with a bone, he stretched a hand up. He got a grip on the next step up, then the next, and then he got a knee on the lowest step and used it to lever himself up.

The bodyguard let out a roar of frustration at the possibility of Silus escaping. He took one step back, then leapt across the gap in the broken stairway.

He clutched the lowest step, elbows and chest on the stair, and began to struggle his way up. The stairway groaned its protest at this new level of abuse, and there was a cracking sound. Silus started to climb, hauled upwards by Daya. The bodyguard hooked an ankle onto the stair and pulled himself higher. Daya nimbly leapt off the stairway onto the roof, still holding Silus' wrist, dragging him with her. Silus got a hand on the edge of the roof overhang just as the bodyguard grasped his ankle.

And then the stairway fell away.

Screams echoed up as the heavy wooden structure fell from a great height on the mob who had waited below.

The bodyguard yelled in anger and fear, hanging onto Silus' ankle with both hands. Silus in turn gripped the edge of the roof, trusting desperately in Daya's grip and the workmanship of whichever roofer had placed the beam that overhung the wall.

But for all Daya's skill and agility, she did not have the strength to support the weight of two men, and Silus' arms were rapidly fatiguing. He kicked at the hands on his ankle, but he could not get the right angle to impart enough force to loosen the grip. So he kicked down, and his heel connected with the bodyguard's face.

He felt the tightness on his ankle relax a little, and he kicked down again. One hand came loose, and Silus could see the bodyguard swinging around in mid-air, arm flailing. He kicked down one more time.

The bodyguard let go, and his scream as he fell three floors was blood-chilling until cut off abruptly by impact.

Silus breathed heavily for a moment, then with Daya's help, struggled up onto the roof, where he lay on his back, gasping for air.

'How...?' was all he could get out.

'You run fast,' said Daya with a chuckle. 'But so do I. I was with the mob, of course, shouting for your head. Then, when I saw they had you trapped, I took another stairway to the roof to help you up here. Or, if necessary, come down there and fight with you.'

'You would do that for me?' asked Silus.

'Of course,' said Daya, looking puzzled. 'We are Arcani.'

From street level, the screams of the injured, the howls of those grieving over the newly dead, and the cries of anger of those who still wanted vengeance and justice reached them.

'Come on,' said Daya, holding her hand out. 'It's time for us to disappear.'

Silus took it and let her haul him to his feet. Together, they jogged along the rooftops until they judged they had put enough distance between themselves and the mob to descend to the streets once more.

Silus tossed his hood back and Daya and he blended into the crowds heading across the Tiber and back into the centre of the city.

Chapter Ten

Dio Cassius grabbed Titurius' arm as he left the Senate meeting and dragged him into the shadows behind a pillar.

'I heard a whisper that you are hosting a party for Antoninus,' said Cassius, without preamble.

'Maybe that should be a warning to us both that little stays secret in Rome,' replied Titurius. 'Who told you?'

'Festus.'

Titurius gave Cassius a hard stare.

'You associate with him? His job is to terrorise and blackmail the likes of us to toe the Imperial line.'

'He serves the Senate and people of Rome, and he sees Geta as the superior of the two Augusti.'

'The question is highly debatable.'

'Is this your answer then? You have picked your side?'

'Absolutely not,' said Titurius. 'This is a favour for a friend.'

'Cilo? What is he playing at?'

'He is playing at peace, Cassius. Maybe we should all be following his example.'

Cassius shook his head. 'Cilo's influence is on the wane. Without Severus to protect him, he is just an old man living off past glories. He will not succeed.'

'Maybe not, but who can fault him for the attempt? You said you were going to speak to Papinianus.'

'Pah. There is another who cannot make his mind up and take a side.'

'If these good men think the best way forward is a rapprochement between the two Emperors, do you really think to know better?'

'Titurius, my friend, I am a historian. My great work starts with the founding of Rome, and tells the stories of the end of the Kings, the Gracchi, Sulla and Marius, Caesar and Pompey, Octavian and Antony and the year of the Four Emperors, and when I eventually reach more recent history, the year of the Five Emperors and the rise of Severus. Rome is no stranger to civil war, and neither am I. Each time of internal strife left Rome stronger than before. Brutus ended the Kings and led to the foundation of the Republic. Caesar took the Empire to a power it had never had before. Octavian stabilised the Empire and made it strong, well-defended and peaceful. Severus reigned long and was a great leader. I have no doubt that the right victor of the current struggle will glorify and strengthen Rome further.'

'And by the right leader, you mean Geta? Your argument seemed to favour the stronger, more military candidate for power.'

'Not so. Look at Octavian. Not a good physical specimen, not a great military leader, but he had strong advisors and generals such as Agrippa, and he was arguably our greatest ever Emperor. With the exception of Severus, of course.'

'Of course.' They might be talking treason and ran the risk of being hurled from the Tarpeian Rock if their conversation was overheard, but there was still no sense in showing disrespect to the recently deceased Emperor. His shade should have long departed, after his interment, but maybe he was still prowling the curia, raging impotently at the senators and his feuding sons.

'Refusing to take a side is a dangerous path, Titurius. Will you support Geta?'

'I'll think on it more,' said Titurius, uneasy with the conversation, especially in such a public place, although he constantly checked no one was near enough to overhear.

'Don't take too long. Soon it will be too late.'

Dio Cassius patted Titurius on the shoulder, looked around furtively, and strode away.

A sick, heavy feeling of dread rose in Titurius' gorge.

—

'It's just not fair,' said Geta. 'He has all the advantages. He is older, bigger, stronger.'

'But not wiser, cousin,' said Aper. Gaius Septimius Severus Aper liked to refer to Caracalla and Geta as his cousins, although in reality they shared not a grandfather but a great-great-grandfather. Many of their relatives used familiar terms closer than they deserved to exaggerate their own status as kin of the Imperial family. Geta didn't mind – Aper had been a good friend to him over the years, and a close supporter. He also had a tendency to say the right thing to make Geta feel better.

'He has the army,' said Geta. 'He has the military experience. Further – and I am confessing this to you in private and in confidence – he has the greater boldness.'

'Which is not necessarily a strength. Charging into battle stark naked, holding only your cock as a weapon, is bold. It is not necessarily wise. Boldness can lose battles, and lose Empires.'

'Still, his boldness has made me look weak. I hate him, but in a way, I have to admire how he feels he can kill Euprepes, one of the most beloved men in Rome, and fear no repercussions.'

'And he is right, isn't he?' asked Aper. 'He will get away with it.'

Geta paced his private chamber, hands clasped behind his back, taking small, rapid steps. If he let this pass, it would weaken his own position further. And he could not have that.

Father elevated me to co-Augustus, he thought, *and named me as co-Emperor as his dying wish. To rule is my right. And my brother would deny me this, because he feels he is so much better than me. But I know he is wrong. I know I would make the better Emperor. And I will not disappoint my father's shade. Or my mother.*

The thought of failing his mother brought a flush to his face, and he turned away from Aper to hide it. He adored her, and hated how close she was to Caracalla, even though he wasn't her real son. He gritted his teeth and turned back to Aper.

'What can I do?'

'Maybe you should do away with one of his supporters.'

Geta shook his head. 'I'm not killing a charioteer or gladiator. That would make me look petty.'

'What about one of his spies?'

'You know someone suitable?'

'I have my sources. Oclatinius is not the only man in the city with secret connections.'

'Oclatinius. Hades take him.' Geta's tone was sour. 'Why is he so loyal to my brother?'

'I don't know, cousin, but I can tell you who killed Euprepes.'

'What? Who?'

'Silus, the Arcanus.'

'Him! Always him! How do you know this?'

'The Commander of the Sacred Bedchamber discovered it through his network and passed it on to me.'

'Festus? I'm not sure where his loyalties lie.'

'You can trust him, cousin. And anyway, I understand this Silus has been a problem to you in the past.'

'Ever since I first encountered him in Britannia. I believe it was his fault that the barbarians rebelled a second time after we had pacified them.'

'So, there is your answer. Have him killed.'

'Could I?' Geta stroked his chin. 'It is a sweet thought. Get my vengeance for all the problems he has caused me, and kick my brother in the balls at the same time.'

'Say the word, cousin. I have a skilled man who works for me – he could take care of the matter in such a way that no evidence points at you, while making it clear why he has been killed.'

'Maybe your man would be better employed taking care of my brother.'

Aper's eyes widened. 'Is that what you want, Augustus?'

Geta hesitated. He saw a fork in the road ahead, and he knew that if he chose the darker path, he would not be able to turn back. Caracalla gone, himself reigning as sole Emperor. All the authority, all the respect. All the love and attention from his mother.

But he couldn't. The temptation was strong, but...

He was scared. Scared of his brother if he failed. Scared of Oclatinius if he didn't. And scared of disappointing his mother. There was no one in the world that he could admit that to. Not Aper. Not even his dear mother herself.

'No. I love my brother too dearly.' He hoped Aper would not see through the lie. 'But we will make him aware that this murder has not gone unnoticed. Make it known to that Arcanus, Silus, that his actions have been noted. Maybe it will restrain my brother's future actions.'

Aper could not hide his look of disappointment, and Geta felt a spasm of shame.

'If that is your wish, Augustus, I will have my man deliver a message. A literal one, rather than a metaphorical one.'

Geta inclined his head. 'Go. I have a headache, and wish to retire.'

Aper bowed and departed from Geta's private chamber. Geta waited until he was out of earshot, and then let out a roar of frustration which echoed off the walls and through the very real ache that was building inside his skull.

–

Silus sat at a table in the street outside a tavern near his apartment. Issa lay at his feet, stretched out to enjoy the late-afternoon sun. Apicula sat beside him. It did not take her long to complete her chores in the tiny accommodation – she had cleaned, scrubbed, done the laundry, brought his provisions and fed the dog. Now she sipped water and silently watched the world go by.

Silus did the same. Rome was an endlessly fascinating place, and he soaked up the street life for his personal as well as professional interest, attempting to understand the little habits of everyday life that the lifelong residents of the city took for granted, but the lack of knowledge of which might mark out a foreigner as someone out of place. He observed daily routines of shopping and washing and bathing, he noted which gods' statues were worshipped and which could safely be neglected, and he watched the haggling over goods sold in the markets and shops and by the wandering street hawkers.

That morning he had gone for a long walk to try to familiarise himself with the local topography. Maybe it was a hopeless task, but he had felt particularly vulnerable the day before, fleeing through streets he didn't know, and his unfamiliarity with his surroundings had nearly cost him his life.

He had had a strange feeling all morning of being watched, but it had come to nothing. He had doubled back, turned suddenly, hidden in shadows and round corners, but had never come closer to catching anyone shadowing him than a movement at the corner of his field of vision. He dismissed the thought from his mind, but couldn't shake an uneasy feeling making his guts clench.

He picked up a date and chewed it, extracting the stone with his tongue and spitting it onto the street. His eyes fixed on a hawker carrying a bag of cooking utensils, walking slowly down the street. His hood was up, despite the fine weather, and he appeared to be making little effort to make a sale, not shouting out his goods and prices like most hawkers. Silus felt for the knife where it lay hidden beneath his tunic, reassured by its solid presence.

A hand touched his arm, and he turned, startled, to see a young boy of no more than seven years, dressed in street-grimed rags, staring at him intently.

'Are you Silus?' said the boy.

'What do you want, child?' snapped Silus.

'Are you Silus?'

'What if I am?'

'I have a message.' The boy looked up, searching his memory for the exact words. '"We know you killed the old man. The Emperor Geta is very unhappy. There will be a reckoning. Let your masters know."'

A chill shot straight down Silus' spine. He grabbed the boy's arm. 'Who sent you?' he hissed.

'Master, you're hurting me.'

'Tell me.'

'I don't know his name. He was selling stuff. He gave me the message and told me to give it to a man called Silus sitting here.'

Silus' eyes darted around. No one was paying him any attention, everyone just going about their usual business. The hawker was no longer to be seen.

'Master, please, can I go now?'

Silus let go of the boy. He would know nothing more. As soon as he released his grip, the boy dashed off like a frightened hare. Silus cursed.

'What is it, master?' asked Apicula.

'Trouble,' said Silus. He needed to see Oclatinius.

-

No expense was spared for the visit of the Emperor. Fine tapestries hung from the walls depicting scenes of famous military victories such as Zama, Alesia and Actium. The tables were draped in linen cloth with broad purple stripes. The plates and goblets were gold and silver, and the silk cushions on the couches were embroidered with pictures of exotic wild animals. Even the slaves had been dressed in expensive tunics for the boys and fashionable stolae for the girls.

The entertainment was refined. Titurius was no fan of bawdy storytellers, or sex shows, or displays of deformed individuals to mock. Instead he had paid for the best flautists, lyre players and dancers that were available, and he watched them perform with satisfaction.

As Cilo had requested, Tituria was reclining to Domna's right, while Cilo was to Caracalla's left, with the Augusta and the Augustus in the centre in the place of honour. Few others had been invited, just a few friends and distant relations of Titurius, Papinianus and some of Domna's inner circle – Galen, Philostratus and Macrinus.

Titurius was familiar with Galen's work and had even consulted him about some ailments of his own in the past. He had met Philostratus the sophist socially in the past, and didn't really care for his preachiness and air of intellectual superiority. Macrinus was a man who he hadn't really encountered except in passing. He knew he was an accomplished jurist, like Ulpianus and Papinianus, and had occupied some important official roles. He was also liked by Caracalla, without being part of his inner circle, at least not yet, and Cilo had suggested Titurius invite him as a friend to the Emperor, but one who was not in a position to be overly influential.

An intricate dance by a troupe of Alexandrian slave girls finished, and the dancers swept out of the triclinium. Low conversation resumed around the room. Titurius' wife, Autronia, reclining on his right, leant forward to speak to Domna.

'Augusta, your hair looks wonderful tonight. How long did it take your ornatrix to style you?'

'Around two hours,' replied the Empress. 'It is so tedious, this fashion, isn't it?'

Autronia had recently purchased a highly expensive ornatrix herself, specifically to copy the style of Domna's tightly curled hair, and she patted her locks and nodded agreement. 'The things we do to make ourselves presentable for our men, Augusta.'

Titurius fought to stop his eyes rolling. Autronia spent half of her day shopping for clothes, jewellery, make-up and perfumes, and the other half wearing it. Yes, she made herself look elegant and fashionable, but Titurius wouldn't have cared if she wore her hair loose and unstyled, and put on no make-up. He still thought the woman he had married fifteen years earlier was beautiful, and he still loved her.

He wished he could swap places with the Empress so he could talk to the Emperor, and leave her to talk to his wife, but it would be poor etiquette. Besides, he knew that Domna could be an interesting conversationalist if he got her on the right topics, such as Greek poetry. On the other side of Caracalla, Cilo was talking, and Titurius strained his ears to filter out the discussion of make-up techniques and eyebrow plucking and hear what Cilo was saying.

'The example of Lucius Verus and Marcus Aurelius is an inspiration, though, don't you agree, Augustus?' Cilo was saying.

Caracalla grunted noncommittally.

'They showed that two brothers can rule the Empire for the benefit of all, with love and peace.'

'Yes,' said Caracalla. 'But Verus always deferred to Aurelius. And Verus died during the Antonine plague. Who knows how their relationship would have developed if he had lived longer? And maybe striking him down with plague was the gods' way of telling us that it is unnatural for Rome to be ruled by more than one Emperor.'

'I don't believe the gods would intervene in that way, Augustus,' said Cilo.

'Maybe we could ask a philosopher,' said Caracalla, and was about to gesture to Philostratus to join them when the next act came in. This was an actor reciting a section from Arrian's *Anabasis of Alexander*, 'The Battle of the River Granicus against Darius III'. It was common knowledge how much Caracalla admired the great Macedonian conqueror. He had even been known to go out and about dressed in ancient Macedonian style to mimic his hero – the flat kausia hat and the crepidae shoes. He shushed Cilo to silence during the performance so he could listen more attentively. Titurius silently congratulated himself on the choice, seeing how entranced Caracalla was.

When the scene had finished, Caracalla applauded loudly and everyone else joined in dutifully.

'Now there was a ruler,' said Caracalla admiringly. 'A brilliant general, and none of his followers would think of opposing him, or of asking to share his rule. His half-brother was never considered as a co-Emperor.'

'Alexander's half-brother was weak of mind,' said Cilo.

'He shares that with my own half-brother,' quipped Caracalla, and a ripple of nervous laughter circulated around the room.

'Augustus, I must speak frankly,' said Cilo, in a firm voice, and a hush fell over the room. It was rare to hear the Emperor spoken to in this way, even in such a small gathering of intimates. Everyone waited to hear what was to come.

Cilo took a nervous sip of his wine, and as he put the cup down, Titurius could see his hand was trembling.

'Augustus, you are a magnificent Emperor. You are strong, powerful, a clever and energetic military leader, and a wise ruler. The Senate, the people and the army all love you.

'But they also love your brother. He resembles your father. And he has some qualities of his own. Where you are a man of action, he is one of reflection. Where you are a man of passion, he is a man of cool judgement. Where you are brave, he is cautious. Maybe he is Fabius Maximus to your Alexander. There is a place in the world for both, you know.'

The room was completely silent now, except for the sound of Cilo's voice, and Caracalla breathing deeply through his nose, nostrils flaring like an angry racehorse.

'Galen would tell you that balance is everything. When there is imbalance in the humours, the body becomes ill. Galen, am I right?'

Galen inclined his head, clearly reluctant to be drawn into the larger argument but looking like he felt he was on safer ground with medical knowledge.

'Quite right, Cilo. Health is the state in which the four humours are in balance with each other, both in strength and in quantity. If there is a marked deficiency or an excess of one of the four humours, then the body shows this as an illness. Even a minor disturbance of the balance can alter one's temperament. So when there is a deficiency or excess in one of the humours, I try to restore the balance by correcting the level of the abnormal humour, while altering its opposing humour in the opposite direction. So if a man has a fever, he has too much yellow bile. We can counter this with treatments that increase yellow bile's opposite, phlegm, such as cold baths, while using medicaments to decrease the yellow bile level. Similarly, we may bleed an excess of blood, or use purgatives for an excess of black bile. Take a patient I had last week—'

'Thank you, Galen,' said Cilo before the elderly physician could take the conversation off on an irrelevant tangent. 'My point is that the Empire thrives on balance, just as the body does. You may think that the Empire would be better with a sole ruler who embodies the attributes of the elements of fire and air, but the world needs earth and water as well.

'Augustus, I beg of you. Make your peace with your brother. Let balance and harmony reign, and together, you will make Rome, and each other, greater than ever before.

'To do otherwise is to mean civil war, destruction and death, when all should be uniting to confront the enemies, internal and external, that the Empire faces.'

He stopped speaking and everyone seemed to be holding their breath, bracing themselves for a Vesuvian response from Caracalla.

The Emperor was looking down into his cup. Muscles on either side of his jaw clenched rhythmically. His face looked flushed. Domna put a calming hand on his arm, but he shrugged it off. He stood slowly, and everyone shrank back from the storm that seemed about to break.

'I think I will retire for the night,' said Caracalla. His voice was tight, but controlled. 'Titurius, thank you for your hospitality, but I am weary. Have your steward escort me to my room.'

Titurius snapped his fingers hurriedly and his steward rushed forward, showing Caracalla the way to the sumptuous bedroom they had prepared.

Low murmurs started as soon as the Emperor had left the room. Titurius looked over to Cilo, who was ashen-faced, head bowed, a fine tremor noticeable from his shoulders down. Next to him, Domna's expression was mournful. Titurius wondered if she had already resigned herself to the loss of either her son or her stepson. It was obvious that Cilo's plea had fallen on deaf ears. There would be no reconciliation.

The next act, a professional jester, seemed wildly inappropriate as he buffooned about, tumbling, falling and making farting noises, and he left, crestfallen, without raising a single laugh. Autronia looked distraught at the way the evening had transpired, but Titurius was philosophical. He had not shared with his wife the true reason for inviting the Emperor, and he had never had high hopes that anything of value would come from the evening. Still, he was pleased he had made the effort. He felt it would ease his conscience, that he could tell himself he had tried, when the storm broke.

Domna thanked Autronia and Titurius for a wonderful evening, lying with ease and grace, and she rose to be shown to her own chambers. Titurius watched her leave, always amazed by how her beauty defied her age. He looked over to his own wife, younger, but more worn by time, smiled, and squeezed her hand.

'Titurius, it was a disaster,' she whispered to him.

He reached out to stroke her face, looking into her eyes with deep affection. 'No, my love. The disaster has not yet reached us.'

Tituria was frustrated. A banquet for the Emperor, and she wasn't invited! She hadn't really expected to be – children hardly ever got to attend such important events, especially girls. There was some discussion as to whether Quintus should be allowed to join them, his mother arguing that it wouldn't be long before he could don his toga virilis and be considered a man. But father was unusually resolute that he should not be there, and no pleading from mother or tantrums from Quintus would sway him. So Tituria stood no chance of being allowed to go, and she didn't even ask.

But what was even more infuriating was how hard it was to snoop. The triclinium only had one entrance, and it was guarded by two menacing-looking Praetorians who moved her on when she tried to peer inside to catch a glimpse of the Emperor and Empress. She considered climbing onto the roof, but the domus was well-maintained as befitted a wealthy senator's house, and she knew from previous expeditions that there were no cracks or gaps in the roof tiles through which she could spy on the party. She even considered getting into the hypocaust and hiding beneath the floor of the triclinium. The recent warm weather meant that the underfloor heating had been turned off. But she wasn't as small as she once had been, and it would be embarrassing, or even dangerous, if she got stuck down there, as had nearly happened on her last excursion there the previous summer.

She wandered listlessly from room to room. She had her hairbrush in her hand, and idly stroked it through her hair as she walked, ever mindful of her mother's instructions to keep her hair well-kempt. She walked into the tablinum, and saw a wax tablet on the desk. She put her hairbrush down and picked up the tablet, struggling to make out the little marks and convert them into words in her head. In the end she worked out it was some tally of supplies, and she threw it back onto the desk and wandered off disconsolately.

In the end she had to satisfy herself with sitting in the peristylium, hugging herself to stay warm in the cool summer evening air, bats swooping past with their high-pitched beeps, snatching moths out of the sky, with her ear pressed hard against the wall that separated the triclinium from the enclosed garden.

It was an unsatisfactory experience. When the musical acts played, she could hear little of the conversation. When everyone was talking at once, it was hard to make out individual voices. But her persistence and patience paid off when a man called Cilo started speaking. His voice sounded old and scared, but he spoke clearly. She listened as he talked about peace and harmony between the two Emperors, frowned when a more distant voice started talking about sickness, then listened intently again as Cilo continued.

When he finished, she waited for a reaction. Surely an impassioned speech like that should be answered with something similar. But she only heard a short, indistinct reply. She gave up. This was no fun. She stood, stretched and wandered back into the main house. Their domus was not a palace, but her father was extremely wealthy like most senators, and she had long ago realised from visits with her mother to other households that their own was enormous in comparison.

She decided she would sneak a look in the Emperor's room before he retired for the night. Her mother had been lambasting the slaves all day to make sure the guest rooms for the Emperor at one end of the house and the Empress at the other end were lavishly decorated, and Tituria decided she wanted to get a quick peek at the place where the Emperor would spend the night. All the other guests would depart for their own homes. Only the Emperor and Empress had been invited to stay.

The Emperor's guest room was down a long corridor. She eased the door open, and closed it behind her quietly. The room smelt of a delicate spicy fragrance. The walls had been freshly painted with pastoral frescoes, and hung with floor-length tapestries of colourful birds and fishes. The bed was covered in silk sheets stunningly embroidered with flowers separated by broad purple stripes. The room was lit by a number of oil lamps that sent multiple copies of her to the walls as flickering shadows. She touched the silk sheets with her fingertips in awe, inhaled the wonderful smell with a deep breath through her nostrils. She was tempted to dive onto the bed – she was sure the mattress was stuffed with the finest down – but she knew that messing up the neatly made bed would lead to unimaginable punishment from her mother.

She heard voices coming down the corridor. The steward.

'This way, Augustus. I do hope it will be to your satisfaction.'

No! It was too early. The banquet was not due to finish for hours. She knew there were several entertainment acts that had not yet performed. Was the Emperor ill?

She looked around wildly. The room had one door and no windows. There were no large cupboards to hide in. She could get behind a tapestry, but the bulge of her body would be obvious.

The sheets over the bed hung down to the floor.

The door swung open.

Tituria dived under the bed, straightening the valance behind her as the Emperor entered the room, accompanied by the steward. She curled herself up into a ball, the sound of her heart pounding in her ears so loudly she was sure the Emperor would hear it. She breathed slowly and steadily, in through her nose and out through her mouth, to keep the volume from her respiration as quiet as possible.

The steward fussed around the room, showing Caracalla the decorations, a jug of water and an empty cup, and the chamber pot which was fortunately placed in a corner rather than under the bed. Soon, Caracalla's patience wore thin.

'Get out. Leave me to my sleep.'

The steward apologised profusely and rushed out. Caracalla sat on the bed with a sigh. For a moment, he just sat there, not moving. Then he unlaced his sandals and tossed them aside, removed his toga and let it fall to the floor. There was a tiny gap where the valance crinkled, and she could see the fine purple woollen garment, with a gold hem, lying crumpled in a mess on the floor. Her first thought was what her mother would have said if she had seen such an expensive item of clothing so poorly looked after. Her mother, of course, thought her tucked up safely in her bed at that moment.

Her second thought, quickly on the heels of the first, was that the Emperor of Rome was lying about two feet above her head completely naked. Her heart raced anew, in excitement and fear. What was she to do? Wait for him to fall asleep, and then try to sneak out without waking him? Or wait there until morning, and escape when he had left, but risk being found by the household slaves? That would be the less dangerous way of being discovered, but it meant her staying there the whole night long, and already she needed to pee.

Either way, she was going nowhere at this moment. She shifted her position slightly, silently, and settled in for a long wait.

Unfortunately, the Emperor gave no indication he was likely to go to sleep any time soon. He turned from side to side, flung his covering sheet about, got up and paced the room before getting back into bed, all the time muttering things like, 'Who does he think he is? How dare he?'

Tituria was pleased that the slaves had cleaned thoroughly under the bed. A little dust provoking a sneeze, and it would all be over. She wondered what her punishment would be for hiding in the Emperor's bedroom. Was it a capital crime? She had always believed implicitly that her father would protect her from any danger. But even he could not protect her from the Emperor's anger, could he?

She fought down a rising panic, reassured herself that all she needed to do was keep calm and still, and the night would pass, and everything would be normal. She resolved to show more caution in her spying activities in the future. She had been foolish, and this could have not only put her in danger, but embarrassed her father too. She would hate to disappoint him.

Eventually, the Emperor seemed to settle. He was less restless, and his breathing became deeper and more regular. She decided to wait a little longer, maybe until he started to snore, before she attempted her escape.

The door gave a quiet creak as it opened, and Tituria held her breath again. She heard Caracalla sit up, let out a sigh.

'Julia,' he said.

–

Caracalla tried to speak, but Domna was in no mood for words. Her stola hit the floor the moment the door closed behind her.

'Julia,' he said again, but she held out a finger and pressed it to his lips, closing them. She reached behind her to take the pins out of her hair and he watched as the movement pulled her breasts back, lifting and tightening them. He licked his lips, then tried again. 'Julia, how dare he? What should I do about him?'

Her arms encircled his neck, and she kissed him long and deep, silencing him. He responded to her, kissing her back aggressively, pushing his tongue into her mouth. She let him take control, slipped easily into the role of submissive Roman woman, let him push her onto her hands and knees, and rode out his anger.

His hands were strong on her body, gripping her hips, breath hissing between gritted teeth, and he satisfied his lust and fury inside her, until they collapsed onto the bed together, both satisfied, exhausted, and their emotions temporarily assuaged.

They lay together, breathing heavily, naked bodies covered in a light sheen of sweat, unaware of the terrified and now shocked little girl a short distance beneath them. Domna ran her fingertip across Caracalla's bearded cheek.

'You had a lot of passion tonight,' she said.

'I didn't hurt you?' asked Caracalla, suddenly concerned.

'No,' she laughed. 'It's one of the things I like about you. You can be tender one time, rough the next. Your father was only ever rough.'

Caracalla huffed. 'How many times, Domna? Will you stop comparing me to him?'

'I miss him, though.'

'As do I. But there is a time and a place to grieve. And that time and place is not when we are in bed together.' Caracalla turned his back on her, his hands beneath his head to form a pillow. She lay against him, breasts pressing into his back, her hands stroking the wiry curls on his muscular chest. Her touch drifted downwards, cupped his groin, squeezed playfully. He turned abruptly, grabbing her wrists, pinning her on her back and looking down into her eyes. She laughed, lifted her head and kissed his nose. He let her go and flopped onto his back.

'You're impossible sometimes, Domna. How do you distract me from my cares so thoroughly?'

'I honestly don't know. You have your choice of so many beautiful women, noble and slave. Why do you choose to bed this old woman?'

'Domna, you know you are beautiful. It is your hairstyles and clothing fashions that the ladies of good society in Rome still follow loyally. Men still turn their heads to watch you walk. I see it all the time.'

'I thought that maybe you were only with me as some sort of... act of defiance to your father. I thought when he passed, you might finish with me, and then I would lose the only two men I have ever loved at once.'

Her eyes were wet, and despite the mention of his father again, Caracalla put his arms around her and drew her close, kissing each eyelid.

'Surely after all these years, you know better, Julia. I love you.'

'I love you, too,' said Domna. They kissed, and the room was silent except for the noise of their mouths working on each other.

And then the sound of a little sneeze.

—

Tituria lay frozen as the Emperor and Empress made love above her. The bed rocked violently back and forward, the wooden frame groaning in protest, and she feared that the whole thing might collapse and crush her to death.

She knew about sex in theory, though she was too young to properly understand it. Some of the older slave girls had told her about the mechanics, and she had witnessed a few acts of love when she had been sneaking around the house. She had even once seen her mother and father together, which had left her strangely unsettled.

But this was different. This was serious, and somehow wrong. The Empress was not the Emperor's mother, she knew, but she was his father's widow. Was that allowed? It was illegal for brother and sister or father and daughter to do it, she knew, but what about this situation? And if it was acceptable, why did they have to do it in secret?

But it clearly was a secret, and if the Emperor wanted something kept secret, it would be foolish to give it away. She resolved to stay silent after she had escaped the situation, and take the details of the Emperor and Empress' private affair to the grave with her.

The rocking stopped suddenly, and she heard them talking to each other in words of love. She flushed. It was so intimate, she felt excruciatingly embarrassed.

There was a movement beneath the bed and she tensed, her eyes coming together as she focused on the thing near her face. A spider, about the size of a coin. Moving forward, pausing, moving again. Her breath suddenly caught in her throat, and she went cold all over.

She knew that spiders were unlikely to hurt her, that the poisonous ones were found in much more exotic places like Africa and the East, but that didn't stop her irrational fear, something she thought she had inherited from her mother. The spider crept closer, and her stillness was her undoing. If she had moved the merest fraction of an inch, the creature might have fled. But taking her for something inanimate, it saw her merely as an obstacle to be surmounted. It stepped onto her hair, walked onto her forehead. From above her were the sounds of kissing. Her breath was fast and shallow as it walked down between her eyes, down her nose, to the very tip.

And then, to her horror, she sneezed.

'Did you hear that?' Caracalla's voice, deep, confused.

'I didn't hear anything,' said Domna. 'Kiss me.'

'I swear to the gods I heard a sneeze.'

'You are overly vexed, dear. Come here.'

'No, it came from under the bed.'

The silk sheet was yanked upwards, and suddenly she was looking into the stern, bearded, upside-down face of the Augustus, Emperor Antoninus, who they called Caracalla. They both stared, neither moving, one from terror and one from blank incomprehension.

Then Tituria rolled out from under the bed and ran for the door.

'Stop,' cried Caracalla, and lunged for her. His hand grasped the hem of her dress, and she looked back at the huge, hairy, naked man, momentarily held back. She gripped the dress and tugged, freeing it from his grip. Caracalla was prostrate, leaning out from the edge of the bed, and Tituria had the barest moment to make the door before he regained his feet.

It was all she needed. She wrenched the door open and fled, fear lending her speed.

She heard Domna's voice behind her. 'Antoninus, stop. You can't raise the alarm. We will be found.'

She ran down the corridor, turned a corner, then another, and ran to her bedroom. The little rag doll her mother had made for her when she was a baby was lying on the sheets. She grabbed it and clutched it to her chest, pulled the bedcovers over her head, and curled up into a ball, tears streaming down her cheeks.

She had been bad. Very bad. She was in real trouble this time, she knew. Not just a stern telling-off, confinement to her room, or even a beating. She had to tell her father what she had seen. He would know what to do. But she couldn't bear to see the look of sadness and disappointment in his eyes.

She clutched her doll tight and wept, as quietly as possible.

Chapter Eleven

Silus had decided he didn't like standing in Oclatinius' office. He reported there twice daily with Daya and Atius, usually to get a nod and a quick dismissal, or if he was lucky, some minor surveillance operation. If he was unlucky, Oclatinius was in a bad mood, such as today, which made it all the more difficult to pass on the message the young boy had given him. But there was no benefit in keeping it to himself, and for all his harshness, Oclatinius was wise and experienced, and would know what to do.

Right now, the old spymaster was ignoring the three Arcani before him, rubbing the bridge of his nose and shaking his head while he read from a wax tablet.

'Cilo, you idiot,' he muttered. 'What are you playing at? This will have consequences.'

Silus remained at attention, correctly surmising that Oclatinius was talking to himself and would not welcome interruption. Atius of course had no understanding of a rhetorical question.

'Maybe if you gave us some details about what the man has done, we could speculate for you, sir,' he said.

'By Venus' tits, will you just keep your mouth shut for once, you dumb cunt!'

That shocked even Atius into silence. Oclatinius roared and bellowed but it was all bluster, and Silus had never seen him lose control.

Oclatinius shook his head. 'Well, the Emperor's response to that is for other people to attempt to moderate. Silus, you asked for an urgent meeting. It's late. What do you want?'

The other two Arcani looked at Silus curiously. He hadn't yet told them about the messenger, or why he wanted this meeting. He wasn't sure how this made him look, in their eyes or the eyes of the spymaster.

'Well,' said Oclatinius. 'Spit it out.' He had been mainly fulsome in his praise of how they had dispatched Euprepes. Silus had been careful to give Atius his due for his diversion, and Daya hers for saving him. Oclatinius had been critical that he had needed saving at all, blaming bad intelligence work by Silus. It was a little unfair given the time they had been allotted, but that didn't make it any less true. Still, he hoped he had enough credit with his boss to soften the impact of his next statement.

'Someone knows I killed the charioteer.'

Oclatinius went quiet. Silus hated it when he did that. It meant he was in trouble.

'Your head was covered, yes?' said Oclatinius.

Silus confirmed it was.

'And your hood remained up the whole time. Even during the chase?'

'One man saw me, but he could not know my name. He would not be able to give my identity to anyone else unless he saw me again.'

Oclatinius thought for a moment. 'One of Geta's spies, then. They must have been following you. Festus is behind this, for sure.'

'Festus? The bedchamber fellow? What has he got to do with anything?'

Oclatinius sighed. 'Leave him to me.'

'Is it a problem, sir?'

'I don't know yet. Time will tell.'

The door to Oclatinius' office flew open, and Caracalla strode in.

Oclatinius jumped to his feet. 'Augustus! What brings you here at such an hour?'

'I need some people dead. Right now.' The Emperor's face was full of fury and something else. Fear?

'Of course, Augustus. Name them.'

'Titurius.'

Oclatinius nodded, a little surprised. 'I thought you were going to say another name. Has Titurius declared for Geta? I hadn't heard. I will have words with my informer.'

'No, he hasn't. At least, not yet. I don't know.'

Caracalla seemed distracted, anxious.

'You said some people, Augustus. Who else?'

'His entire familia.'

There was a pause. 'I see.'

'Everyone in that house. His wife. His son. His daughter. All the slaves too.'

Silus risked a glance at Daya. Her face was impassive. Atius looked troubled, but he knew that with his broken hand, he would be playing no part in this slaughter.

'Would it be helpful to know why, Augustus? I can dismiss my Arcani if you wish to tell me privately.'

'One of them… saw something they shouldn't. It only just happened, so they shouldn't have had time to pass on what they saw to anyone outside the household. Make sure everyone inside that house dies, and do it now.'

'Augustus, is it not so that the Empress and her attendants are staying at Titurius' domus this night?'

'They have returned to the palace. She informed her hosts that she was unable to sleep in the bed they had provided, and has left.'

'So the Empress concurs with this action?'

Caracalla's eyes narrowed. 'Why would the Empress' approval be required?'

'Oh, of course, it isn't, Augustus,' said Oclatinius quickly. 'I just know how much you value her counsel.'

'I instructed the Empress to leave Titurius' house. She does not know why.'

'There will be some suspicion around the fact that you and the Empress have both excused yourselves when you were expected to stay. Do you have any concerns about who people believe are responsible for this?'

'No, I don't care what people think!' Caracalla clenched his fists, breathed hard through gritted teeth, and slowly regained control of himself. 'Can we make it look like an accident?'

'Four family members and ten slaves? Not easily.'

'Burn it down,' said Daya.

Oclatinius and Caracalla turned to look at her, as if they had both forgotten the presence of the Arcani.

'Daya,' said Oclatinius, a warning in his voice. 'You are speaking to the Emperor.'

'Apologies, Augustus. I merely wanted to point out that destruction of the house and its contents will make it hard to ascertain the cause of death of its occupants, and will at least make it plausible that their deaths were an accident.'

'Get it done,' snapped Caracalla and swept out.

Oclatinius stood to attention until he had left, then his shoulders slumped and he let out a long breath.

'Well, Daya, Silus. You heard our Emperor. Do you know which one is Titurius' domus?'

'I do,' said Daya. 'I visited with my master when he went there on business, when I was a slave.'

'You know the layout of the house?'

'Some,' said Daya.

Oclatinius considered. 'You know I normally expect my Arcani to do their own intelligence work, but there is no time for that, given the urgency of the mission.' He gave the Arcani a detailed account of the floorplan. 'There are four family members, Titurius, his wife Autronia, his son Quintus and his daughter Tituria. Besides that, there are two porters, one of whom will be awake, four kitchen slaves, three cleaning slaves and a steward. There must be no survivors. And make sure the place burns well. Any questions?'

None that Oclatinius would answer, Silus thought. 'No, sir.'

'Silus, Daya, go and report back to me as soon as it is done. Atius.' He looked at the big Arcanus' broken hand and shook his head. 'Just go home.'

–

The Esquiline Hill was quiet. It was the opposite side of Rome to the Tiber, where much of the trade arrived in the city, and was mainly a high-class residential district, with well-tended public gardens and baths, as well as the fine houses of the rich. The vigiles patrolled occasionally, looking out for fires and people up to no good, but as they were far more likely to find both these problems in the centre of the city amongst the narrow streets and insulae, they were seldom seen.

There were two main ways into a domus in Rome. The frontage of the house facing the street had a narrow doorway, leading to a vestibule and then the atrium. Either side of the front door were shops, using the valuable street frontage to make money. In the case of Titurius' house, the shops either side were a jeweller and a perfumier. Both were shut up tight, but they did not connect to the domus in any case.

The door to Titurius' domus was thick wood with metal crossbars that would put up a good resistance to a strong man with an axe. It would be impossible to enter quietly that way.

The other entry point was the wall of the peristylium, climbing into the open-roofed enclosed garden, and Daya led Silus to a street that ran along the back of Titurius' domus. The wall was smooth, stuccoed, and ten feet high, but Daya was light and agile. She found handholds and footholds in cracks, and shinned up the wall like a monkey. Once she was on the roof, she dropped a rope down for Silus, and he scaled the wall, walking up it as he hauled himself upwards.

They paused on the tiled roof for a moment, looking down into the garden, confirming it was empty, then dropped silently down off the roofed colonnade. The peristylium had a number of rooms leading off it – kitchens, storerooms and some small bedrooms for the slaves. Silus and Daya moved through the shadows cast by a half-moon and slipped into the first bedroom. Two female slaves were sleeping together on a straw mattress, covered by a single sheet. The two assassins drew their knives, and in perfect synchrony clamped their hands over the slaves' mouths and slit their throats.

They repeated this twice more, with two male slaves in the next bedroom, and two more female slaves in the one after that. Silus tried to remain dispassionate about these brutal murders of innocents, but his heart was racing, from the fear of being caught, of waking the household, and at the guilt for his actions. Daya seemed to have no such compunction, brutally efficient as always.

The next small bedroom held an older man, and his mattress was feather instead of straw. Silus presumed this was the steward. He had his arms around a young woman, another of the household slaves, he presumed. In moments, they were dead too.

That left just the two porters and the family. They approached the main part of the house.

–

Tituria swung her legs out of her bed, and walked to her bedroom door, clutching her doll in her hands. She hesitated, then opened the door and padded out. She wore a short wool tunic, but her feet were bare, and the floor tiles were cold on her soles. She passed her brother's door, paused to hear his deep breathing, then continued on to her parents' bedroom.

She heard the sound of her mother crying, and unable to break her lifetime's habit, she opened the door a crack and peered through with one eye, even as a voice at the back of her mind reminded her how much trouble her curiosity had created for her this night.

'I don't understand,' sobbed Autronia. 'What did I do wrong?'

'Nothing, dearest,' said Titurius, putting his arm around her shoulders. 'It's politics, I'm sure.'

'The Empress said the bed was uncomfortable. That mattress was stuffed with goose down! And why did the Emperor leave? Did the food make him ill?'

'I don't know. I think Cilo upset the Augustus quite markedly. Maybe they left because of his speech at dinner.'

'But that wasn't our fault.'

'Well, it was a little.'

'What do you mean?'

Tituria's father looked sheepish. 'Cilo asked me to invite both him and the Emperor, so that he could plead for reconciliation between Antoninus and his brother.'

'You knew?' gasped Autronia. 'This disaster was planned?'

'I had to, my love. My duty is to Rome. I was trying to avoid a civil war.'

'And have you?'

Titurius looked glum. 'I doubt it. Now, I think it's just best to keep our heads down, and hope the storm blows out above us.'

Tituria pushed the door open wide, and her mother and father looked up at her, surprised.

'What is it, darling?' said Autronia. 'Bad dream?'

Tituria pressed the rag doll to her mouth, and shook her head, eyes wide and brimming with tears.

'What then? What has upset you?'

'I've been bad.'

'I'm sure it's nothing awful, darling.'

'Why don't you go back to bed, and cuddle your dolly, and we can talk about it in the morning.'

'I went into the Emperor's bedroom.'

Autronia and Titurius went quiet.

'You did what?' asked Titurius, voice low.

'I wanted to see what you had done to it, Mother, so I sneaked in while you were all at dinner.'

'Did the Emperor see you?'

Tituria nodded, not daring to speak.

'He came in and found you there?'

She shook her head, swallowed. 'I hid under the bed when he came in.'

Titurius knelt in front of her, put his hands on her shoulders. 'Tell me exactly what happened.'

'I stayed quiet, and he didn't notice me. Then someone else came in.'

'Who?'

'It was the Empress. The Augusta.'

Autronia's hand flew to her mouth. Titurius' face was as white as a freshly fulled toga. 'Go on.'

'They got on the bed together, and they... did things.' Now the words came out in a rush. 'I could hear them, and the bed rocked a lot. Then they stopped. And I was going to wait until they fell asleep so I could escape, but then I sneezed, and the Emperor saw me, and I ran, and he chased me, but the Empress told him to stop, and I ran to my room, but I wanted to tell you, Father, because you always know what to do, and I'm so sorry...'

She dissolved into tears, and Titurius grabbed her and held her tight. But only for a short moment. He pushed her away, held her by the shoulders at arm's length, looked into her eyes sternly. 'It was an accident, darling, I understand that. But we are going to have to leave Rome now. Tonight. Go to your room and get what you need for a journey. Only absolute essentials, clothes, hairbrush, dolly. Autronia, you start doing the same. I'm going to send the porter to Geta for help. If Antoninus is after us, Geta is the only person in Rome we can turn to. Go now, Tituria, quickly.'

Tituria fled to her room, a feeling of doom pressing down on her. She pulled out a couple of dresses, a practical tunic, a couple of pieces of jewellery and some pots of make-up. She looked around for her hairbrush, then remembered she had left it on her father's desk in his study. She knew that they were in a hurry, and it was all her fault, but she was sure she had time to fetch it. She ran lightly, still barefoot, still clutching her doll, to the study, and looked around in the gloom for a moment. She spotted it on the edge of the desk when she heard voices approaching.

Her father had instilled a terrible dread into her, and her immediate thought was that it was murderers come to kill them all. She rationalised that it was stupid, that it was probably a couple of the slaves, but she decided to err on the side of caution, and she nimbly squeezed herself into the vase she had used in the past as a hide to spy on her father.

She immediately identified the voices as her father and the night porter. She thought about revealing her presence, but she decided she was in enough trouble already without her father finding her hiding away yet again. She was ready to go; she could wait until they left, grab the hairbrush, and then fetch her other belongings that she had got ready without holding anyone up.

'Take this message directly to the Imperial palace on the Palatine,' her father said, and she heard him scuffling on the desk for his wax tablet and a stylus. 'Make sure you go to the Emperor Geta's wing, not the Emperor Antoninus'. Do you understand?'

'Yes, master,' said the porter.

'Put it in the hands of Geta's personal guard. No one else.'

'Yes, master.'

There was a pause as Titurius scratched out a message, then handed it to the porter. Then he gave a sudden gasp, and Tituria heard the tablet fall to the floor.

'Who are you?' asked Titurius, voice full of fear.

They decided to leave the family until last – they were the least threat. So they bypassed the bedrooms at the main part of the house which were near the triclinium and tablinum, and went straight for the rooms off the atrium. It was not hard to find the off-duty porter. He was snoring as loud as a thunderstorm. He did not stir when Silus slipped into his room, and thrust the dagger through his heart. The sleeping doorkeeper never even woke.

They circled round the atrium in opposite directions, checking rooms, until they converged by the front door.

'Where's the other porter?' hissed Daya.

The night porter should have been sitting in the vestibule just off the atrium, guarding the front entrance. It would not have been surprising to find him dozy or even asleep. The chances of him being required to perform his duties as a nightwatchman or doorman were remote in such a nice area, in a well-protected house, at that time. But not to be there at all – that was odd.

'Maybe he is having a piss,' suggested Silus.

'Well, the front door isn't open, so he hasn't gone out that way. And look, there is a chamber pot, so he doesn't have to leave his post.'

'Let's head back into the main house. He must be there.'

They retraced their steps back through the atrium, and heard sounds from the main bedroom, drawers being opened and closed hurriedly. Silus approached the half-open door and glanced in.

'It's the wife,' he whispered to Daya.

'I can hear someone asleep in the bedroom next door,' she said. 'I think it's the son.'

'I'll deal with the wife, you take the son, meet you back here.'

Daya nodded and eased herself into the adjacent bedroom. Silus entered the room before him.

Autronia had her back to him. She was letting out sobs and muttering to herself as she pulled clothes out of a drawer and threw them over her shoulder.

'Titurius, what have you done? What have you done? Letting that man into our house. Letting him threaten our family. And Tituria, why couldn't you keep your nose out of everyone else's business for once in your life.'

Silus approached silently, dagger drawn. He was within a foot of her and ready to strike when she turned. The wig she had in her hand dropped to the floor. Her shoulders sagged in acceptance.

'Please,' she whispered. 'Not my children.'

Silus took a quick step forward, pushed her backwards over her dressing table, hand over her mouth, and thrust his dagger expertly through her ribs into her heart. He held her, looking into her terrified eyes, until she was dead. Then he eased her to the floor, and stepped back outside.

Daya was already there, wiping the blood from her dagger.

'The boy's dead,' she said.

'And the wife,' he replied.

'Just the porter, the father and the girl to go.'

Voices reached them from the tablinum. Silus nodded towards it, and together they crept to the study. Inside, they could see the father, Titurius, scribbling on a wax tablet.

'Where's the girl?' hissed Daya.

'Probably hiding,' whispered Silus. 'We finish these two, then we find her, burn this place to the ground and get out of here. I'll tell you something, Daya, I'm getting tired of this shit.'

'Keep your focus. Get the mission done. If you want a change of career, you can talk to the boss about it after.'

He smiled at her, and she smiled back, and for a moment his heart skipped a beat. Then he gripped his knife tight, and stepped into the tablinum.

Titurius and the porter turned together as they entered, and Titurius let the tablet fall to the floor with a clatter that was deafening in the deathly quiet of the domus.

'Who are you?' he asked, tremulous. The Arcani did not answer. Blades drawn, they advanced on the two men.

The porter, a large, dark-skinned Numidian, let out a roar and charged at Daya, who was nearest him. She took a step back, sat down hard with her foot up into the porter's midriff, and tossed him over her head. He clattered across the floor, and Daya sprang to her feet, whipped around and advanced on him as he struggled to regain his feet.

Silus moved forwards, blade out and low. Titurius reached behind him onto the desk for a weapon of any sort. His fingers touched the stylus, grasped it. It was made of bronze, its point sharp. As Silus came within reach, Titurius whipped it round, stabbed it down hard towards Silus' neck.

Silus reacted quickly, ducking and rotating his body to the side. The stylus stuck into the muscle in his upper arm. He grunted in pain, slashed out with his knife. Titurius jumped sideways, away from the desk, edging towards the door. Silus circled, keeping himself between his prey and the exit.

Behind him, Daya kicked the supine porter in the face. His head snapped back, hitting the floor and stunning him. Before he had a chance to shake it off, Daya was on him, straddling his chest, plunging her knife down into his neck repeatedly.

Titurius looked like a cornered animal, eyes darting around desperately for any escape, any help.

'Please,' he said. 'Spare my wife, my children. If I have wronged Antoninus or Geta, let the punishment fall on me alone.'

Daya, back on her feet, walked up beside Silus. Blood coated her blade.

'I'm sorry, it's too late for that,' she said.

Titurius' brow creased in anguish. 'No,' he whispered.

'It's time to finish this.' She took a step forward, arm raised to strike the final blow. Her arm came down.

But Titurius was no fat, idle senator who had never known exercise. He practised regularly with the sword, spent time lifting weights in the gymnasium, sparred and boxed with trainers. As the blade descended, he ducked inside the arc, reached forward with both hands and grabbed Daya by the neck.

She brought her knife down again, but she no longer had the right angle, his firm forearms restricting the amount of motion she could achieve. She made small ineffectual stabs as she tried to gasp air. Silus moved to intervene, but Daya's back blocked him. He moved to go round the desk to attack Titurius from the other side, but before he got there, Daya found purchase with her feet. She drove Titurius backwards, and he crashed into a large vase, which toppled sideways and smashed on the floor. She continued the momentum, the skilled little fighter using her speed and her opponent's own weight to drive him backwards. As his back thumped into the solid wall, his hands came away from Daya's throat.

She thrust upwards.

Her wickedly sharp dagger sliced up through guts, into liver, slicing major vessels. Titurius clutched her as he bled out, dropping to his knees, then slumping face forward.

Daya stepped back, and the eyes of both the Arcani were drawn to the wreckage of the smashed vase.

Later, when Silus looked back on what happened in the next few moments, it was not a blur. His senses were heightened with excitement and fear, and he could remember every little detail. There was a smell of fresh blood in the air. Titurius' last gasping breaths were the only sounds. The walls of the room were decorated with large abstract diamond patterns on a background of vibrant red. The floor was a fine mosaic of scenes of hunting, deer and boar, chased by men on horseback with spears. The smashed vase was terracotta, painted in the red-figure style of Ancient Greece with a black background, though it was no longer possible to make out the subject of the painting.

And sitting among the wreckage, a little girl was staring at her dying father with wide, terrified eyes.

It was Tituria, the last surviving member of Titurius' family. But it was also Sergia, his daughter. It was Hortensia, Plautilla's child. It was every little girl who had died in Caledonia of hunger or disease or the sword.

His heart stuttered in his chest. Time seemed to stop, and yet the moment was too brief for deliberation, for conscious rational thought. He looked at the little girl, and her danger bit deep into his soul, bringing out a father's instinct to protect, no matter what the cost.

Daya took a single step forward with her knife raised.

'No!' cried Silus, and as the knife descended towards the little girl's exposed neck, he threw himself at Daya.

His superior weight and the surprise of his attack knocked her off her feet, and she sprawled forward, face down. She was instantly on her feet, facing him, dagger pointing at his guts. Her eyes blazed with fury.

'Wait,' said Silus, blade in his right hand pointing down, left hand extended, palm up.

'Traitor,' she hissed, and lunged at him. He danced back as she swung, once, twice, rapidly reversing across the small room until his back was to the far wall. She feinted, thrust, and this time he defended himself, fending her knife away with his own.

'Stop this. Please.'

His chest felt like there was a stone slab pressing down on it, and it was not fear or fatigue but anguish.

'Don't make me do this.'

'She must die. There must be no survivors.'

Daya thrust once more, and this time, he let the blade pass by his body, before trapping her wrist against his side with a strong forearm. With the fist that clutched the knife, he punched her hard in the face, snapping her head back, stunning her. She staggered back two steps, blood pouring from her nose.

She wiped the flow away with the back of her hand, and stared at him with a hatred he had never seen, even from Maglorix. Tears sprang to his eyes as he realised what he must do.

She flew at him like an enraged cat. Whether it was the blow that had stunned her, or she had lost control in her anger, she fought with none of the skill which she usually displayed. She screamed as she flailed with knife and fist and nails. Silus blocked and parried each attack, and although none of her attempts hurt him, he could feel himself tiring, while she showed no sign of slowing.

He took a deep breath, grabbed her knife wrist, pulled her close to him and thrust the blade into her chest.

She was instantly still. Her hand opened and her weapon clattered to the ground. She looked him straight in the eyes and he saw no pain or fear there, only incomprehension and betrayal.

'I'm sorry,' he whispered, his vision misty. 'I couldn't. Not another...'

She said nothing as she went limp in his arms. He didn't let go, held her body against him, felt the warmth of her blood spreading from the mortal wound in her chest and seeping into his tunic, against his skin. Her head flopped backwards, eyes still open, staring at the ceiling. He kissed her once, lightly, on the lips, almost breaking down as he did so. Then he lowered her gently to the ground, and laid her on her back.

She was still beautiful in death, the only differences from life the red blossom on her chest and the pallor of her skin. He bowed his head over her and cried silently, letting the tears drip onto her bloody tunic. What had he done? He had killed his colleague, friend, someone he... He couldn't bring himself to express his feelings for her, even inside his own mind. But what were the other consequences? He had betrayed Oclatinius, Atius. Caracalla.

Fear suddenly shot through him. This would be the end of him. He would be executed without trial and without question when the Emperor was informed what he had done. He didn't know why every member of the household needed to die, but Caracalla had been completely explicit. And Oclatinius would not tolerate the murder of one of his own, by one of his own.

He stood slowly, turned to where the little girl was huddled on the floor with her knees drawn up to her chin, hugging her shins. She was of course the only witness to what he had done. He could still complete his mission. He could kill the girl, tell them Daya had died in the raid. He would be commended by Oclatinius and Caracalla. He would be rewarded. He would be spared.

'Are you the man my father sent for to protect us?' The girl's voice was tiny, but clear in the silence. She was not crying, too shocked probably right now. What did she mean? Then Silus realised that she had not seen him kill anyone apart from Daya. All she had witnessed was him defending her, and killing the assassin who had murdered her father.

She thought he was her rescuer.

Silus had tried to save his daughter, and had failed. He had stood by while Hortensia died. He would not let it happen again.

He put out a hand to her. She didn't move. He stepped towards her, squatted down. He must look a terrifying sight, a rough stranger in her house, covered in blood, amongst all this slaughter. But right then, he was all she had. He took her hand, and helped her to her feet. Her whole body was shaking.

Amongst the debris of the broken pottery was a rag doll. Silus bent down and picked it up, brushed the dust and shards off it as best he could, and handed it to the girl. She clutched it tightly.

'What is she called?'

'Helen,' she said.

'Beautiful. And what is your name?'

'Tituria.'

'I'm Silus. Now listen. I am going to get you out of here. But I need to take care of some things. I'm going to carry you to the atrium and leave you there for a few moments. I want you to close your eyes until I say it's fine to open them, understand?'

She nodded, and he picked her up, one arm beneath her. She was a little older than Sergia, a little heavier, though not by much. She put her arms around his neck, and buried her face in his chest as he walked out of the tablinum, past the bedrooms containing the corpses of her mother and brother, past the room with the sleeping porter, into the luxurious atrium, where her father would have conducted much of his public business. He sat her on a marble bench and said, 'You can open your eyes now.'

She did as she was told, staring blankly at the impluvium full of ornamental fish. 'Wait here,' he said. 'Do not move.' He left her there, and went back into the domus.

Working quickly, he dragged all the bodies into the tablinum. That meant moving one porter, the mother and son, and eight other slaves, one at a time. It was hard work, but he was well-conditioned from his training, and soon he had the bodies piled up together.

Although the building was constructed partly in stone, as expected for a wealthy senator's house, there was still plenty of wood and other flammable material to make a fire. He pulled down some tapestries, gathered some wooden furniture and threw some scrolls into a pile around the bodies. Then he collected as many oil lamps as he could find and emptied their contents onto the tapestries. Finally, he took a lit lamp and applied the flame.

It might look suspicious that all the occupants of the house were in a single room, although maybe it could be argued that they had all fled to the one room as the conflagration took hold. He wasn't sure how good the vigiles were at reconstructing the causes of a fire, or even whether they cared. But the important thing was that all the bodies were burnt sufficiently to conceal the causes of their deaths, and give a plausible alternative explanation.

The flame spread across the cloth tapestries, the oil from the lamps accelerating the process. Daya's face was exposed, and he watched for a moment as the fire advanced on her, then took her. He stepped back as the heat became more intense, and knocked something with his heel. He bent down and picked up a wax tablet, hinged in a double-leaved diptych style. It was the tablet that Titurius had dropped when the Arcani had first entered the room. He looked at the markings on the wax, scribbles that were hard to make out in the flickering firelight. He closed the leaves and tucked it into his belt. He gave one last look towards the fire consuming Daya, and all the others that she and he had killed that night. Then he went quickly back to the atrium, and to Tituria.

The young girl was sitting on the bench, holding Helen tight, rocking rhythmically backwards and forwards.

'Come on,' he said, his voice as calm as he could make it. 'It's time to go.'

He held out his hand and she took it without resistance. He led her to the front door, unbarred it and pushed it open. It was long past midnight, and the street was as quiet as it ever got. He looked behind him, and saw smoke billowing out towards the atrium. The fire had caught well, and should spread beyond the tablinum, making it hard to see where it had started or what had caused it. Other nearby buildings might even catch, although it wouldn't be as dangerous as a fire in the poorer districts where the houses were closely packed and shoddily constructed with more flammable materials.

The vigiles would be alerted soon, either a patrol spotting the fire themselves, or being fetched by alarmed neighbours. They needed to be a long way away by then. He picked Tituria up, and she sat on his hip with her legs around his waist, one arm around his neck. He put his head down and walked fast, descending the streets down the Esquiline Hill.

As they moved into the centre of the city the streets became busier. Rome never truly slept. Wheeled carts, banned during the daylight hours, rattled along the cobbles, carters and merchants shouting warnings and curses at each other. Silus kept his head down when patrols of vigiles passed, though he doubted he was of interest to them. A glow developed on the horizon, the merest suggestion of dawn, which was still a couple of hours away. At least, that was what Silus presumed. He had been walking west away from the Esquiline, so he wondered if it was actually a spreading fire. He hoped not. There would be an investigation if the fire turned into an out-of-control conflagration, and the penalty for arson was, appropriately, burning alive.

He felt a strange relief as he entered the narrow, winding, maze-like streets of the Subura. He was a new resident, and yet it felt like a safe haven. With only a couple of wrong turns, he found his way to his apartment. Tituria had been quiescent for the whole journey, not asleep but silent, but she was becoming quite a burden, and carrying her up the flights of stairs to the top floor was exhausting. He managed it without stopping, though, and when he reached his own apartment, he kicked the door three times to rouse Apicula.

Issa started yapping at the disturbance, and after a few moments, Apicula opened the door. If she was surprised to see Silus carrying a young child into the apartment, she said nothing to show it. Silus laid the girl down on his mattress, and Apicula came over with a cup of watered wine and helping Tituria sit up, held it to her lips.

Tituria swallowed, coughed, then swallowed again. She looked from Apicula to Silus, her eyes full of questions, but unable to formulate them in her fear and shock and grief. Issa came over to her cautiously, sniffed her hand, then cuddled up to her, nestling under her arm. Tituria looked down at the little dog and stroked her head absently.

Silus went to the door and barred it, then slumped down on the floor, his back against the wall. The wax tablet that he had shoved into his belt dug into his belly, so he pulled it out and tossed it to one side. It came to rest beneath the table.

He was aware that he smelt of smoke, that he was covered in blood, mainly other people's, much of it in fact Daya's. And that he had just appeared at his apartment in the early hours of the morning with a strange child.

He had not had much time to have any long chats with Apicula, if that was what one did with slaves. He wasn't sure – he had never been able to afford one before. But he understood that a slave's loyalty to their master was absolute, that the master held the power of life and death over them, and besides this, he felt deep down that Apicula was someone he could trust.

So he spoke to her in a low voice, telling her as much as he thought was necessary.

'The child is in danger. She must be kept hidden. You are to tell no one she is here. She is not to leave this apartment, and neither are you unless I am here to watch her. You are to admit no visitors. Not even Atius. You are to look after her as if she were your own.'

That last caused a flash of pain to cross Apicula's face, and he wondered if she had children of her own. As a prostitute, there were precautions that could be taken, but it was hard to avoid pregnancy completely. But a brothel had no use for children, and they were likely to have been sold at an early age. Her children, if she had been fertile, and any had survived the dangerous early years, could be anywhere in the Empire right now.

This wasn't the time to ask about her past, though.

'Do you understand?'

'Yes, master. I will care for the child.'

'Sit with her now. She has experienced horror tonight.'

'Yes, master.'

Apicula settled herself beside Tituria and stroked her hair. The little girl was staring into space, her doll clutched under one arm, Issa snuggled under the other. Her shallow, panicky breathing began to calm, and though she fought it, exhaustion overcame her, and she slept.

Silus knew he had to report to Oclatinius. He also knew he would have to lie convincingly to the wily spymaster, and he wasn't sure how. He mentally prepared himself to leave. But first he would close his eyes, just for a few moments. His head sank down onto his chest.

Chapter Twelve

Silus decided he was really coming to hate Oclatinius' office. He had woken with a start when the light of dawn broke through the small window in his apartment. Oclatinius would be wondering where he was, might even send someone to find him.

Tituria had been fast asleep. Apicula, lying on the hard, cold floorboards, dozed lightly beside her. He had touched his slave's shoulder to wake her, put a finger to his lips, and indicated that she should bar the door behind him. He had then hurried out and rushed to see Oclatinius, stopping only to urinate in a public toilet.

Atius was waiting for him outside when he arrived.

'What happened, Silus?' he asked urgently. 'Where have you been? Where's Daya? Oclatinius is furious.'

'Silus, is that you?' came a voice from within the office. 'Get in here.'

Silus took a deep breath, let it out slowly, then entered, Atius at his back.

'Report,' snapped Oclatinius. Then his eyes narrowed, looking beyond Silus through the open door into the corridor behind. 'Where is Daya?'

Silus bowed his head. 'Sir, I'm sorry to report—'

'Atius,' interrupted Oclatinius. 'Shut the door.' Atius did as he was told. 'Continue.'

'I'm sorry to say that Daya lost her life in the action last night.'

Oclatinius pressed his fingertips together, touched them to his lips. For a moment, he said nothing. Silus wasn't sure whether to carry on with his report.

Oclatinius wiped one hand over his face, ending the motion with his palm pressed to his mouth. Then he said, 'Start at the beginning.'

Silus related the mission honestly, all the way to the fight with Titurius. Oclatinius interrupted intermittently to ask for details, which Silus easily supplied. It was when he got to the point where Daya faced Titurius that he diverged from the truth. He had rehearsed the story in his mind on the hurried walk over from his apartment, had examined it for holes, and thought it was watertight. But Oclatinius was an expert. Would he accept Silus' version of what happened?

'Daya underestimated him. She thought he was unarmed and helpless, but he was stronger and faster than she realised. When she stepped forward to finish him, Titurius grabbed the blade and turned it on her. I couldn't get there in time. I rushed around the desk and cut his throat, but it was too late for Daya. She died in my arms.'

That much was true, and Silus' eyes blurred with tears again as guilt and grief accentuated by exhaustion threatened to overcome him.

Oclatinius looked sceptical. 'This senator managed to disarm her. Disarm Daya?'

'As I said, she underestimated him. She was complacent.'

Oclatinius looked deeply into his eyes, and Silus held the gaze, willing himself not to break down, not to tell his superior everything. Not for himself. At that moment, he would have been happy to confess all, and take whatever punishment he was due. But that would mean the end of the little girl. And Daya's death would have been for nothing.

'Fine,' said Oclatinius. 'You have accounted for everyone except for Tituria, the child.'

'She had been hiding in a large vase in the tablinum during the fight. When I killed Titurius, he crashed into the vase and smashed it, and I found her.' The best lies were as close to the truth as possible. Oclatinius had taught him that.

'And? Is she dead?'

'Yes, sir,' lied Silus. 'I stabbed her in the heart myself.'

'That must have been difficult for you,' said Oclatinius, though his tone held no pity.

'It was.'

'And then you burnt the domus. I understand the vigiles did not arrive before the whole house and two neighbouring houses were ablaze. They stopped a conflagration developing, but Titurius' domus was razed to the ground. It's still too hot for them to look through the rubble for bodies, and as the house collapsed, they are unlikely to be able to identify much about the remains. That was well done, Silus.'

'Thank you, sir.'

'Why did you leave Daya there?'

'Sir?'

'What if they find an extra body – it will arouse suspicion. Why didn't you bring her to me for burial?'

Oclatinius' voice was thick, and Silus realised that the spymaster had also been fond of the young assassin.

'I reasoned that walking through the streets carrying a body that had clearly died a violent death might have aroused more suspicion than losing her in a jumble of bones which would likely never be properly identified after the fire and heat and collapse of the house had done their work.'

Oclatinius frowned. 'Are you being sarcastic with me?'

'No, sir,' said Silus hastily. 'Just letting you know my reasoning.'

Oclatinius nodded. He seemed satisfied, although of course the head of the Arcani was impossible to read with any certainty.

'And where have you been since the mission finished?'

'Sir, I'm sorry. I was fatigued. I meant to come straight to you, but I rested briefly, and fell asleep.'

'That's poor, Silus. I ordered you to report to me as soon as you were done.'

'I know, sir. I apologise.'

'Still. I can inform the Emperor that the mission was a success, despite the loss of an Arcanus?'

'You can,' said Silus and wondered what sort of retribution, from man or god, he was owed.

'You did well,' said Oclatinius. 'Go and clean yourself up, and make a sacrifice to Daya's shade.'

Silus nodded, suppressing a shiver at the thought of Daya's restless ghost coming to visit and castigating him for his crime. He bowed his head, and left with Atius. Outside the office, Atius patted him gently on the back.

'I'm sorry, friend. It sounded really hard. And I know you liked Daya.'

Silus squeezed Atius' arm, not trusting himself to speak.

'You look like shit. Let's go back to your apartment. Apicula can clean you up, you can put on some fresh clothes, and I can have a drink while you get some rest.'

'No!' said Silus, and Atius looked surprised at the vehemence. 'No, I really want to go to the baths. Clean this muck off me, soak myself, get a massage.'

Atius looked doubtful. 'You have blood all over you.'

'We can clean the worst off in a fountain before we go in. Come on, let's go, and then let's offer a libation to Daya and the other manes.'

'I'll offer a prayer to the Christos and his mother,' said Atius. 'Apart from that, I agree.'

He put his arm around Silus' shoulder and they walked towards the nearest bathhouse.

–

'You're sure?'

'Yes, Augustus. The whole household.'

'Including the girl?'

'Yes, Augustus.'

'And you don't think they had time to tell anyone outside Tituria's familia?'

'I don't see how, Augustus. The Arcani struck that night. I doubt they would have believed there would be such a swift response, nor have even considered the right course of action in that short time.'

Caracalla sat back and let out a breath. It was highly unfortunate that this action had been necessary. Domna had initially advised against it, but it didn't take much to change her mind. The consequences of their affair being made public were unthinkable. It might even be worse if the secret was held privately, especially by his brother, for then he would be Geta's hostage.

But it seemed the drastic action had been successful. The relief was almost ecstatic.

'I'm sorry for the loss of your girl,' he said. Oclatinius bowed his head in acknowledgement of the sympathy.

'Augustus,' said Oclatinius. 'I have served you for many years and you have always considered my counsel in the past. Might I offer you some advice now?'

'Speak.'

'I don't know what it was that the young girl saw that provoked this reaction. I believe it would have been of a private nature. And sufficiently damaging that a senator and his family had to die to keep it private.'

Caracalla had a suspicion that Oclatinius knew or strongly suspected exactly what the girl had witnessed. Oclatinius knew everything about everyone.

'Go on,' said Caracalla, but his voice was low, urging caution.

'Perhaps that private activity should be carried out with more... discretion.'

Caracalla regarded him with a chilly glare.

Oclatinius swallowed but continued. 'There are ways of arranging liaisons away from spying eyes and ears. I can assist if you wish. But those meetings must become less frequent.'

'Must?'

'The more often this private matter takes place, the greater the risk of discovery, Augustus.'

'Did you just say your Emperor "must" do something?' Caracalla's voice was getting higher, louder.

'Augustus, I would never suggest that you be compelled to do anything, of course. I was merely suggesting—'

'How dare you, Oclatinius? I should have the Praetorian Guard come in here right now and—'

There was a loud knock at the door. Caracalla breathed fiercely through his nose, nostrils flaring. Then he shouted, 'Enter!'

The Praetorian on guard duty opened the door, entered and saluted.

'Augustus. The deputy urban prefect, Gaius Julius Asper, is here to see you as you commanded.'

'Choose your words more carefully in future, Oclatinius,' said Caracalla.

'Yes, Augustus. I apologise for any offence.'

'Send Asper in,' Caracalla said to the guard.

Gaius Julius Asper was descended from nobles from Antioch and though he had been many years in Rome, including as a consul under Commodus, he still had the olive skin of his ancestry. He was approaching, but had not yet reached, old age, and had been around in politics long enough to have been a consul under Commodus. Now he acted as the deputy urban prefect under Cilo.

'Augustus, how may I serve?'

'Tell me about Cilo,' said Caracalla.

'Augustus? What in particular did you want to know?'

'I know you are loyal to me, Asper. Oclatinius here has vouched for you. But we have concerns regarding the urban prefect. Where do his loyalties lie?'

Asper became guarded, seeming uncertain what answer Caracalla was looking for.

'He is a dedicated servant of Rome, Augustus.'

'And of Rome's Emperor?'

'Of course, Augustus.'

'Which one?'

'I think…' Asper hesitated. He looked to Oclatinius for help, but the spymaster's face was impassive. 'I think he keeps a foot in each camp.'

'I thought as much. He whines about peace and harmony, but really he doesn't want to commit to either side, and risk backing the loser.'

'I'm not sure,' said Oclatinius. 'Cilo appears to be a man who genuinely wants the best for Rome.'

'I am the best for Rome!' snapped Caracalla.

'Of course,' said Oclatinius quickly.

'I think Cilo needs a lesson in loyalty. Asper, you are dismissed. You too, Oclatinius.'

The two men bowed and left promptly.

Caracalla watched them go, thoughts in turmoil. It had been a close call with Titurius' girl. Oclatinius was right, he would have to be more circumspect. At least as long as the Imperial throne was still disputed. Without Geta to destabilise him, to use his love for Domna to his advantage if he found out, then maybe it wasn't so important. Maybe he could even marry her. Would Rome stand for that? Would Domna accept if he asked?

He stood up and paced. He had sacrificed a noble Roman family to protect his position and his relationship with Domna. He asked himself how much further he was prepared to go.

He knew the answer: as far as necessary.

–

Silus returned to his apartment feeling clean on the outside and filthy in his soul. Atius had been his usual chatty, light-hearted self, and had tried to cheer Silus up. When that failed, he had become serious, attempting to get Silus to open up to him about what happened. He had known that Silus was becoming attached to Daya, maybe before Silus had realised it himself, and understood how devastating it was that he had lost her — especially in a mission he was leading, where the blame and responsibility would fall on him.

Silus knew he had been sullen and uncommunicative, and it pained him to see the hurt in his friend's expression at being shut out. They had bathed and one of the bath attendants had washed Silus' tunic for a copper coin while he had a rub-down with oil and a strigil. But when Atius had suggested they get some lunch and a drink, Silus had pleaded exhaustion.

Atius, clearly worried, had again offered to take Silus back to his apartment, and suggested they eat and drink and dice there. He had looked confused and dejected when Silus had declined, and they had walked away with Atius watching him in puzzlement.

At the top of his stairs, he knocked on the door and called out Apicula's name. He heard the door being unbarred, and it opened just enough to admit him, without showing the occupants of the apartment to prying eyes.

Apicula held a hairbrush, and Tituria sat on a stool, her back to her. The slave was running the brush gently through Tituria's long hair, easing out the tangles. The young girl had Issa in her lap, and was stroking the old bitch's head between the ears. She stopped the fussing and looked up when Silus entered. Issa protested about the interruption to her attention, and butted Tituria's hand with her head. Tituria gave a half-smile and carried on stroking.

'Apicula, take this purse and go and buy some supplies. Wine, bread, cheese, some honeyed pastries. Some ox liver for Issa. She can't manage anything tougher with her old teeth.' He looked at Tituria, dressed in a tunic of fine wool, but covered in grime and dust. 'And buy a change of clothes for our young guest.'

Apicula gave one last stroke of the brush, patted the girl's head, then took the money from Silus before leaving. Silus looked at the hairbrush and considered picking it up before thinking better of it. Instead, he poured himself a cup of water from a jug and sat on the floor on the far side of the room. Tituria watched him uncertainly, still subconsciously smoothing the little dog.

'We haven't introduced ourselves yet, have we?' he said. He kept his voice quiet and gentle, the sort of tone he had used when telling Sergia bedtime stories. Calm and unthreatening. 'I'm Silus. Your name is Tituria?'

She nodded cautiously.

'This is my home,' said Silus. 'I'm sorry it isn't what you are used to. But you are welcome here as long as is necessary.'

Tituria said nothing.

'The little dog is called Issa.'

Tituria looked down, as if only just remembering she was holding the pet. 'Issa,' she repeated.

'She is older than you, I would think,' said Silus. 'How old are you? Eight years?'

'Nine.'

'I had a daughter. She was younger than you.'

'Did she die?'

'She did.'

'Is my father dead?'

Silus had no idea what he was supposed to say. Lie? The truth, or at least as much of it as he was prepared to reveal? He decided there was nothing to be gained from delaying her discovery of the awful facts.

'He is.'

Silus watched for a reaction. Tituria said nothing, betrayed no emotion except an acceleration in the rhythm of her stroking. Then, not looking at Silus, she said, 'Is my mother dead too?'

A memory of the matron pleading for the life of her children, just before his knife pierced her heart, flashed through his mind.

'Yes.'

She breathed through an open mouth, her nose snotty and blocked. Her voice became even smaller, even quieter. 'Quintus?'

Silus presumed that was the name of the brother. Now his own voice was thick with emotion.

'Yes.'

He stared at the child, wondering why she didn't cry, why she didn't scream and beat her fists on his chest, and yell that she hated him. He felt as though he couldn't stand what he had done to her, what Caracalla had ordered be done to her. That he had saved her life felt like scant comfort at that moment.

Of course, she believed he was her saviour. That he had come to their rescue, but arrived too late to save the rest of her family. Was that true? Had he really saved her, or just delayed the time when Caracalla discovered she still lived, and ended her life?

'Why did that woman kill him?' she asked.

'I don't know.' That was true, beyond the obvious answer that she had been ordered to. Someone had seen something they shouldn't? What? Who? Was it Tituria herself? He was desperate to ask, but if it had been her, then she would be the reason for the death of her entire family, and that wasn't a burden he wanted this child to bear.

'Do you know how to play knucklebones?' he asked, looking for anything to distract her.

'Father wouldn't let me gamble. But Quintus and I played the game where you toss them in the air and catch them on the back of your hand.'

Silus knew the version. He had played it with Sergia. The throw and catch were repeated as many times as possible until they had all been dropped. He found his knucklebone set after a short search, as Apicula had tidied them away somewhere. They were old, their surfaces worn by time spent rubbing against each other in the same bag. One had tooth marks from when he had rescued it from Issa's mouth after he had foolishly left her alone with them for the merest moment.

He sat on the floor and indicated that Tituria should join him. He took his turn first, tossing and catching the four bones until they had all fallen.

'Six,' he said. 'That's not bad, is it? Your turn.'

Tituria hesitated, then set Issa down. The little dog stared intently at the bones, licking her lips. Tituria picked up the bones and threw expertly, dropping the last on her eighth toss.

'You're good at this. I need to up my game.' Silus picked the bones up and had another go.

The game required just enough concentration to be a distraction without being so complex that the miserable Tituria would give up easily. Every time it seemed that Tituria's thoughts were wandering, Silus brought her attention back to the game, and this way they played on until Apicula returned with the supplies.

When she offered Tituria some bread and cheese, the girl looked up at her and said, 'I'm not hungry.' But when she offered her a honeyed sponge cake, Tituria took it with a timid 'Thank you' and put a small piece in her mouth. The sweetness was enough to overcome her lack of appetite and soon, one morsel at a time, she had finished the whole cake.

Apicula had bought some goat's milk and she poured a cupful. Tituria took small sips from this while the slave brought out the clothes she had purchased. Although not as expensive as Tituria was surely used to, the little girl looked appreciative when Apicula passed her a light blue linen tunic with a woollen belt, and a matching palla to drape over her head and shoulders.

Apicula instructed Silus to turn his back, and he stared at the cracks in the wall while his slave helped Tituria out of her clothes of the previous day and into the new purchases. Apicula cleaned Tituria's face with a damp cloth, and then told Silus he could turn back again.

Silus regarded the little girl standing before him, chin lowered, looking up at him with wide, bloodshot eyes, and felt as though something inside him crumbled. His legs started to tremble, and he dropped to his knees and took her hand.

'I'm so sorry, Tituria. So sorry for your loss. For... everything. But I swear to the gods, and to my daughter's shade, that I will not let any harm come to you. You are safe. Do you understand?'

Tituria nodded. Then she turned and picked up Issa, and sat cross-legged on Silus' mattress. He saw that the tears in Apicula's eyes matched his own. He gave her a nod, and she pursed her lips and nodded back. Apicula didn't know the circumstances of the girl's bereavement, or her background, but Silus could tell that she would protect her as one of her own. He desperately hoped that between the two of them, it would be enough.

–

Silus met Atius near the Praetorian barracks, well away from the Subura, away from his apartment and Tituria. Sitting on chairs in front of the tavern on the street, they drank and diced, and watched the citizens go about their day.

'I was drinking with a chap I met from the vigiles last night. They are all talking about the fire on the Esquiline.'

Silus sipped his drink and said nothing as a heaviness settled in his stomach.

'They are speculating that the fire might have been started deliberately, but they don't know, and they say it is just as likely that it was an accident – an overturned oil lamp or suchlike.'

'Have they been through the embers?'

'They had a poke around, and found a few bodies. None were identifiable. The heat had burnt too fiercely, and the collapsing walls and roof had smashed up the bones too much to even be able to sort them into individuals. Not that I think they tried too hard. They don't get paid much. They will put some bones in a box and present them to the relatives as if they knew who was who. The nobles will be cremated and placed in the family tomb, and the slaves will be no doubt be tossed into the Tiber.'

The tightness in Silus' guts eased a little. They hadn't counted the teeth to confirm the number of corpses. Why would they? So Tituria was presumed dead with the rest of her family. That much at least helped with her safety. For now.

Atius reached out a hand and gripped Silus' shoulder. 'If you like, I can ask them to go through the bones more thoroughly, see if they can identify Daya.'

'No,' said Silus quickly. Then he took a deep breath and said more calmly, 'She is gone. We have no need of her body to honour her memory.'

'I'll pray that she gets resurrected with the Christians when the Christos returns,' said Atius.

'If you like,' said Silus.

Atius looked over Silus' shoulder, and his eyes narrowed.

'Where are they going, I wonder?'

Silus turned to see a detachment of a dozen legionaries from the Urban Cohorts marching purposefully down the street, led by a military tribune in full dress uniform. They had got used to seeing patrols of two to four strolling around the city, keeping a watchful eye open for civil disturbances, but as Silus had learnt quickly, for most minor offences the citizens policed themselves. It was unusual to see a larger group of legionaries looking as though they had somewhere important to be in a hurry.

'Should we follow them?'

Atius smiled. 'We're spies, aren't we?'

–

Cilo lay in the warm water of his bath, situated in his private bathhouse which opened onto his peristylium, and inhaled the scent of roses and lavender. It was not like the large public baths in the city as it lacked the pools of different temperatures, the gymnasium and the massage rooms, but it also lacked the crowd, the noise, the commotion and the smell.

Bees buzzed around the flowers in the garden. Evergreen bushes pruned into neat cones were interspersed with statues of Hermes and various nymphs. A gentle splashing sound came from the central fountain, where water spurted out of the mouth of a dolphin into a surrounding pool. Cilo's town house on the Aventine had been gifted him by the Emperor Severus, and the garden and bathhouse had always been a peaceful retreat for him, a place of tranquillity where he could contemplate the beauty of nature shaped by man's artistry. He needed it now more than ever.

Sacked.

He had never suffered such a humiliation in his long life and his heart cried with the insult to his dignitas. But his head told him it could have been far worse. At least he still had a head. He had taken a risk in addressing Caracalla the way he had, and if losing his job as urban prefect was as far as his punishment went, he could consider himself fortunate.

Caracalla had been cold to him that morning, rather than angry, when he had informed him he was being stripped of his position. He did not give a reason, but he did not need to. Cilo's words in the triclinium of the unfortunate Titurius had given offence, as he had feared. Caracalla wanted to hear no counsel of peace and harmony. If you weren't behind him alone, then you were behind Geta, and Caracalla would clearly no longer tolerate that.

He couldn't believe the news about Titurius. Fire was an ever-present danger in Rome, with minor fires a daily occurrence and even larger conflagrations experienced on a regular basis. But it was unusual for a fine house to burn down, given the preponderance of stone over wood in the superior construction, and the separation from neighbours in the richer districts making the spread of the flames harder. He felt fortunate that he had not been invited to stay the night at Titurius' domus. That Caracalla and the Empress had left before the fire seemed some sort of miracle, a divine intervention of sorts. Cilo would have been suspicious that it was an act of arson aimed at himself if it wasn't for the fact that Caracalla knew he was not staying the night. As far as he was aware, Titurius had given neither Emperor offence. He presumed, therefore, it was a tragic accident.

Maybe his sacking as urban prefect was a blessing in disguise. It was all becoming too much. He looked down to see his hands shaking, a fine tremor he couldn't still, even when he clasped them together. It was time to retire. Take his family and go to his villa in Campania. Grow vines and olive trees. Go for long walks in the country with his wife, Cilonia Fabia.

A loud hammering from the front door reached him, disturbing his reverie. He sighed and rose from the bath, donning a short tunic and a pair of slippers, and walked into the peristylium. Then he sat on a marble bench and waited for his porter to find out who was disturbing him. If it was someone sufficiently important, the porter would escort them to the atrium and then inform him of their arrival.

Instead, a tribune and two uniformed legionaries from the Urban Cohorts strode straight into his peristylium.

He stood at their approach, confused. He thought at first they had come to report to him in his official capacity. As he had only just come from Caracalla, they couldn't yet know that he was no longer their commanding officer.

'Tribune. What is the meaning of this intrusion?'

'Come with us,' said the tribune roughly. His tone was insolent, disrespectful.

'Watch your tone, tribune. You will pay if you speak to me that way again.'

'Take him,' said the tribune, and the two legionaries grabbed him by the shoulders. The porter stepped forward to intervene, but the tribune half-unsheathed his sword, and the porter backed away, hands spread in a gesture intended to show he wasn't going to get involved.

The legionaries dragged Cilo out of the peristylium, through his atrium and onto the street. A number of soldiers waited for him. A small crowd had gathered, curious to find out what was going on.

The tribune spoke loudly, for all to hear. 'Lucius Fabius Cilo. You have committed treason against the Emperor. We are here to administer your punishment.'

Cilo went cold, but he stood straight and kept his voice steady. 'On whose orders?'

'On the orders of Gaius Julius Asper.'

Asper? His deputy? That snake.

'Wait,' said Cilo. 'Tribune, I command you—'

The tribune struck him across the face, and Cilo dropped to his knees, aghast at the assault. The officer signalled to his soldiers, and before Cilo's disbelieving eyes, they went into his house and started to plunder it, bringing out silver plate, plush robes, his wife's gold jewellery and his coins.

'We will show you how traitors in Rome are treated,' said the centurion. 'Bring him.'

The soldiers hauled him to his feet and marched him, resisting weakly, down the Sacred Way towards the palace.

–

'Who is that?' Silus asked a fellow bystander in the crowd as the old man, dressed only in a short tunic and slippers, hair still wet from bathing, was dragged out of his house.

'That's Cilo, the urban prefect.'

Silus turned to Atius. 'Cilo. Caracalla told us that he was one of his supporters.'

Atius called out to the soldiers, 'Hey, what are you doing to him?'

'Shut your mouth and mind your business, you foreign scum,' came the reply.

'Is this Geta's doing?' Silus wondered aloud. 'Atius, run to Oclatinius and tell him what is going on. I'll try to keep Cilo alive until we have orders from the boss. Go!'

Atius took off at a run. Silus watched as Cilo was struck down, and as the soldiers plundered his house of all its valuable goods. It didn't take long before the legionaries had brought sacks of riches out of the domus. Then they lifted Cilo up onto his feet and started to march him down the Sacred Way.

Silus stood in front of the soldiers, barring their way. 'On whose authority have you arrested the urban prefect?' he said defiantly.

'None of your business. Get out of the way, or you will feel my sword in your guts.'

Silus stood his ground, but when the tribune put his hand on his hilt, he stepped aside. He couldn't fight them all, and besides, he didn't fully know the rights and wrongs of this situation.

Word spread rapidly that something interesting was happening, and a sizeable gathering lined the streets to watch the rich nobleman being marched towards the palace. Fevered speculation and imaginative rumour circulated as to his crime. Some said he had attempted to murder one of the Emperors, or the Empress, or he had violated a Vestal Virgin. Some even made bets on what he had done and what his punishment was to be.

Silus kept pace with the soldiers, hoping that Atius would return quickly with orders from Oclatinius. He hated the feeling of helplessness and uncertainty. Should he try to intervene again?

At a crossroads, Cilo stumbled, and fell to his knees again. A few legionaries laughed, and some of the crowd joined in the mockery. The poor of Rome were always happy to see the rich and powerful humbled.

The tribune ordered Cilo to his feet, but the nobleman continued to kneel, head bowed, breathing heavily. The tribune struck him with the back of his hand, but Cilo simply took the blow passively. He looked up.

'If you feel you are worthy enough, end my life, tribune. I, who have been legate, military prefect, consul, proconsul, urban prefect. Do you think you have the dignitas and auctoritas to murder someone so far your superior?'

The tribune turned red. 'Seize him,' he commanded. 'Strip him.'

Two of the legionaries hauled him up with hands under his arms. Then they ripped his tunic down the front with sharp tugs, revealing a ribby chest with white curls of hair. They pulled the rest of the clothing away, and even pulled off his slippers, so he was naked.

There was more laughter from the crowd, but it faded as Cilo stood straight, arms by his sides, making no effort to cover his nakedness, looking the tribune straight in the eyes.

The tribune could not take the defiance and became enraged. He drew a knife from his belt and slashed it across Cilo's cheek, opening up a deep gash which dripped red profusely. Cilo did not flinch, nor put his hand to his face. The crowd was silent now.

Cilo's dignity infuriated the tribune further and he slashed him across the other cheek.

'Leave him alone, you coward!' shouted Silus. Others joined in the shouts. 'Let him go! Bully! Bastard!'

The crowd's sympathies turned completely at that moment, now perceiving a dignified old man taking undeserved punishment from a bully. Some threw stones at the soldiers and the tribunes. The soldiers closed ranks, drawing their swords. Silus realised the scene was about to turn ugly. But he was not prepared to see this helpless old man die. He gritted his teeth and stepped forward, drawing his knife.

'Soldiers! Stand down!'

The voice carried clearly through the growing din, and was full of absolute authority. Silus turned, as did the crowd and soldiers, to see the newcomer.

It was Caracalla, riding down the Sacred Way on a night-black stallion, in full military dress, escorted by twenty Praetorians.

The tribune stared at the Emperor in disbelief, then bowed his head. 'Augustus.'

Caracalla dismounted and strode to Cilo's side. He removed his cavalry cloak and draped it around Cilo's shoulders, covering his nakedness. He turned to the Urban Cohort legionaries in fury.

'This man was once my tutor. How dare you insult his dignity this way!'

He flicked his fingers at the centurion in charge of the Praetorians.

'Disarm these disloyal men and bind them.'

The legionaries threw their swords to the ground and submitted immediately to the Praetorians, who tied their hands behind their backs and forced them all to their knees.

'Augustus,' said the Urban Cohort tribune. 'We thought we were doing your bidding. We had orders—'

'Silence!' snapped Caracalla. His eyes locked on Silus for the first time. 'I see I have one man here who is loyal to me. This man obeys my orders without question, with bravery and skill. Is that not so, Silus?'

Silus bowed his head. 'Of course, Augustus.' His thoughts went to Tituria, hiding in his apartment, and he hoped the Emperor couldn't read his thoughts.

'These men who have plotted against Cilo have plotted against me. They are traitors. I condemn them to death. Silus. Carry out the sentence.'

The legionaries stared in horror at their Emperor. The tribune stammered. 'But Augustus, we only strived to do your will...'

Silus swallowed. 'Augustus, wouldn't it be better to pass them to Oclatinius to get more information about their plotting?'

'Do you defy me as well?' roared Caracalla.

Silus looked at the knife in his hand that had already drawn so much blood. When would it end? But his Emperor had just given him a direct order. He moved behind the tribune, took his hair and pulled his head back, exposing his throat, and looked at Caracalla. Caracalla nodded peremptorily.

'Augustus, we were acting on orders from—' The tribune's words were cut off by the sharp edge slicing deep across his neck. Silus held him until his convulsions stopped, then moved on to the next man.

Some of the legionaries started to resist, to struggle to their feet, but they were bound, unarmed and outnumbered by the Praetorians, and they were clubbed back into a kneeling position with the butts of spears and the hilts of swords. Silus moved down the line, cutting throat after throat. Some took their deaths stoically, some babbled for mercy, some just shook and soiled themselves. They all bled and died the same.

When it was over, Caracalla did not even acknowledge Silus' work. He ordered a litter brought, and the Praetorians bore Cilo away with the Emperor following solemnly behind. Silus looked at the dead bodies strewn around the crossroads, lying in a lake of their pooled lifeblood. What would happen to them?

It wasn't his problem. He used the hem of the tunic of one of the dead soldiers and wiped his hands and his knife. Then head down, dark thoughts in his head, he went to find a drink.

Chapter Thirteen

It was unusual for Silus to be the drunk one, and Atius to be the voice of reason and sobriety.

'Come on, mate, take it easy.'

'Are you fucking deaf? I said get me another.'

Atius sighed and ordered another cup of wine from the serving slave, making sure they knew to water it well. It seemed that seeing his friend in this state had driven the will to drink from him, at least temporarily, and he ordered water for himself.

When Silus drank the diluted wine, he spat. 'What is this piss? Has it even seen a grape? You, fetch me a cup, and make sure there is none of your sewer water polluting it this time.'

The slave nodded and replaced his drink with a stronger one, ignoring the dark looks from Atius.

'Listen, mate. There is no need for this. I get that today was tough—'

'Tough? Are you fucking kidding me? Tell me, *mate*,' he emphasised that word with a snarl, 'when was the last time you cut the throats of a dozen men and watched them all twitch and bleed out at your feet?'

Atius reached out to place a hand on Silus' shoulder, but he shrugged it off angrily.

'What the fuck are we doing, Atius? When Oclatinius took us on, we were soldiers, fighting an enemy in Britannia that wanted to destroy us, kill our families, steal our possessions and burn our homes. That was a real purpose, an honourable reason to risk our lives. Then we became Arcani, spies for the Emperor, killing traitors and enemy leaders, getting revenge for atrocities and saving Roman and British lives. But it's changed. From soldier to spy to assassin.'

'We do what we do because we are loyal to the Emperor.'

'Killing the weak and innocent, because Caracalla wills it?'

Atius looked around nervously. There were only a few in the tavern, most engrossed in their own conversations or games, and fortunately no one seemed to be paying them particular attention.

'Watch your words, friend. Talk like that could get you thrown to the beasts.'

'What do I care? I've lost everything. I've had my revenge. I thought serving the Emperor would give my life meaning. But this morning... Atius, I was a simple executioner. Those soldiers were following orders, and because they followed the wrong leader, they died.'

'That has always been the way, Silus. Pick the wrong gang in your village or the wrong side in battle, or just the wrong country to be born in, and you will suffer through no fault of your own. The Christos knew that man was born to suffer. That is why he came to us, to offer us a better life to come.'

'Fuck the Christos too.'

Atius frowned and sat back. 'It's one thing to insult the Emperor. Or me. But you will put yourself at odds with me if you insult the Christos.'

Silus made a sour face and took a drink. Then grudgingly he said, 'I apologise. To you, and to the Christos.'

Atius looked partially mollified.

'Why don't I take you home?'

'No!' snapped Silus.

'Why not?'

'Because I don't want you to.' Silus knew he was drunk. Not so drunk he had forgotten that he didn't want Atius in his apartment, but too drunk to come up with a plausible explanation.

'I don't understand. If I didn't know that you have nothing of any worth, I would think you were hiding something from me.'

A chill went through Silus, enough to make him shiver despite the fear being attenuated by the drink.

'Go home, Atius. I want to be alone.'

Atius shook his head. He stood, his stool scraping backwards on the floor tiles.

'I'll see you tomorrow, friend. I'm sorry you feel like this. Just remember where I am if you need me.'

Silus didn't look up from his drink as his friend left, but just swirled the contents around the cup and watched the dark liquid circulate. He was torn between tiredness, a deep exhaustion in his soul making him desperate to lie down on his bed, and fear of returning to his apartment and looking into the empty eyes of Tituria, then waiting for the shades of twelve dead legionaries of the Urban Cohorts and their tribune to come to him with accusations and recriminations.

He threw his cup across the tavern. The contents sprayed a couple of old men gossiping nearby, and they sent curses his way. The cup smashed against the wall, and the tavern keeper shouted at him.

'You, get out, or I'll call the vigiles.'

For a moment Silus was tempted to confront them all, provoke them into a fight, so he could punch and kick and bite. But he was done with violence for the day. He stood, steadied himself with one hand on the table as a moment of nausea and dizziness swept over him, then made for the door when it passed.

He took a slow, gently weaving walk towards his home. Though night had fallen, it was not late, and the streets were crowded. As well as the wheeled vehicles threatening to crush anyone too slow to move, and the various drovers and carters bringing their goods to market, there were plenty of citizens of all ranks, from the wealthy borne in litters by slaves, to the poorest sitting on street corners and begging for coins, food or wine.

Silus was conscious that he was below his usual level of alertness. It was dangerous for anyone to be alone and drunk on the streets of Rome at night – it was just asking for a mugging. It was doubly dangerous for Silus, who had started to make enemies. He shook his head to clear it, and forced himself to pay attention to his surroundings. For a while, nothing seemed out of the ordinary.

Then he realised he had seen the same man twice, a short distance behind him. The man's hood was up, and he recalled the hawker who had been nearby when he had received the threatening message, ostensibly from the Emperor Geta. He had been dressed similarly, if his drink-hazed memory could be relied upon.

Silus took a turn down a narrow alley, then stepped into a doorway and waited. The hooded man was only a short distance behind, and when he took the same turning, he stopped, confused, looking around for Silus.

Silus stepped out of the shadows and grabbed the man from behind, placing his blade against his throat. He pulled back his hood and got a good look at his face, olive skin with fine Egyptian features.

'Why are you following me?' he hissed.

The man tried to protest, but Silus dug the knife in deeper, drawing blood, and he yelped.

'In three heartbeats I'm going to bring my count of throats slit today to fourteen. Honestly, my heart isn't in it, but I will do it all the same. One, two...'

'Wait. I have orders.'

'From whom?'

'Aper. He is working for Geta.'

Aper. Silus racked his drink-befuddled brains. There were so many politicians and nobles in Rome. Maybe if he were a native, he would know them all. As it was, he had to rely on Oclatinius' lessons. Aper. Wasn't he a cousin to Geta and Caracalla? He had obviously picked his side. Useful information for Oclatinius and Caracalla. If Silus still owed them his loyalty. He wasn't sure any more.

'And why me?'

'You are marked, Silus. You have been a thorn in Geta's side for a long time now, since Britannia. He wants you monitored closely. He hates you.'

'Were you going to kill me tonight?'

'I don't have orders for that yet. You are under Caracalla's protection.'

For now, thought Silus. And anyway, the protection of an Emperor had done Euprepes no good.

'What is your name?' asked Silus.

The man hesitated, then said, 'Bek.' Silus had no idea if it was his real name or not, but at least he had something to call him.

'Are you going to kill me now?' asked Bek. His voice held only a trace of tremor.

Silus took the blade away from the spy's throat and stepped back.

'I've had my fill of blood for today. Go away. And tell your master that the next man I catch following me will be dead before he knows he has been discovered.'

Bek nodded, then turned and ran. Silus waited for a while to make sure no one else was tailing him, then exited the far end of the alleyway, sobering up slowly as he took a long, winding walk home.

–

The initial shock had worn off. It was the bit where she didn't believe it was true, despite what she had seen with her own eyes. She had barely spoken a word since the rough man had brought her to his house, and his slave had started caring for her.

253

The slave was kind, like the one who had helped her mother raise her. She had cleaned her, shopped for her, cooked for her, brushed her hair, dressed her, and held her when the tears had begun to flow. Once she had started crying it was hard to stop, but eventually the torrent had slowed to a trickle, then ceased.

And then an anger grew inside her.

Tituria had rarely been angry in her life. She had had little need to be. Tantrums, yes, shouting matches with her brother, strops at her mother. But not real anger like this. Rage against the murderers of her family, the injustice that had ripped her away from everything she loved and that kept her safe. And now the questions started.

'Who did it?'

Apicula looked startled. She had hardly heard the child speak, and the blunt enquiry took her by surprise.

'Did what, child?'

'Who killed my father? My brother and mother. Burnt down my house?'

The look on Apicula's face told Tituria she would be getting no answers from the slave.

'Child,' breathed Apicula, a hand on her chest. 'Oh, child, is that what happened to you? I'm so sorry. I know nothing about any of it.'

Tituria pursed her lips. 'How long am I to stay here? When will Silus take me to friends of my family, or to relatives who can care for me?'

'I don't know these things either. I'm sorry.'

Tituria looked away, clenching her fists and digging her fingernails into her palms.

'Thank you for your hospitality. I think it is time to take my leave.'

'But you can't!'

'Am I a prisoner here?'

'No. Yes. The master said—'

'You know I am a freeborn daughter of a senator?'

'No, I didn't know, but I—'

'I'm going to go now.'

'Where will you go?' Apicula looked desperate, uncertain.

'To the house of Dio Cassius. He was a friend to my father. He will know what to do. He will look after me.'

'Child, the master said that you were in danger. That you had to stay here. I can't let you go.'

'You are a slave. You have been kind to me, but that doesn't alter the fact that if you lay a hand on me or try to hold me here against my will, I can have you crucified.'

Apicula blanched. 'Please don't...'

'Goodbye, Apicula. Thank you for your hospitality.'

Tituria stroked Issa between the ears, walked to the door, unbarred it, picked up her doll and stepped out into the night.

–

When Silus returned to the apartment, he found Apicula sitting on the floor, weeping into her hands, while Issa stood on her hind legs and tried to reach her to lick her face. He looked around the room in puzzlement, pulled back the curtain to the bedroom, then turned to face Apicula again.

'Slave! Where is she?'

'Master, I'm so sorry. She left.'

'She what?' Silus' fury threatened to overtake him until he saw the scared and pitiful expression on his slave's face. He controlled himself with an effort.

'Didn't I say to keep her here? That she was in danger?'

'She wouldn't stay, master, and she said she would have me crucified if I tried to stop her.'

Silus clutched at his hair in frustration. 'And you thought I would be pleased that you had disobeyed my orders?'

Apicula got onto her knees and clutched the hem of his tunic. 'Master, forgive me, please.'

'Stop it, slave. I'm not one of these rich Romans. I'm not going to punish you. Did she say where she was going?'

'To the house of Dio Cassius.'

'How long ago?'

'Mere moments, master. You must have just missed her.'

'Why didn't you say straight away?'

Silus rushed for the door, hearing Apicula start to cry again behind him. He ran down the rickety steps two and three at a time until he reached the street. He looked up and down, realising he didn't know where Dio Cassius lived. He had heard of the senator from Oclatinius' teaching, but couldn't recall his address. Was it the Palatine or the Esquiline?

He took a gamble and ran in the direction of the Palatine. He covered distance quickly, but was conscious that with Rome's multiple intersecting streets, Tituria could have taken a different route, and he might easily breeze straight past her along a parallel road. He estimated he had run nearly half a mile when he saw a patrol of vigiles, strolling casually along with their belted tunics and axes at their sides.

'Sirs,' he said, out of breath. 'Do you know where the senator Dio Cassius lives?'

Their leader looked suspicious. 'What's it to you?'

'I... have an important message for him. From my patron.'

'And your patron neglected to tell you his address?'

'He did, I just... forgot. And my patron will have his men beat me if I don't deliver the message he asked.'

The leader of the vigiles looked at his men. 'Dio Cassius? Isn't he the big house on the Esquiline?'

'That's the one, boss.'

Jupiter's hairy cock, he was going the wrong way. He thanked them, and retraced his steps. He wondered how quickly a nine-year-old girl could travel at night in Rome. Or how much danger she would be in. Maybe her air of authority coupled with innocence would keep her safe from the dark men of Rome's night. But it wouldn't keep her safe for long when she reached her destination.

He recalled Oclatinius telling him that Cassius Dio was likely a Geta loyalist. Perhaps that would save her – after all, it was

Caracalla who wanted her dead. But he didn't know what information she carried in her head. Maybe it was as dangerous to Geta as to Caracalla. Or maybe it was of benefit to Geta, with Tituria being used as an expendable pawn in the game between the two brothers.

He redoubled his pace through the city, and started the climb towards the Esquiline. He realised his route was similar to the one he had taken so recently when he had killed Tituria's family. Cassius Dio must live in the same region as Titurius had, so Tituria would know his house well.

As he ascended the incline at the foot of the Esquiline, he passed a tavern keeper picking up dirty plates and cups from the tables outside his store.

'Hey. Which way to Dio Cassius' domus?'

The tavern keeper was much less suspicious than the vigiles had been and gave him detailed directions.

'Have you seen a young girl on her own heading that way?' Silus asked, more in hope than expectation. But the tavern keeper confirmed that he had been surprised to see a child going that way a short time before.

Silus broke into a run. The domus was close now, and if Tituria got there before he stopped her, she would be recognised, and it would all be over. Not only her life, but his, when Oclatinius and Caracalla found out he had lied and spared her.

He rounded a corner and sprinted down the street, narrowly avoiding a cart trundling the other way, then running into a litter and spilling a finely dressed lady into the ordure in the gutter. He kept going, her screams and the curses of her slaves echoing behind him, and took the next turn as the tavern keeper had directed. At the end of the street was the town house of Dio Cassius, and striding purposefully towards it, head down, her doll clutched in her hand, was Tituria.

A porter was standing outside the senator's domus, leaning against the house with one hand while he held his cock in the other, a hiss of urine splashing against the wall. Tituria headed straight for him, and was maybe a dozen yards away when Silus grabbed her from behind, covering her mouth with his palm, and lifting her off her feet into a tight hug.

Tituria's surprised and outraged scream was too muffled to disturb the porter, who didn't turn. Silus dragged her down a side alley, pressed her against a wall and leant down in front of her.

'Tituria. Are you hurt?'

'Let me go, Silus,' she said calmly. 'Or I will scream for the vigiles and the Urban Cohorts and the Praetorian Guards, and they will arrest you and throw you into the arena.'

'Tituria, I know you are hurting. I know you must be full of questions. But you have to trust me. It's not safe...'

'Why do I have to trust you?'

'Why? Because... because I am the only one looking out for you right now.'

'Silus, I need to know what happened. And why.'

Silus nodded. 'I will tell you what I can. But I need you to talk to me, too. Maybe we can piece this together between us.'

Tituria looked towards Dio Cassius' house, and considered. Silus wondered what he would do if she decided she still didn't trust him. How could he keep her safe in his little apartment if she didn't want to be there? It even crossed his mind that he might have to kill her himself. If she insisted on running, then his crime against Caracalla would be revealed, and soon after that he would be dead himself. But he quickly dismissed that idea. He hadn't been able to let her die before, and had killed Daya to prevent it. He would not kill her now, not after that.

'I'll come home with you, Silus,' she said.

Silus breathed out a sigh of relief. 'Thank you. It's late. We will sleep. And in the morning, we'll talk.' He held out his hand. Tituria hesitated, then took it, and he led her back towards the Subura.

–

When Silus awoke, he ached. He had slept uncomfortably, although the straw mattress which was new and therefore free of bedbugs and fleas was no worse than he was used to, and in fact better than many of his beds when he had been on field missions in Caledonia. But he had a crick in his neck, a dry mouth and a banging headache. A heavy drinking session followed by a foot race across the city was probably not the healthiest way to spend an evening.

He swung his legs over the side of the bed, the wooden frame creaking as he did so. He pulled the curtain separating the bedroom from the rest of the apartment aside, and blinked in the sunlight that shone through the small window. Tituria, Apicula and Issa were curled up together on the mattress in the main room.

Apicula was awake, and she gave him a look which Silus interpreted as an apology for not having risen earlier, but as her arm was trapped beneath the sleeping girl, Silus gestured that it was no matter. He rubbed his face hard to get his circulation moving, and then poured himself a cup of water from the jug on the table. He downed it in one, then drank a second more slowly. He used the chamber pot, then tipped the contents out of the window before the smell stunk up the apartment too badly. He knew he had been drinking a lot last night, but by Vulcan's arse, what had he been eating? Some curses came from below, but he ignored them. Getting covered in the slops from chamber pots was apparently an occupational hazard of going for a walk in Rome.

Tituria stirred, stretched, slowly opened her eyes, then sat up with a gasp. Apicula sat up next to her and put a comforting arm around her shoulder. For a moment the little girl seemed unable to catch her breath, her respiration panicky, rapid and shallow. Then she swallowed and got herself under control. She looked up at Silus with big wet eyes.

He was glad that she had fallen asleep straight away the previous night – he had been in no state to have a coherent conversation. Although he didn't relish the prospect of the talk any more this morning than he had the previous night, he at least felt less muddled in his thoughts, and was less likely to say something stupid.

He passed Tituria his cup of water, and she sipped at it.

'Apicula. Go and get us something to eat for breakfast. Take your time.'

She pulled on her tunic and a pair of sandals and took the coins Silus offered. She kissed Tituria on the top of the head, and then left Silus alone with the little girl.

Tituria sat on the mattress, her knees pulled up under her chin, hugging her shins. She looked at Silus expectantly.

Silus picked over the words he would use, knowing that he would have to lie, and lie well. He barely knew this girl, she had spoken very little since he had taken her from her home, and yet her eyes were alert and shone with intelligence. He knew the question she wanted answered was very easy to ask and very hard to answer. The simple interrogative: why?

'I am a foreigner in Rome,' he began, stating the obvious. 'You can tell from my accent and my looks that I wasn't born here. I come from Britannia, where I was with the army. I don't understand much about politics in Rome. In fact, you probably know way more than me about the subject.'

Tituria said nothing. Issa nuzzled up to her, and she stroked the little dog's muzzle absently.

'There is a war going on in Rome right now. It may not be obvious. There may not be soldiers fighting in the streets, or sieges of forts. But people are dying all the same. Men are being asked to choose a side.

'Your father I think was a powerful and rich man. He was also honourable. His opinion was respected. It mattered. I think your father chose the wrong side. Or chose no side at all, which might be worse, as he would then have the protection of neither.'

'Who ordered him to be killed?' asked Tituria.

'I don't know,' lied Silus.

'Who sent you to save me? Did my father's message to Geta get through?'

Titurius was sending a message to Geta? That was news, and would be useful to Oclatinius, if there was any way he could tell the spymaster without revealing his own crime. It also gave him a helpful reason for his actions that he could tell Tituria.

'I don't know. My boss sent me to rescue you all.'

'Why only you?'

'He sent others. They were coming behind me. I just got there first.'

'Why do I have to hide? Why can't Geta protect me?'

'Because I don't know who wants you dead, and I don't know why.'

'Why do they want me dead? My whole family? Why not just my father?'

'I was hoping you could tell me.'

Tituria looked away, and her eyes filled with tears.

Then she said, 'Might it be my fault?'

'Why would you say that?'

'Because I saw something. Something I shouldn't have. Something bad.'

'What was it, Tituria?'

She shook her head. 'I can't say. If that was the reason, then telling you might put you in danger too.'

'Tituria, do you trust me?'

Tituria looked at him for a long moment. Then she said in a small voice, 'Yes.'

'So tell me. Then we can decide what to do.'

Tituria took a breath.

And there was a loud knocking.

Silus looked at the door in alarm. It couldn't be Apicula. She wouldn't need to knock. And there was no one else he trusted.

'Get in the bedroom,' he hissed. 'Under the bed.'

She scurried into the small room, looked at the bed and hesitated. She turned to look at him, uncertainty on her face. He had no time to ask why.

'Do it, now! And keep quiet. Both our lives depend on it.'

Tituria shuffled under the bed, and Silus pulled the curtain across, then opened the door a crack and peered out.

Oh, shit.

It was Oclatinius.

He opened the door wider, and stood in the doorway.

'Sir, this is an unexpected pleasure.'

'The day I become predictable is the day I should retire, don't you think?'

'Yes, sir.'

'Well?'

'Well what, sir?'

'Well, are you going to make me stand on your doorstep like some supplicant client begging his patron for a handout?'

'No, sir. Please come in. But I warn you, it is not what you are used to. And I have precious little to offer – I have just sent my slave for supplies.'

'Your good company will suffice, Silus.'

Silus stepped aside and let Oclatinius enter. The spymaster looked around him, taking in the cracked walls, the peeling paint, the tiny window, the splintered wooden door.

'Aren't you going to show me around?'

Silus thought he was joking, given that the apartment was only a few square feet, but Oclatinius just raised his eyebrows.

'Well, sir, this is the area where my slave sleeps, and where I eat and dress. And behind that curtain is my bedroom.'

'Let me see.'

Silus hesitated. 'Sir, it is just a bed and mattress.'

Oclatinius glared at him. Silus' heart started to thump, but he kept his expression neutral. The old spy was a master of reading faces. But Silus had also had training in how to make a lie convincing, and how to master his emotions. He pulled the curtain back to reveal the wooden bed with its mattress and scruffy unmade sheet pulled halfway down. Oclatinius glanced in, then looked away, uninterested. He walked to the window and looked down into the street far below, already thronged with the usual crowds shouting, pushing and fighting. Silus let the curtain fall back into place with a suppressed sigh of relief.

'Lovely place you have. I can see why you want to spend so much time here.'

'Thank you, sir. Do you have a mission for me?'

'No, no, just checking in on the welfare of one of my best operatives.'

'Do you have cause for concern, sir?'

'Let's just say that a friend of yours thought you weren't yourself. Acting out of character. That you were erratic, and wanted to be alone.'

Thanks a fucking bundle, Atius, thought Silus.

'Before you take it out on him, I have to tell you he came to me because he was worried, not to report you. Silus, the things you have seen and done. They can wear on a man's soul.'

Juno's tits, please don't go into detail about what I have seen and done. Not with Tituria listening to every word. Could she remain silent if she found out he had been responsible for her family's death?

'I'm fine, sir.'

Oclatinius looked at him, and the old man's eyes seemed to spear into his soul. Could the wily spymaster drag his secrets out of him without him even speaking a word? Silus swallowed.

'If that's all, sir?'

The door opened, and Apicula entered, looked at Oclatinius in surprise, then around the room in confusion. While Oclatinius turned away from Silus and towards her, Silus gave her a subtle warning shake of his head.

'This is your slave, Silus?'

'Yes, sir, Apicula.'

Oclatinius looked her up and down, seeming to take in every detail, and despite her past profession, Apicula blushed at the attention.

'Sir, I have brought supplies for... for you.'

Oclatinius looked in her basket. 'Goat's milk? Honey cakes?'

'I had a heavy night last night, sir. I thought the sweetness might be good for my head. I asked her to get me fried canary – I understand the Romans swear by it as a hangover cure. I'll punish her when you leave, for the poor performance of her duties.'

'As you see fit. I will take my leave.'

'You won't stay for a honey cake, sir?'

'Most kind, Silus, but no. Report to me as usual this evening.'

Oclatinius nodded to Apicula and left. Silus shut the door behind him, then put his hand against it and let out a long breath that whistled through his teeth.

'Where is Tituria, master?' whispered Apicula. Silus nodded to the bedroom, barely able to speak with relief. Apicula opened the curtain, and got on her hands and knees to help the little girl out from under the bed. Tituria stood and dusted her tunic off, then looked at Silus curiously.

'What did he mean, the things you have seen and done?'

Silus glared at her, feeling irritation at the way she challenged him, head cocked to one side, hands on hips.

'Nothing to concern a child. Apicula, give her some food. I'm going back to bed.'

Chapter Fourteen

Silus wrenched the door open to find Atius on his hands and knees, his eye pressed against a crack in the door. Silus grabbed him by the collar of his tunic.

'Atius, you bastard. You really are a hopeless spy. I could hear you breathing.'

Atius looked past him into the apartment. Apicula was out on errands, and the room was empty, but the curtain to the bedroom was drawn.

'I saw, Silus. I saw her in here. Where is she? Under the bed? Was that where she was hiding when Oclatinius came round?'

Silus sagged, let go of the tunic and took a step back.

'Atius, I thought you were my friend.'

'I am, Silus. I was genuinely worried about you when I spoke to Oclatinius. But after he visited you, he came away more suspicious than before.'

Silus reflected that he should have known he had not pulled the wool over his boss's eyes. Maybe after the spymaster visited him he should have just taken Tituria and fled Rome. Or done that right from the start. But that would have marked him as guilty, and he would spend the rest of his life a wanted man. And the gods alone knew what he could do with Tituria. Adopt her?

'He sent me to spy on you. To find out what you were hiding. I couldn't say no.'

'You could have asked me.'

Atius raised his eyebrows.

'Tell her she can come out, Silus. It must be dusty under that bed.'

Silus said nothing, but Tituria emerged from the bedroom anyway. She looked at Atius with wide scared eyes.

'Who is she?'

Silus pressed his lips together.

'Tell me she isn't the senator's daughter? The one you—'

'Atius, shut it.'

'Silus, we need to talk about this.'

Silus took a deep breath. Then he turned to Tituria. 'Stay here. Do not leave this apartment. I need to talk to this man. Understand?'

Tituria nodded.

'You promise?'

'I promise.'

—

She counted to a hundred heartbeats before she tried the door. Silus had locked it, so she went to the window. It was small, but so was she, and she wriggled out of the gap and with her feet on the sill clambered up onto the roof. From there it was simple to drop down onto the stairs outside the apartment and hurry down.

Silus and Atius were walking slowly and she soon caught sight of them. Silus clearly didn't intend to go far from the apartment, and when they got to the nearest crossroads, they stopped at the central fountain and sat side by side on the retaining wall that held the pool. Slaves and the poorer matrons filled buckets of water to take back to their homes, and others washed in the pool or drank from the stream spouting out of the mouth of a finely carved fish.

She weaved through the crowd of taller adults to bring herself closer to the two men without being seen, and sat on the far side of the fountain from them. The noise of the street and the splashing of the water made eavesdropping harder than she was used to. But she was young, with acute hearing, and when she closed her eyes and filtered out the extraneous noise, she could make out their words.

'You aren't serious?' It was Atius speaking. 'Please tell me you aren't serious. Did you lose your mind?'

'Keep your voice down,' said Silus.

'She is Tituria? The senator's daughter?'

'I already told you. And you guessed before that.'

'But how? Why?'

'I couldn't do it, Atius. She reminded me too much of my own Sergia. And after Daya killed that little girl on Lipari... I know why Caracalla said she needed to die, but that didn't make it any easier. I couldn't let it happen again.'

There was a pause, and Tituria wished she could see their expressions.

'So how much of what you told Oclatinius was true?'

'Most,' said Silus.

'So you killed the slaves. You killed the porters. You killed Autronia and Daya killed Titurius.'

Tituria held her breath. No. Please, no.

'Yes,' said Silus.

Tituria thought her heart had stopped. The man who had saved her life, who she had watched kill the assassin who had killed her father. He had been sent to kill her. And he had murdered her mother. Her fingers and toes started to tingle as she lost control of her breathing, taking deep gulps of air as though she had just come up from almost drowning.

'And Daya?' said Atius. Even through her distress, she could hear the threat in his tone.

Silus was silent.

'Did you kill Daya?' asked Atius, pronouncing each word slowly.

'Atius.' Silus sounded like he was pleading. 'I cared about Daya. You know that.'

'Did you kill her?!' Atius was shouting now.

'I had no choice. I couldn't let the little girl die.'

Tituria's head spun and she thought she would pass out. It was too much to take in. He had been sent to kill her? He had saved her? He had killed her father's assassin? He had loved her father's assassin? She stumbled to her feet, walked away from the fountain, away from the apartment, in a daze.

Passers-by gave curious looks to the little girl alone with tears streaming down her face. A woman in a toga, heavily made up, stopped in front of her.

'What's wrong, little one?'

Tituria just shook her head and waved her away, carrying on her aimless walk. Through the fog of her misery, she realised for the first time in her life she had nowhere to go. No one to turn to. She couldn't trust Silus. It didn't matter that he had tried to save her – he had killed her mother. And she could trust no one else. She didn't know whose side anyone was on. She wasn't entirely clear what the sides were. Should she visit Dio Cassius? Silus had thought it would be dangerous. But Silus was a liar.

One thing was clear from what she had just heard. Caracalla was the one who had ordered their deaths. And she suddenly realised why. It had nothing to do with her father's politics. It was because of her. Because of her snooping and exploring, because of what she had witnessed. Caracalla had decreed that she and everyone in her household must die.

Her family was dead because of her.

She stumbled against a stall selling brass pots and pans, and was cursed by the vendor when she knocked a saucepan to the ground with a clatter. He shook his fist, rounded his table to chase her, and she ran, turning left and right until her pursuer was gone. Then she slumped against a wall, curled up and shook uncontrollably.

She didn't know how long she sat there before she stopped trembling. There was a dull ache at the back of her eyes, and her legs were shaky when she stood. But she had made a decision.

Caracalla wanted her dead.

Caracalla was at war with his brother, Geta.

Father had been sending Geta a message for help.

She had to go to Geta, and tell him what she had seen. Then she could beg him for protection. And revenge.

Setting her shoulders, she began to walk towards the palace.

—

Atius' mind was in turmoil. He had stormed away from Silus, leaving his friend, if he could still call him that, at the fountain calling after him. He turned a deaf ear to him.

Where did his loyalty lie now? To Emperor and Empire? Or to his friendship, that he had fought and nearly died for? It wasn't that if he didn't report what he had found out, he would be complicit in his friend's crime. But he had taken an oath of loyalty to the Arcani, as well as one to the Emperor when he had signed up for the auxiliaries – albeit the old, dead Emperor.

He wanted to ask his best friend for advice. But he was the one person he couldn't talk to. So he had to go to Oclatinius. He was wise. He would know what to do. And the problem would no longer belong to Silus alone.

But Oclatinius wasn't at his quarters, and his secretary informed Atius coolly that the head of the Arcani had business with the Emperor Antoninus, and that he was welcome to wait, but he had no idea how long it would be. Atius decided that he couldn't delay. Now that Silus knew his secret was out, Atius couldn't predict his actions. He would either throw himself on the mercy of the Emperor, or attempt to flee the city. If it was the former, then what Atius did now didn't matter. If it was the latter, then speed was of the essence.

So he hurried across the city towards the palace. Doubts crowded his mind. He had to betray his friend or betray his Emperor. Surely friends came first. And yet Daya was a friend. He had been fond of her, though not to the extent that Silus had clearly started to fall for her. Silus had killed their friend, their comrade. But he had done it to save a child, one who reminded him of his own daughter.

Atius wanted to scream. He didn't like to think beyond the next drink, the next fight or the next fuck. He was a follower of Christos, as his mother had taught him to be, and he prayed to the God of the Jews and to His son, and the Mother Maria, but he didn't give it much thought. It was just an unquestioned constant in his life, and the fact that not all believed the same as him did not particularly bother him or give him pause for thought. The only deep thinking he ever had to do was how to complete the mission he had been given, and recently he had had Silus to do that for him. Now he had a real choice to make, with terrible consequences whichever path he took.

It was in this state of mind that he turned a corner and ran straight into Tituria.

—

When Silus returned to his apartment, Apicula was waiting on the doorstep with an armful of laundry fresh from the fuller. Of course, he had locked the door after he left to stop Tituria from absconding. He turned the key in the lock, opened the door and saw immediately the empty apartment and the open window.

'Where is she, master?' asked Apicula, puzzled and concerned.

Silus groaned. This time he had no leads. This time she had a huge head start. He would not find her. It was over. He slumped to the floor and put his head in his hands, staying in that position until Apicula offered him some bread and cheese and a cup of wine. He took them, then ate and drank numbly. He contemplated flight, but was hit by an overwhelming sense of ennui. What did it matter any more?

The little doll, Helen, was lying on the floor beneath the window. Tituria had obviously needed two hands to escape, and had left her beloved toy behind. Silus picked it up and turned it over in his hands. It smelt musty. The hair was ragged and sparse, and the colour of the dress had faded. She had obviously had the doll a long time.

Sergia had had a doll when she was younger, which she had treasured. Silus had cremated it with her. His eyes misted. When he had started to recover from the throes of grief at losing his family, he wondered how long it would take to be able to think about them without wanting to howl and scream and punch walls. He realised now that the answer was never. Nor did he want that feeling to end. Because that would mean he was forgetting them. And that would never happen.

He had failed to save them. And now he had failed to save Tituria, despite risking everything to do so. He let the doll fall from his hands. Then he noticed, in a corner beneath his table, a wax tablet. Wood-backed with two hinges in a diptych style. He frowned, then recalled he had picked it up from Titurius' tablinum. He had tossed it aside when he first arrived home with Tituria, and had not seen it or thought about it since. He picked it up, opened it, and saw there was writing engraved into the wax.

Silus was not an accomplished reader, but he had a basic grasp of letters, as was necessary for a scout who from time to time had to send and receive written messages. The words were small, but written in a neat, angular script which was perfectly legible. He read each letter individually, mouthing the words they spelt.

> *To Publius Septimius Geta Augustus, from your loyal servant Titurius,*
>
> *I bring you grave intelligence regarding your August brother and your honoured mother. It grieves me to inform you that my daughter spied them together in congress contrary to the will of the gods, given the Empress' relationship to both your father and your brother.*

I fear that the Emperor Antoninus discovered my daughter's knowledge of their illegal act, and that consequently my whole family is in mortal danger. I throw myself on your mercy, and beg that you extend your protection to my household in exchange for this intelligence I have now bequeathed to you, however distressing you find it. Encircling your Imperial cloak around my family will leave me for ever in your debt, and for ever your most devoted follower.

Silus closed the tablet and stared at the far wall. He felt as though a curtain had been ripped aside in his mind, revealing the mystery behind it, a mystery that had been obvious all along, with the benefit of hindsight. He suddenly recalled an experience in Britannia, in the Emperor's palace when he had overheard an act of passion behind closed doors. Could that have been Caracalla and the Empress? If he had waited longer for them to emerge, would it have been him in Tituria's place, privy to a fatally dangerous secret? The poor girl, what must she have been through? Did she realise it was she who had made her family targets, had caused their deaths?

What to do about it? He could go straight to Geta. Show the younger Augustus what his brother had been up to and let him use it to bring Caracalla down. What would that mean for Rome, if Silus effectively presented the opportunity to take the throne for himself to the less experienced, weaker brother? At that moment, he realised, he didn't really give a fuck about Rome. He only cared about Tituria and himself. But could he rely on Geta to free Tituria, in either ability or trustworthiness? Geta hated him personally, he knew, and Silus was strongly associated with Caracalla now, for right or wrong. He gripped the closed tablet tightly in his hands and pursed his lips, racked by indecision.

There was a loud hammering. Plaster flaked, and the wood cracked, only the bar stopping the door caving in.

'Open up in the name of the Emperor Antoninus!'

Silus looked at the door in alarm. Atius! You bastard!

He thrust the tablet at Apicula.

'Put this under your tunic. When they take me, go and hide somewhere safe. Take the rest of my money. They will probably come back for you. You need to disappear. Guard this tablet, and let no one else know of its existence. One day it might save your life. There is no more time. Do you understand?'

Apicula nodded, taking the tablet and stuffing it down the top of her tunic.

'Open up, Silus, or we'll break this flimsy door down.'

'I'm coming,' Silus shouted at the door.

'Be brave,' he whispered to Apicula.

Silus unbarred the door and opened it. Two uniformed Praetorian Guards stood there, faces stern and menacing. At the bottom of the stairs he could see half a dozen more. There was no real point in resisting. Where would he go anyway?

He stepped forward, and they laid rough hands on his shoulders, leading him down the steps, not paying any attention to his slave or his apartment. He gave one last pleading look to Apicula, hoping desperately she would be safe. Then he let himself be taken.

Chapter Fifteen

The holding cell in the Praetorian barracks was six foot square, with a bucket in the corner, sawdust on the floor and nothing else. There was no window, and the only light was filtered through a grille in the solid wooden door. Unlike the door in Silus' apartment, this one wouldn't come down with a good kick. It would need a hefty axe to get through it.

Silus' mouth was dry, but he didn't think it was from thirst. His stomach cramped and clenched, and he didn't think it was from hunger. He looked over to the bucket. It was malodourous from his having just used it, but he felt as though he might need to make use of it again soon.

He was scared, but he was also resigned to his fate. What hope was there for him? To go against the Emperor's explicit orders so egregiously. There would be no forgiveness. And anyway, what did he have to live for? No family. The girl he had tried to protect was gone, and would probably be dead soon. No career. If by some miracle he survived, he would surely be dishonourably dismissed from the military, and then what was he good for? Banditry?

There was one glimmer of hope, one small chance. The tablet. With the secret engraved into the wax in Titurius' hand. But how to make use of it? He shifted to scratch an itchy bite on his back against the wall, grimaced as his stomach spasmed and relaxed, and thought once more about using the bucket.

The door to the cell opened, and though the illumination was minimal, he could see it was Atius.

His friend stood there, his bulk taking up most of the doorway, looking at him.

Silus looked away.

'Silus.' Atius' voice was strained, choked. 'Silus, please. Speak to me.'

'I've got nothing to say to you.'

'You don't understand. You don't know everything.'

'Ha.' Silus' barking laugh was bitter and humourless. 'I know way too much, Atius. That's the problem.'

'Tituria is safe, for now. I found her and took her to Oclatinius.'

Silus' head dipped forward. He had not really expected the girl to survive, but confirmation that she was in her enemy's hands extinguished the last tiny spark inside him.

'Atius.' His tone was full of disappointment. 'Why?'

'I... I had to. He is our commander. I took an oath...'

'They will kill her, Atius.'

'No, they have no need. It was her father who Caracalla wanted dead, and the son so he didn't try to avenge him. The little girl doesn't matter.'

'Did Oclatinius tell you that?'

'No, but I assumed...' Atius trailed off.

'It was all about the girl, Atius. The whole thing. Her father, her family, her household, burning down her house. It was all because she saw something she shouldn't have. Even Daya died because of it.'

'Daya died because of you,' said Atius darkly.

'Yes. She died so an innocent child could live. I had to choose between them.'

'You chose the daughter of a stranger, who we had been ordered to kill, over our friend and comrade.'

'Yes, I did. Could you have done the same, Atius? I don't think you have the inner strength, despite your belief in the god of that Jewish cult, and all the mercy and forgiveness you say that he commands.'

For a moment the only sounds were dripping water and the scurry of an exploring rodent.

'I am to take you to Caracalla.'

Silus nodded. His friend was to take him to his execution. Maybe he would even be his executioner. He stood.

'Let's go.'

'Silus, what did she see?'

What did it matter now? thought Silus. He would soon be dead. Tituria would soon be dead. Maybe he shouldn't put his friend's life in jeopardy by passing the secret to him, but what did he owe Atius now? He was the reason Oclatinius had first become suspicious, the one who had betrayed Silus to the Emperor, the one who had given Tituria over to her death. He felt a surge of anger.

'She saw Caracalla and his stepmother fucking, Atius. That innocent little girl saw the ruler of the Empire committing incest, and the Emperor decreed she and her entire family had to die to keep the secret. And now myself too. Now you know it as well. Will the Emperor spare your life, knowing you have had a chance to talk to me?'

Atius looked thoughtful.

'Did they send you back for Apicula?'

Atius nodded reluctantly. 'I was to kill her as well. But she was gone. Issa too.'

Silus' eyes welled with tears that he would never see his little dog again. He hoped Apicula would look after her. He also hoped Apicula had found somewhere safe, to keep away from danger, and to live out her life in freedom and comfort. She deserved it.

'Shall we get this over with?'

'Silus, I'm sorry. I was angry. And I didn't know what to do...'

Silus extended his hands to be bound, but Atius shook his head. He stood aside, and Silus left the cell in front of him, his best and only friend in the entire world behind him, armed to cut him down if he tried to escape.

Silus squeezed his buttocks together, stupidly wishing he had used the bucket in the cell before leaving. If he died while he had diarrhoea, would he always have diarrhoea in the afterlife?

There were only four of them in the throne room – Caracalla with Oclatinius to his side, while Atius stood behind him. Caracalla looked thunderous, Oclatinius grave.

As soon as Silus had come to a standstill, Caracalla started to shout.

'You were one of my most trusted men, Silus. How dare you disobey me? How dare you place your Emperor in danger with your actions?' He rose from his throne, pointing his finger angrily at Silus.

'I told you I am not to be questioned. That there are reasons why I give orders that may seem distasteful. It is not your position to doubt them. And disobedience to your Emperor is treason. Punishable by death.'

'I know the reason,' said Silus quietly.

Caracalla's face dropped, and he visibly paled.

'You will address your Emperor as Augustus,' snapped Oclatinius.

'Why? I'm a dead man. What difference does it make now?'

'There are many ways to die, Silus, you know that. Some are much worse than others.'

Caracalla held up a hand to stop Oclatinius.

'What do you mean, you know the reason?'

'The little girl told me.'

Caracalla sat back on his throne and stared. Oclatinius looked at Caracalla, uncharacteristically uncertain. Atius stood very still, trying not to be noticed.

Caracalla held out a hand. 'Oclatinius, give me your knife.' Oclatinius passed his blade to the Emperor without hesitation. Caracalla took it, tested the edge with his thumb, a thoughtful look in his eye. Then he rose and advanced on Silus.

'Get on your knees,' he hissed. Silus did as he was told, sinking down, just wanting it to be over. Caracalla put a hand on Silus' shoulder, and pressed the tip of the blade to his throat. He leant forward and whispered in Silus' ear, 'I trusted you.'

Silus braced himself, looking forward to the ending. Whatever happened next couldn't be worse than this existence, even if it was just a long and final sleep.

And yet, despite this, he found himself whispering back, 'I have proof.'

Caracalla held still.

'I don't believe you,' he said.

'Then kill me.'

Silus closed his eyes and waited.

The pressure of the point at his throat disappeared. He opened his eyes again. Caracalla was looking down at him, the knife clutched so tight in his hand the tip was trembling.

'Oclatinius, Atius, leave us alone.'

Oclatinius stood and Atius turned, but Silus said, 'I told Atius, and I'm pretty sure Oclatinius knows already. He is very good at his job.'

Caracalla turned to Oclatinius, eyes wide. The head of the Arcani lowered his eyes submissively. He looked at Atius who was staring intently at his feet. Then he turned back to Silus.

'What proof?'

'A wax tablet. In Titurius' handwriting. Detailing exactly what his daughter saw. It is clear evidence of your crime, and also a clear motive for the death of Titurius and his household.'

'Where is this tablet now?'

'Safe.'

'Oclatinius. How was this missed?'

'My profound apologies, Augustus. I had no knowledge that this tablet even existed.'

'So where is it now?'

'No doubt in the safekeeping of his slave, but she absconded as soon as Silus was arrested, and I have not been able to locate her.'

Silus smiled to himself. Good girl.

Caracalla took a few faltering steps backwards and sank down onto his throne.

'I should cut you down, Silus. This betrayal is so deep, from someone I thought loyal. Have I not been kind to you? Have I not supported you in every way I can?'

It was true, Caracalla had favoured him, although Silus was sure he had not done so out of pure altruism, but for his own personal gain. Nevertheless, he did feel a pang of guilt at the hurt in his Emperor's eyes.

'Augustus, I never intended to betray you. But I couldn't allow another child to die. Not after losing my own to violence.'

Caracalla nodded. 'And what if I tell you that Tituria is my hostage, and I will kill her if you don't hand over the tablet to me?'

'What if I tell you that if anything happens to the girl, the wax tablet will be handed to Geta?' Answering the Emperor back like this might have been the bravest thing Silus had ever done, he realised, and his loose bowels nearly opened at the magnitude of what he had just said. Caracalla was staring at him in disbelief, and he could feel Atius' eyes burning holes in the back of his head. Only Oclatinius looked thoughtful.

'It seems we have an impasse,' he said. 'Both of you have the ability to do great harm to the other.'

Caracalla and Silus waited for the old man to say more. He considered, stroking his chin. 'Would an exchange be acceptable? The tablet in return for the girl?'

'No!' said Caracalla and Silus simultaneously.

'The girl was the original problem,' clarified Caracalla. 'If she is released, Domna and I will be in perpetual danger that one day she will open her mouth and spill our private secrets.'

'If I give him the tablet in exchange for the girl,' said Silus, 'he will destroy it, and then send assassins after the girl again. She will never be safe.'

Oclatinius nodded. 'Then there is only one solution. The Emperor must keep the girl, and Silus must keep the tablet.'

Silus and Caracalla both looked like they wanted to speak, but couldn't find the words.

'It works for me,' said Atius.

'Shut the fuck up,' snapped Silus.

'It's not enough,' said Caracalla.

'It is the deal on the table,' said Silus, still wondering at his boldness.

'I am the ruler of the civilised world. I command the legions. Senators and kings bow to me.' Caracalla's voice was rising. 'I will not be dictated to by a lowly assassin!'

Silus bowed his head, trying not to tremble at the anger in the Emperor's voice, only just holding himself together enough not to run from the room in terror.

'Augustus,' said Oclatinius tentatively. 'I believe that Silus could still be a loyal servant to you. He has served you well in the past, with bravery and skill. He can still be useful to your cause.'

Caracalla narrowed his eyes. 'Go on.'

'Maybe an oath of personal loyalty to you from Silus would renew the bond between you. You are losing no dignitas by forgiving Silus his crime – only the people in this room will ever know about it. Be mindful, Augustus, that the true struggle for the throne has yet to come. Silus could be an invaluable weapon in that fight.'

Silus remained on his knees, head bowed, waiting for Caracalla's answer with bated breath, a racing heart, and gurgling guts.

'Silus,' said Caracalla. 'The girl will remain my hostage. She will be taken to an island and guarded. She will be raised in good conditions, provided you remain loyal to me. You will keep this wax tablet, and will take steps to ensure it can never be found by anyone except yourself. And you will swear to obey me and serve me in all matters from here forward. Because if I discover the slightest disobedience, the slightest disloyalty, the girl will suffer. She will live, as assurance that the tablet will remain hidden. But her well-being will depend on you, Silus. Life can be made very unpleasant for a girl while still keeping her alive. And finally, if anything happens to me, if I die unexpectedly, of any cause, the girl dies too.'

A chill ran down Silus' spine. He didn't doubt that Caracalla meant every word. He knew how ruthless he could be in protecting and advancing his own position.

'Do we have an agreement?'

'Yes, Augustus,' said Silus. 'I ask one favour, prevailing on your mercy. May I see her before she is taken from Rome?'

Caracalla considered. 'Very well. Oclatinius. Administer the oath of loyalty.'

—

The small cubiculum was clean and freshly decorated, the walls painted with a fresco of fruit trees and songbirds. The bed was clean, with a soft mattress, and there was a table with a hand mirror and a selection of make-up, hairbrushes and jewellery.

When Silus entered, Tituria was holding the mirror in one hand and combing her hair with the other. It seemed at first a scene of normality for a young girl alone in her room, but as he watched, he realised she was combing the same strand of hair over and over, repetitively, though it was completely tangle free. In fact the over-grooming was so marked that the hair was beginning to come out.

'Tituria,' he said softly.

She turned, startled. When she saw who it was, she returned to the repetitive combing.

'I've brought Helen.' Silus held out the doll. He had gone back to his apartment to find it. The place had been ransacked of course, soldiers or others sent to look for the wax tablet in case he had been stupid enough to leave it in his apartment. But they had taken nothing of value, and the doll had remained where it had been discarded.

Tituria snatched the doll from him, then retreated to her bed. She sat, knees pulled up to her chest, the doll pressed to her face, and looked at him with eyes full of fear and hate.

Silus moved towards her but she shrank back, so he sat on the stool by the dressing table.

'I want you to know how sorry I am. For everything. I thought I was doing the right thing. For the Emperor, for the Empire. But when I saw you there, all I could see was my own daughter, who I miss dreadfully.'

Tituria said nothing, but her eyes were fixed intently on Silus.

'The woman who killed your father. I loved her, you know. And I chose you over her. It was the only way to save you.'

'You killed my mother,' said Tituria, speaking at last, her tone dead.

Silus nodded, and his eyes filled with tears. 'She died as bravely as any Roman matron, thinking of her children.'

For a moment, Tituria was silent. Then she said, voice so quiet Silus could barely hear, 'Was it all because of me?'

Silus grasped for words. Should he lie? Could he? But could the child live with the truth?

'It isn't your fault,' he said, the words sounding lame to his own ears. 'The Emperor did wrong, and you found out. He sent me to... to cover up. The sin is all his. Not yours. Not even mine.'

'You killed my mother. You saved my life. Should I be grateful to you, or hate you?'

'I don't know,' said Silus truthfully.

'What will happen to me now?'

'I made a deal with the Emperor to keep you alive and safe. But part of that deal was that I have to keep working for him. Doing things I don't want to do any more.'

'Should I thank you?'

'I don't know,' he said again. 'You are to go to an island somewhere. I don't know which one. You will be looked after.

You will live in grace and comfort. You will have everything you wish for.'

'Except my family.'

Silus bowed his head, and tears dropped from his overflowing orbits onto the mosaic floor.

'Silus,' said Tituria. 'I have nobody in this world who cares whether I live or die. Except you.'

She put her doll down and stood, then tentatively stepped forward. Silus looked at her, eyes full of sadness. Then she ran into his arms, and hugged him. The floodgates opened, and both of them wept, great sobs from the depths of their misery.

When they had both cried themselves out, Tituria stepped back.

'I will never forgive you for what you have done. But you are all I have. Silus, I don't want to go. Will you come with me?'

'I can't,' he said, desperately wishing he could do more to make amends. 'The Emperor has demanded my service in exchange for your safety.'

Tituria nodded. 'Maybe when your service is over, you could come and find me.'

'I will. I swear to all the gods, and on the shades of my family, that I will do everything in my power to come to you when I can.'

'Thank you. You can leave me now.'

Silus desperately wanted to hug her once more, but he knew the time had passed, that the outrushing of emotions was a momentary release that was unlikely to be repeated.

'You will have a fine family of your own one day,' said Silus. 'And when you do, I will be very proud.'

Tituria picked up the hand mirror and the comb, and turned away from him. He closed his eyes for a moment, then walked to the door.

Chapter Sixteen

Tituria looked out across the sea, watching the sun slowly sink beneath the horizon. She clutched her doll against her belly with both hands. She was bored. It had been months since she had been brought here, to the island of Lipari. She lived in a beautiful villa, with plenty of good food, fruits and sweet treats. There were baths on the island she could use. Her guardian, a Greek freedwoman called Myrtis, cared well for her, continued her education in Greek and Latin, in rhetoric and philosophy, and played games of ludus latrunculorum or knucklebones when she wanted.

Silus had seen her off at the docks at Ostia on the boat that was to take her to her prison. She was under no illusion that this was a gaol for her, and she felt she deserved it, for the tragedy she had brought on her family and herself. Silus had warned her to say nothing of what she had seen to anyone ever again. Not the guards on the island, not her tutor, not any visitors. He had made it clear that if she did, it would be the end of her.

Tituria had not been told where she was being taken, and Silus didn't know either, but the sea journey had lasted a few days, including stops at various ports along the coast.

The poor girl was bored. No children her age. No adults to eavesdrop on, although she doubted she would do that again even if the opportunity arose after what had come of her spying before. This was it. A golden cage, like that of a songbird kept for the amusement of a young woman.

She had heard that another family had been exiled here before, including a young girl. She had found some of her toys when she went exploring. She wondered what had happened to them.

She also wondered if Silus would ever come to visit. Whether he would be allowed, whether he could even find her. Whether he cared. She wasn't sure how she felt about seeing him again. But at least it would break the routine.

She sighed, bid Myrtis goodnight, and went to bed.

–

Myrtis clutched Tuccius tight, her arms and legs around him, as he groaned and bucked above her. He wasn't a particularly good lover – no real interest in her pleasure and far too quick, but she wasn't exactly spoilt for choice on this island, and the Praetorian Guard was the best she could get.

When he had finished, she stroked his hair while he lay slumped, breathing heavily, murmuring sweet words to him that she half-meant. When he rolled over onto his back, she put her head on his chest and stroked his arms. She liked his arms. They were strong with a nice covering of wiry hair.

'She was talking in her sleep again tonight, you know.'

'Uh-huh.'

Tuccius showed little interest. His eyes closed, his breath deepening as he drifted away.

'I could make it out a bit more clearly this time.'

'Right.'

'It was quite strange. She said, "It's one of the things I like about you. You can be tender one time, rough the next. Your father was only ever rough."'

Tuccius let out a short laugh. 'Odd dreams for one so young. Do you think she saw a couple of her slaves together? Sounds like one woman was sampling two generations.'

'And then she said, "How many times, Domna? Will you stop comparing me to him?"'

Tuccius propped himself up on one elbow, looked at his lover quizzically.

'Domna? She said, "Domna"? You're sure?'

'Fairly sure. She was asleep. Why? What do you think it means?'

'Probably nothing. Best to forget it.'

He turned over, and within moments started to snore. Myrtis looked at his back in annoyance, then closed her eyes and waited for sleep to come.

—

'It's a crap posting, that's for sure, Kyriakos,' said Tuccius, and took another deep draught of wine.

'How much longer are you here for?' asked Tuccius' drinking partner.

'Another nine months, curse my luck.'

'It doesn't sound that bad. You have nice weather, nice quarters, as much food and drink as you want, no danger, and a good woman to fuck.'

'Yeah, true, but she's a bit needy and demanding. And the other lads get jealous and give me a hard time. It's so boring. I'm a Praetorian Guard. I should be in Rome, looking after the Emperor, marching in parades, getting all the girls. Instead I'm a glorified babysitter. Your visits when you sail into harbour to bring supplies are all that keep me sane.'

'You never did tell me why you have to guard that little girl. Why is she so dangerous?'

'Apollo may know, but I don't. Although get this, Myrtis heard her talking in her sleep last night.'

'What did she say?'

'Something like, "You are a much better fuck than your father." And then, "Stop comparing me to my father, Domna."'

'"Domna"? Really? How interesting.'

'That's what I thought. I don't know how much to read into it, though. Anyway, keep it to yourself, right? I don't want to get into any trouble.'

'Of course.'

286

'When do you need to leave?'

'We'll sail with the morning tide. Enough time to get a bit of drinking done. It's a long way back to Ostia.'

–

Domna looked around the triclinium at her dinner-party guests. She loved being surrounded by intellectuals, although there were times when they could be argumentative and tedious, and in those moments her mind drifted to thoughts of Caracalla: his broad, hairy chest and thick muscular thighs.

At that moment, Ulpianus was holding forth about the upcoming Saturnalia celebrations. While it was tradition that masters should serve their slaves during the festival, this was rarely followed beyond a token display. After all, the festival lasted six days. Which master would be prepared to be a slave for that long? Ulpianus, however, argued that all men are equal, except the Emperor of course, which was just as well, since Geta was looking on. He argued that the behaviour exhibited in the Saturnalia should be extended throughout the year – free speech to be able to criticise their masters, wearing clothes that reduced the distinction between master and slave, rich and poor.

Papinianus laughed at the idea. 'You sound dangerously like a follower of the Christos cult,' he said. 'At least you agree that our Emperor here is above this strange equality you are talking of.'

Domna was glad that Caracalla wasn't there. He had become less and less tolerant of Geta being referred to as Emperor in his presence. But of course, there was no way Caracalla would attend a meal at which Geta was a guest, and vice versa. Their relations had become so low that they never spoke or were ever found in each other's company.

'You will be telling us that women and men are equal next,' commented Philostratus, the sophist, and this earned a chuckle from around the table.

'Hippocrates taught us that, according to their humours, women are physiologically cold and wet, where men are dry and warm,' said Galen. 'It leads to many of their problems.'

'Do tell me more,' said Domna, and Galen failed to notice the acid bite in her tone.

'Their character makes them prone to putrefaction of the humours, and this causes the uterus to become sick, leading to all the symptoms of hysterical passion. This is of course a particular problem in those that abstain from sexual intercourse, widows and virgins and the like, since the sexual act widens the woman's canals and allows cleansing of the body. If this doesn't happen, the uterus produces toxic fumes and migrates around the body, causing symptoms of anxiety, tremors, a sense of suffocation and paralysis.'

'It may have escaped your notice, physician,' said Domna coldly, 'that I am a widow. Do I display any of the symptoms you suggest? Do I need my canals widening?'

'No, no, Domna. You are the picture of health. Physiology is an inexact science. But that you remain hale while clearly abstaining from male relations is a puzzle. Maybe the undoubted prowess of your much missed husband has protected you thus far. But for your health, there will come a time when you should remarry.'

'Physician, you are impertinent. Let us change the subject. Dio Cassius, tell us how progresses your book?'

It was a topic that the historian could talk about at great length, and so the conversation veered away from an increasingly uncomfortable discussion. Domna took a sip of wine while Dio Cassius droned on about the war between Pompey and Caesar, and her thoughts turned back to Caracalla's chest.

She didn't notice Geta looking at her thoughtfully.

–

'Augustus, I have heard some news that will be of interest to you.'

Geta looked up from his tablet.

'Bek, do you have any idea what supplying the army with boots costs every year?'

'No, Augustus.'

'I'm willing to bet my brother doesn't either. All he cares about is glory on the battlefield. What sort of Emperor would he make?'

'A bad one, Augustus.'

'Exactly. Rome needs someone to rule it wisely, take care of its laws and its finances, not just its legions.'

'Yes, Augustus.'

'What were you saying?'

'I received some information, Augustus.'

'Well?'

'You... may not like it. And it is only hearsay, at this stage.'

'Go on.'

Bek looked at Festus doubtfully. Festus stood on Geta's left side, with Aper on his right. Festus was around fifty years old, completely bald, with a thin face and piercing blue eyes. His official titles were Commander of the Sacred Bedchamber and Keeper of the Emperor's Daily Record Book, but his real role involved bullying senators and military officers with physical threats and blackmail to keep them in line. For these purposes he employed his own set of spies and enforcers. Bek reported to Aper, but feared Festus and didn't trust him.

'You may speak freely in front of these men,' said Geta impatiently.

'Yes, Augustus. Some captain on the docks was telling stories while he was in the tavern. One of my men heard what he said from another. We tried to question the captain himself, but he had already set sail.'

'And? What was he saying?'

'He had a voyage to take supplies to where a young girl is being held captive on an island. By Praetorians.'

'Praetorians? Who is she?'

'I don't know, Augustus, nor where she is being held. But it was what she said that was most interesting. She speaks in her sleep. She said... Augustus, you might find this upsetting.'

'Spit it out, spy.'

'Augustus, she said in her sleep, "You make love better than your father." And then said, "Stop comparing me to my father, Domna."'

Geta's brow furrowed in confusion.

'Father? Domna? What does it mean?'

'It's very speculative, Augustus. But she hasn't been exiled by you, so in some way she must have wronged your brother, as she is guarded by a Praetorian. And if she is dreaming of some trauma she has witnessed for real, then maybe...'

Geta's eyes widened. 'Are you saying... are you implying that she witnessed my brother and my mother in bed together?'

'It is a possibility, Augustus. I'm sorry.'

Festus and Aper exchanged glances. Geta stared into space. 'My mother and my brother. Surely not. And yet. All those times Mother took his side instead of mine, her real son. And then there are Galen's words – if my mother is not sexually active, why is she not displaying signs of hysteria?'

'I am not a physician, Augustus,' said Bek.

'Can we prove it, Bek?'

'No, Augustus. It has no more status than a rumour, easily denied and dismissed as slander.'

'I will not let him get away with this. How long has it been going on? Since before Father died?'

'I have no way of knowing, Augustus. It may not even be true.'

'I believe it is. And it will not stand. That he refuses to acknowledge me as his equal is bad enough. But that he defiles my mother, his own stepmother...'

Bek kept his face impassive.

'Aper, you have agents in his part of the palace?'

'Of course, Augustus.'

'Then it will be poison. It is fitting for his toxic character. Do it at the feast on the last day of the Saturnalia. It is time. He must die.'

—

These days, Caracalla found the Saturnalia feast farcical, and paid the merest lip service to its traditions. He had his secretary arrange gifts for the whole Imperial household, and he put in a brief appearance at the public banquet that the Senate arranged for the population of Rome. But when it came to serving slaves himself, he restricted this to a token where he poured a cup of wine for the Saturnalis princeps, who was master of ceremonies at the banquet. He took more seriously the offerings to Saturn, and attended the sacrifice at the god's temple, although his allegiance was much stronger to eastern gods such as Serapis. But once his public duties were done, he retired to his part of the palace for a private meal with a few close friends.

It was a marked contrast to his childhood love of the celebration, when he had taken the gifts from his father – dice, writing tablets, a hunting knife – and passed them on to his tutors and to his clients. But he had grown up, and adulthood had a tendency to leach away childish joys, especially when you grew up in the Imperial family.

Domna was present, sitting on his right. It was difficult for her to choose whether to visit Caracalla or Geta on this important occasion, but she had compromised by attending Geta at lunchtime and Caracalla in the evening. Papinianus, Marcellus, Julius Avitus, Dioga, and even Cilo were present. Cilo's face was badly scarred, the marks from the stitches that had reattached the flap of skin on one cheek and sewed up the gash on the other still visible, and it seemed to give him some pain when he ate. Marcellus' wife Julia Soaemias, Julia Domna's niece, was beside her husband, to Caracalla's discomfort. Throughout the feast she fired winks and suggestive smiles in his direction, and he could feel the frostiness radiating off Domna when she noticed.

Jesters, fools and acrobats were the main entertainment for this Saturnalia feast, and while Caracalla clapped at appropriate moments, his heart wasn't in it. Maybe it was the long nights of the midwinter that were depressing his spirit, or the stalemate with his brother and the frustration of his ambitions. Whatever it was, he just felt tired, and wanted to retire to bed with Domna.

He flicked his fingers for some mulled wine that one of the serving slaves was bringing round. He passed it to his taster first, who sipped it, swilled it around his mouth, then passed it back with a nod. A taster was a major inconvenience when feasting, but he had employed one since his father's death, and he was sure Geta did the same. It was only prudent.

He took a sip of the spiced wine himself, but it was both strong and hot, and he clicked his fingers for it to be watered. A nearby slave poured cold water from a jug into his silver cup, and he swirled it around, then raised it to his lips.

To his surprise, a hand on his arm prevented him from drinking. He looked around to see Oclatinius. Damn, that man was quiet. How had Caracalla not seen him come up behind him?

'What is it, Oclatinius?'

'Augustus, I have just had some intelligence of a possible threat to your life.'

Caracalla frowned and looked around. The men at the banquet were loyal, he was sure, and there was a strong Praetorian presence both inside and outside the dining hall.

'Are you sure?'

'It came from a reliable source in... a rival's employ. But it is easily proved. You!' Oclatinius gestured to the slave who had poured the cold water into Caracalla's cup. 'Come here.'

The slave looked suddenly very pale, but he walked over slowly. 'Master?'

'That water in your jug, which you just used to cool the Augustus' wine. Drink it.'

'Master, I don't... I can't...'

Oclatinius took the jug from the slave's unresisting hands. He proffered it to him, close to his lips, and the slave shrank back.

'Guards, seize him.'

Praetorians grabbed the slave, and at Oclatinius' instruction, pushed him to the ground and pinned him there, one guard holding each limb firmly. Oclatinius advanced on him, bent over and pinched the slave's nose shut. When he opened his mouth to breathe, Oclatinius poured in the water from the jug. The slave struggled and spat and coughed, but lying on his back, he couldn't help but swallow as Oclatinius continued to pour.

When the jug was empty, he gestured to the guards to let the slave go. He got to his feet, looked around wildly, then ran for the door. Praetorians barred his way. He turned back to Oclatinius. 'Please, Master. Let me see a physician. I had no choice. They said I could see my son again if I did what they said.'

'Who gave you the order?' asked Oclatinius coldly. 'Who supplied the poison?'

'Please, I can't say, they will—'

He got no further. In front of the horrified and fascinated guests, his legs abruptly gave way. He pitched onto his hands and knees, and started to salivate profusely, his mouth spewing foam. He tipped over onto his side, and his body was racked by convulsions, forceful jerks of every limb, jaw chattering, eyes wide with dilated pupils. A strong ammoniacal smell of urine flooded the room as his bladder voided. Then a few more jerks and twitches and he lay still.

The room was silent, stunned. No one moved except Oclatinius, who remained composed.

'Remove this body,' he ordered two guards, and seeming to snap out of a trance, they came to attention and dragged the dead slave away.

Caracalla pointed a trembling finger at the body. 'That was meant for me?' he asked in a shaky voice.

'I'm afraid so, Augustus.'

'My brother?'

Oclatinius pursed his lips.

Caracalla looked at the door that the slave had been pulled through. He rose to his feet, putting one hand on the couch to steady himself. His voice became tight with anger. 'Papinianus, double the guard on my quarters tonight. Attend me at dawn tomorrow morning. You too, Domna. And you, Oclatinius. I will retire now.' He pulled his toga tightly around him, and swept out, leaving a room full of guests suddenly terrified of what the next day would bring.

Chapter Seventeen

'He must die. I cannot give him more chances. I cannot forgive him for this.' Caracalla was calm and fully in control, but his tone was icy. He sat, back straight, the only sign of tension his hands gripping the arms of the throne.

'Please, Antoninus,' said Domna. 'He is my son. Have mercy.'

'At what cost? To what end? So he can try to kill me again?'

'Do we know for sure that Geta was responsible for this outrage?' asked Papinianus. 'Without wishing to cause offence, Augustus, there are numerous people who might wish you dead. Just by virtue of your position. Maybe adherents of Geta, acting without his knowledge. Or maybe someone else with their own agenda. Maybe even a supporter of the Greens. An admirer of Euprepes...'

Caracalla looked to Oclatinius. 'Well?'

'My intelligence is solid, Augustus. The order came from Geta himself.'

'Then can anyone here tell me why I should spare him?'

His Medusa-like gaze swept the three standing before him. Oclatinius' expression was inscrutable. Papinianus looked grim, while Domna was clearly distraught. She stepped forward and put a hand lightly on his forearm.

'I went to see him last night, Antoninus.'

Caracalla's face darkened even further. 'You did what?'

'I had to. This will end with one of you dead, and I couldn't bear it.'

'I've tried, Julia,' he said, voice softening marginally. 'You know I have. But how can I let this pass?'

'Listen to me. He has agreed to a peace conference.'

'A what?'

'I talked to him. Made him see that it doesn't have to be this way. He is proud, Antoninus, like you. He hates the idea of being second best for the rest of his life. Yes, you are co-Emperors, but he knows that you are the older, the one the military look up to, and let's face it, you are the more forceful of the two of you. You are the one most likely to get your way. If you could find a way to rule together, with both of you retaining your auctoritas, your dignitas and gravitas...'

'There is no such way. I am the senior Augustus, and he should defer to me.'

'But if you made some show of compromise. This could be a turning point. If you just talk to each other. After all, you are brothers. You have a bond of blood. You should be able to trust each other.'

'Oclatinius, how easy would it be to assassinate Geta?'

'Give the order and he will be dead before sundown, Augustus.'

'No, please,' gasped Domna.

'Papinianus. Your opinion?'

Papinianus hesitated, pressed his palms together and touched his forefingers to his lips as he considered. 'Augustus,' he said slowly. 'You have been grievously wronged. You have every right to anger, every right to wish for justice and retribution. But it is my duty to counsel you, paying regard to two imperatives – your well-being, and the well-being of Rome. And it may be that in this regard those two imperatives are aligned.'

Caracalla frowned, but indicated that he should continue.

Papinianus gathered his thoughts, then spoke again. 'Rome faces unprecedented challenges at this time. There is pressure on its borders like never before. Subduing the north of Britannia took three years and the attention of three Augusti. Meanwhile the Alemanni and other Germanic tribes are restless. The civil war in Parthia has destabilised Armenia and the region may require intervention in strength in the near future. Yet our manpower has never fully recovered from the Plague of Galen that ended three decades ago, and our economy is feeling the strain of funding the military we need to keep the Empire safe. We can only devalue the currency for so long before it starts to have a serious effect.'

'I am fully aware of the threats the Empire faces, Papinianus. That is why it needs a strong leader in sole charge.'

'What if the job is too much for any one man?' He held up a placating hand as Caracalla opened his mouth in anger. 'Hear me out, please, Augustus. Who would not acknowledge Marcus Aurelius as one of our greatest ever Emperors? And yet he ruled the Empire with his brother Lucius Verus, dividing responsibility so they could together face down threats such as the plague and the Marcomanni and Quadi invasions. Maybe Rome would benefit from two strong leaders, to face its challenges and bring it even further glory. And if Geta ruled in Rome, you could concentrate on the military, which is your main interest and your main strength. Let Geta worry about grain supplies and the economy while you bring Rome victory against the barbarians.'

Caracalla looked uncertain. 'We talked about dividing the Empire before. The Augusta persuaded us against it, and it has brought us to this moment.' He gave Domna a reproachful glare, and she flushed and looked down.

'I am not proposing to divide the rule of the Empire geographically, but in terms of spheres of responsibility.'

'Would Geta accept this? Would he allow me this degree of glory? Wouldn't he fear that I would ultimately eclipse him?'

'It would be better than he has now, if you were to acknowledge him as fully your equal, and swear an oath to rule in harmony with him.'

Caracalla looked up, as his mind raced with possibilities. Though his personal sense of outrage demanded justice and revenge, Papinianus spoke sense. He had no real interest in the minutiae of rule. He was desperate to be away with the legions, emulating his hero Alexander, expanding the borders and defeating the barbarians. But there was a risk to being absent from Rome – that a usurper might try to seize power. Having his brother ruling in the city should prevent that. If only he could trust him.

'Please, Antoninus,' said Domna. 'Meet him. Hear what he has to say.'

'I don't know.' Caracalla was torn, the pride in his heart warring with the sense in his head.

'There is another issue, Augustus, if I may,' said Oclatinius.

'What is it?'

'The loyalty of the Praetorians.'

Caracalla scowled, then glared at Papinianus.

'Is it suspect?'

'No, Augustus,' protested Papinianus.

'Yes, Augustus,' said Oclatinius.

'You dare question my allegiance to the Emperor?'

'Not you, prefect. The men themselves. They know there is conflict between you and your brother. They don't like it. And while they respect you most for your military prowess and your willingness to share their hardships, they have a love for your brother based on his youth and his close resemblance to your father, whom they adored. And of course, Papinianus' co-prefect Laetus is questionable, to say the least.'

'What are you saying?' asked Caracalla.

'If it came to open conflict between yourself and your brother, I could not guarantee which side the Praetorians would choose.'

'And if Geta was dead?'

'Then I couldn't guarantee that they would follow you.'

Caracalla stared at him. 'But... the men love me!'

'They do, Augustus. But perhaps it is prudent not to test the depth of their love.'

Caracalla slumped back into his throne, shaking his head. 'If we had reached the end of all possibility of compromise, I would test their love to destruction. But I can't take the final step without one last chance at reconciliation. I must try just one more time to follow father's last advice to Geta and myself.'

'"Live with each other in harmony. Enrich the soldiers. And damn the rest,"' quoted Domna.

Caracalla nodded. 'What does he propose?'

'A family meeting. Just you, me and him. No guards. No attendants. No weapons. No voices to whisper in your ears, to manipulate or provoke. Just the wife and sons of Severus, in a room alone.'

'Are you serious? When he has tried to kill me? How do I know it isn't another plot against my life, luring me into a trap?'

'He wouldn't use me like that,' said Domna with certainty. 'He loves and respects me too much. I believe this is a genuine offer. One last chance to avoid bloodshed and have peace.'

Caracalla hesitated, his brow creased with deep furrows as his mistrust of his brother warred with his affection for his stepmother.

'Please, Antoninus. For me.'

Caracalla shook his head. Achilles had his heel. He had Domna.

'Very well. Tell him I agree.'

–

Silus shuffled disconsolately down the alleyway. He kicked at a chicken that got too close while on its hunt for worms in the gutter muck, and it squawked and leapt into the air with a flutter of wings and flurry of feathers. It landed a few feet away and looked at him reproachfully before continuing to peck in the dirt.

He was trapped now. If what he had done was to mean anything – killing Daya, defying Caracalla – then he had to follow through and be the Emperor's loyal servant, or Tituria would suffer for it. And how many others would die at his hand to keep Tituria safe? He needed to harden his heart, turn himself into a monster, to protect this girl that he hardly knew, but had decided to care about. Whom he had promised to visit, as though she was a favoured niece that he would pop over to see for a vacation.

It was just past dusk, and the wheeled vehicles were once more allowed into the city. He stepped aside and breathed in to allow a donkey cart laden with grain, almost as wide as the alley, to squeeze past. He was on his way to meet Atius. They were reconciled, but their relationship was strained now. Both of them had done things the other found hard to forgive – Silus in killing Daya, Atius in betraying Silus. They hoped that gambling and drinking would help put it behind them. It hadn't yet, but they kept trying.

Suddenly everything went dark, and his face was covered with linen material that made it hard to breathe. He reached up instinctively to clear his vision, but his wrists were grasped by strong hands and pulled behind him. Rags were stuffed into his mouth through the material, making him gag. His nostrils flared as he struggled to breathe through his nose, partially blocked by the linen, and panic rose in him. He started to flail, but a kick to the back of his knees sent him stumbling to the ground. In moments, his ankles were tied too. He felt himself lifted, then tossed onto the back of a cart. He found he was rolling from side to side as someone yelled for the mule or ox pulling the cart to get moving. He wriggled, flapping like a fresh-caught fish in the bottom of a boat, until someone punched him in the side of the face and told him to stay still.

The journey wasn't long, and he lay quiescent as his mind raced. Had Caracalla changed his mind? Surely not. The deal was favourable to the Emperor. He was in no danger if he stuck to the terms, but he could be if something happened to Silus. At least, Silus was fairly sure he had convinced Caracalla of that. The reality was that if Silus died, Apicula would probably stay hidden, and the tablet would never surface. And even if he was well, he actually had no idea where Apicula had disappeared to.

But if it wasn't Caracalla, who could it be? Random muggers? A fan of Euprepes, a Green?

The cart trundled uphill, and Silus had a vague sense that they were ascending the Palatine, but neither his sense of direction while blindfolded nor his mental map of Rome were sufficient for him to be more precise. They arrived at their destination, and Silus was hoisted off the back of the cart and carried like a dead body, someone with hands under his shoulders, someone holding his ankles. He considered struggling or shouting, but decided it would only earn him punishment, with no realistic chance of reward, so he stayed compliant and allowed himself to be taken inside a building.

Once he was off the streets, his ankles were untied and he was allowed to stand on his own two feet. He was propelled forwards with shoves in his back down several long corridors, and two flights of stairs, bumping his face or shoulders painfully into walls as he went, until he heard a heavy door opening, and was dragged into a room. His hands were untied, then manacles were clamped around his wrists. He tugged on them, and found that he was chained to the wall behind him. Then the linen bag was pulled from his head and he found himself staring into the olive-skinned face of Bek.

'You?' said Silus. 'What the fuck is going on?'

'That's what your friends asked,' laughed Bek.

Silus looked around him. To his left was Atius, and to his right was Oclatinius, both of them similarly manacled to the wall. Oclatinius looked stony-faced. Atius gave a half-smile and an apologetic shrug. Two men with no uniforms but with long knives at their belts stood behind Bek, one tall and skinny with a pox-scarred face, the other shorter and wider with a patchy beard.

'There goes your hope of rescue, eh?' Bek laughed and left the room, and the two guards followed him, slamming the door shut and barring it behind them.

Silus turned to his commander and his friend, incredulous.

'Jupiter. What is this?'

'We have been captured, Silus,' said Oclatinius simply. 'By adherents of the Emperor Geta.'

'How? Why?'

'For the how, I was snatched from the bathhouse, naked and unarmed, in the middle of a rather therapeutic massage. Whereas young Atius here was snatched, naked and unarmed, from a whorehouse in the Subura. As for the why, I expect we will find out more soon.'

'But you must know, Oclatinius. You know everything that happens in the city.'

'I like to give that appearance, yes. And I have my suspicions. It might help you to know that two nights ago, Geta made an attempt on the Emperor Caracalla's life. And that tomorrow, there is due to be a peace conference between the two of them, hosted by the Empress.'

'Then why take this action? Why now?'

'Patience, Silus. I'm sure it will all become apparent. Now I suggest you get some rest and gather your strength. I have a feeling that we have something of an ordeal to face.'

–

As Silus had become accustomed to, Oclatinius was right. They were woken in the night by the door banging wide open. Their cell was windowless, and when the door had closed the only light filtered through cracks in the planks and under the gap between the door and tiled floor. Opening the door seemed to flood the cell with the light of oil lamps from the hallway beyond, making him blink, though in reality it was not bright. Bek walked in with the two guards and, without preamble, walked up to Silus and punched him in the gut. The guards followed suit, as the tall, pox-scarred one made a beeline for Oclatinius, and the shorter taking Atius, immediately laying about them with punches and kicks to the head and body.

After a few moments of beatings carried out wordlessly, their three captors left and the door slammed shut. The room held only the noise of their wheezy breathing, and groans.

Silus spat a bloody gob onto the floor. One tooth felt loose, but he couldn't reach his mouth with his chained hands to check. 'What the fuck was that about?'

'Just softening us up,' said Oclatinius. 'The questions will come.'

'I hope they are on a subject I know something about, like beer or girls. If they ask me about Greek plays, I'm screwed.' Atius' words were slurred, spoken through a thick lip, and Silus wondered why Oclatinius wasn't showing more signs of pain and injury. But then, he was a tough old bastard.

Silus realised he was going to need a piss before the night was out, and decided he might as well get on with it. He certainly didn't want to be beaten with a full bladder. Not only would it hurt, but there was a risk the wrong blow could rupture it, with fatal consequences. He opened his legs to avoid soiling his tunic and let the stream go. It pooled at his feet, then trickled down the slight incline of the floor towards Atius.

His friend yelped when the tepid liquid touched his toes. 'Silus, you little shit, when I get out of here, I'm going to piss all over you.'

'Atius,' said Oclatinius wearily. 'You would be better working out how we get out of this, rather than planning your celebrations.'

Silus chuckled despite himself. His mind went back to another time in captivity, in the depths of Caledonia, with Atius and their old commander. It was a strange contrast. Back then he was held by enemy barbarians who wished to sacrifice him to their gods in the middle of hostile territory. Now he was being held by Romans, in the middle of the capital of the Empire, and the gods knew why, although it was something to do with the complex politics of Rome. His position was no less hopeless than when he was captive in Caledonia, and yet the presence of Oclatinius was strangely reassuring. The man always had something up his sleeve.

At that moment, though, shackled and imprisoned with his only allies in the city, he couldn't see what that could be.

'Where are we?' he asked.

'In a holding cell in one of the vigiles stations,' said Oclatinius. 'Where the guards are used to the prisoners screaming and shouting for help.'

Atius started to sing a song about Christos and his disciples. Silus closed his eyes and tuned it out.

—

They were beaten twice more, with no questioning, no commentary. Just blows that crunched and smacked and bruised, and left them panting and moaning and bleeding. Time passed, but it was impossible to tell how much.

The next time the door opened, Silus braced himself for more, while wondering how much he could take. If they moved on to serious torture rather than just beating, with flame or knife or hammer, he thought he would break, although at that moment he had no indication what he could offer them to make it stop.

But this time, Bek and the two guards were accompanied by another man. Silus squinted at him in the dim light, through swollen eyelids.

'Augustus,' said Oclatinius. 'I'm sorry not to be able to greet you more formally.'

'There's no need, Oclatinius,' said Geta. 'I'm sorry you find yourself in such a predicament.'

'Your sympathy is appreciated, Augustus, though I'm not sure how or why I have found myself in this situation.'

'I suspect that will all become clear. But in the meantime, I would like the answers to some questions, if you would be so kind.'

'I will assist as best I can, Augustus, as will my men here.'

'Excellent. That will prevent the need for unpleasantness. Or at least, unnecessarily drawn-out unpleasantness.'

'Why don't you just say what you mean?' Silus was tired, hurting, and moving beyond fear to anger. He felt no great love towards Caracalla at this time, but this man, Caracalla's brother, had been a stone in his boot from the first time he met him. From the time he had arranged the release of Maglorix, the murderer of Silus' family, for some political prisoner exchange, to their arrest on returning from their last mission in Caledonia, to his situation now, Silus' allegiance to Caracalla had put him at odds with Geta. 'What is this unpleasantness shit? You are talking about torturing and killing. Be a man and stop hiding behind weaselly words.'

'Silus...' Oclatinius' voice held a note of gentle admonishment. 'You are addressing one of our Emperors. You should really show more respect.'

'I see nothing to respect.'

Bek stepped forward and drove his fist into Silus' midriff, knocking all the air out of him, leaving him struggling for breath and incapable of speech.

'Silus,' said Geta. 'The one who killed Euprepes. There was a real hero. A fearless champion of the Circus. Cut down in his old age by a coward.'

'Euprepes should have known how dangerous it can be to meddle in politics or to cross the Emperor Antoninus,' said Oclatinius. 'It was a salutary warning that should have been taken seriously by all.'

Bek moved towards Oclatinius, fist back, but Geta stopped him. 'Wait. I want to ask the old man some questions. I don't want him broken. Not yet.'

Then he said, 'Tell me about Titurius.'

Silus' heart sank. Why was Geta asking about him? Did it mean Tituria was in danger?

'Ah, the late senator,' said Oclatinius regretfully. 'What would you like to know?'

'Why don't we start with how he died.'

'I understand he died in a fire that consumed his domus, along with his entire household. Tragic.'

'How did the fire start?'

'I don't believe the vigiles could determine a cause.'

'And his entire family died?'

'I believe so.'

'Every one? Because soon after the fire, a young noble girl appeared on a remote island, seemingly imprisoned and under guard by Praetorians.'

'Really? Your information is better than mine, Augustus.'

'And there are rumours that this young girl has seen something unpleasant. Something unsavoury that concerns my mother and my brother. Have you heard such rumours?'

'I have not, Augustus.'

Geta let out a short laugh. 'I find that hard to believe. A spymaster with your ability and resources.'

'You flatter me, Augustus. I am a simple servant of the Senate and people of Rome.'

Geta shook his head. 'Let me be blunt with you, Oclatinius. You are a talented man, and I would like to have your service. But you are also loyal. I don't expect you to serve me while you are still bound to my brother. That situation is about to change, though.'

'Oh?'

'After tomorrow, you will be released from your oath to my brother.'

'That would only be possible if he was dead, Augustus.'

'Precisely.'

Oclatinius thought for a moment. 'The peace meeting?'

Geta smiled. 'Just myself, my mother and my brother. And half a dozen of my men outside the chamber, ready to break in and finish him.'

Silus' mind whirled. With Caracalla dead, where would that leave him? Released from the man he was finding it increasingly difficult to serve. But Tituria? If Caracalla died, she would be killed immediately. It was Caracalla's protection against Silus ending their agreement with assassination. He yanked at his chains, but they were solid, tight on his wrists and firmly attached to the stone wall. Geta saw him testing his bonds and smiled.

'Ah, you fear for my brother, Silus? Such loyalty is commendable. I am half-minded to demand such loyalty to me. But you have defied and annoyed me far too much. For that, you are to die, along with your fool of a friend.

'Now, Oclatinius, will you aid me? When my brother is dead, I need to be able to give a good reason to the soldiers and the populace, to gain their approval for the deed. Confirmation from you that my brother and my mother were engaged in foul and unnatural acts together would give me all the justification that I need. So, tell me what Tituria's daughter saw, and swear to me that you will testify on oath about the disgusting relationship between Antoninus and Domna.'

'You are prepared to sacrifice your mother's reputation as well as your brother's life, Augustus?' asked Oclatinius.

'You don't seem to understand, Oclatinius. I will sacrifice anything to have the throne to myself.'

Oclatinius gave a short nod. 'Very well. When Antoninus is dead, I will testify that he was engaged in unnatural relations with your mother, and I will pledge my loyalty to you.'

'I have your oath?'

'On the shades of the departed, and the gods of the underworld.'

Geta smiled. 'How easily you are turned, Oclatinius. I thought you would be cursing my naming and swearing revenge if I hurt a hair on Antoninus' head.'

Oclatinius shrugged. 'I am a servant of the Emperor. Whoever he may be.'

'It's late,' said Geta. 'I must depart soon for the meeting. And ready myself for the beginning of my sole rule. Oclatinius, you have a short while to say goodbye to your two subordinates here. After the deed is done, we will meet, and you will tell me how you can be of service to me.' Geta gave Silus a hard stare. 'Goodbye, Silus. We won't meet again.'

He exited the cell with Bek and the two guards, leaving Silus, Atius and Oclatinius alone in the near darkness. Silus searched for words, but it was Atius who spoke first.

'Curse you to hell, Oclatinius, you fucking coward.'

Oclatinius said nothing, offered no defence, and Atius continued, his voice loud in his fury. 'You have served Caracalla, been his trusted friend. And I have served you with dedication Silus too, as best his conscience allowed. And you are to cast us all aside for convenience. For your own ambition. To save your own skin. I respected you, I thought you were better...' He broke off, his voice choking with emotion.

Silus stared into the darkness. He felt completely helpless. Bek would be back soon, with those guards, to kill Atius and himself. When Caracalla was dead, the Praetorians would kill Tituria. Of those he had the slightest care for, only Apicula and Issa would survive. He supposed it was for the best that he was to go now. He had had enough. The killing. The death that followed him everywhere. It was time for him to join his family.

An indeterminate amount of time passed before the door opened again, and Bek entered with the two guards. He looked doleful, head bowed. Once in the cell, the tall thin guard lit an oil lamp, and the other closed the door.

'This gives me no pleasure,' said Bek. 'It saddens me more than you know when Roman is forced to kill Roman. I wish this conflict between the two Emperors had ended peacefully. But it wasn't to be.'

'If you're so sad, why don't you let us go?' said Atius.

'Would you, in my position?'

Atius opened his mouth, but clearly couldn't think of a suitable retort.

'Just do it,' said Silus. 'Don't drag it out.'

Bek looked at him for a long moment, then nodded. He gestured to the two guards, who drew short swords from their scabbards.

'Kill those two,' said Bek. 'The old man is not to be touched.'

The two guards each took a step forward. The one before Silus was the shorter, wider man with the patchy beard. He looked into Silus' eyes and drew his sword back, preparing to plunge it deep. Silus kept his eyes locked on his executioner, gritting his teeth and preparing himself for the pain.

The sword struck deep, skewering through skin, through abdominal muscle, through guts, severing vessels and lacerating visci. Silus stared in shock at the sword, buried to the hilt.

The executioner's eyes were wide, and he grasped the sword, then collapsed to his knees with a guttural groan, and then to the floor.

The speed, the gloom and the shock meant it took Silus a moment to realise that the tall, skinny guard had run the other through from side to side. Even as his mind tried to process what his eyes had just seen, the guard was tugging his sword free, rounding on Bek.

Bek had frozen for the briefest of moments before reacting. He pulled his knife from his belt and lunged at the guard. The guard jumped backwards, and as he did so the sword came free from his dead colleague with a wet sucking sound.

Bek followed up his attack with a series of swipes with his blade, quick cuts designed to incapacitate and make for an easy kill. But the guard had a weapon with a longer reach, and he was able to keep Bek at arm's length.

Bek clearly had the greater skill, and as they circled, feinted and parried, Bek's superior weaponcraft started to show. Nicks and cuts appeared on the guard's forearms, upper arms and chest, making him bleed, making it harder to wield his heavier weapon. The smallness of the cell made it difficult for him to use the longer blade to its full advantage too, with a full swing or an overhead cleave impossible. The short sword was best used for stabbing, but Bek was agile, and cunning, keeping out of the reach of the guard, and of Silus and Atius, who strained at their chains and shouted encouragement to the guard who had unexpectedly come to their aid.

But Bek had discounted Oclatinius. The old man, with the bowed back, age-atrophied musculature and arthritic joints seemed no threat. Silus knew better.

Bek circled so his back was to Oclatinius. And Oclatinius kicked his feet upwards into the air, using the chains as leverage like an acrobat. His legs locked around Bek's neck, and he squeezed tight.

Bek struck like an asp, jamming his knife into Oclatinius' upper thigh, making the old man relax his grip enough for Bek to wriggle free.

But it was all the guard needed. He thrust forward hard, and the sword ran Bek through, just under his sternum, straight through his liver and bursting out of his back. Bek gripped the hilt of the sword, opened his mouth, vomited a gutful of blood, and crashed down to the ground.

'Well done,' said Oclatinius, as the guard used his key to unlock the shackles of the three prisoners. 'Do you happen to have a bandage?' The guard tore a strip off his tunic and tied it tight around Oclatinius' bleeding thigh. Oclatinius experimented putting weight on the injured leg, but it gave way and he put his hand out to steady himself on Silus' shoulder.

'You two need to get to the Empress' chambers, straight away.'

Silus looked at the two dead bodies on the floor, then back to Oclatinius.

'What just happened?'

'This fellow is one of mine, of course. I had a feeling that Geta was planning something. This was the best way to find out what, quickly. You don't think I would let myself get captured unless it suited me, do you?'

Silus shook his head. Oclatinius never ceased to amaze, and indeed to frighten.

'Now, get moving,' said Oclatinius. He gave them directions to Domna's private quarters. 'Take both the swords. Go and save the Emperor. With the will of the gods, there may still be time.'

Silus pulled the sword from Bek, and Atius retrieved the other guard's weapon. The two friends looked at each other.

'Are we good?' asked Silus.

'Always,' said Atius.

They ran.

—

Silus and Atius emerged blinking into the daylight in the bustling Transtiberim region on the west side of the Tiber. They took a moment to orient themselves, but soon located the Via Aurelia and the Pons Aemilius that led back towards the centre of the city. Elbowing and shoving, they rushed through the traffic across the bridge towards the Circus Maximus, which stretched out along the south side of the Palatine Hill.

A chariot race was obviously scheduled for later in the day as the roads around the Circus were crowded with fans of all four factions drinking, singing and taunting their opposition. Much of it was good-natured, but here and there fights broke out as a thrown apple or cup of cheap wine made contact and led to a physical retaliation.

Silus and Atius, aching, tired, bruised and in pain, skirted these brawls as best they could, pushing through the fans as they desperately tried to reach the Palatine in time. At a crossroads, two men grappled and rained punches at each other's heads. One hard jab to the cheekbone sent the unfortunate loser of the fight stumbling backwards into Silus. Silus grabbed on to him, a piece of material pinned to the fan's tunic coming away in his hands. Then a tangle of legs and feet caused Silus to tumble to the dusty street, face down.

'Apologies,' said the victor of the brawl, reaching a friendly hand down to lift him to his feet. Silus took the hand gratefully, and let himself be hauled upright. He stood before the man, who had a green piece of cloth attached to his tunic, opened his mouth to thank him, and looked into the face of a balding man with wall eyes.

A moment of mutual recognition passed between them, that heartbeat where you know you have seen someone before, and are struggling to remember where. Then both their eyes grew wide at the same time.

'You!' said the fan.

'Oh, shit!' said Silus.

Atius hopped from foot to foot. 'Come on,' he urged.

'Lads,' shouted Wall Eye to the surrounding fans. 'This is the one that killed Euprepes!'

A dozen Greens turned to the voice, faces full of menace and anger. They advanced on the two Arcani, making a ring around them. None had swords, but most drew dangerous-looking weapons from folds in their clothes – knives, clubs with nails through them, knuckledusters, all the protection you might need if the rivalry between factions turned serious.

Silus and Atius backed against each other, swords low and pointing forwards.

'Is that the bugger who saw you?' growled Atius.

'It is.'

'Silus, we don't have time for this.'

The angry Green fanatics were holding back, throwing curses and pebbles, but they weren't soldiers, and none had yet plucked up the courage to be the first to attack. It would only be a matter of time though, Silus knew, before they had goaded each other sufficiently to rush at them. He looked at the piece of material still clutched in his left hand. It was blue.

'Follow my lead,' muttered Silus over his shoulder.

'Silus, what...'

'For the Blues!' yelled Silus at the top of his voice, and rushed towards the wall-eyed Green who had continued to curse him for killing Euprepes.

Atius, not slow on the uptake, charged at the opposing side of the circle of Green fanatics, roaring, 'Blues for ever.'

Both Arcani swirled their blades over the heads, making the Green fans back off, and leap out of the way. It was not a recognised battle tactic – they should be thrusting, twisting, pulling back. But they weren't trying to kill. They were trying to attract attention and sew confusion.

Sure enough, more Greens started to congregate at the sight of two armed and maddened Blues fans assaulting fellow Greens.

But so did the Blues fans. As Silus swung and feinted at any Green who came near, he saw tunics in the crowd with blue badges, heard confused queries and shouts.

'What's going on?'

'Hey, guys, there are Blues fans in trouble over here.'

'Fight!'

The atmosphere changed from convivial rivalry to a furious maelstrom of outright hate in a heartbeat. Neighbour grabbed neighbour, brother wrestled brother. Clubs swung and knives flashed. The circle of Green fans that surrounded Silus and Atius suddenly had to turn to protect themselves as the brawl spread. Cries of pain and anger filled the air, and the crossroads was a full-blown riot.

Silus and Atius forced their way forwards, ducking punches and club swings, shoving rioters aside, using the hilts of their swords to clear away anyone who delayed them too long. Slowly, they made progress through the chaos.

Two guards from the Urban Cohorts appeared before them, looking nervous. Silus pointed his sword tip at the ground, but his expression was every bit as threatening as his weapon.

'We aren't the problem here,' he said. 'You need to wait for reinforcements, then get in there and do your jobs. Don't force us to ruin your day.'

The guards exchanged glances and stepped back, taking them away from the riot and allowing the Arcani to pass. Silus nodded to them, and they broke into a run once more. He wondered how many would die or be maimed in this riot. But he felt little guilt. The factions rioted and fought each other regularly. He had just given them another excuse. Besides, inciting a riot was a small price to pay for saving an Emperor's life.

He prayed they would be in time.

Chapter Eighteen

Caracalla arrived in Domna's audience room before his brother. The Empress was alone, and he stopped and just stared at her beauty. She sat on her throne, straight-backed, with empty thrones to her left and right, angled inwards. She was delicately made up, skin pale with lead powder, highlighted with kohl eyeliner, rose lipstick. She wore a loose blue stola, and small gold earrings.

He loved her. He always had, but what might once have been a hormonal, slightly Oedipal crush on his stepmother had grown into a deep adoration that her age and her relationship with his father did nothing to diminish. He hated that it had to remain secret. He wished he could parade her in front of the world as his wife, not his stepmother. Maybe, if he was sole ruler, he could consider it. His predecessors had done worse. Claudius had married his brother's daughter and, if the gossips were to be believed, Caligula had slept with his own sister and Nero with his own mother. Emperors unchecked by Senate or family members seemed to be able to do what they liked, as long as the army supported them, and they could avoid assassination.

Domna smiled at him, and his heart missed a beat. He stepped forward, took her hands in his and kissed each one.

'Thank you, Antoninus. From the bottom of my soul. I know you are only doing this for me.'

That was partly true. Much as he loved her, though, he had not lost his wits to her charms, and Oclatinius' words about the uncertain loyalty of the Praetorian Guard had shaken him more than he would admit.

'He is my brother,' said Caracalla. 'I don't want this to end in bloodshed.' And that was partly true as well. He really did want an agreement with his irritating brother, even to the point of forgiving him the recent attempt on his life. But things could not continue as they were. He hoped that something meaningful would come from this peace meeting.

'What is he actually going to suggest?' he asked. 'Is this going to be a waste of time, or is he prepared to offer something of substance?'

'First I have asked him to beg for your forgiveness for the poisoning.'

'He admitted it to you?' Caracalla raised an eyebrow.

'He did.'

Caracalla sighed. 'What else?'

'He is going to bring a proposal to divide the responsibility for ruling the Empire, not on geography, but along the lines that Papinianus suggested. And you seemed open to this too.'

'I may be. It depends on the detail. But that sort of division, leaving me in charge of the military, effectively makes me the senior Augustus, with the power to enforce that position if I wished. Will he accept that?'

'He says he would. Honestly, Antoninus, he seemed different. He was desperate for this meeting to happen. I think he really wants to find a solution that will work.'

'We'll see.'

'Please, say you will do your best, Antoninus. For me.'

'I promise,' said Caracalla.

She looked deep into his eyes, then leant forward and kissed him impulsively, deeply, her tongue seeking his tongue, her hand on his chest. His passion stirred inside him, suddenly feeling the way only she could make him feel.

The door opened and they stepped back guiltily from each other. Caracalla turned to see Geta enter the chamber. He paused, giving them a long, appraising stare.

'Geta, you're late.'

Domna stepped forward with her arms outstretched. 'My son, I'm so glad you are here to find a new friendship with your brother.'

Four men stepped through the door behind him. They wore short swords at their belts, and nondescript tunics, indicative of no particular branch of the military. Caracalla noticed now that his brother too was wearing a sword.

Domna stopped dead, her arms dropping to her sides. Caracalla took a step backwards.

'Brother,' he said in a low voice. 'What is the meaning of this? The arrangement was that it would be just the two of us and the Empress. Unarmed.'

The men closed the door behind them, and drew its bar across.

'Thank you for agreeing to meet me, Bassianus.'

Caracalla frowned. Geta only used his childhood name when he was being insulting. His brother was clearly in no mood for conciliation, whatever his words to the Empress. Which made the presence of the armed men even more alarming.

'The Augusta said that you wished for a genuine solution to our conflict.'

'Oh, I do, brother, I do. And I think I have found one.'

'What are you talking about? Why are these men here?'

'Mother,' said Geta, turning to Domna.

'Geta. What are you doing? I vouched for you. I promised your brother you had too much respect for me to use me as bait in a trap.'

'Respect? Hmm.' Geta gave her a quizzical look. 'You are looking very well, Mother. Oddly well, in fact. Galen is the world's foremost physician, would you not say?'

Domna looked puzzled at this seeming non-sequitur. 'Undoubtedly, but I don't see—'

'And it is Galen's assertion that a woman who is chaste will soon begin to show signs of hysteria. You were there when he said this.'

'He accepted that your father's vigour was sufficient to protect me from such issues. But Geta, this is not seemly.'

'No, it really is not seemly. Bassianus, where is Titurius' daughter?'

Caracalla went cold. 'What... who...?'

'Please, brother. Your denials are pointless. You disgust me, both of you. How could you disrespect Father in this way? Was it happening when he was alive? Mother, were you cuckolding him with his son?'

'Geta, listen, you don't understand, it's not—'

'Silence!'

Caracalla and Domna both took an involuntary step back, shocked at the forcefulness that was so rare in the younger Augustus.

'Maybe I would have been open to some sort of solution. Some division of rule that acknowledged me as your equal while giving you the greater responsibility and power. But I will not rule with the man who made a cuckold of my father. Nor will I suffer him to live.' Geta drew his sword and held it in front of him in his right hand, point angled towards the floor. Then he lifted it above his left shoulder and stepped quickly forward, slashing in a downward backhand. Caracalla flinched backwards, and as he did so, Domna stepped forward, arm outstretched, palm raised, crying, 'Geta, no!'

Geta tried to pull the stroke away, but the edge of his blade sliced through his mother's palm. She clutched it to her chest, blood staining her dress. She stared at her son, her eyes full of hurt, the emotional pain worse than the physical.

'Mother, I'm sorry, I didn't mean to—'

'Stop this, Geta. End this now. Take your men and leave.'

He looked down, and for a moment it seemed that he might acquiesce. But when he spoke, his voice was full of regret. 'I'm sorry, Mother. There is no going back from this. Now please stand aside.'

'No.'

'Brother, come out from behind my mother. It is not befitting of your dignity to hide beneath her skirts.'

Caracalla gently eased Domna to one side, though she resisted.

'You know, brother, I have always admired you. You were stronger than me, faster, braver, and not just because you were the elder. And I would be for ever in your shadow, no matter how equal we agreed to be. I think I could have accepted that. But I can't accept your character, your anger and ruthlessness, your moral baseness. Your relationship with my mother. I'm sorry it has to end this way. But it must.'

He lifted his sword, and Caracalla tensed, staring at the point, preparing to move, to take whatever slight chance of survival he might have by fighting back, even though he knew that Geta had four armed men backing him up.

And then there was a huge crash at the door, and the wood splintered.

–

'Again!' urged Silus. 'Put your whole weight into it.'

Atius shoulder-barged the door again, and the wood splintered inwards. He stepped back, rubbing his upper arm and prepared to charge again. Silus pushed him aside and aimed a kick at the door by the jamb. On the other side, the metal hoop that held the draw bar in place exploded into the room, and the door flew open.

Silus dived through the gap, staying low, reducing the possibility of an arrow or sword swing that had been lined up finding him. He rolled, came instantly to his feet, sword in hand. Behind, Atius charged through, his blade held ready before him.

Silus took in the situation in the briefest moment. Four armed but unarmoured guards faced them, swords drawn, expressions surprised but resolute. Behind them, Geta had his sword out and was facing Caracalla who was unarmed. Behind

Caracalla was the Empress Julia Domna, bleeding freely from a wound on her hand.

All eyes had turned to Atius and himself, which was all Caracalla needed to save his own life. The muscular Emperor rushed forward, grabbing the wrist of his brother's sword arm, and they struggled for the weapon.

Silus knew he couldn't get to Caracalla until the guards had been dealt with, and in any case Atius and he had their work cut out staying alive against the four men. But he could keep the guards off Caracalla to allow him a fair fight with his brother.

Atius looked to Silus for guidance. Rush in, swords flailing? Spar and keep them occupied? It was Silus' decision. The guards had no clear leader, especially with Geta occupied with Caracalla, and so they failed to take advantage of their natural superiority in numbers.

Silus gave Atius a hand signal, and Atius nodded his understanding. Silus dodged left, Atius right, bringing them to opposite corners of the room, backs to the walls. The audience chamber was not vast, and now it would be hard to come at them more than one at a time.

Hesitantly, a young guard approached Silus, pushed forward by an older colleague. He was fit, well-toned, but no more than twenty years of age. Too young to have built much muscle, and too young to have learnt how to fight dirty.

'You're not old enough to die,' said Silus. 'Drop your weapon and fuck off.'

The young man, not much more than a boy, looked terrified, but he gripped the hilt of his sword tight, and raised it up high for a heavy cleaving stroke.

Silus ran him through before his sword could even begin to descend. Silus twisted, the sword tearing internal organs and lacerating vessels, and pulled it out, a gout of blood following. He kicked the young man in the chest, and he toppled backwards out of the way. The older guard who had pushed the younger into conflict stared in dismay at the corpse of his comrade, but he had no time to grieve. Silus was on him in a heartbeat, forcing him to lift up his sword to parry a thrust.

The older guard was wilier than the younger had been, and kept Silus at bay, not committing to a killing blow that would leave him vulnerable, content to keep Silus back and occupied.

Silus took the opportunity to glance around. Atius had likewise dispatched his first opponent, who was writhing on the ground clutching a mortal gut wound, and was forcing his second opponent back with heavy, axe-like swings of his sword. Behind them, Caracalla and Geta were wrestling, the sword swinging around them wildly as they pushed and pulled, trying desperately for an advantage. Julia Domna had retreated to her throne, where she looked on in horror while clutching her injured hand.

Silus decided he had to bring things to an end. Caracalla was strong, but Geta was still the one holding the sword. If Caracalla died, Tituria would die too. It would all have been for nothing.

He feinted, a high thrust towards his opponent's eyes, and when the guard pulled his head sideways to avoid the blow, he kicked him hard in the leg, scraping his hobnails down the shin. Silus had had this low trick performed on him in a barracks brawl in the past, and he knew how excruciating it was. The guard howled and hopped backwards, momentarily off balance. Silus swept a foot round hard to catch the guard's standing leg, knocking it out from beneath him. The guard crashed hard to the floor, lying on his back, winded. Silus stepped astride him and thrust downwards, putting all his weight through the hilt of the sword so it cracked ribs as it transfixed his chest.

He stepped back, panting. Atius had battered his opponent to his knees, and as Silus watched, a vicious side swipe cut the unfortunate guard's sword hand off at the wrist. He stared at the pumping stump for only a moment before Atius cleaved his sword into the side of his neck, almost decapitating him. The guard with the gut wound was already dead.

Behind the dead guards, Caracalla had forced Geta up against a wall. He used his superior weight and strength to hold his brother there, his left hand gripping Geta's right wrist so the sword was pinned uselessly. His right hand found Geta's throat, and he started to squeeze, while the grip of his left hand tightened powerfully and painfully on Geta's wrist. The only sounds in the room came from Geta as he gurgled, and Domna as she sobbed quietly. His eyes widened in terror as he failed to draw breath into lungs desperate for air.

The sword dropped from his hand and fell to the floor with a clatter that seemed deafening in the small room. Caracalla looked at the fallen weapon, not easing the pressure on his brother's throat.

'Antoninus.' Domna's voice was pleading, desperate. 'Stop.'

Caracalla turned to her, and the look in his eyes was full of anger, but also anguish. He released his grip on his brother's throat. Geta fell to his hands and knees, gulping air into his chest as a man rescued from the desert drinks cold water. He crawled on his hands and knees over to Domna, where she still sat on her throne. She leant forward and took his arm, and he dragged himself into her lap, breathing noisily through his damaged windpipe.

Caracalla looked thoughtfully at the sword on the floor, the one that his brother had been about to kill him with. He bent down and picked it up, hefted its weight experimentally in his hand, squinted along its length to check it wasn't warped.

'This is a fine blade, brother.' He made a couple of practice swipes and thrusts. 'Yes, very fine.'

Domna's arms were wrapped around her son, and she watched Caracalla with eyes brimming with tears, wet rivulets carved through the lead make-up revealing the darker skin beneath.

Caracalla turned to the throne. The sword tip was angled towards the ground. Geta stared at his elder brother.

'Antoninus...' began Domna, but Caracalla held up a hand and stopped her.

'You're bleeding, Domna.'

322

'It's just a scratch. Please put the sword down.'

'No, Domna. I'm sorry.'

'Antoninus, this can be fixed. Geta will submit to you. Acknowledge you as sole Emperor. Go into exile.'

Caracalla shook his head sadly. 'He will always be a rallying point for discontent as long as he lives. And how can I ever forgive him for this base betrayal?'

'Mother,' said Geta. He sounded like a little boy, seeking solace from a nightmare. 'Don't let him hurt me.'

'Show me your hand, Domna,' said Caracalla.

'It is nothing...'

'Show me!' he yelled.

Hesitantly, Domna held up her palm. There was a deep diagonal gash, the skin drawn back to reveal white tendon and bone among glistening redness. Caracalla stared at the wound.

Then he let out a wordless roar, charged forwards and thrust his sword deep into the side of Geta's chest.

The sword penetrated between two ribs, just below Domna's arm which embraced him protectively around the shoulder, and stopped when it lodged against the inside of his ribcage on the other side. Geta let out a single, choking cry. He looked up into his mother's eyes, and opened his mouth to speak. Instead of words, dark blood bubbled out and over his mother's dress, mixing with the bloodstains from her wounded hand.

Caracalla released the hilt of the sword and stepped back, whole body shaking.

Domna stared down at her dying son, and cradled him like a baby, stroking his face and crooning soft words to him. Geta tried to breathe, but just coughed out more blood. His body stiffened, head going back in a spasm, and then he was still.

Domna looked at Caracalla, and let out a single, disbelieving, hysterical laugh.

'Gods, Antoninus,' she said. 'He's gone.'

Caracalla bowed his head. Then he dropped heavily to his knees, put both hands to his face, and started to howl.

Much to Silus' relief, Oclatinius arrived a short while later. Atius and Silus had been looking at each other awkwardly as the mother wept over her dead son, and the brother who had killed him cried out his grief and guilt.

Oclatinius limped in, supporting his weight on a crutch, and surveyed the scene, quickly taking in the details. He neither needed nor asked for any information from Silus, although Silus was sure an in-depth debrief would be required later. Oclatinius moved over to Caracalla and put a hand on his shoulder. After a moment, the distraught Emperor looked up at him.

'Oclatinius. I had to do it.'

'I know, Augustus. He left you no choice.' He looked over at Geta's body, pallid from the blood loss. 'I'm sorry that I let this situation arise. I sent my men as soon as I found out.'

Caracalla slowly got to his feet with Oclatinius helping support him despite his own injury. The new sole Emperor turned, as if seeing Silus and Atius for the first time.

'You two. Again. I owe you my thanks.'

Silus bowed his head in acknowledgement. The Emperor's thanks meant nothing to him. He was at best ambivalent towards Caracalla. But Tituria's life depended on the Emperor's health and his goodwill, and Silus had just preserved both.

'Silus, Atius, relieve the Empress of her burden.'

Silus swallowed, and the two of them approached Domna. She looked at them piteously, and gripped her son's body tighter.

'Augusta,' said Silus and took a hold of Geta. Domna gripped him even more tightly. 'Empress, please. I know what it is like to lose your only child. But you have to let go.' Domna gave one more squeeze, then let her arms drop to her sides. Geta started to roll out of her lap, but Silus and Atius were there, and they caught him and eased him to the floor, straightening his legs and folding his arms over his chest.

'Augustus,' said Oclatinius. 'I know you are grieving. But you have to act now. This event will unsettle the city, and in particular the Praetorians. You must go to them and explain what happened.'

Caracalla took a deep breath, then let it out slowly through his nose.

'Very well.'

'Silus and Atius will accompany you. I will attend the Empress and... take care of things here.'

Silus and Atius looked at each other. They were grimy, bloodstained, bruised and dishevelled. Hardly an appropriate honour guard to accompany the Emperor to the Praetorian barracks. But at that moment, it was all he had.

'I should change,' said Caracalla, sounding a little dazed. 'Dress in the purple.'

'No, Augustus. With respect, let them see the blood upon you, so that the truth of the attempt on your life is self-evident.'

'You are right.' Caracalla looked across to Domna, who was still sitting on the throne, drenched in congealing blood, her own and her son's. The look she returned was coloured with anger, loss and the hurt that only a loved one could inflict. Caracalla's mouth worked as he searched for words. Then he shook his head, and flicked his fingers at Silus and Atius. 'Come.' He strode out of the chamber.

–

They had gathered some Praetorians from the palace before they walked to the Praetorian camp. It was a long walk across the city from the Palatine to the Castra Praetoria – it was situated to the north-east of the city, outside the Servian walls, behind the Viminal, and the sun had fallen by the time they arrived. The party of pristine Praetorians escorting two blood-covered men out of uniform, and a similarly blood-soaked Emperor, who hurried through the city on foot calling out intermittently that he had narrowly escaped an attempted assassination, had collected a large crowd of curious and concerned citizens.

The Castra Praetoria was an impressive structure with thick masonry walls, similar in style to a fortress in the hostile provinces, but far more ornate and luxurious, its temple and baths more suitable for their situation in Rome rather than a far-flung outpost needed to hold back barbarian hordes. They entered through the Porta Praetoria, leaving the crowd of civilians behind. Caracalla went straight to the camp temple, where the standards of the guard were worshipped, ascended the steps and threw himself onto the floor.

As a crowd of stunned Praetorians grew at the bottom of the steps leading up to the colonnaded temple entrance, Caracalla prayed in a loud voice in front of the altar.

'O Mars, O Jupiter, I give thanks here for my safety, that you have seen fit to spare me from this terrible attempt on my life by my brother.'

A shocked murmur went through the guard. Silus, crowded in with the soldiers, saw the idea dawning that something of real significance and import was happening this evening.

Caracalla rose, and with the help of the temple priest who attended him nervously, sacrificed a white dove and a white rooster in gratitude for his delivery from danger.

Praetorians from all over the fort scrambled to attend as word about what was happening got around. Some had been asleep, some in the bathhouse, so they had wet or untidy hair and beards, and were still adjusting their uniforms as they reached the temple. Caracalla walked out of the temple, and stood at the top of the steps, so he could address them in a loud voice.

'Loyal soldiers, my Imperial guard. Tonight, an attempt was made on my life, by my very own brother. He invited me to peace talks: just me, him and the Empress. He came wearing a sword and with armed men to kill me. The Empress tried to defend me and was injured.'

This drew a gasp from the collected soldiers. To inflict an injury on the sacred body of the Empress was sacrilege, and a palpable sense of anger washed over the assembled guards like a wave. Caracalla held up a hand.

'The Empress is well. The injury is not fatal. But while defending myself, I struck my brother Geta dead, with the very sword he brought to kill me.'

The soldiers went silent at the news. Then roars broke out, and Silus found it hard to tell whether the anger was directed against the actions of Geta or Caracalla.

Caracalla held his hands up again, and when the noise didn't die down, he shouted to be heard.

'My loyal guard, you are most happy. Because Fortuna has chosen me to be your sole Emperor, and now I, the one who loves you most, am in a position to reward you greatly. I say to you now, I am rewarding your loyalty with a bonus of two thousand five hundred denarii.'

This got a reaction, as those who had heard passed the information to those who had been shouting too loudly to hear. The roars of anger died out to be replaced by cheers of celebration at the award of this vast sum.

'Furthermore, your rations are increased by one half. See how I reward those who are faithful to me!'

More cheers, applause, laughter. Silus swallowed bitterly, the happiness so incongruous after the scene of grief and death he had just left.

'Now go and claim the gift I have given you, from the temples and treasuries, and let no man stop you, for I, Imperator Caesar Marcus Aurelius Severus Antoninus Pius Augustus Britannicus Maximus, whom men call Caracalla, decree that it is your due.'

The Praetorians started chanting, 'Imperator, Imperator,' and Caracalla waved his hand in acknowledgement. Then the guards dispersed, flooding into the city to ransack the temples and the depositories of the Imperial treasure. Silus doubted that they would demand the exact number of coins that was strictly owed, but instead they would loot as much as they could. Rome would be a chaotic and dangerous place that night.

Suddenly alone with Atius in a rapidly emptying camp, Silus felt overwhelmingly tired. He squatted down on his haunches, and pressed his face into his hands, fingers massaging his sore eyes. After a moment, Atius nudged him with a thigh, and he looked up. Caracalla was standing over them.

Silus struggled to his feet, leaning on Atius as a wave of dizziness struck him.

'Augustus,' he said, bowing his head.

'Silus,' said Caracalla. He looked grave, morose, like a man defeated rather than one who had finally got what he had craved for so long. 'My brother is dead, at my own hands. I have bought the loyalty of the Praetorians, for the time being. But there will be many in the city who despise me now. Many of my brother's faction who wish me ill.

'You have served me well. Time and again. Though once you defied me, I can forgive that. I need your loyalty now, more than ever. Can I depend on you?'

Silus bowed his head. 'Of course, Augustus. I am your man.'

And he meant it. As long as Tituria was held hostage, her life in the hands of this impetuous and ruthless man, then Silus' faithfulness to Caracalla was as solid as the Tarpeian Rock. He would do whatever was commanded of him, however it made him feel, however distasteful.

And he knew that there was a lot of distasteful work ahead. He had begun this journey as a scout, a soldier, a sword for the Emperor. He feared what would be demanded of him next.

A cold wind blew through the evening air of the parade ground, and a chill ran down Silus' spine.

Epilogue

'So, that is how it ends, old friend.'

'I fear it is just a beginning.'

Festus and Oclatinius were standing at the top of the Tarpeian Rock. Two old men, well over a century of years in combined age, and barely enough hair between them to make a rat's toupee.

'How long have we known each other now?' asked Oclatinius.

'Too long.'

Oclatinius wasn't sure whether that was a comment on their age or their acquaintanceship. He wasn't prepared to reciprocate his colleague's appellation of friend. He simply nodded agreement.

The Tarpeian Rock was their habitual meeting place, usually late at night, where they grudgingly shared intelligence when they thought it was beneficial to their individual ends. Though both were the heads of clandestine organisations reporting directly to the Emperor or Emperors, their activities much less conspicuous than the agents of the legions, the Urban Cohorts, the frumentarii, the speculatores, the Imperial bodyguards or the Praetorians, they were also rivals, with little trust between them. The Tarpeian Rock, the promontory at the southern summit of the Capitoline Hill, was the traditional site of the execution of traitors, as well as murderers and other criminals. Although it had fallen out of use for this purpose – why give a criminal a quick death, when a more protracted one could entertain the crowds in the arena? – it still carried the aura of the punishment of treachery. The phrase, 'The Tarpeian Rock is close to the Capitol,' was still in use, and was both literally true and a reminder that even the highest were never far from a fatal fall. As such, it had always seemed a fitting meeting point for the two spymasters.

'There will be a slaughter,' said Oclatinius. 'How can it be otherwise? The Emperor must consolidate his position. Whether it is from a place of fear, anger or good sense, will not matter to those whose heads are sent rolling.'

'Will you come for me?'

'Not I.'

'Does the Emperor trust me?'

'He trusts almost no one. But he will not hear of your support for Geta from me.'

Festus nodded.

The wind ruffled Oclatinius' sparse hair, and he pulled his cloak tighter. He felt the cold so much more keenly now than in his youth.

'Will he be a tyrant?' asked Festus.

Oclatinius shrugged. 'I am no more a seer than you. He has it in him certainly. But he has the character and ability to be so much more. Time will tell us.'

He looked down to the Velabrum, the valley between the Capitoline Hill and the Forum Boarium. A few years before, the money-changers and merchants had dedicated an arch to the Severan family. Although Oclatinius could not make out the detail from this distance, in the dark, with his old eyes, he knew that on one side there were images of sacrifices involving Severus, Domna and Geta, and on the other side Caracalla, his wife Plautilla and his father-in-law Plautianus. Of those depicted, only Caracalla and Domna still lived, and Oclatinius doubted that the images of the traitorous father-in-law, the unfaithful wife and the treacherous brother would be left undisturbed for long.

Shouts and cries rose up from the city below as the soldiers rampaged, looting the temples and treasury. No doubt there would be rape and murder tonight. What else could be expected when thousands of soldiers were let loose on a city? It would be as if Rome was being sacked by barbarians.

'One thing I can predict,' said Oclatinius, 'is that we are going to be busy.'

'I don't doubt it, my friend.'

Oclatinius ground his teeth at the second use of the epithet.

'We will need to meet again soon, I'm sure,' he said.

'We will,' agreed Festus. 'I'll send a messenger with the time.'

Oclatinius turned his back to the cliff and began to walk away, in the direction of the Forum Romanum. 'Are you coming?' he called over his shoulder.

'I think I'll just stay a while and collect my thoughts,' said Festus.

Oclatinius waved a hand and disappeared from sight. Festus turned back to look out over the cliff edge. After a while, another figure joined him. They stood in silent contemplation for a time. Then the figure spoke. The language was Greek but the accent was Syrian.

'Do you trust him?'

'He won't betray me. Too much has passed between us. But someone else? Aper will not live long. But will he be executed immediately, or tortured first, in which case he may give up my name?'

'I doubt the Emperor is in a mood to look for confessions and hear pleas for mercy right now.'

'Maybe not. So we lie low for now. He will consolidate his position with the army first, and he will likely make some grand gesture for the masses to make sure they love him too. But he alienates the Senate, and there is mutual distrust and hatred there. My position is precarious. But things will come to a head. And when the mood has shifted against him sufficiently, we must be ready.'

'I am always ready. This will be the greatest revolution in the history of Rome, since the time of the Kings.'

Festus nodded. 'And its time has come.'

The wind swirled around them, and they remained in silent contemplation, looking down at the rocks that had ended the lives of so many traitors.

Author's Note

That history is written by the victors is a quote attributed variously to Churchill, Machiavelli and Hitler, and is often considered a truism. Yet there are many examples in which history was written by the losing side, such as the Athenian Thucydides' account of the Peloponnesian War, which Athens lost; the Greek scholars who fled to the west after the fall of Byzantium; or even, controversially, American depictions of the Vietnam War (although of course many Americans such as Otto in *A Fish Called Wanda* claim that was a draw).

Whether or not Caracalla should be counted as a victor after the death of his brother, he certainly was the survivor of that year of conflict, yet the contemporaneous, near contemporaneous and more recent historiography is almost universally hostile. I have explored Caracalla's reputation further in the essay below, but for this historical note, I will concentrate on a few contentious points that are found in this novel.

The most important, of course, is whether Caracalla planned to kill his brother at the peace meeting in Domna's chambers, or whether it was Geta who attempted to murder Caracalla, and Caracalla was merely defending himself. The two main sources, Herodian and Dio Cassius, were markedly hostile to Caracalla. Dio Cassius was a senator during Caracalla's reign, and no doubt resented the Emperor's dismissive treatment of the Senate. However, both historians acknowledge that the two brothers were plotting against each other, or at least believed this was the case. Both historians also record that Caracalla claimed he had been saved from a plot against his life by Geta. So it is equally plausible that Geta really did instigate a murder plot against his brother at the peace meeting as that Caracalla may have been the guilty party. We will never know for sure, but fortunately, as I have said before, as a historical novelist I can choose the possible version of events that suits my narrative best.

Another area of doubt in the history is whether Plautilla, Caracalla's estranged wife, had offspring. This is not recorded in the contemporary records, but numismatic evidence from before the downfall of Plautilla and her father in AD 205 shows a coin of Plautilla holding a child. If this is a representation of her own child, and it is illustrated on a coin, then officially at least the child must have been Caracalla's. But Caracalla hated Plautilla, whom his father had required him to marry to cement his ties with the Praetorian prefect Plautianus. When Plautianus was executed after a failed plot against Severus, Caracalla was able to have her exiled with her brother and presumably, if it existed, her child.

Herodian says that Caracalla refused to eat or sleep with his wife, and Dio called her a most shameless creature, so it is reasonable to assume that it is at least possible that the girl was not Caracalla's. He may not have been sure himself, but would likely want the whole family disposed of to avoid any future threats to his rule, including ones claiming a hereditary right to rule by someone marrying his supposed child. If he is not the monster that history makes him out to be, then he no doubt felt remorse at this act, but equally felt it was necessary.

Silus and Atius are fictional characters, but many of their actions are attested in the sources. I have mentioned the murder of Plautilla and her family. Also, the murder of Euprepes, the famous charioteer, is noted in Dio Cassius – killed, so it was said, for supporting a faction opposing his own. If by faction Dio is referring to the teams of Circus supporters, then it seems a bit arbitrary to kill off a famous old man, even if he was a fan of the other side, notwithstanding the passion with which the Circus fans supported their teams. (The Blues, Greens,

Reds and Whites moved with the capital of the Empire to the Hippodrome in Byzantium/Constantinople, and a riot between fans in AD 532 led to nearly half the city being burnt and tens of thousands dead.) However, Geta and Caracalla supported opposing Circus factions, as they did the opposite in most things, and so if Euprepes had been vocal in his praise for Geta, the most prestigious of the Green fans, then Caracalla might have taken that as a personal slight.

The attack on Cilo is also historical, with Caracalla intervening to save him. I have therefore represented this as a sort of St Thomas of Canterbury/Henry II moment, with frustration being misinterpreted as an execution order.

Galen is another fascinating historical figure, as he was the most prominent doctor of his time. He was the personal physician to several Emperors, and his theories of disease and the workings of the human body were hugely influential until well into the sixteenth century. He was present in Rome when the Antonine plague, named after Marcus Aurelius, struck, and it is sometimes called the plague of Galen due to his attempts to understand and treat it. His descriptions have allowed modern researchers to identify this lethal pandemic as smallpox. He was a member of Julia Domna's circle of intellectuals, and was Severus' personal physician until his death.

I have mentioned one or two other historical figures who were to become important players on the Imperial stage. Macrinus became increasingly influential under Severus and Caracalla. Julia Soaemias was one of the Syrian women related to Julia Domna who had an unusually large influence and power in Severan Rome. And we have also now briefly met Sextus Varius Avitus Bassianus, who later became the controversial Emperor Elagabalus. And he is to play an important part in the story of Silus yet to come...

Bibliography and Further Reading

I have consulted too many texts in the research for this novel to list here, but some of the principal books I have relied on are:

Bowman, A. K., Garnsey, P. and Cameron, A. (2005), *The Cambridge Ancient History: Volume XII, The Crisis of Empire AD 193–337*, 2nd edition, Cambridge University Press, Cambridge.

Grant, M. (1996), *The Severans: The Changed Roman Empire*, Routledge, Abingdon.

Levick, B. (2007), *Julia Domna, Syrian Empress*, Routledge, Abingdon.

Southern, P. (2001), *The Roman Empire from Severus to Constantine*, Routledge, Abingdon.

Swain, S., Harrison, S. and Elsner, J. (2007), *Severan Culture*, Cambridge University Press, Cambridge.

Sylvänne, I. (2017), *Caracalla, A Military Biography*, Pen & Sword Military, Barnsley.

Historical Texts

Emperor Caracalla: Does He Deserve His Reputation?

According to Edward Gibbon, Caracalla was 'the common enemy of all mankind'. Further, Gibbon says that 'although not destitute of imagination and eloquence, [he] was equally devoid of judgment and humanity'. Dio Cassius (or confusingly, Cassius Dio), the Roman senator and historian writing in the early third century CE, knew Caracalla personally and seemingly hated him. He said that Caracalla 'belonged to three races; and he possessed none of their virtues at all, but combined in himself all their vices; the fickleness, cowardice, and recklessness of Gaul were his, the harshness and cruelty of Africa, and the craftiness of Syria, whence he was sprung on his mother's side'. Not a fan then. Herodian, a minor Roman civil servant writing at a similar time, said Caracalla 'was harsh and savage in everything he did, scorning the pursuits mentioned above [contrasting Caracalla's behaviour with his brother Geta's supposed interest in physical exercise and intellectual pursuits], and pretending a devotion to the military and martial life. Since he did everything in anger and used threats instead of persuasion, his friends were bound to him by fear, not by affection.'

But did Caracalla deserve all this disapprobation? He certainly committed some evil acts by modern standards, but if we compare them to the deeds of beloved Emperors such as Augustus, Diocletian and Constantine the Great, was he any worse? Does he deserve to be hated and reviled more than Sulla, Tiberius and Maximinus Thrax?

Much about the history of this period is murky, and there is a possibility of many inaccuracies in the accepted narrative of events and 'facts'. These arise from all the usual problems we see in history, exacerbated by the huge distance in time separating us from the third century. So we see bias and contradiction in the sources and patchy archaeological and epigraphic detail. It is made worse that for the period of Caracalla's life, the best contemporary history of the period, Cassius Dio (or Dio Cassius!) is available to us only as fragments and a brief summary made by the eleventh-century monk John Xiphilinus on the orders of the Byzantine Emperor Michael VII Doukas. Herodian, another important source, is relatively brief, while the other main record, the *Historia Augusta*, written by an unknown author or authors in the fourth century, is at least partly a work of fiction. The estimate for its accuracy of the history of Caracalla's brother Geta is put at only 5 per cent!

Of course, to an author of historical fiction, this can be seen as an opportunity rather than a problem. If the sources are missing, contradictory, or can be interpreted in multiple ways, then the novelist can choose the version that suits the story best. I have a personal rule that as far as possible I do not alter the known history when it comes to my books, even if the plot suffers as a result. Other authors are happy to change events, for example the dates, to improve the narrative flow, and this is a personal decision and certainly not wrong, especially if the reality is explained in an author's note. But what I am happy to do is pick a possible but less probable version of the facts.

For example, let's look at Caracalla's date of birth. It is generally believed that Caracalla was born in 188 CE, the child of Julia Domna and Septimius Severus, and full brother to Geta. However, Dr Ilkka Syvänne, associate professor at the University of Haifa, and the author of the only full-length text on Caracalla, contends both in his book and in personal correspondence to me that it is possible he was born to Severus' first wife, Paccia Marciana, in 186 or 174 CE, and that 174 CE, the date attested in the Historia Augusta, is the more likely. For me this is convenient, as it is more believable that Caracalla is having an affair with his stepmother Julia Domna if he is a bit older.

Stepmother? The accepted history is that Julia Domna was Caracalla's mother, but Dr Syvänne says that if there was a larger age gap between the brothers, because Caracalla was born to Severus' first wife, it would explain why he was promoted to Augustus so many years before his brother. He also speculates that the sibling rivalry would be more pronounced if they had different mothers, and less plausibly, he thinks that biologically the gap of twelve months between children is unlikely. In favour of Julia Domna being Caracalla's mother was his original name of Bassianus, which was the name of Domna's father. However, Dr Syvänne notes that Caracalla could have been renamed Bassianus when he was adopted by Domna.

I believe the conventional stories about Caracalla's date of birth and parentage are probably correct, but the controversy over these two seemingly firm facts helps illustrate how much of history is uncertain, and is just a best guess.

So we return to Caracalla's reputation. He was hated by his two main historians, a senator and civil servant, who he likely snubbed and paid insufficient respect to, preferring the company of the legions and the common soldiers. One of his most generous acts, his extension of citizenship to every free man in the Roman Empire, the Constitutio Antoniniana, may have rankled with the senatorial elite, who characterised this as a way of increasing the taxable population. This may be true, but as the majority enfranchised in this way would have been poor, it was unlikely to have contributed much to the Imperial coffers. He also gave all freeborn women the same rights as Roman women, which doesn't seem to have brought any significant financial advantage.

What of Caracalla's worst deeds? He was rumoured to have wanted to put a premature end to his father's reign. The main documented attempt on his father's life was during a meeting with surrendering Caledonian nobles, when he drew his sword behind his father's back. Others present shouted a warning, and Severus turned and saw it. Severus later put a sword in Caracalla's reach, in the presence of the Praetorian prefect Papinianus, and told Caracalla to use the sword or order Papinianus to murder him. Caracalla declined. However, another explanation is that Caracalla actually intended to kill the unarmed Caledonians, who he considered had been lured into a trap. This was consistent with his later behaviour as a general and Emperor. On the other hand, it may be that Caracalla genuinely wished to kill his father, and was suffering from the Oedipus complex so well known to classical history.

Some time after Severus died, Caracalla ordered the murder of his wife Plautilla, and her brother and child. Although the child was nominally his, he had hated his wife, who was thought to be unfaithful to him, and it is possible Plautilla's child actually had a father other than Caracalla.

The next most egregious deed of Caracalla is the murder of his brother in his mother's arms at a peace conference in which both brothers were supposed to be alone and unarmed. Dio Cassius puts the blame for this firmly in Caracalla's court, but it is entirely possible, given the animosity between the siblings, that Caracalla's claim that he was defending himself against an attempt on his life by Geta is true. Herodian says that both brothers repeatedly tried to murder each other with 'every sort of intrigue,' including poison. So even if Geta's murder was planned and plotted by Caracalla, he may have considered it pre-emptive given that his brother was trying to do the same to him.

After the death of Geta, it becomes harder to defend Caracalla's actions. He embarked on an orgy of slaughter of Geta's family, friends and associates. Herodian says, 'Geta's friends and associates were immediately butchered, together with those who lived in his half of the Imperial palace. All his attendants were put to death too; not a single one was spared because of his age, not even the infants. Their bodies, after first being dragged about and subjected to every form of indignity, were placed in carts and taken out of the city; there they were piled up and burnt or simply thrown in the ditch.'

Caracalla may have become unhinged with guilt and grief at the death of his brother, or may have been shrewdly and ruthlessly securing his position, but in the modern day, no one would attempt to defend a mass slaughter. Put in the context of his time, though, it may have been no worse than the actions of other respected and not-so-respected rulers. The following are some examples of heinous acts of other Emperors and rulers of Rome that compare with Caracalla's actions, with the disclaimer that some of these 'facts' may be malicious stories made up by hostile contemporaries.

1. Mass slaughter/proscriptions. Caracalla is reported to have slaughtered 20,000 of his brother's adherents after Geta's death, though this may have been exaggerated by his hostile biographers. Sulla's proscriptions are estimated to have resulted in the deaths of between 1,000 and 9,000 of Rome's upper classes. Gaius Marius, the great Roman general, at the start of his seventh consulship, began a hideous massacre of his enemies in Rome, and it was only his death seventeen days into his consulship that brought this to an end. Octavian/Augustus, as part of the Second Triumvirate, was responsible for a more modest 300 deaths in his proscriptions, but these deaths were aimed at silencing political rivals and acquiring wealth. Diocletian, the saviour of the Empire who ended the Crisis of the Third Century, massacred Christians, with the Great Persecution estimated to have resulted in the

deaths of 3,500, although earlier sources put the number as high as 17,000 in a single month.

2. Uxoricide (I had to look this one up – it's the act of killing one's wife), fratricide, matricide, etc. Nero kicked Poppaea, his pregnant second wife, to death, and had his mother assassinated. Messalina was ordered to be executed for infidelity and treason, though this was on Narcissus' instructions rather than Claudius'. As for the murder of other family members, Constantine the Great ordered the execution of his own son, Crispus, Nero poisoned his brother Britannicus, and even the founder of the city, Romulus, murdered his own brother.

3. Incest. If Caracalla did commit incest with his stepmother or mother, he was in good company in ancient Rome. Although incest was illegal, Caligula was rumoured to have sex with his sisters, Claudius married his niece, and Nero was thought to have sex with his mother.

Caracalla undoubtedly had positive character traits. He was a good general, waging a brutal but successful campaign in Scotland under his father's oversight. He won victories against the Alemanni in Germania, and also the Parthians, which weakened the Empire that had been a thorn in Rome's side for centuries sufficiently enough that it fell to the Sassanids. He is described as launching surprise attacks under the guise of peace negotiations, which Dio Cassius characterises as treachery, but others may see as good strategy. Whatever the motivations for his Constitutio Antoniniana, it was clearly welcomed by the poor who strived to be Roman citizens. Unfortunately, it weakened recruitment to the legions, since citizenship on discharge was one of the big attractions of serving your lengthy term. He was also cultured to an extent, learning to play the lyre later in life and able to quote Euripides at length. The *Historia Augusta* characterises the young Caracalla as intelligent, kind, generous and sensitive, although he became more reserved and stern in later life. He was physically in good shape, enjoying swimming in rough water and long horse rides. He enjoyed the company of the army and the common soldier.

But he also had many characteristics, and performed actions, that modern readers would consider reprehensible. My contention in writing this article is not to be an apologist for Caracalla's actions, but to set them among those of his contemporaries. Even if the worst actions and motivations for them ascribed to him are true, which is a big if, does Caracalla deserve his reputation for being one of the most despised of all the Roman Emperors, and 'the common enemy of all mankind', when so many other Roman Emperors, both hated and loved, behaved similarly?

Dio Cassius on Caracalla

Adapted from an English translation of Dio's Roman History, *Book 78, by Earnest Cary PhD, 1914, taken from the LacusCurtius website.*

Epitome of book LXXVIII I–II

After this Antoninus assumed the entire power; nominally, it is true, he shared it with his brother, but in reality he ruled alone from the very outset. With the enemy he came to terms, withdrew from their territory, and abandoned the forts; as for his own people, he dismissed some, including Papinian, the prefect, and killed others, among them Euodus his tutor, Castor, and his wife Plautilla, and her brother Plautius. Even in Rome itself he killed a man who was renowned for no other reason than his profession, which made him very conspicuous. I refer to Euprepes the charioteer. He killed him because he supported the opposite faction to the one he himself favoured.

So Euprepes was put to death in his old age, after having been crowned in a vast number of horse-races; for he had won seven hundred and eighty-two crowns, a record equalled by no one else. As for his own brother, Antoninus had wished to slay him even while his father was still alive, but had been unable to do so at the time because of Severus, or later, on the march, because of the legions; for the troops felt very kindly toward the younger brother, especially as he resembled his father very closely in appearance. But when Antoninus got back to Rome, he killed him also. The two pretended to love and commend each other, but in all that they did they were diametrically opposed, and anyone could see that something terrible was bound to result from the situation. This was foreseen even before they reached Rome. For when the senate had voted that sacrifices should be offered on behalf of their concord both to the other gods and to Concord herself, and the assistants had got ready the victim to be sacrificed to Concord, and the consul had arrived to superintend the sacrifice, he could not find them and they could not find him, so they spent nearly the entire night searching for one another, and so the sacrifice could not be performed then. And on the next day two wolves went up to the Capitol, but were chased away from there; one of them was found and slain somewhere in the Forum and the other was killed later outside the pomerium. This incident also had reference to the brothers.

Antoninus wished to murder his brother at the Saturnalia, but was unable to do so; for his evil purpose had already become too obvious to remain hidden, and so there now ensued many sharp encounters between the two, each of whom felt that the other was plotting against him, and many defensive measures were taken on both sides. Since many soldiers and athletes, therefore, were guarding Geta, both abroad and at home, day and night, Antoninus induced his mother to summon them both, unattended, to her apartment, with a view to reconciling them. Geta was persuaded, and went in with him, but when they were inside, some centurions, previously instructed by

Antoninus, rushed in a body and struck down Geta, who at the sight of them had run to his mother, hung about her neck and clung to her bosom and breasts, lamenting and crying: 'Mother who bore me, mother who bore me, help! I am being murdered.' And so she, tricked in this way, saw her son perishing in the most impious fashion in her arms, and received him at his death into the very womb, as it were, from where he had been born; for she was all covered with his blood, so that she took no notice of the wound she had received on her hand. But she was not permitted to mourn or weep for her son, though he had met so miserable an end before his time (he was only twenty-two years and nine months old), but, on the contrary, she was compelled to rejoice and laugh as though at some great good fortune, so closely were all her words, gestures, and changes of colour observed. Thus she alone, the Augusta, wife of the Emperor and mother of the Emperors, was not permitted to shed tears even in private over so great a sorrow.

Herodian on the death of Septimius Severus and the co-reign of Geta and Caracalla

Adapted from Herodian's history of his own times, original translation J. Hart 1749.

Book III, Chapter XV and Book IV, Chapters I–IV

Antoninus, having now taken power, began to perform cruelty and murders. He put to death the physicians who had refused to murder his father as he ordered, together with all his own and Geta's tutors, because they attempted to reconcile him with his brother. Nor did he allow one man of honour or authority among all his father's servants to long survive their old master. By large bribes and larger promises, he tempted the principal officers to persuade the army to declare him sole Emperor, and by all kinds of artifices he plotted his brother's ruin. But the soldiers would not comply. For remembering that Severus had educated both with equal care, they resolved to pay the same respect and obedience to both.

When Antoninus therefore found that he could not get what he wished from the army, he made a treaty with the barbarians and granted them peace. Having received hostages of their faith, he left the enemy territory and marched back hastily to his brother and mother. She, with the assistance of the chief officers and counsellors, her husband's friends, tried with all her power to bring them to agreement. Antoninus, at length, when all opposed his plans, was prevailed upon to make a show of reconciliation, more out of necessity than choice, for his malice still remained in his breath, somewhat smothered, but not extinguished.

The two brothers, co-partners in Imperial affairs, agreed to embark their troops and hasten to Rome, carrying with them their father's remains (for the corpse was burnt and the ashes enclosed in an alabaster urn with all kinds of spices and sweet smells), in order to inter them among the sacred tombs of the Emperors. They set sail with the army in triumph for their victories over the Britons, and having crossed the sea, landed on the opposite coast of Gaul.

This Third Book ends with the account of Severus' death and the joint succession of his two sons to the Empire.

The memorable actions of Severus, during the whole eighteen years of his rule, have been related in the preceding book. His sons, both still very young, together with their mother, proceeded to Rome with haste, quarrelling frequently along the way. They did not stay in the same inn or use the same table, and took strict care when eating or drinking for fear that the other may have secretly mixed some poison in the food, or corrupted some of the other's slaves to poison their master. These suspicions made them pursue their journey with greater speed, for they believed they might have better security in Rome, because, having divided the sovereignty, they imagined that in a spacious palace, greater than any city, and containing so many separate apartments, they should be able to live each as they pleased.

When they arrived in Rome, the people, with laurel in their hands, gave them a joyful reception, and the Senate addressed them in the usual manner. The two princes went first, clothed in Imperial Purple. Next came the consuls, bearing the urn in which were the remains of Severus. The senators and magistrates, after saluting the new Emperors, paid their respects to the urn. Then all in their respective ranks joined the procession and followed with the urn with great pomp to the temple, where it was deposited among the sacred monuments of Marcus and the former Emperors.

After performing these ceremonies, as the law required, the two Emperors retired to the palace, which they divided between them, and took care to block all the private avenues and passages, and permitted none to enter or leave except by the public gates and entrances of the court. The brothers never met, except when they decided to appear together in public, and this was seldom.

The first thing they did was to perform the funeral rites for their father. It is a custom among the Romans to consecrate those of their Emperors who die and leave sons or designated successors, and they call this apotheosis. At this ceremony there is a big show of mourning, feasting and worshipping throughout the whole city. The corpse is buried the same as any other man, but in a very costly manner, with an image made of wax representing very closely the size and form of the deceased which lay on a magnificent bed of state made of ivory, with coverings richly embroidered with gold. The bed is raised and exposed to view in one of the galleries of the court. The image has a pale, languid countenance like a sick person, and is attended for most of the day by the most illustrious of people, for on the left side of the bed the members of the Senate sit in black mourning robes, and on the right, the women of quality, whose husbands or fathers are the principal officers of state. None of these ladies has any ornament of gold or jewels, but they are all dressed in plain white, and in every way resemble mourners. For seven days, the image lies in state, during which the physicians pay constant visits, approach the bed, inspect the fictitious patient, and every time declare that he grows worse and there appears no hope of recovery.

At last he is said to be dead, and the highest of the equestrians, together with some young senators, take up the bed and bear it along the Sacred Way to the Old Forum, where the principal magistrates of the Romans give up their authority. On each side are stairs, raised in the form of ladders, on one side a choir of boys picked from the sons of the best families, and on the other, young ladies of similar quality and distinction. These sing funeral dirges and hymns in honour of the deceased, with words and tunes adapted to the mournfulness of the occasion.

This done, the bed is taken up again and carried out of the city to the Campus Martius, where it is raised in the widest part of the plain, a large square building composed of no other materials than wood, representing a fort. The inside is filled with dry combustible matter, but the outside is beautifully decorated with rich hangings wrought with gold, ivory statues and all kinds of paintings. Above this is another floor, built in the same form and equally embellished, but smaller than the first, with open doors and windows. Then a third and a fourth, smaller as they rise, till the top appears sharp and pointed, like those pyramids which are erected at the entrances of certain ports to light ships safe into their harbours by night. They are commonly called phari or lighthouses. The bed is carried up and placed in the second storey of the edifice, amidst great quantities of rich spices and odours of every kind the earth offers, to which they add the most delicious fruits, fragrant herbs and sweet juices brought from all parts of the world. For there is neither nation nor city, nor person of distinction or honour, who is not proud of bestowing some costly presents on this fort, in honour of the Emperor. When these spicy and fragrant oblations are amassed to an immense heap, so that the whole place is filled with them, a kind of cavalcade is performed by all the Roman equestrians, who ride around the building keeping exact time, doubling and redoubling in a sort of course they called the Pyrrhichian Rhythmus. Chariots likewise circle the structure, keeping the same regular time and measure. Their conductors are clothed in purple robes, personifying the most illustrious generals or Emperors of the Romans, adorned with all the badges and ensigns of their respective dignities.

After these rites have been completed, the successor to the Imperial throne takes a lighted torch to the edifice and sets fire to the dry, combustible matter on each side, which conveys the fire to the spices and perfumes. Soon the whole fabric is in flame. Out of the last and narrowest floor, as if from the summit of a lofty tower, an eagle is let fly, and this ascends with the flame and smoke into the air. It is believed by the Romans to soar into the heavens, bearing the soul of the departed Emperor, who from this time forth is worshipped as are the other deities.

When the divine honours had been performed for their father, the young princes returned to the Imperial Palace, where they continually quarrelled, hated, and plotted against one another. Each of them spent his whole time in contriving means to murder his brother and make himself sole ruler of the Empire. This gave rise to factions and feuds among all who had honour or authority in the city. Each of the princes, by secret letters, bribes and promises, endeavoured to bring followers over to his side. The greatest part favoured Geta because he showed moderation in his temper, was civil and accessible and employed himself in serious studies. He conversed with men of learning, was frequently in the palaestra and was very fond of the best gymnastic exercises. Word of his pleasant character to those about him gained him the love of most of the people. On the contrary, Antoninus was imperious and turbulent, and rejecting the exercises mentioned above, pretended to be a lover of military discipline and the life of the warrior, acting always with rage. He seldom persuaded and frequently threatened, and he was fonder of making friends by fear than winning them by gentleness and affability. Their mother did everything in her power to bring her sons closer, but they still showed an irreconcilable enmity in all their actions, and quarrelled about the most trifling and petty things. At last, they decided to divide the Empire, so that each brother might be safe from the treachery of the other, of which both were afraid while they remained in Rome.

They therefore called together their father's friends and their mother, and proposed that the Empire be divided according to the following stipulations:

I. Antoninus to be sole master of all Europe and Geta to rule Asia (for they said these continents seemed to be so divided on purpose by some divine providence, by the straits of the Propontis.

II. That Antoninus have a camp at Byzantium and Geta at Chalcedon in Bithynia, that the army on either side of the Propontis might guard the frontiers of their respective realms, and prevent any invasion from the opposite side.

III. That the Senate be likewise divided, so those under the dominion of the European sovereign to remain in Rome, while the rest would follow *Geta to Asia*.

IV. That Geta could keep his court either at Antioch or Alexandria, both of which are very large cities and not much inferior to Rome.

V. That of the Southern Nations, Mauretania, the Numidians and the adjoining part of Libya belong to Antoninus, while the rest of the countries to the east remained under the government of Geta.

While the two princes were debating these propositions, everyone around them seemed dejected and hung their heads in silence. But Julia the mother vented her grief, saying, 'You find means, my sons, to divide the Earth and Sea between you and the stream between, you say, severs the two continents. But how will you be able to divide your mother? How am I, your unhappy parent, to be torn asunder and shared between you both? There is just one way. First, sheathe your swords in my breast, and then let my body be cut into two, that each prince may bury half his mother in his own territory. So I shall be equally parted between you, together with your Empire of the earth and sea.'

These words were uttered with tears and cries of grief. She took them both by the hand, embraced them in her arms, and with all the tenderness of a mother's love, begged them to lay aside all thoughts of separation. This scene was so affecting that all present were moved to pity. The assembly was dismissed and the scheme abandoned, and the youths retired to their separate apartments.

But their hatred and disagreements still increased. Whenever a post of honour or power fell vacant, each endeavoured to fill it with his own friends, or if they sat in court on judgement, their findings were always opposing, sometimes to the ruin of the parties concerned, for their love of opposition was more powerful than their regard for justice. The same spirit appeared in all their public appearances. No kind of treachery was left unattempted, but each tried to persuade his brother's cooks and cup-bearers to mix poison into his food. This was difficult, though, because they both ate and drank with the strictest caution.

At last, Antoninus, tired with frequent disappointments and increasingly desiring sole rule, resolved to put the finishing stroke to his black design with the sword, or else to die in the attempt. Since secret means had proved ineffectual, he decided to proceed to dangerous and desperate measures. He therefore entered the chamber where he had an appointment to meet his mother and her son, and when some centurions who had been posted there for that purpose, rushed out with their weapons, the horror of the boy and his mother, hers from maternal love and his from the sight of instant death, Geta was fatally wounded, and poured out his blood on his mother's breast, and died.

After this murder was perpetrated, Antoninus rushed out of the room and ran through the palace, crying that an attempt had been made against his life, and with much difficulty he had escaped the treason. He ordered the Praetorians on guard at the court to come to his rescue and take him directly to the camp, that the army might guard him, for it was no longer safe in the palace. The guards, believing him and ignorant of what had been committed, seeing him flee with such speed, fled with him, while the people were worried to see the Emperor running through the streets at dusk. When he arrived at the camp, he went straight to the temple where all the ensigns and images of the army are worshipped, and fell prostrate on the ground, and gave thanks for his deliverance.

But when the soldiers heard about this, even though some were bathing and some were at rest, they all ran to the temple. Antoninus came out and concealing what he had done, exclaimed that he had just escaped from imminent danger from an enemy and traitor (meaning his brother), and that he had managed to get the better of his adversaries, and after both parties had fought to the death, he had remained the sole surviving Emperor. By these hints, he tried to make the murder understood, and he promised, if they would keep him safe, he would give each soldier 2,500 denarii, and their ration would be increased by half. He then bid them to go and take the money which was deposited in the temples and treasury, and thus, in one day, he squandered all the wealth Severus had accumulated from the ruin of other people in the space of eighteen years. The soldiers, tempted by the offer of so much money, and understanding what had been done (for the murder was now shouted about by those who had fled there from the palace), saluted him as sole Emperor and declared Geta an enemy.

Acknowledgements

Thanks again to Michael Bhaskar, Kit Nevile and everyone else at Canelo for support in the writing and production of this book. Thanks to my fellow authors for support, particularly Simon Turney, whose *Marius' Mules*, *Praetorian* and *Damned Emperors* series you should really read. And thanks of course to my family, Naomi and Abigail, in supporting me through another big project.

The Imperial Assassin

Emperor's Sword
Emperor's Knife
Emperor's Axe